HETCH

MEN OF SWAT

RIVER SAVAGE

First edition: May 2016

Edited by Becky Johnson, Hot Tree Editing
Cover design ©: Louisa Maggio at LM Creations
Image: Furious Fotog
Model: Chase Ketron
Information address: riversavageauthor@gmail.com

DEDICATION

To anyone who has ever had suicidal thoughts.
I am glad you're still here. Keep holding on.

AUTHORS NOTE

This novel contains adult/mature young adult situations. It is only suitable for ages 18+ due to language, violence, and sexual situations. Hetch explores the damaging effects of suicide, its aftermath, and the possible issues associated with mental illness and PTSD. Despite being a HEA, Hetch and Liberty's journey may cause possible triggers related to suicide and other mental health issues.

PROLGUE

HETCH

I once heard you can trace who you've become in this life to three external factors: ten defining moments; seven critical choices; and five pivotal people. I'm not sure how true it is, but it's one of those things that always stuck with me. Sure I've had moments, both positive and negative, that one could say redefined the type of person I have become. But I've never had a moment which entered my consciousness with such authority it changed the core of who I thought I was.

Until I did.

1

HETCH

"Before we begin, I need to form a baseline. I'm going to ask you to state your name then tell me two truths and one lie, in that order." I shift in my seat, jostling the cords I'm attached to before answering.

"My name is Liam Hetcherson. I have one sister. I drive a black Ford F150. And I'm really excited to be here today." An unhurried smirk appears on the psychoanalyst's chapped lips, and I get a small sense of satisfaction knowing I managed to break through his stony composure.

"Good. Now, let's try some word association. I say a word, you give me the first word that comes to mind. For example, if I say cat, you may say dog." I nod, already aware of how these things work.

"Ask?" He kicks it off without any warning.

"Answer."

"Gun?"

"Shot."

"Responsibility?"

"Mine."

"Red?"

"Blood."

"Help?"

"Late."

"Respect?"

"None."

His assessing gaze behind his rimless bottle-cap glasses moves from the polygraph machine and connects with mine. A surge of silence pulses around the four-by-six interview room we sit in as I wait for his next word.

"Father?" The word drawls from his mouth and crashes through my steely resolve.

My father.

What this psych evaluation will come down to today. Imagery floods in of the man, who for twenty-nine years, I called Dad. The man who taught me how to drive, to work hard, to value family. The man who I looked up to, who I aspired to be.

Until I didn't.

"You're thinking too hard, Sergeant. Let's try it again. Father?" He presses when I don't answer.

"Coward." My honest answer slaps the air. It's years of hurt, years of suffering, years of unanswered questions that weigh the one word down with pain.

"Your father... he took his life."

It's not a question. It's a true statement. A fact.

My defining moment.

"Would you like me to word associate it, Doc?" If I was expecting some kind of reaction from him as he notes something down on my file, I would have been left disappointed.

I was prepared for this line of questioning. I've dealt with it plenty of times throughout the last three years. The polygraph machine monitoring my stress while answering these questions, however, is new.

It's my psych evaluation. Department forced counseling at its finest. Part of the selection process I must endure if I want to be team leader. An entire day where written tests are issued and various interviews are conducted to find out if I can make the cut.

Everything I've been working toward rests on this.

"Let's talk about it for a minute. It's what, the third anniversary of his death next month? How are you coping?"

"What's your machine tell you?" It's no surprise I dislike talking about the death of my father. What I dislike more is being hooked up to the fucking machine and being asked to talk about it so they can overanalyze my answers with their psychobabble bullshit.

"You know this isn't how it works, Sergeant Hetcherson." He's right. I do. I know how this fucking works. I know every time tactical requalification comes up, I'm evaluated. Every time I discharge my weapon, hell, every time I can't talk a subject down, I'm being assessed, put through the wringer to make sure I'm coping.

"Tell me, Doc, how do you measure how well I should be coping?" I decide to indulge him. It's not the first time I've played this game.

"Well, coping does not represent a homogeneous concept. It's a diffuse umbrella term. Coping can be described in terms of strategies, tactics, responses, cognitions, or behavior." There he goes with his psychobabble bullshit.

"I use sex, beer, and my job. However, I liked sex, beer, and my job before he shot himself in the head less than five feet from me. So where does this leave me?" While there is some honesty to my answer, I am fucking with him.

"Listen, Liam." The pen falls to the desk in frustration, and he takes a moment to remove his glasses. "I'm not trying to be the bad guy here. My job is to determine if you're mentally stable for this position. This line of work leaves little room to be complacent."

"I don't have PTSD if that's what you're asking." He doesn't

4

comment, doesn't show signs of agreeing or disagreeing, just adds a note to my file before continuing.

"Let's talk about incident 9837." He flicks through his paperwork, pulling out a file and opening it up.

"You'll have to refresh my memory, Doc."

"Richard Fallon." He starts reading through the transcripts, but truthfully there is no need. I can recall the incident in clear detail.

"Hetcherson. 11:15 a.m. Do you need me to tell you how this plays out? What happens when you put a bullet in your head? The mess you will make when the bullet leaves the chamber and explodes into your skull. What's worse, you might not even die. Then what, Richard? Do you want your family to see you like that?"

The scene plays out in my head as he reads the play-by-play of the incident, yanking me back to the night I witnessed the second suicide I couldn't prevent.

"Sterling. 11:20 a.m. You're losing him, Hetch."

"Heterchson. 11:21 a.m. No, the risk is low. Give me more time."

He continues to recite the transcript, and to anyone who wasn't present that night, his monotone recap almost makes it seem boring. Inconsequential in the grand scheme of things. But I know differently. They're my words. That's me trying to save a distraught man who had just lost his wife.

It was far from boring.

"I remember the case." I cut him off, not wanting to hear any more.

"Five minutes later Richard Fallon discharged his weapon."

"Yes."

"Do you think there would have been a different outcome had anyone else on your team taken lead negotiator?"

"No." I speak the word with the utmost certainty. "Regardless of who took lead negotiator, Richard Fallon went there to die. He wasn't responding to compassion or understanding. We didn't have much time to begin with. I had to go in with hard reality."

"But you still lost him."

"Yes." I hate the way my fist clenches on that word, my

5

body's reaction to the failure coursing through me because of the truth. His eyes track my movement, landing on my clenched fist with a knowing glance.

"How do you feel when you're called out for a possible suicide?"

"About as excited as having to sit here and answer these questions."

"Deflecting with humor is a sign of negating the real issues at hand." His jab shuts me up, and I wait for the next question. "Do you think what happened to your father hinders how you handle a negotiation situation?"

"I don't believe so, but I'm not the professional. You tell me. You have my file." I know I'm not helping my case here, but I'm growing tired. Never mind I've been a member of Team One for the last two years. Our unit has the top success rate in the force, and yet even with a record number of high-risk call-outs, today still comes back to him.

"You still hold a lot of anger toward your father." Again, with his carefully crafted observation. It's not a question, but he's baiting me to respond.

"Of course I'm fucking angry." My still-clenched fist finds the metal table in front of me with a resounding thud. "Is that what you want to hear? I'm pissed? Even three years later? Well, there you have it." I squeeze my fingers open and closed a couple of times to calm myself down.

"And what exactly are you angry about, Liam?"

"I don't know. Take your pick. I'm angry because he chose a permanent solution to a temporary problem. Or that he brought me into it, and subsequently what it did to my family. There is a lot to be angry about. And maybe I don't have a right to be angry, but you know what? The anger keeps me holding on. It keeps me caring. You may think I can't do this job because of what happened. Go ahead, write up your recommendation. But let me tell you something, the minute I stop being angry is the minute I stop caring. And the minute I stop caring is the minute my emotional capacity starts to hinder how I deal with this job."

"You don't think this anger affects how you respond to a high-risk situation?" I almost envy his composure, his ability to not react to the tension.

"No, I don't." I want to believe my words more than anything, hope I am skilled enough to fool him, but a small part of me isn't sure. "Tell me, Doc. Have you ever lost a loved one?" I don't expect him to answer. This isn't about him, but for some reason he does.

"My daughter passed away five years ago."

I school my features and ask him the same question he put on me. "And does her death affect how you're doing your job in this room today?" He doesn't acknowledge my question this time, but he doesn't need to. I still get my answer.

I may have blown my chance at being team leader, hell, maybe even jeopardized my spot on the team, but I refuse to sit here and be torn down while he looks for something that isn't there.

Yeah, my father took his life.

Did it change who I thought I was?

No.

It changed who I thought he was.

And therein lies the issue of what his death had over me.

I just wasn't ready to address it.

* * *

"I think it's your last one, Hetch," RJ, my favorite bartender, tells me later that afternoon, when my fucked-up day is over and I'm sitting back with a beer or ten at my local bar, The Elephant. Since it's close to Trebook's police station, the team often comes in after a long shift. Sometimes we might stay for one round, other times it might end up an all-nighter. I've already been here for a few hours, trying to drown my demons with one too many beers.

"Nah, man, can still remember too much." I think I slur, but can't be sure. I'm pretty certain I'm about to be cut off.

"Maybe it's time you start remembering," he offers before moving down to the other end of the bar.

My mind tries to fight it, the beer helping to numb it a little, but like every time I get to this stage, broken memories of three years ago start flashing back.

His vacant stare holds my gaze as a flicker of something passes between us.

Him understanding my fears.

Me accepting his weaknesses.

"I love you, Liam, always know that."

It happens so fast.

The change of his aim.

The discharge of his gun.

The fall of his body.

The agony of my screams.

The roar of sirens.

Yet nothing is as deafening as the stillness of the moment.

"I take it from the state you're in, it didn't go well." Sterling's voice startles me from the past.

Fuck, I'm not sure what's worse. The fucked-up interview, the memory of a past I continue to run from, or this present moment that has my best friend breathing down my neck.

It takes me a few minutes to rein in my raging heart before responding. "It went fucking awesome, Sterlin'," I slur while slapping the stool next to me for him to sit on. "In fact, I'm celebrating." I lift my beer and salute it to no one in particular.

"Yeah? What are we celebrating tonight?" He takes a seat on the stool and waves off RJ. I cough out a humorless laugh, unable to come up with some bullshit line.

"Jesus, that bad?"

"You know how it is. What it always comes back to." I don't need to say my father's name. Sterling knows what I'm talking about. It's always been this way between us, always will be. Best friends for thirty years. Fellow beat officers for six, SWAT teammates for two, brothers for life. We've been through everything together.

"The fucker didn't think about anyone but himself," I whisper when he doesn't respond. "Didn't think what it would do to me, how it would fucking hinder me." I'm rambling, but it's not the first time in the last three years Sterling's found me this way. I'm lucky he has my back and doesn't report my ass.

"Come on, let's get you home." Sterling drops a hundred on the bar, closing out my tab.

"I'm not fucking ready to go." I try to call RJ back over, but Sterling has me up and out of my stool before I have a chance.

"Yeah, well you gotta. RJ cut you off. You're shit out of luck now."

The fucker.

"What a piece of shit, let me have a word with him." I try to turn back, but Sterling's hold on me doesn't waver.

"You can have a word with him another night. Come on, don't you have a shift tomorrow? You need to sober the fuck up."

"No point in even fucking going," I tell him, throwing an arm over his shoulder as he walks me out to his truck.

"You need to stop this bullshit, Hetch." He scolds me like I'm some petulant child while pushing me into the cab of his jacked-up Ford. He's right. I'm a fucking mess; I know it. I just don't know how to control it.

"Yeah," is all I say instead. It's probably not the most comforting endorsement of my mental wellbeing, but after today, it's all I have to give.

"I'm fucking serious, Hetch," he warns before closing the door and walking around the front of his truck to the driver side.

"You speak to your mom or Kota today?" he asks, starting the truck up.

"Not in the last week or so." I try to think back to the last time I had a conversation with my mom and sister.

"Spoke to Kota yesterday," he admits, pulling out of the

parking lot. I rest my head back and close my eyes, waiting for another lecture. "She's worried about you."

And there we have it. What this time of year always brings. Concern.

"Kota is always worried." I brush off his remark. My little sister wears her heart on her sleeve. If a few days pass and she doesn't hear from me, she rings my best friend to check on me. She's always been this way, even before our father took his life and shocked us into our new reality.

"You need to check in with her. I can't keep dealing with her calls." He acts like it's a hardship for him. Far from it. If I had the balls to call him out on it, I would. But it's an unspoken thing between us. He's in love with my sister. My sister is in love with him. I always wonder when they will act on it… if they will act on it. I'm probably an asshole for not putting him out of his misery, but I've never been one to put my nose where it doesn't belong. If Sterling and Dakota end up together, then I'll support them, but until they find themselves there, I'm staying out of it.

"I'll call her tomorrow." I appease him, knowing I should check in with both my mom and sister. After Dad died, we grew closer, opting to keep each other near, but as the years have gone on, they've moved on too, sometimes making me wonder if I'm the only one stuck.

"You fucking better, Hetch."

"I told you I would," I murmur, not in the mood for his threats. He grumbles a reply, but I don't take it in; instead, I block it out. I block it all out. The day, the interview, the last fucking three years, every thing that brings me down is pushed aside as I let the beer-induced sleep take me to the place I've been searching for.

Oblivion.

* * *

"It cuts like a knife, son, knowing it's you, but it is what it is."
"Dad, no!"

I wake with a startle what feels like hours later. It takes a few breaths to get my bearings before I realize I'm home, on my bed, fully clothed and not back in the past trying to save my father's life.

The night's activities filter through my mind as I try to sort them in order: the interview I fucked up; Sterling coming to The Elephant and paying my tab before driving my drunk ass home, dragging me up to my apartment and telling me to get my head out of my ass.

"Fuck." I roll and groan. My head is throbbing like I survived a brass knuckle punch, and the slight buzz filtering through my ears confirms I definitely had too much to drink.

Fucking idiot.

After breathing through a wave of nausea, I manage to find my feet and pull myself up to sitting position. The clock beside my bed tells me it's only just midnight. I guess it's what happens when you get drunk before five.

Finding the strength to stand, I make my way to the bathroom. I don't bother looking in the mirror. The asshole staring back only reminds me of an older version of my thirty-two-year-old self. Instead, I head for the toilet. After the longest piss known to man, I undress down to my boxers, pop two double-strength Tylenol, brush my teeth, making sure I scrape along my tongue to remove the funky taste of beer and God knows what, then take my sorry, drunk ass back to bed.

My head is still throbbing, but the buzzing has cleared so I flick my lamp off and roll over to my side. It doesn't take long to slip back into a light pre-sleep, and I'm almost out when the buzzing starts up again.

What the hell?

I roll over, flicking the lamp on to search out the source of the buzz. I might be drunk or in the early stages of a hangover, but it doesn't take too long to realize it's not coming from my room but through the wall.

Fuck me, it's the new neighbor.

The walls of this damn place are so thin. They need to put this shit on the lease before another sorry bastard signs their privacy away.

Flicking the lamp off again, I settle back into bed, the buzzing sound growing louder as the seconds tick by.

Is that a toothbrush or a fucking vibrator?

A soft gasp confirms my suspicion, followed by the loud cry of her release.

Holy shit, the little minx is getting off.

Not at all embarrassed by my actions I roll closer to the wall and place my ear up against it. I don't know if she's alone, or if the guy's she's with is a quiet fuck, but all I can hear is the sound of a vibrator and her. My bet is she's alone.

Becoming more alert than I care to be after midnight, I press my ear harder against the wall. Her soft whimpers grow louder, and my dick hardens with pleasure when she shouts out.

Fuck, I should have foregone the beer and went with pussy tonight.

Regretting the decision now, I do what any respectable single male would do in this situation. I slide my hand down my boxer briefs and wrap my fingers around my cock. Stroking slowly and deliberately at first, I then build up to deep, rough and needy strokes as soon as I realize she's going for a second release.

"Fucking greedy little thing." I groan when her whimpers start becoming desperate. The buzz of the vibrator dying off interrupts me from my own pleasure.

Unsure what to do, I stay quiet, wanting more than anything to talk to her, maybe even try to see if I can get her to come over, but I can't imagine she'll respond all that well if I let her know I've been listening in. But fuck me, the thrill of what I'm doing turns me on more than I've ever been turned on before.

After another few beats of silence, the vibrator starts back up again. My fist moves back in rhythm, this time faster and rougher to catch up. She's louder this time, more vocal and it only takes a minute or two for her to find her release, the deep moans of her orgasm not quite enough to pull me over with her.

"Fuck, woman, wait for me this time," I say on a groan, unable to hold back my frustration. I don't know if I do it on purpose, or maybe I'm too lost in the moment to control what I'm saying, but whatever the reason, the words still come from my lips, halting any chance of me getting my happy ending.

Fuck me.

Again.

LIBERTY

"What the hell am I doing?" I think I speak the words aloud, but I can't be sure. A thick fog encases my head in a pre-orgasm high. I'm not sure of anything anymore as I barrel toward some kind of alternate universe where I do crazy shit and don't give any fucks.

Until the rational part of my brain finds its way through the fog, and clarity finds its way back into my normal universe.

They say moments of clarity hit you hard. Like suddenly a deep understanding smacks you in the face. Your vision becomes unclouded, and a truth that's been out of your reach rushes at you. It's in that second your perception of reality becomes so clear you can't begin to describe it.

Some call it beautiful, some say it can be saddening, some even compare it to the moment your drug of choice washes over you, offering a moment of escape.

I wish I could say my moment of clarity is an epiphany or some kind of life-defining moment that showed me where my messed-up life is going.

No, my moment hits me as the first wave of the orgasm I've been chasing the last few minutes washes over me.

"Fuck, woman, wait for me this time." His voice pulls me from my haze first, reminding me how messed up I am.

Heat covers my body, not from the life-altering orgasm, but from embarrassment.

Without thinking rationally, I throw my vibrator to the floor and freeze, afraid to move, as a low moan pauses on my lips. The thump of my beating heart, almost syncing in perfect rhythm to the throb drumming between my legs.

Jesus, please tell me he didn't hear me.

"Don't go shy on me now, babe." He half chuckles, half growls, and even though there is a wall between us, the words wash over me; Goose bumps prickle my skin as if his warm breath whispered over me.

Shit.

Shit.

Shit.

Slowly, as if by some freak of nature, apartment nine can see me through the wall, I roll off the bed and find myself on all fours.

Really, Liberty?

Fully committed to my actions, I slowly army crawl my way to the nearest exit.

A strong tap on the wall halts my escape followed by, "You still there?" Another wave of humiliation crashes over me when I take stock of my predicament.

If I don't get out of here fast, I'll be drowning in so much embarrassment, nothing will resuscitate me.

Unable to form a coherent thought, and not willing to engage with the pervert, I continue to low crawl my way out of my bedroom and into my bathroom. Closing the door, I stand, and quickly walk to the shower. After turning the faucet on, I strip the rest of my clothes off, then step under the spray of the water.

Jesus, that was close.

I have no idea what I was thinking. In fact, I know I wasn't.

Which scares me even more.

I, Liberty Jenson, would never take risks like this. If asked what prompted this change in me, I'd answer with two things.

Apartment nine.

And a self-appointed sex sabbatical.

It all started when I moved into my new apartment. At first, I was excited, ready for a fresh start. After a messy break-up, which included dealing with a douche ex who didn't know how to keep his dick in his pants, I needed a new place. Somewhere closer to town this time, secure, and most importantly, affordable. However, finding a place close to the city, which was secure enough to make me feel safe and would still leave me enough money left over from my program director's wage, proved to be a feat. After searching for five weeks, I was about to give up, accept defeat and move in with my mom and dad again. I mean it wasn't the worst thing that could happen to a single thirty-year-old woman.

Right?

Luckily for me, I didn't have to resort to such desperate measures when this place came up two weeks ago. After a quick walk through, I fell in love with the two bedrooms, one bath, and open kitchen living area. I filled out the paperwork, paid my deposit, a month's rent in advance, and moved in five days later.

Everything seemed perfect.

That was until I realized how paper-thin the walls were between apartments.

It started out subtle, a sneeze in the early evening on my first night here as I settled into bed. A soft murmur of a man's voice the third night.

But then came the sex.

The hot, wild, filthy sex.

The fourth night in my new apartment, I was woken to the low moans of what I assumed to be a needy woman.

My face heats up remembering the screams, the grunts. The deep baritone of apartment nine's voice as he told the 'bitch' to keep it quiet.

Unsure what to do, I laid silent, listening to my new neighbor fuck some lucky woman into submission.

I'm not going to lie; I wasn't turned on by it. I was set alight.

I never thought I would be *that* kind of person, the kind who got off from listening in on someone get off, but something in the way he spoke to her, something in the way he spoke to all the other women since, stirred a new want in me. Soon I found myself seeking out my room for a chance to hear him.

It was wrong.

So wrong.

But it didn't stop me from wanting it.

The screams.

The deep grunts of pleasure.

I wanted it all.

I wanted it to be me.

"I'm officially going to hell." I groan under the water, trying to wash the stupidity off me. Stupid would be the nice way of calling me a fucking idiot. And an idiot is what I am. Especially after tonight.

I had finished my last case study for the evening and was settling in bed for a couple of chapters of a new book when I realized the familiar deep rumble of my next-door neighbor was absent tonight. For the first time in eight nights, I had the privacy I wasn't sure I wanted.

I want to blame the hot scene I was reading at that moment, but in the interest of being honest, I wasn't strong enough. A week of listening to a real life sex show had threatened my sabbatical. I was barely through my first orgasm when I thought I heard the familiar deep rumble floating through the wall. I paused, shutting down my vibrator listening out for any signs of life only to be met with silence. I wasn't sure if what I had heard was my imagination or real. Maybe if I wasn't so highly strung, I would have stopped then. I mean one orgasm is enough, right? But after a few beats of silence, a thrill ran through me when the thought that maybe he was home, and perhaps like me, he too may have been listening out for me, his hand wrapped around what I imagined was a huge cock, getting off like I was. The image took hold of me, and then I couldn't stop myself from allowing my fingers to flick my vibrator back on and permitting myself to get off knowing full well he may be listening.

It turns out I was right.

How hot and exceptionally disturbing.

I groan in frustration, knocking my forehead to the cool tile of the shower wall.

Deciding there's only so much dwelling one can do in a shower, I gingerly turn the faucet off and step out. Too chicken to go back to my room, I dress in my bathrobe and quietly walk out of my bathroom.

I eye the hall to my bedroom with shame. Only an hour ago, the thought of walking to my bed seemed like a simple task, something I wouldn't think twice about. Now the thought makes me want the floor to open up and swallow me whole. Deciding I can't deal with what happened tonight and sleep in my room, I head toward my living room. My three-seater sofa isn't the most comfortable piece of furniture, but desperate times call for desperate measures. I fetch a quilted blanket—one my grandmother made me—out of the hallway cupboard and settle on two of my throw pillows. For a second, I think I hear footsteps at my front door, and I freeze midmovement. When nothing comes of it, I flop down on my sofa.

Jesus, what is wrong with me? Hiding in my own apartment.

This is not normal behavior for me. I mean, it's not like I can't get a man. It's just I don't want one. Not after recently getting out of a messed-up relationship. Sure, no strings attached sex would be nice, as would an orgasm or two that didn't come from a vibrator. I mean, clearly I'm wound up ready to combust if the sound of a man's muffled voice makes me want to finger myself. But it's not what I need. I need time to decompress, time to find myself.

Hence this damn Sabbatical.

It wasn't some fly-by-the-seat-of-my-pants decision. Five weeks of living in the same room I grew up in can do a lot to a person. Tristan and I had been seeing each other for three years. I honestly thought he was it for me. I was thinking marriage and maybe kids while he was off fucking some twenty-year-old pussy. Not once in my carefully thought-out plans did I expect to be single at thirty again. It's depressing and somewhat sobering. I mean I could have gone down the party-and-fuck-everything-with-a-penis road, but honestly, where would it lead me? More alone and feeling sorry for myself when the self-loathing finally kicked in.

Instead, I made a promise. No men and no sex for six months.

The first five weeks were a breeze.

The last two weeks have been hell.

If only apartment nine would get the memo and quit fucking like a porn star on a reunion show.

"Ugghh." I scream into my pillow. Every detail of the night plays over in my head, and before I know it, I've worked myself up into a mess.

Needing someone to talk me down from my impending freak-out, I reach for the phone and dial my best friend, Payton.

"Hello?" She answers on the third ring.

"I knew you would still be up," I greet, not caring it's after midnight.

"Yeah, Arabella is teething."

Arabella is Payton's four-year-old daughter. She's also my niece and goddaughter.

"Again?" I don't know much about teeth, but it seems like the poor kid is too old for new teeth.

"Ahh, yeah. These ones are her second molars. It's hell."

"Ugghh, I bet." I shudder, not sure how she does the mothering gig most days. That shit is scary.

Payton and I have been friends since high school. Even though we weren't the best of friends in the beginning—since she was captain of the cheer squad and I was captain of the debate team—we soon got to know each other when she started dating my older brother, Jett.

Jett and Payton, the cliché, high-school sweethearts.

Payton and I grew closer when we left for college, even living in the same dorm. No one, especially me, would have guessed Payton and Jett would have survived high school and college,

19

but they proved us all wrong five years ago when they married. They beat the odds, had the perfect relationship, fell pregnant right after their honeymoon, and nine months later welcomed Miss Arabella.

They had it all.

Until last year when my dipshit brother went and ruined it by cheating on her.

"What are you doing up?" she asks, oblivious to my personal dilemma.

"One word: neighbor."

"What? Again? Are you kidding me? What's that, every night this week?" She's trying not to laugh, but failing miserably. I've been filling her in on my neighbor's activities, even calling her on Sunday to let her listen in on the fuck-a-thon. "I think it's time you need to address this, Lib. What about a note?"

"Yeah, I don't think a note is going to fix this."

Could it?

"You never know. You could write something like, "Hey, neighbor, I've heard you like to fuck a lot, maybe you can ball gag the next bitch you bring home, so I'm not being woken at one every morning."

"Umm, no. That's not happening." I laugh, knowing Payton isn't joking. She would have had a note pinned up on apartment nine's door, signed and dated after the first night here if this were happening to her.

"Why the hell not? Maybe he doesn't know the walls are stupidly thin."

"Nope, I'm pretty sure he knows."

"How do you know?"

"Because something happened," I offer, still unsure how I even begin to fill her in what happened tonight.

"What? Did you finally meet him? He's hot, isn't he? I knew it. No man fucks the way you described and isn't attractive. Tell me how hot is he?" Her voice rises with each question.

"I don't know. I still haven't met him." She's quiet for a beat, something which doesn't often happen to Payton before she catches up.

"Okay. Then what the hell happened?"

"Well—" I begin.

"No wait, don't tell me, you picked up a one-night stand, didn't you? Please tell me you gave him a show in return?" She cuts me off, her mind clearly making up her own scenarios.

Patience has never been Payton's strong suit.

"Focus, Pay."

"Sorry. Okay, go ahead."

"Well, I was lying there, minding my own business, with my vibrator—"

"SHUT THE FRONT DOOR." She shouts loud enough that I'm afraid apartment nine could possibly hear her.

"Shhh, keep it down. I thought it might help to relieve some of my own pent-up frustration."

"Sorry, sorry. I'm shocked. What happened to your sabbatical?"

"Well, it's not like it's penetration, Pay," I blurt, only to hide my face in my hand. I can't believe I said that.

"If you say so." She laughs, still not understanding my need for a sabbatical. She's been against it since week one. "So what happened next?"

"Well, next thing I know I'm coming, and he tells me to wait for him."

"OH, MY GOD. THIS IS FUCKING EPIC." She cackles in hilarity before I hear the sound of a male's voice.

"What the hell, Pay? You have company?" I sit up faster than needed.

She could have told me before I admitted to getting off.

"Ahhh, yeah. Umm, Jett dropped in to see Arabella." The way she casually says it, tells me she's full of shit.

More like dropped in for a booty call.

"Jesus, what the hell are you doing, Payton?" I can't keep the annoyance out of my voice. The last thing Payton needs right now is Jett sniffing around.

"Well, right now, I'm listening to my best friend tell me about her messed-up life."

"Don't deflect. You and I both know this can't be good."

I love my brother, but I'll never be okay with what he did. Not only did he cheat on Payton, but he also walked out when she finally confronted him. Left her and Arabella for the skanky little whore.

"Can we can talk about it later?" she whispers so only I can hear. I decide to leave it be, and not push. If there's one thing I know about Payton, it's that there's a fine line when it comes to getting her to open up. Cross it and she will only close up tighter.

"Later," I repeat, knowing my later and Payton's are so far apart. It will be weeks before I get any more info from her.

"Thanks, B. Now tell me what happened next."

I continue my story, telling her everything from the moment I went to bed, down to the army crawl, to hiding in the shower. I even admitted to the low blow of sleeping out on my sofa. After she spends far too long reliving my horror with too much glee, I come up with a plan to write a note letting him know he needs to keep it down and mind his manners.

Payton's not sold on it.

"Trust me. I guarantee we'll be laughing about it next week over drinks on our girls' night out. Give it a few days. All will blow over, and your humiliation will fade with it," she promises.

I'm not sure if I can see that happening, but wanting to be done with the conversation, I let her words reassure me and tell her I won't leave it.

"Yeah, we'll see. Anyway, I'll let you go. Give my shithead big brother a hug for me."

"Will do. Love you, girl."

"You too." I hang up, dropping my phone back on my coffee table. I don't bother trying to head back to my bedroom; instead, the rest of my night is filled with lumpy sofa cushions, a small, scratchy pillow, and one sexy, mystery man who follows me into my dreams, telling me to wait for him.

* * *

Hey, douche bag, maybe keep it down.

22

I read over the note written in my neat handwriting and cringe at my choice of words.

"Oh, God, that's terrible," I tell myself and tear off the piece of paper, scrunch it up into a ball, and drop it into the trash bin beside my desk.

It's been seventy-two hours and I still can't find the right words.

Thinking it over for another few minutes, I start again.

I'm not sure if you're aware, but I can hear you fuck.

Ugghh, that's worse.

"Ahhh excuse me, Liberty, your mom is here to see you." My eyes move off the crude note I'm working on to find Renee, the newest member of our team, my mother and my niece at the door of my office at Boys Haven.

"What's wrong, Mom?" I stand almost instinctively. She knows she can't just turn up here unannounced. While Boys Haven isn't as strict as some of the other group homes I have worked in the past, we do have structured visitor rules for privacy reasons.

"Working on your day off, how shocking." She steps past Renee, ignoring my panicked question.

"I'm sorry, Liberty. She said it was urgent. I thought 'cause you're on your day off…." Renee offers in explanation.

"Thanks, Renee, I'll sort it out." I step forward, motioning my mother and niece into my office before closing the door behind me.

"Seriously, Mom. You can't show up here unannounced." While my office here at Boys Haven is not part of the main residential quarters, I still don't like to receive visitors. As program director, I take my job seriously, but I'm also very hands on. I don't like to mix my personal life with my work life.

"Well, maybe if you answered your phone and stopped ignoring me, I wouldn't have to drop in to see my only daughter." She takes a seat across from my desk, making herself comfortable.

"I'm *not* ignoring—" I start to argue, but abandon that route when her eyes roll back at me the same way my younger self did to her fifteen years ago.

Deciding I need to rush this impromptu visit along, I take a seat back at my desk and motion for Arabella to come to me.

"Hey, sweet girl, how are you today?" I lean forward and kiss her milky white forehead. The amber curls, which match her mother's, sit on top of her head, sticking out in all directions.

"Good. Nana said bad word." Arabella turns and points her cute chubby finger at my mom.

"Did she now? Well, isn't she a naughty nana." I throw a smirk Mom's way.

"Uh huh. She called Daddy a bad word."

"Okay, that's enough kid. Don't go telling all my secrets." Mom cuts her off before she can spill anything else.

"What bad words have you been saying about your only son?" I wonder if she knows Jett and Payton have been seeing each other. Both Mom and Dad have been vocal about their opinions on Jett and his bad decisions. It doesn't mean they don't love him anymore. One phone call to Mom and she would be there for him, but there is no denying if ever it was broken down to sides, they'd stand by Payton.

"Ask me no questions and I'll tell you no lies." I hold her eyes, the same green as mine, and wait to see if she elaborates. She doesn't, so I put a pin in the conversation for later and move on.

"So what are you guys doing here?" I let Arabella climb off my lap, and walk over to the corner where I keep a small box of coloring books and pencils.

"Well, Arabella and I are heading out to lunch. We tried calling you, seeing as it's your day off, but then I remembered how much of a workaholic my only daughter is and I thought we'd drop in to drag you away." She leans forward, her eyes gliding over my desk to see what I've been working on.

"Ha ha, and where is Payton in all this?" I pick up the notebook I was writing in and place it in the top drawer of my desk. I'm a little annoyed with Payton. I haven't heard from her all week. I know she's avoiding me, but I still have issues to go over with her.

One being I'm tempted to do the most stupid thing I've ever done and tape the crude, mean note I told her I wouldn't write on apartment nine's door.

Not that she wouldn't be all for it.

"She had some errands to run," Mom answers, unaware of the impending drama or my near future meltdown.

"Well, as much as I'd love to come to lunch with my favorite niece and mom, I already have something plan–"

"I'm serious, darling. You work too much." She cuts me off, probably not believing I really do have plans.

"Please, I work a normal eleven-hour day like most people, Mom."

"Statistics show people who work eleven hours a day or more have a 67 percent greater chance of suffering from coronary heart disease." She folds her thin arms across the front of her, her cute little self being swallowed up by the chair.

Why couldn't I have gotten my mom's genes? She's so petite and angelic. At fifty-six, she's all class and style. Blonde hair, fair skin and a fashion sense to rival the best of the best.

"I'm thirty years old, Mom. I'm not going to have heart disease. Relax."

"I'm just saying." She unfolds her arms and offers me an unapologetic shrug.

"What's heart dibeebs?" Arabella's sweet, high-pitched voice asks.

"It's what happens when you work way too much," Mom replies, a smug smile on her face.

"Do you have heart dibeebs?" Her head tilts to the side, giving me a once over, searching for this elusive heart disease.

"No, sweetie. Nana was being silly," I assure her before Mom puts any crazy ideas in her head. I already get it from my friends and family; I don't want it from my sweet Arabella.

"So, what are these plans of yours that are stopping you from lunching with us?" Mom drops the morbid work statistics and

25

moves onto trying to wear me down.

"I have an outing with one of the boys. He's been getting into a little trouble at school, so I need some one-on-one time with him. Give him some positive reinforcement."

Mitch is our newest resident. He's only been in care at Boys Haven for the last six months and since he's been here I've grown a little fond of him. I know it's not smart, getting attached to the kids who come through the doors, but something about Mitch has struck a chord with me.

He first entered the system with his older brother, Dominic, at nine, when his father murdered his mom. With no other living family, there wasn't anywhere else for them to go. The first few years they were kept together—bounced around from foster care to group homes—but soon it became apparent Dominic wasn't interested in playing by the rules. With a bad attitude, some serious anger issues and an opposition to authority, Dominic continued to find himself getting involved with the wrong crowd. The boys' case workers tried to keep them separated, but Dominic's hold over Mitch is strong. Always finding a way to drag him down. It's only since Dominic turned eighteen and left the system that we've seen Mitch slowly come into his own.

"You get too involved, Liberty. You need to be careful." Mom's face takes on the don't-mess-with-me look that worked so well back when I was a teenager.

"Mom…." I think I manage the same tone I used to reply with back then—bored with my best I-know-better-than-you attitude.

"I'm serious, Bertie. I worry about you."

"Mom, one, please, for the love of God, don't call me that. I'm not three years old anymore. And two, I can handle myself. Besides, I think I'm getting through to this one. He's a good kid. He just needs someone rooting for him." I offer more than I probably should. My need to prove the good I do here outweighs my responsibility to keep my cases confidential.

"Darling, it doesn't matter if you're three or thirty. Hell, in another thirty years you'll still be my Bertie." I shouldn't give her a hard time about the name. I know she'll never stop calling me it. It's been my childhood name since birth when Jett couldn't pronounce Liberty. The real problem I have is being treated like I don't know what I'm doing.

"Well, try to refrain from calling me it here," I compromise. The last thing I need is someone to catch onto the hideous nickname.

"Okay, dear." She too concedes, before standing. "We should probably get out of your hair." I check the time, cringing when I see I was meant to meet Mitch inside five minutes ago.

"Yes, I need to head out. We'll rain check for sure."

"Okay, I'm holding you to it. Come on, Arabella, Aunt B has to work now, time to say good-bye." Mom stands and picks up her bag.

Arabella packs up her book before walking back over to me.

"You always have to work." She pouts as I take her in a hug.

Jesus, she spends too much time with my mother.

"How about I take you on a picnic next weekend to the park with the big slide you like?" I ask her, already knowing the answer.

"Yes, please." She claps her hands, clearly excited at the prospect.

"Don't forget you have that girls' night thingy next Saturday night," Mom reminds me. The look on my face must convey my forgetfulness because her easy smile sets into worried lines. "You cannot cancel on Payton. She's looking forward to a night off." Her tone pushes me to appease her.

"Of course I won't. I promise."

Shit. I was looking forward to a quiet night in.

"Good, she needs this, darling, a good night out with some friends."

"I agree." I also think she needs to stop letting my brother use her as a booty call, but I don't say anything on the matter. Mom probably doesn't need to know the finer details.

"Okay, you guys have a nice lunch."

"Would be better if you were coming." She folds me in her arms, and even though I have a few inches on her, she still embraces me the way only a mother does. Gently and fiercely. Comforting and knowingly. The kind of hug where you physically feel your worries leave your body.

"Mom—"

"I'm proud of you, Bertie." She cuts me off. "What you're doing here, how passionate you are. I may worry, but never forget how proud your father and I are of you," she whispers before releasing me.

"Jesus, Mom. Get out of here before you make me cry." I wave her off, not needing this kind of moment here at work.

"I'm going. I'm going." She takes Arabella's hand and leaves me alone to process her words.

It's moments like this, in the comfort of my mom's reassurance, I realize how lucky I truly am and that makes me want to be here, working closely with these boys. Offering the same kind of love and support to them when no one else can.

Sometimes I might not be able to make them feel a fraction of what my mom gives me in a simple hug and a few words, but I'll always try.

Because it's what her love taught me.

HETCH

"Why don't you put the gun down and we can talk about it?" I keep my voice low, controlled, and free of any hostility.

"Don't fucking play me. You think I don't know what you're trying to do?" His voice is harsh, panicked, but I don't relent. I need to stay in control.

"I have a clear shot," Fox speaks into my coms, letting me know he's in position.

Mason Fox, our go-to weapons and training specialist. Fox has been on Team One for longer than anyone else. The best of the best and one mean son of a bitch.

I hit the mute button on the phone and speak into my earpiece. "Not until you get the order," I reply, letting him know I'm still in control here. The air is thick with tension. My team is in place, ready to move at a moment's notice. We've been going at it all day. I'm tired, the team's tired, but in situations like this, tired doesn't enter your vocabulary.

"I've given you my demands. I want this now. I'm the one in

control. Do you understand?"

"I understand the situation, Devon." I unmute the phone to answer. "But you need to know what you're asking for is not what I can give you right now."

"Then you leave me no choice. I'm gonna have to start shooting."

"You don't want to do that, Devon. Work with me on this. Give me something more, something I can go back to my bosses with. Then maybe I can give you what you're asking for." It's all bullshit. Devon isn't getting what he wants. In fact, Devon isn't real. Devon is being played by Sergeant Kaighn, Team Two's tactical leader, and while Team One and I are in place ready to eliminate the threat he's posing, it's all for training and review purposes.

"I've already given you FIVE hostages! What more do you fuckin' want?" He's escalating, and for the sake of today's training session, I'm not going to be able to talk him down.

"You did, and it worked in your favor, Devon. We sent in food and some drinks. What about the injured guard? How is he holding up?" I press for more information, while Walker, our coms guy, works on getting us a better view inside the warehouse we're training in.

"He's doing good. He's sleeping right now."

Fucking Kaighn is busting my balls here.

"That's not good, Devon. I need to get my men to him."

"He's fine!"

"Let me break it down for you here, Devon. If the guard dies, things are going to get a whole lot messier for you."

"Oh, yeah? How much messier?"

"Well, for one, if he dies, you'll be looking at murder. You don't want that, do you?"

"I didn't shoot him! It was an accident. He wrestled me. If he sat down as I told him instead of trying being a hero…."

"I'm in and I have a clear shot." Tate lets me know his position.

Preston Tate, the youngest officer on Trebook's tactical team, is ex-special ops, five years on the force, and first year

30

tactical. Tate's fresh, but it doesn't mean he's not one hell of a good marksman.

One of the best I've seen.

Ignoring the coms, I continue to engage with Devon. "I know, and those witnesses in there will be able to vouch for you. We need to get him help now." I can see him wavering on the video feed. His pacing has slowed as he rubs the palm of his hand down his face.

"Fine. But only the guard." He gives me a chance to make my play.

"Good decision, Devon." I hit the mute button and switch my coms.

"Okay, boys, we're going in. He's probably expecting a front entry, but we'll continue as planned. Let's hit 'em hard and smoke him out."

The two teams will breach the building. Team One-alpha, consisting of Hart and Sterling, will go through the air vents. Team Two-bravo, comprising of Fox and Tate, will enter through a window on the fourth floor. Sterling and Hart will release a flash bang, creating enough distraction to get both teams down on the ground. Sterling and Hart will then cover the hostages while Tate will cover Fox, giving him enough time to secure Kaighn before he has a chance to use his weapon.

That's the plan. We just need to pull it off.

"Copy. Alpha team in place." Hart checks in for the first time, letting me know he's on board.

Ryan Hart is the oldest member of the team. Before I made the team, he was the top negotiator the force had. Then four years ago, the poor bastard lost his wife to cancer. Mourning his loss, and trying to figure out the ropes of being a single dad to his two kids, he stepped down from the team and took a leave of absence. It took a few years for him to return. First coming on part-time, and then working his way back up. After passing his physical and mental exams last month, he was offered a full-time spot back on the team.

"Bravo team in place," Fox whispers, confirming both teams are ready. Even though this is the second run through of the day, it's a new play, one I want to make sure we get right.

"Alpha team on my count. Three, two, one."

"Alpha team breaching now," Sterling speaks through his coms. The flash bang is loud enough for me to hear it outside the perimeter.

"Bravo team down," I order, watching them all unfold the play on the small feed in the command unit. Hart's flash bang is enough to get the boys on the ground while Fox and Tate manage to secure the weapon and place Kaighn in custody. It all happens fast like we've trained.

In and out in ninety seconds.

"Subject secure. All hostages safe." The final coms come from Sterling, letting me know the play worked, and our team pulled it off.

"Good job, Sergeant Hetcherson." My lieutenant taps me on the back, reminding me today's training session was being closely watched. "Risky to split the team up like that, but it played out for you."

"Thank you, sir." I release the earpiece from my ear. Today's training drill was to assess if the team is cohesively working as a unit. While each and every one of us is an asset to the team, we still need to make sure we're working as one. I think after that run-through, both teams, not just ours, proved where we belong.

"Tell me. You've been acting team leader for three months now?"

"Yes, sir." I nod, wondering where he's going with this. It's been a week since psych evaluation, and so far, I haven't been removed from duty.

Is today the day I get pulled?

"You still feel like you're the best person for the job?"

"I can't answer that, sir. Only you and the team can." I don't know what to say, or if I should say anything. I want to say when I'm on the job, I'm focused, I'm switched on, and for the most part, I am, but when you're constantly questioned on your mental ability in these sorts of situations, you can start to doubt yourself.

"You passed your physical, you requalify at the top of your team every year, but as you are aware, we had over twenty applicants for new team leader."

"Yes, sir. I was aware."

"Your psych testing." He pauses.

Fuck, here we go.

"The guy was a pompous ass. Got in my head." I come right out and say it. No point beating around the bush. He's gotta know I fucked up.

"They all are. It's their job." He's right; it's their job, but a fucking polygraph to test my stress? I call bullshit.

"The department outsources to different companies. I had no idea what went on until after the fact. Seems to me you received the short end of the stick." I don't say anything as I nervously wait for the setback I've been expecting all week.

"Is your head in the right space, Hetcherson?" he questions, and it takes everything in me not to say I don't know.

"Yes, sir."

"Good. The decision will be made next week. I suggest you think long and hard about what it is you can bring to the team, Hetcherson, because from what I saw today, you have a team ready to follow your lead. It's only you holding yourself back." I nod, releasing a quiet and steady breath.

"I'll see you back at headquarters." He leaves me standing there more confused than what I was last week.

Does this mean I'm being considered, even though I blew my psych evaluation? Or is his warning a preparation for things to come?

All the questioning in the world won't give me the answer I'm looking for; all I can do is wait.

"You doing okay, Hetch?" Sterling steps into command as soon as the lieutenant steps out.

"Yep, good job out there." I don't relay the lieutenant's conversation, opting to keep it to myself for now.

"The team is heading to The Elephant after debriefing, you in?"

"Yeah, I'm in." I school my features the best I can and act

like I didn't get a warning to sort my shit out. The truth is the lieutenant's words have me stuck in a gray area.

Maybe team leader holds too much power over me. Or maybe I am the only one holding me back.

I have to figure out what it is I want.

'Cause right now, I'm not sure.

* * *

"I want her." I signal as the woman I've been eyeing stands from her table and moves toward us. Her short blonde hair hangs below her jaw in soft, loose curls.

Fuck, just enough to hold on to.

Her sharp green eyes find mine briefly before she drops her gaze to the floor. A small, possibly shy smile drags my eyes down to her mouth. She's wearing red on her lips, and the small dip in the top pout has my cock wanting to claim every inch of her fuckable mouth.

Jesus, she's fucking beautiful.

I noticed her as soon as we walked into The Elephant twenty minutes ago, and I haven't been able to keep my eyes off her.

"You keep going at this rate, you'll blow through all the available women in town." Sterling throws back the remainder of his beer. He's not gonna fight me on it. He just wants to give me shit.

"You going to start on me too?" I continue to watch the blonde. Her hips sway from side to side as she makes her way to the restrooms. I'm not fucking stupid; the little sway is for show. Like a fucking peacock displaying her feathers. Presenting herself to me.

"You won't hear any complaints from me. Who's giving you a hard time?"

"Who isn't? Mom, Kota, my new fucking neighbor." My mind skips over my mom and sister and flashes to the mystery woman who's managed to turn me on and surprise me at the same time.

"I still don't know why you're in that place when you have a perfectly livable house." Sterling nods to RJ, signaling for another beer. He doesn't bother checking if I want another. He's picked up my vice for the evening will be pussy, not alcohol.

The truth is I've had the house for over three years. Before my father killed himself, he was helping me renovate. The first two years after his death, I couldn't go back. The reminder of him around the place was too raw. Too fresh. It's only been in the last twelve months I've started spending days off out there. Slowly working on it. Of course, I don't tell Sterling any of this.

"I told you, I'm not living there until I'm done fixing it up." I know it's counterproductive, paying a mortgage on my own place and paying rent in town, but the house needs major work, and I refuse to live in the mess of construction while I renovate. The job most days takes it out of you, coming home to chaos won't cut it for me. I don't need the clutter in my life.

"So what about this new neighbor? Nosey old bat is she?" The bastard smirks, probably looking forward to the story.

"Not that I know of." I shake my head, still unable to get her out of my mind. Her soft whimpers the other night when I heard her pleasuring herself, the sharp gasp of air when she realized I was listening. It all keeps replaying over and over.

Jesus, I need a do-over.

"What do you mean?" Fox asks, drawing me out of my own personal wet dream. The whole team is here, and even though I didn't want to head out after training, I'm glad I did.

"I've never seen her," I tell him, knowing it's only going to generate more questions. These little team get-togethers are the only time I see the moody bastard relax enough to drop the permanent scowl he wears and open up enough to know behind the steely attitude, he's genuinely a good guy.

"How is this possible?" His eyes fill with suspicion like he thinks I'm keeping something from them.

"Well, she only moved in a few weeks ago, you know how it is. Between training and late night call outs, I barely see anyone these days." They all nod, agreeing with my summary of the life of Trebook's tactical team.

"So what is she doing to piss you off?" Sterling presses for more information.

I'm not sure pissing me off would be the correct word to describe the woman in apartment seven. I'm not even sure she realizes she's pissing me off.

"Let's say she's a bit of a prude." It's the only way I can describe the issue with the mystery woman since I'm still trying to wrap my head around the strange turn of events.

It all started the night when I fucked up and talked to her. I should have let her get off, but my need to want to come with her had me calling out and scolding her.

My demand was met with silence, followed by a thud to the floor.

I nearly laughed. I managed to contain it, but I did give a tap on the wall and asked her if she was still with me. I didn't hear anything back and after a few minutes waiting around, I realized I was alone.

I thought about heading over and knocking on her door. But this situation is not something I've ever experienced before and, to be honest, part of me wasn't sure it happened the way I had imagined it. It wasn't until I received the anonymous note a few days later letting me know I was too loud, that I knew it really happened. At first, I thought her smartass letter was funny, maybe a little sassy, but then the more I thought about it, the more it pissed me off. I mean, why would she care how loud I am? Clearly, she needs to work on that issue herself if her fucking vibrator is waking me up.

I should have marched over and knocked on her door the day I received the note, but that didn't excite me. Instead, I found myself being louder, more obnoxious, hoping to rile her up and get some kind of reaction.

"Earth to Hetch!" I cop a slap up the back of my head.

"Sorry." I stall, not sure I should go there with them. If my promotion goes through, conversations like this will need to simmer down.

"Come on, you gotta give us more. How is she a prude?"

Hart enters the conversation, making it harder for me not to spill.

"She left me a rather interesting note about my extracurricular activities." Hart, Sterling, and even Fox laugh, understanding my meaning right away, but Tate is slow on the uptake.

"What sort of extracurricular activities?" he pushes, making the guys laugh harder.

"His fucking activities," Hart answers, and we wait for Tate to catch on.

"Jesus, Hetch." He blushes slightly, reminding me he's still fresh.

"All I can say is it's the thin walls." I shrug, not in the least apologetic about it. She wasn't so fucking worried how loud she was when she was getting off last week.

"So what are you gonna do?" Sterling leans in closer, more invested in the story than the others. Of course he is. The fucker lives for my discomfort.

"What do you think? Fuck louder." The boys burst out in laughter, and I earn myself a slap on the back from Fox. The truth is I'm not sure I know what I want to do. Part of me wants to replay the night over, preferably with no wall between us. The other part wants me to say fuck you and make her regret the stupid note.

Fuck, I need to fuck her out of my head.

As if on cue, the blonde woman from earlier takes my attention again when she walks past our table and heads back to her friends.

Maybe she can help me stick it to the prude in apartment seven.

"What's the tall blonde drinking?" I ask RJ while watching her take her seat next to a pretty redhead.

"Rum and coke." RJ answers, already knowing my game plan. "But, you're wasting your time. She already sent one back from that douche." I follow his gaze and eye the sorry fucker who struck out.

"Send her a rum and coke." I ignore his warning. I'm pretty sure her earlier display of feathers tells me I'm not wasting my time. RJ smirks as I sit back and watch the waitress walk over with her drink.

She doesn't turn like I expect her to; instead, she whispers something into the waitress' ear. I wait for another beat, before she returns back to the bar, drink still on her damn tray.

"Ohhh, burn." Tate smacks me on the shoulder, offering me some bullshit comfort.

"What the hell was that about?" I try to think of the last time I struck out.

Besides the mystery neighbor last week, never.

"I told you it wasn't going to work." RJ offers no sympathy as he moves on to serve another customer.

Not prepared to accept defeat, I stand and reach for the drink.

"Where the hell are you going?" Sterling calls out when I head toward the woman in question.

"Going to ask her what her deal is," I call back.

"Oh, Jesus, here we go." Fox laughs, no doubt shocked at my play. Normally, I don't have to work this hard. The badge alone gets me the pussy I need. Chasing after a woman with huge effort is not my normal play, but something about the way she is sending mixed signals has my attention. Sure, it may also be the way her legs look in her tight-as-sin jeans. It might even be the hint of a fucking delicious cleavage that has every guy in the bar's attention. Or maybe I just want to see those red lips wrapped around my cock, while I fuck her mouth into submission.

Whatever it is, I'm not giving up.

Not yet at least. .

LIBERTY

"What is your deal? At least that one's cute." Payton scolds me as the waitress walks back to the bar, drink still firmly on her tray.

"I'm not interested." I shrug, knowing they won't understand.

"Please, we just watched you walk past him, adding a little extra sway in your hips." My cousin Sophie cuts in.

"What? I was walking." I don't try to hide my lie.

Seriously, could I have been any more obvious?

"I'm with the girls. That was rude. You've been eye-fucking him since he walked in, sending the poor guy mixed signals and then you send the drink back." Fiona, the final link in our foursome, adds her opinion to the table.

Tonight we're out for a girls' night. Something we're not able to do too often these days.

Between Payton's time restraints with Arabella; Fee and Sophie's new business venture, and my heavy caseload at work, we've barely seen each other in the last few weeks.

"Please, I'm a grown woman, Fee. I can admire the view. I can also buy my own drink." I place my straw in my mouth and watch them all shake their head in disbelief.

"You're crazy. I get the first guy's brushoff, but this one, he's sexy as fuck." Sophie sets her disappointed eyes on me.

Sophie's mom and my mom are sisters. Extremely close sisters. This meant we spent practically every moment of our lives growing up together. Born only a few days apart, it was almost like we were twins. Growing up with a built-in best friend was awesome. The first day of school was always less stressful, heading off to college was less daunting. Christmas was always fun and the few times we've had a fight, we knew there was no getting rid of each other. Even now, thirty years on, she may be my cousin, but she's also one of my best friends.

"Come on, guys, I told you all, I'm on a sabbatical." They all groan, clearly thinking my sabbatical is a bad idea.

"Accepting a drink doesn't have to lead to sex," Fee presses, in the mood to argue with me on this tonight.

Fiona is the type of friend who gives it to you straight and isn't about to apologize for it. I met her six years ago when I moved back from college. I had just started at Boys Haven. She was the house cook. The boys loved her cooking, and I loved her carefree, no-bullshit personality. We hit it off right away, and even if some days she pisses me off with her bluntness, I know she'll always be there for me.

"It does when the guy is that hot," I admit, knowing damn well he's too dangerous for me. Sure, looking is fine, but accepting a drink will only lead to having to speak. And by the looks of the guy in question, I can almost say with certainty talking would lead to more.

I need to stay strong.

"Hang on a minute, rubbing one off to a stranger behind a wall is okay, but accepting a drink from a cute guy isn't?" Sophie questions.

"No, 'cause her sabbatical only includes penetration," Payton mocks me.

Bitch.

"I'm never going to live this down, am I?" I look to each one of my friends, wishing I didn't trust them with the stupid shit I do.

"Girl, you think we'd let you off the hook? Hell no. This is too much fun." Payton winks.

"What happened with apartment nine anyway?" Sophie takes the conversation back to my issue with my neighbor.

"You still haven't met him?"

"No, she left him a note, telling him to keep it down," Payton tells them before I can.

"But you were the one who was loud." Fee points out the lack of logic in my actions.

"It was a personal moment. He shouldn't have eavesdropped." I tell them my reasoning behind the little note I left. It wasn't like I was rude about it. I just said maybe he should be a little quieter.

"So it's okay for you to listen to him fucking, but because he joined in with you, he's in the wrong?"

"Yes." I nod, unsure to what I'm agreeing.

Fuck me. I need another drink.

"Girl, you need to get your vibrator back out. I think you're losing rational reasoning every week you don't have an orgasm." The table erupts in laughter, and I let it wash it over me.

"Ha ha. No, I don't need cock. I need to find myself. This issue with the neighbor is a setback. It's done. It's over. We need to move on."

"Well, if finding yourself is what you're after, I think you're about to find it in another setback." Fee's smug look confuses me for a second until Payton's eyes find mine.

"Ah, B. He's coming over here." Her mouth barely moves over the rim of her glass, but I hear her loud and clear.

"Shit." I groan under my breath. I didn't think about how he was going to react to my brushoff, but having him come over here wasn't one of the scenarios.

"Evening, ladies." His voice is clear, calm. The smooth baritone dances over my skin and down my spine.

"Good evening." Payton smiles up at the mystery man, then back to me.

"I wanted to know if there was something wrong with the drink I sent over?" He places a drink, the one I just sent back, down in front of me.

I take the opportunity to turn and look up at him. Dark blond hair, green eyes, strong jaw, slightly visible under a five o'clock shadow. A healthy ego more visible the closer he steps into me.

"No, nothing wrong. I'm just not looking for a drink right now." His left eyebrow arches as the start of one of the sexiest grins I've ever seen starts to pull at the side of his kissable mouth.

"Seems to me you're about ready for a refill anyway." He motions to my almost empty glass.

"Like I said, I'm good." I set my lips into my best get-lost-now smile and turn back to face my girls. The table is silent, and for a second, I fight my body's response as I work through some conversation starters.

"You know, where I come from, a man offers to buy you a drink, you say thank you and don't be rude about it." It takes me a second to forcibly let his bullshit mentality slide, before turning back to him.

"Well, where I come from, accepting a drink from a stranger is dangerous." The grin I thought was sexy, spills wider over his face, rendering me stupid.

Fuck, not dimples.

Case in point, Fee. Talking leads to dimples. Dimples lead to sex.

Hot, sweaty, dimple-filled sex.

"You think I laced your drink?" It takes a second to work through the words that filtered into my mind before I can answer.

"For all I know—" I begin.

"I didn't." He loses the dimples, his pinched mouth masking them.

"Yeah, I'm sure all serial killers say that before drugging their victims," I counter. Payton clears her throat, fighting a snort, but

I don't waver.

"I'm a cop."

Wow, three words I wasn't expecting from him.

"I bet a few have used that line too," I fire back, still not cracking.

Jesus, I'm dealing with dimples, arrogance, and a cop.

I sure know how to pick them.

"I can show you my badge." He pulls out a chain from the neckline of his shirt and presents it to me like the good kid in class, handing in an essay a day early.

"Is this supposed to impress me?" At this point, I don't know why I'm still engaging. Sure he's hot, dangerous dimples, and looks amazing in the tight jeans and dark Henley he's wearing, but the man is cocky as hell.

That combo never mixes well.

"You always this bitchy?" He tucks his badge back in his shirt and brings back the dimples.

"And strike three, you're out." I spin back to face my friends. If I wasn't so set alight, I would find their slack jaws almost comical.

Seriously, did they expect anything less from me?

"Aww, come on, B. I thought he had, at least, one more strike in his favor." Payton offers him a lifeline, and I have to hold myself back from kicking her under the table.

"My thoughts exactly." Dimple's tone is playful, but I still catch an air of arrogance.

I turn back, happy to lay it out for him. "Buying me a drink without asking." I raise one finger and count them off. "Showing me your badge and expecting me to drop my panties at the sight of it." I raise a second finger. "And calling me a bitch." I raise a third. "You're so out it's almost laughable."

"Hey, now, I didn't call you a bitch. I said bitchy." His hands move to his narrow hips, drawing my eyes down to his package.

"Same thing." I force them back up.

"It's not." He fires back, not giving in, and even though I struck him out, and he's still arguing with me about it, I find myself awfully attracted to him and surprisingly, this

43

conversation.

"What's your name?" he asks, tilting our banter on its axis.

Don't engage.

Don't engage.

Do not engage.

"Liberty." My stupid tongue answers without permission. Because let's be honest, deep down, she knew the second he walked over my self-appointed sabbatical was in danger.

"Nice to meet you, Liberty." He leans in closer. "Can I buy you that drink?" The smooth baritone of his voice deepens at the change of volume while his hot breath moves over my skin. A strong awareness of my heartbeat takes over, as again, I find myself having to work through the words to find the question he asked.

"I think I'm good." I manage past the excessive moisture my mouth seems to have collected.

"Jesus, woman, I'm not sure if you're always this difficult or it's me, but you have some serious attitude."

"I'm not sure if you're always an ass, or it's me, but being a huge dick won't make yours grow bigger," I counter, my comebacks growing bolder the longer this goes on.

"Invite me to sit with you for a drink and find out." I open my mouth to turn him down, but Fee beats me to it.

"Would you and your friends like to join us for a drink?"

That bitch.

"I'd like that. Let me grab a water and I'll introduce you to my friends." His smug gaze rakes down my body, those stupid dimples deepening when I raise a brow at his blatant checking me out.

When he doesn't move away from me, I press. "Take your time." He shakes his head with a soft chuckle before he steps away back toward the bar.

"Holy shit, Lib." Payton pounces as soon as sexy-as-sin cop walks out of earshot.

"What the hell, Fee?" I ignore Payton and set my scowl on Fee.

"Sorry, I slipped." She doesn't look sorry; in fact, she looks satisfied.

Uggh.

"You can't be angry." Sophie comes to Fee's defense. "If the roles were reversed, you would have done the same damn thing." She's not wrong. I probably would have.

"Yeah, besides," Fee pipes back up, "maybe you were too busy eye-fucking cocky McCocky pants, but did you see his friends? A girl's gotta do what a girl's gotta do." She fans herself with the bar coaster. I turn in my chair and catch a glimpse at the rest of the guys sitting at the bar with Dimples.

Jesus, she's not wrong.

"Ugggh, fine. But you owe me." I turn back, reach out, snatch the coaster from her grasp, and start waving it in front of my face. The light fan of air does nothing to cool me down after the encounter, so I drop it back to the table.

"Please, by the end of the night you'll be thanking her." Payton raises her glass in a toast, encouraging us to follow suit. "Here's to saying fuck the sabbatical, and hello wild sex to piss our neighbors off."

Jesus, why did she have to go there?

***

"And then what happened?" I ask Hetch, more enthralled in his story than anyone else sitting at the table. Thirty minutes, three drinks, and one interesting story later, my sabbatical is more in danger than I care to admit.

After Dimples had returned to the table with his water and friends, he offered me his name.

Liam Hetcherson.

Hetch.

Ugghh, even his name is worthy of abandoning a sex ban.

"We had to wait it out. Then I was able to talk him down. We got there in the end." He shrugs like it's no big deal while I'm left looking at him in a different light.

Hetch is a badass.

A sexy-as–sin badass.

I'm officially ruined.

"So, what do you do, Liberty?" he asks, taking the attention off him for a minute. Since the moment he sat down, he's had my full attention, walking me through the craziness of his work. I think it's part of his game plan, since talking about a day in the life of a SWAT officer equals panties melted.

"Well, I can't say it's anything as exciting as your line of work, but I'm a youth worker. I'm the program director at Boys Haven." There's a slight shift in the tilt of his head, before some kind of understanding flashes in his eyes.

"The big house over on 5th, right?"

"Yeah, you been there?"

"No, but I've driven past it a few times." The easy smile he's been wearing twists into a grim line.

Ignoring his shift in attitude, I continue to chat about the kids I work with and how much I love it. He listens intently for the most part but doesn't engage with any questions. Eventually, I fall quiet, the silence between us growing more awkward than comfortable.

"You okay?" I finally ask, wondering where I lost him.

"Ah, yeah." He clears his throat before taking a sip of his drink. "Just remembering someone." I don't push on his weird reaction; instead, I let the silence grow between us and take in the rest of the table's conversation.

Payton has been in deep conversation with one of Hetch's workmates, Hart, since they joined the table. He's the oldest of the team, not that you can tell. Other than a few gray flecks around his hairline, you wouldn't know the gentle-looking giant is almost forty years old.

I'm not surprised Payton and Hart are getting on. As soon as he said he was a single father, he and Payton had a level ground. Though they seem to have hit it off, I know it's an innocent conversation. As much as Payton likes to play the outrageous friend who acts like she's into everything, and anything, for reasons still unknown to me, she's still madly in love with my stupid brother.

If only he wasn't such an idiot.

Sophie has been talking with Tate, the cute younger member of the team. Tate is quiet, a little shy, Sophie's type down to a T. Add in his blond hair and blue eyes, I wouldn't be surprised if something more ends up happening after tonight.

And Fee has been sharing her attention between Sterling and Fox.

If ever there were two men polar opposite, these men would be it. Where Sterling is light, Fox is dark.

Clean shaven, to a full beard.

Green, gentle eyes to brown, assessing ones.

Soft smiles to deep scowls.

Sterling ticks all the boxes for a good guy. Fox screams fuck-your-checklist; I am the ultimate bad boy. In fact, I'm still not sure how to take him. He's barely said a word, other than a few grunts, but it hasn't slipped my attention the few times he's thrown one of his scowls Payton and Hart's way.

I'm not sure how to read him, considering he seems to be the type of guy who looks pissed off all the time, but I'm definitely getting a vibe.

"So, is the tactical team a full-time unit?" Fee asks the guys, still interested in their line of work.

Sterling answers first, and I listen to him rattle off how they technically are a part-time unit, but practically train and work as a full-time unit, until I feel Hetch's gaze on me. I try harder to stay engaged in the conversation, nodding along like I'm taking in everything he's saying, but after a few more minutes, the soft touch of Hetch's finger starts to glide over my jean-clad thigh.

Jesus.

Ignoring his touch makes it harder to stay focused. And staying focused makes it harder to ignore his touch.

Hetch seems unaffected, answering another question Fee asks. All the while his fingers are innocently stroking my thigh, in the most devilish way.

"You okay, Liberty?" Sterling asks me when Hetch's finger inches closer toward the middle of my legs.

"Ahh, yeah." I squeeze my thighs together, locking him out. It's like he teased me into a trance.

Jesus, get it together.

Needing a moment to compose myself, I stand from my chair.

"Excuse me, I'm going to the bathroom." I find Payton's eyes, letting her know where I am.

"You okay?" she mouths. I nod once with a reassuring smile and then make my way to the bathroom.

The line to the restroom is short, and after using the toilet, and washing my hands, I take a minute to force some deep breaths into my lungs.

"Keep it together, Lib," I coax myself through the mirror, trying to talk myself down from the arousal he's stirred in me. "Do you really want a one-night stand right now?" My body is saying yes, but my head says no. Deciding on an action plan, I take one last look in the mirror, fix my lipstick, tell myself to stay strong, then step out into the hall, only to find Hetch waiting for me.

Shoulders to the wall, hands in the pockets of his deliciously tight jeans, which fit his ass perfectly, he smirks when our eyes collide.

Yep, dangerously perfect.

"Hey, you." He pushes off the wall, and steps forward, invading my space.

"Ahh, hey, back at ya." I try to keep some distance, but his overpowering presence makes it hard. I've never seen myself as short. I mean five feet seven's not model tall, but with heels these days, I find I'm around eye level with an average male. Standing in front of Hetch, it's not the case. The guy has to have a foot on me. Even with my heels.

"You want to get out of here, Liberty?" His face lowers to mine in a slow, measured pace. My mind is screaming at me, reminding me about a certain sabbatical I promised myself, but my body is melting against him, ignoring all rational thought.

"Yeah," I think I reply, or maybe I sigh. I can't be sure, nor do I have a chance to figure it out, before the soft touch of his lips find mine and wipe any and all thinking from my capacity. At first, it's a ghost of a touch, then a little more. Expecting to be consumed with the sweep of his tongue, and anticipating the power of his lips, I'm rather disappointed when, after a modest graze of our lips, he pulls back.

What the hell?

Self-doubt sneaks its way through my subconscious. Self-preservation and maybe shame forces me to take a step back. Hetch doesn't let me get far. His hands move to either side of my face, forcing me back into his space.

"Been thinking about owning these lips since the second I saw them." His gaze locks onto my mouth, and his fingers tighten in my hair. "Just didn't want to rush it." He's close, close enough I can breathe in his need and let it sink into my bones. The whole scene is almost too intense. The way he studies my lips, as if he's committing every small line, every dip to memory. The hardness of his body pressed against mine, imprinting me with his presence, commanding me with his strength. His fingers, tightly wrapped in my hair, hold me hostage while still caressing my need.

"So fucking perfect." He drags his hungry gaze from my lips and gives me his eyes. "Almost too perfect." Before I can ask what he means, his mouth brushes over mine. Once, twice, three times before his tongue dives between my lips and meets mine in hungry need.

I groan at the contact. Hetch hums at the sound, the vibration sparking an intense fire burning through my veins. Eyes open, gazes locked, he continues to own my mouth, my body, like it's never been owned before.

"Fuck me." He pulls back slightly, his eyes flash with confusion, before flicking back to hunger. Then his lips lock back to mine, diving his tongue back in my mouth and branding me like he owns me.

It's like being thirsty on a hot day, and downing a bottle of water in twenty seconds. You swallow every last drop, suck every bit of air until you're out of breath. Only then are you satisfied, fulfilled.

Relieved.

That's what kissing Hetch is like.

Pressed together, mouth-to-mouth, tongue-to-tongue, I can't quench my need fast enough. I drink, he drinks, our tongues dance, dueling together, thrusting us forward to drink some more.

Finally, after the need no longer feels desperate, and the want hurts a little less, the kiss slows, and the perfect way his lips found mine in the beginning, becomes the end.

"Jesus, Lib." The whisper of his tongue tracing my top lip and the way he shortens my name in a hungry need only turns me on more. I don't know what makes my knees weaker. The kiss or the way my name rolls off his tongue. If I'm honest, it has to be the kiss. I've never had a kiss hit me so hard before.

"Yeah." I open my eyes, not realizing I closed them. Hetch keeps me pressed to his front, but detangles his hands from my hair. His thumb moves to my lips, and in the gentlest way a man's ever touched me, fixes what I'm assuming is the mess of my red lips.

"Get your shit, tell your girls you're going home and meet me at the door." He breaks the connection first, and bosses in a way that doesn't bring my bitch out. Unable to utter a word, I nod faster than my normal, respectable self would have liked to and let my feet follow through with his order. All previous promises of my sex ban have flown out the window as I make my way back to the table.

"I'm heading home, guys. You all okay to get home?" I manage to wake my tongue from its kiss-induced haze and force it into conversation.

"Yeah, girl. Your mom and dad have Arabella tonight. I'm going to stay." Payton eyes me up and down before searching for Hetch.

Please, God, I hope he's still in the hallway.

"You sure?" I flick my gaze back around the table. I'm sure I look like a hot mess, but no one calls me on it.

"Yes, I'm sure. Hart was telling me about his daughter." It's a hint to say she is fine and to let it go. "Now, go, or your vagina might combust if you wait any longer." She laughs, forcing my blush into a new shade of red.

Yeah, she knows what's happening.

Not needing to have any more attention on me, I take her for her word and lean in for a quick hug. "Love you. Message me when you get home."

"Message me when *you're* done," she quips, before pushing me away then turning back to her conversation. I say good-bye to the rest of the table, grab my coat, and then leave. It only takes me a few seconds to find Hetch waiting for me outside the front door. When our eyes connect, I know there's no going back. The need outweighs the concern. The want overpowers the reasoning.

Maybe tomorrow I will regret this decision and wish I held on stronger, but tomorrow's Liberty will be biased. She'll already know what it feels like to have Hetch between her legs.

Today's Liberty doesn't. Today's Liberty needs it more than the next breath.

5

HETCH

Her eyes lock with mine the second she steps outside and my pulse quickens, almost in the same way it does before I'm about to go out on a SWAT call.

Jesus, what is it with this one?

"Ready?" she asks, stopping short of an arm's length in front of me.

"My place or yours?" I answer, reaching forward and pulling her flush to my front. The swell of her breasts press against me, and it takes everything in this good guy persona not to push her against the wall and bury my face between them.

"Yours," she squeaks. Her earlier confidence seems to have faded, but it doesn't stop me from taking her hand and dragging her out of the pub and over to my car. If I'm desperate or too pushy, she doesn't say anything, just follows along, her fingers wrapped tightly around mine.

"I'm not far from here," I tell her as we walk up to my black pick-up truck. She doesn't say anything as I open her door. Only giving me a slight grin before climbing up into the cab.

My dick rejoices for the up-close and personal view of her ass before she plants herself in the seat.

"Buckle up, babe," I order, then close the door and walk around to my door. I'm not sure if the kick in my step is from having less alcohol through my body or the fact for the first time in a few months, I'm taking a woman to bed, and I'll be able to remember it.

"You always this way?" she asks when I climb in. The click of her belt tells me she followed my request and isn't going to sass me, but the tone of her question tells me her confidence is coming back.

"You mean following the law?" I offer a wink then watch the small pout of her lips spread into a reluctant grin.

Fuck me, she's a cute thing.

"Smart ass," she mutters under her breath, looking out the window. The conversation stays light; she asks me questions about Trebook's tactical team and protocol, and I even dare to ask some more questions about her working at Boys Haven. Earlier when she said she worked at Boys Haven, I was taken back. My father was a youth worker for thirty years and at one point growing up, I almost followed his career path. Until my thirst for police work took over.

"You doing okay over there?" I ask as I turn down my street. She fell silent midconversation about two streets back, her fingers tensing over the strap of her purse.

"No." She shakes her head, her color dropping to a shade of white. I'm not sure if she's having second thoughts about coming home with me or she's had too much to drink.

"You feel sick?" I ask when she doesn't say anything else.

"No, no, no, no, no." Her clear eyes narrow, looking from me to my apartment building.

"What is it?" I pull into my parking space and cut the engine.

"Apartment nine?" She spits the two words out like it leaves a bad taste in her mouth.

"Yeah?" I look at her horrified face and then the freshly painted nine above my parking spot.

"You have to be kidding me." She pushes the release on her seatbelt and exits my truck, slamming the door behind her. I follow her out and watch as she walks around the car and stomps her way up the stairs.

"Want to tell me what the hell is happening here?" I race to catch up with her. A part of me starts to panic. I would never have picked her to turn out crazy, but by the looks of things, I might have an issue on my hands.

"Oh, not much, Hetch." My name has never been delivered with such animosity before, and it takes a second to process it. "Just the fact I almost had sex with my annoying new neighbor who changes his women nearly as often as his underwear."

What the fuck?

"Apartment seven?" I stop midstep as it all becomes clear. The change in her the closer we got home. The angry way she spat out my apartment number and the way she stomped up those steps like she knew her way.

"Oh, please. Don't say it like I'm the pain in the ass." She throws her sass over her shoulder and starts taking the steps two at a time.

Jesus Christ. This is the woman who's had me messed up the last couple of days.

"What the hell are the chances? Of course, it's my luck." She keeps muttering, placing more distance between us. Shaking my shock away, I continue my pursuit.

"Are you shitting me right now?" I'm torn between laughing at the turn of events and watching the way her fuckable ass moves up the steps.

"Jesus, it's like a bad joke. The man who rudely interrupted my Jill session last week is you. You!" I don't think she realizes what she just blurted or how loud she's being; instead, she continues to rant, "No fucking way you can make this shit up. This is just my luck."

There are many comments I could lead with right now about the *Jill* session we had, but I decide I'm better off keeping my mouth shut.

"I almost gave up my sex ban for *you*. God help me." She

54

pushes her key in the door. The same door I've been walking past every day this week wondering when we would meet.

"Wait, Liberty. Come here and take a brea—"

"Like hell I'm going anywhere with you, Hetch." She cuts me off.

"And why the hell not?" I fold my arms over my chest, waiting for whatever bullshit she comes up with.

"Because one, I happen to like where I live. Even if my new neighbor is some manwhore who likes to fuck hours on end, and then listen in when he isn't welcome. Two, I have a lease I cannot get out of for another year. And three, you don't shit where you eat and all that jazz." She holds her hand out, offering me some friendly bullshit gesture. If I wasn't so fucking turned on right now, I'd be offended she insulted me with a fucking handshake.

I just had my tongue down her throat, my dick pressed up against the softness of her belly, and she offers me her fucking hand.

I'd be less offended if she used said hand to help me get off.

"So that's it?" My hard dick dies a slow, sad death, knowing this isn't ending the way he envisioned.

"Of course, that's it." She huffs, only making me want her more.

"Well, fuck, babe. Can't say I'm not disappointed."

"I'm sure you'll get over it when your next fling comes around." I don't know what's worse: the undertone of her disgust or the lip curl that follows when she looks me up and down. "Good night, Hetch." She opens her door and steps inside.

"Liberty," I call out before she closes the door. She doesn't turn around, but I know she's waiting to hear what I have to say.

"You're wrong about the women."

She spins, mocks me with her judging eyes, daring me to deny it all.

Quit while you're ahead, man.

Instead, I elaborate. "I don't change women more than my underwear."

She scoffs, "Please, in case you forget, I can hear all."

"I don't wear underwear, babe," I clarify with a grin.

"Ugghh. See, you're an ass." The door slams closed before I can let out a full belly laugh.

It's not lost on me that it's something I haven't done with sincerity in a long time.

Nor is it lost on me how much I like that she pulled it from me.

Well, this is fucking interesting.

* * *

"Hey, you still awake?" I tap on the wall a little later on. After staring at Liberty's door for longer than I should have, I dragged my ass into my own place, had a shower, and then climbed into bed. It's the first time I've been knocked back so vehemently; I don't know what to do with myself.

"Go away." I hear her huffed reply.

"Can't really go anywhere." I snicker, feeling all kinds of messed up talking through a wall. A reminder of last week filters through my memory, reminding me of how she sounds when she comes.

Fuck, I want a replay now.

"How about you go to sleep."

"Can't sleep."

"Well, I'm trying to, so be quiet."

I don't say anything for a few minutes, the silence growing between us.

"Wanna jack off again?"

"Ugghh, seriously, Hetch. Don't talk to me." A bang on the wall follows, and it brings a smile to my face knowing I rile her up.

"I like you, Liberty. You're unexpected." I don't know why I say it; the fact I'm not fucking a woman like my cock thought it would be is messing with me.

"I don't like you, Hetch," is her reply. I don't bother correcting her. We both know she's more than affected by me. Instead, I rest further back into my pillow.

"We'll see," I whisper, not sure what it means, but I'm happy to wait it out. I wasn't lying when I said she was unexpected. She excites me, intrigues me, and even if the night ended the way it did, it's the first time in a long time I'm looking forward to more.

More what, I don't know. But I can't wait to find out.

LIBERTY

"So, I've let you hold off for as long as physically possible, spill it, sister." Payton starts on me the next morning when I meet her and Arabella for breakfast.

"Seriously, let me have at least half of this coffee before I can begin to get my head around last night." I drop my face into my hands and let out an undignified groan.

"What! That bad? Say it isn't so." She kicks at my foot under the table, needing more information.

I drop my hands and sit back up. "You know the manwhore next door?"

"Don't tell me you got into a fucking contest to see who could scream the loudest?" She lowers her voice on the word fucking, for Arabella's sake.

"Jesus, Payton. No. Where do you come up with this stuff?" She shrugs, not giving me a true answer. "Hetch *is* apartment nine."

"SHUT THE FRONT DOOR. Loud-as-fuck is none other

than sexy Officer Fucks-a-lot?" She forgets to sensor herself this time and manages to garner the attention of the old couple next to us, the two guys behind us and one little four-year-old.

"Lower your voice. And don't call him that." If I wasn't so embarrassed, I would snicker at her nickname for him.

"Uh-oh. You said bad word, Mommy," Arabella blurts with her mouth full of toast.

"Bad Mommy." Payton smacks her own hand then passes her another piece of toast.

"Sorry, I'm having a moment. So was he as good as he sounds then?" She turns her attention back to me, not done with her interrogation.

"I didn't screw him, Pay." *Jesus, what does she think of me?*

"And why the hell not?"

"Why do you think? He's clearly a manwhore," I answer with the most logical reason.

"Aww, come on, he's not that bad. A few different women over the course of two weeks barely constitutes being a manwhore. Besides, who cares? You weren't looking for anything serious, right?" She has a point, who am I to judge him when I was clearly ready to do the same thing? Still, it doesn't sit right.

"I'm not comfortable knowing what I know about him. The whole idea of a one-night stand is you don't have to see them again. Besides, he wasn't impressed when he found out who I was either."

"Please, I saw the way the man was looking at you. I don't think he would give a flying nun who you are."

"It's easier to keep things separate, you know. I mean, the last thing I need is to have things awkward between us."

"Oh, you mean like they are already after Wallgate?"

Seriously, I don't know why I tell her anything.

"Ha ha, you're so funny. Anyway, it's done. Over with. It didn't happen the way I was expecting it to happen so enough talking about him, please. It is what it is. I want to know what happened to you." I change the subject. I spent all night thinking about Hetch; I don't want to continue into today. "Hart, was it?

Did you get his number?"

"Oh, God, no. It wasn't like that." She gives an innocent shrug, completely unaware how clueless she is.

"Why not? He seemed nice, Pay. A little older, yeah, but has a good head on his shoulders. Single dad. You guys have a bit in common."

"He was nice, but I didn't see him like that. Besides, Jett and I are still trying to work it out." She drops a little tidbit of information in there.

"Ahh, since when?"

"A couple of weeks."

I shouldn't be so surprised by her need to keep it quiet. I have been particularly forthcoming with my opinion on the matter of her and Jett. But it still stings a little she kept it from me.

"You didn't think you could tell me." I'm not asking. It's more for my own understanding.

"Well, you really haven't been pro-Jett." She's not kidding. My stupid brother had the perfect life with a wife and daughter who worshipped him. Instead of appreciating what he had, he gave it up for some little hussy he had working as his assistant.

"Do you blame me?"

"No, but this isn't about you." She has a point and the moment I realize my selfishness, I try to curb my attitude.

"Are you sure it's what you want, Pay?"

"I don't know yet. But don't I owe it to him to at least try? I mean, I took a vow."

"A vow he crapped on." My vocabulary is limited with Arabella at the table, but crapped on is a fairly accurate account.

"Lib," she warns, but I've never been good at curbing my attitude.

"No, Payton. That's bull and you know it. You don't get to be in my face about my business, and I can't tell you how I feel." I want to be the good friend here and tell her I'm so happy for her, but at the same time, it's getting to the point where tough love is needed.

"He's your brother, Liberty, you of all people should be on

his side."

"Side? This isn't about sides. Yes, he's my brother, and I love him, but what he did is wrong."

"He's trying, Lib. For real. He's been going to counseling."

I want to say counseling doesn't make a new man, but what sort of sister would it make me? "And it's not just me I have to think about, you know. What about Arabella? If there is a chance I can give her the family I never had, don't you think I should try?"

I get what she's saying. I do. Payton never had a good relationship with her parents, but I know my brother. I remember how devastated Payton was, and how cold he was. The last thing Payton or Arabella needs is to be hurt by him again.

"You know I love you and Arabella. I'm just looking out for you. I don't want my dipshit brother hurting you again. If you think you owe it to me or Arabella, I can tell you now, it's not going to work. You haven't lost his family. We're still here. We always will be here. But if you really want this for you, then I'll support you."

"Honestly, I don't know what I want, Liberty. I wish we could go back to before, you know?" She reaches out and runs her finger along Arabella's cheek.

"So he fired her I take it?" I can't even say her name; the little whore doesn't deserve one.

"Well, not exactly."

"What does that mean? She's still working there?"

My dipshit brother.

"Well, it's not like he can fire her. He would be opening himself up to a lawsuit."

"So you're paying this home-wrecker, and he's still seeing her every day. Can't you see how messed up this is?" I know I said I would support her, but this is ridiculous.

"I don't know what you want me to say, Liberty. It's okay for you to sit there and tell me what is best for me. You're not the one living this. I love him, okay. And maybe that's stupid, but I can't stop it." She stands from her chair and starts packing up

Arabella's stuff.

"I don't want to go, Mommy." Arabella notices her mom's rush to leave.

"Payton, sit down." I try to reach out to her, but she ignores me and continues to ramble. I didn't envision our breakfast ending like this.

"He messed up. But if I can forgive him, then you should be able to. We all make mistakes. You're not perfect either you know." She reaches for Arabella and picks her up out of the chair.

"No, Mommy. I not finished."

"I never said I was. I just don't want to see you get hurt."

"Well, it's a risk I may have to take."

"Okay, I'm sorry. I won't say anything else about it, okay?" We stare at one another for a beat. Her standing, me seated. We've never argued like this before, and I'm having a hard time getting my head around it.

"Look, I need to go." She breaks the silence.

"Payton, don't—"

"Thanks for breakfast. I'll speak to you later. Say bye, Aunt B." Arabella looks as confused as I am, and before I can call her back, she's out the door, leaving me sitting there feeling like an asshole.

"And that's what happens when you dish out tough love," I whisper to myself.

* * *

"Liberty?" A knock on my office door a few hours later has me almost jumping out of my chair.

"Hey." I look up from my paperwork, checking the time.

Crap, after seven. I was meant to finish an hour ago. I promised myself I was going to stop staying so late, but time keeps getting away from me.

"Sorry, didn't mean to startle you, but we have an issue." Sue, one of Boys Haven's full-time youth workers, steps into my office.

"What's up?" An issue in a house like this can be as little as a fight between the boys, or as huge as one of the kids getting into serious trouble.

"Mitch hasn't come home for curfew."

Shit, not what I want to hear today.

"What about the other boys?" I stand, packing up my desk.

"All in and accounted for."

"Has anyone seen him since school let out?" I try to think back to what his schedule looks like on a Monday. Four of the six boys we house here are old enough to work. On Mondays, Cam, Jonah, and Will head off to work, while the other three boys, Mitch, Garrett, and Brooklyn come home, check in, and start on their homework.

"He checked in, then was cleared to leave with Garrett for the library. Garrett says he thought he saw some of The Disciples hanging around."

Shit.

The Disciples are a local street gang Mitch's brother hangs with.

"Are you kidding me right now?" I reach for my keys.

"Where are you going?" she asks, following me out of my office and inside to the house.

With the capacity to house up to nine boys, Boys Haven is a big house. Built for the sole purpose of what we do here, we have the luxuries not a lot of other houses like ours do.

Two bathrooms, one large kitchen. Two recreation areas, a large back yard, plus the garage, which was turned into two offices. The boys and the staff have it very good here, all things considered.

"I'm going to get him," I tell her when I step into the house and make my way down the hall to one of the recreation areas.

"I don't know, Liberty." She seems unsure, but what are the other options? It's not like Mitch to miss curfew. After spending the day with him last week, I know he's having a tough time, but he's trying really hard. He wouldn't throw it all away. If he's missing curfew for his brother, it's for a reason. If he's missing curfew for The Disciples, then he's in deep shit.

"Excuse me, boys." I interrupt the conversation in the main recreation room. Even though we're not to capacity, most days we're kept on our toes. Situations like this make it tenfold.

"What's up, Liberty?" Brooklyn, one of the oldest boys, looks up from his homework.

"You know where I can find Mitch's brother?" He looks from me to Sue, then back to me. Brooklyn is a good kid. With a dad who left before he was born and a strung-out mom who stopped giving a shit, he was placed in the system when he was five. Now almost seventeen, he's worked his way up from being in serious trouble, to serious potential. And with my recommendation, he will stay at Boys Haven until he turns eighteen. Then with the help of our team, we'll help transition him into independent living.

"I don't know exactly where, but word is he hangs downtown on Lexington." He gives me something to work with.

"Thanks." I nod and then keep moving back through the house to the front door.

"Liberty, wait," Sue calls out before I can make it out the front door.

"I'll be safe. I'll drive around. Maybe Garrett was wrong and he's still there. Caught up in his work. God knows it happens to me." I know she wants to believe me, but like me, she's worried.

"You know protocol here. We need to call this in," she gently pushes, always one to follow the book. I know the protocol, but right now, my only concern is Mitch.

"Let's give it half an hour before we go making any formal reports." She looks so unsure, I almost tell her to call the cops, but she ends up giving me a nod. "I'm gonna head to the library first. I bet you he's there." Deep down I know he's not, but one can only hope.

"Okay, well, call me if you find him." She's as invested in these boys as much as I am. Boys like Mitch have it difficult to start with and watching them walk down the wrong path is a hard pill to swallow.

"Will do." I wave as I walk out the front and get into my car. Trebook is the type of place where it's big enough to have a big city feel, but still small enough someone knows someone. On my own, my search could last all night, but with a few connections on the street, I may have a good chance of finding him.

I head to the library first, my concern growing when I don't find him there. I drive around for another fifteen minutes, almost too afraid to head in the direction Brooklyn told me. Knowing I have no other option, I suck it up and make my way downtown to Lexington. My trust is shattered when after driving down the street twice, I notice a group of boys standing at the side of the convenience store.

Mitch.

He's there, clutching a metal bat in his hands, the group of guys crowding him.

Pulling off to the side of the road, I put the car in park, and unbuckle my seatbelt.

"Jesus, Mitch. What the hell are you doing?" I whisper to myself as I reach for my phone and dial Sue's mobile.

"Liberty?" She answers on the first ring like she's been sitting there anticipating my call.

"I found him," I tell her in greeting.

"Oh, thank God. Is he okay?"

"I don't know. He looks fine, but I think he's with his brother and his gang."

"Crap."

Yeah, crap all right.

Gangland culture in Trebook and the surrounding areas of Arizona has increased dramatically in recent years. Gang violence and youth involvement have particularly grown. Gangs like The Disciples have contributed to the increasing levels of youth violence and incarceration numbers. The guys Dominic's been hanging with are bad news, and I refuse to let Mitch get involved with them.

"I'm putting a stop to this right now," I tell her.

"Now hang on a minute, Lib. Maybe you should come back

to the house. I don't want you getting yourself into trouble."

"Well, I can't leave him here," I argue. If he gets caught hanging with these boys while in the program, there will be no helping him.

"I'm calling this in, Lib. Don't you get involved."

"The police will take too long. Besides, as of right now, he's not doing anything wrong other missing curfew and meeting up with his brother. If I want to stop Mitch from fucking up his clean record, then I have no other choice."

"Liberty, you can't save them all, and you can't put yourself into a position that is going to hurt you. You know Dominic's history. He's not someone to mess around with. Just stay in your car and call it in." I consider what she is saying, but still something compels me to reach out.

"Maybe I can scare them off. Can you stay on the line for me?" Sue starts to argue, but I pull the phone away and get out of the car, slowly walking over to them.

"Mitch!" I call out when they all start to walk toward the convenience store. Mitch's head comes up, his eyes growing wide at the sight of me.

"Liberty?" He freezes, looking at Dominic then back to me.

"I've been looking all over for you. You missed curfew." I keep my eyes on him, hoping he's not about to go into the convenience store wielding a metal bat with this gang.

"Well, well, look who we have here. Liberty, is it?" Dominic steps into my path before I can reach his brother. With the height of a man and none of the bulk, Dominic looks only marginally older than his younger brother. His dark hair sticks out from under a red bandana and, unlike Mitch, his Latin skin is branded and scarred. My eyes briefly collect the visible marks, knowing each one tells a story you wouldn't want your children to ever hear. Each one proof as to why Mitch has to stay away.

"I think you're in the wrong neighborhood, little lady." The boys in his crew snicker at his attempt of intimidation while I keep my gaze on Mitch.

The last time I saw Dominic was five months ago when he was told he couldn't come to the house to visit. He lost his shit, swearing and threatening bodily harm. We ended up calling the police when he refused to leave. In the end he left, but not before telling me I would pay for keeping his brother from him.

"Mitch, get in the car." I ignore Dominic's tactics and focus on what needs to be done.

Get Mitch safely back to the house

"Sorry, Liberty. Mitch isn't going anywhere right now. He has some business to attend to." Dominic answers for him, stepping out of my path and walking toward his brother.

"Mitch, you know the rules. The police have been called. Go get in the car now." I stay strong. This is all a power struggle for Dominic. The last thing he needs is for his crew or his brother to have a run in with the police.

"You're full of shit." Dominic calls my bluff, his earlier bravado marginally slipping.

"Stick around and find out then." I keep my composure and hope Sue has already made the call. "Mitch, I'm not going to tell you again. You're already in a lot of trouble. So get in the damn car before I can't help you." I may have a potty mouth outside of work, but don't normally speak to the boys like this. Desperate times call for desperate measures.

Mitch looks torn. I can see he wants more than anything to get into the safety of my car, but something is holding him there. Something Dominic has over him.

"Mitch is done taking orders from you, Liberty. So I suggest you turn your tight ass around and get out of here before you find yourself in trouble." Dominic takes a step toward me.

"Why are you doing this, Dominic?" I ask, not giving in. I can't walk away from Mitch. Not if I know for sure this isn't what he wants.

"We're family. Family stick together."

"Family also support each other, Dominic. Mitch is doing so well at Haven. His grades are improving. He's top of his class. He doesn't need to go down this path."

"Ahh, Liberty." His condescending tone is almost comical. "What's wrong with this path? I got myself a good life." My heart thumps in my ears, as the gaze he sets on me tells me he's hiding something.

"If you're happy with your choices, then I'm happy for you, Dominic. But don't you think Mitch deserves more?" I notice two of the guys come around the side of me, starting to box me in. One larger than me, the other around Mitch's size.

"You gonna teach this uppity bitch a lesson, Dom?" A prickly unease filters through me, and an overwhelming urge to run tingles into my toes. He steps forward as I step back.

"Come on, guys, leave, Liberty alone. She has nothing to do with this." Mitch shrugs off one of the guy's arm and steps in front of me. It's the worst thing he could have done. Not one to be told what to do, the guy brings his fist back and connects it with Mitch's face.

A tight scream pushes from my mouth as I reach out for Mitch.

"Please, Dominic, don't let them hurt him." I cringe as blood spurts from Mitch's nose, but he doesn't react like I expect him to. Instead of cowering away, he stays strong, standing tall between us. Protecting me.

"Mitch, you best be moving," Dominic warns before his crew can do more damage.

"You need to teach your boy a lesson." The guy who just punched Mitch tells Dominic.

"Kid, you need to move." Mitch doesn't budge. Standing in front of me, he holds his brother's stare.

"Why, are you going to hit me, too?" Not two seconds pass before Dominic's fist comes out, and punches him, this time knocking him down. Mitch rolls to his side, groaning in pain.

Oh, God, what the hell is happening here?

I don't have a chance to help him up before Dominic sets his sights on me. Reaching for me, I outstep him only to back into the hardness of another body.

Shit.

"You know what, Liberty? If you think you can keep my family away from me, then you and I have some business to sort out." Mitch tries to stand from the ground, but another one of Dominic's boys steps in and keeps him down with a boot in his back.

"Dominic, you don't want to make threats. You know the system," I warn. It's not much of a deterrent for a man like him in his position, but there isn't much more I can do.

"I think you telling me what to do, isn't in your best interest." Arms come around me, holding me in place. The hard body I found myself backing into keeps me from retreating.

After struggling in his grasp, my fight finally dies when Dominic steps in closer.

"You need to know your place, *puta*. You stepping in, putting your nose in where it doesn't belong, is messing up my plans. Now Mitch is *my* family, not yours, and I'm not gonna take too kindly to you stepping in again. So I'm gonna give you a warning, and you're going to listen to it." His hand reaches out and wraps his fingers around my jaw, squeezing tightly.

I hold my composure. It's not the first time I've been confronted by a group of boys or dealt with physical assault. Working in an all-boys home makes you tough.

"You're gonna back the fuck off and let Mitch do what he needs to do. If you don't, then you and I are going to have problems. You understand me?" His fingers dig deeper into my face.

Unable to move my mouth, I nod instead.

"Good. Glad we see eye to eye on this." He releases my face with a push, then steps back. "Mitch, Liberty's right. It's late. Past your curfew. We'll pick this up next time." He nods to his crew then turns and starts walking away.

The guy holding my arms releases me with a push, forcing me down to the ground.

"And keep your mouth shut, bitch." He delivers a kick to my ribs, followed by a boot to my face. A throbbing ache radiates through my face and a scream dies in my lungs almost immediately as an almighty sharp pain shoots up through my side, rendering me breathless.

"Liberty." Mitch crawls forward, trying to help me to sit up, but the movement only causes me to yell out in pain.

"I'm so sorry, Liberty. It's all my fault. I'm sorry." Mitch

69

starts crying, his hand raking through his hair and pulling at the ends in a frenzied state.

"It's okay, Mitch. Just get me to the car." My words come out in small bursts of air as I fight against the pain, against the fog threatening to take me under. My head is spinning, the blow to my ribs having altered my ability to stand, but I know if I don't get up soon, I may pass out.

"Liberty? What's happening? Do you need to go to the hospital?" He picks up something is wrong at about the same time realization hits me.

Something is definitely wrong. And not so much with him, but with me.

"Mitch, I-I…." My words slur and eyes blur as warm blood trickles down my cheek.

The last thing I hear before passing out is, "Police."

7

HETCH

"You know what I think? I think she's the first woman to knock you back, and you can't handle it." Sterling continues to give me shit hours after telling him about Liberty turning out to be the annoying woman in apartment seven.

"No, you know what I think?" I answer with my own question.

"What?" He sits a little straighter. He's been waiting all night for me to bite. Ever since we started our shift, he's been on my case about whether I've heard anything from my neighbor.

"I think you should mind your own damn business." He laughs, not deterred from pissing me off.

It's a quiet Monday night, and while Trebook's tactical unit is closer to a full-time unit than part-time, we are still required to work patrol shifts on a rotating roster. Tonight is our shift.

Accident reports and domestic disputes have taken up half our night, add in Sterling's bullshit prodding about my new neighbor and I'm about done. Give me training, give me drills,

71

give me a twelve-hour hostage negotiation over this shit.

"Just fucking admit it. She has you messed up."

"Control to 347, we have reports of an assault at the front of a convenience store, over on 6th and Lexington." The call comes in over the radio, halting Sterling's interrogation.

"347, 10-4, en route," Sterling responds, while I take my next left, and pull the cruiser around to make my way back up to 6th. We're only three blocks away, and within two minutes, we pull up out the front of the convenience store.

The parking lot is quiet and dark, but as I park and exit the vehicle, I spot movement over to my right.

"There." I point out to Sterling on our left. "Police," I shout out, letting our presence be known. "Let me see your hands. Show me your hands." Sterling comes around the cruiser, and we walk forward, flashlight in one hand, gun in another. My flashlight lands on a male, hunched over, while Sterling's lands on a woman who appears to be passed out.

"Step away from her now and show me your hands," I repeat my order, this time closer. I'm expecting him to run, can see him seriously thinking about it, but he complies with my order and steps back.

"Don't shoot." He raises his hands in front of him, showing me he's not armed. My flashlight shines on his face, and I get a good look at him.

Jesus, he's only a kid.

"I'm not gonna shoot you. Keep your hands where I can see them." I walk forward to pat him down while Sterling checks on the woman.

"Please, you have to help her." The kid doesn't have any weapons on him, but I'm still not taking any chances, considering he was about to run, and his face looks like he's been attacked.

"I'm just gonna put these on until I know what's happening here." I place the cuffs on his wrists. It's not normal protocol, but considering the situation, and the area, I'm not taking any chances.

"What's your name kid?" I ask, spinning him back around to

face me.

"Mitch." His voice is shaky, but he holds my eyes in a way that tells me he's not afraid of me.

"You have a last name?"

"Westin."

"347 requesting a 10-57 on Lexington and 6th, we have an unresponsive woman," Sterling calls in for an ambulance while I tell the kid to take a seat on the ground.

"Okay, Mitch, want to tell me what happened here tonight?" I ask when I take stock of the scene and where we are. Trebook houses some shifty areas, and downtown is definitely one of them.

"I missed curfew. I didn't mean to. I was at the library studying, and then my brother cornered me. Liberty turned up and tried to get me home." Her name cancels out the kid's story and has my head spinning around to get a better look at her.

"Liberty?" Sterling looks up at her name, and then back down at the woman he's been giving me a hard time about, taking in a better look of her.

"Yeah, it's her," he confirms, brushing a stray blonde hair off her face.

"Stay there." I point down at the kid and make my way over to her.

"Liberty?" I kneel down and place my hands on either side of her face.

Fuck me. She's been hit pretty hard. Blood coats her face, dripping down her neck onto her shirt. Hot rage fills my veins seeing her like this while panic weighs me down next to her.

Who the fuck would do this to her?

"Lib?" I call again, hoping to stir her.

"W-what are you doing here, Hetch?" She starts to come to and the fucking pussy who's taken up residence inside of me since meeting her, enjoys that she recognizes me first.

Fuck me. Keep your dick in your pants.

"Mitch?" She tries to sit up but, but I stop her from moving too far.

"Whoa, hold on there, sweetheart." I force her to look at me

73

so I can get a better look at her injuries. "You're bleeding." Her left cheek has a quarter-inch graze; it's raised with the start of a bruise already appearing.

"Hetch? What?" She's still disorientated. My anger thickens, pulsing through me at a sluggish pace from seeing her like this.

Who the fuck did this to her?

"The kid do this to you?" It's the first thing I ask, still uncertain how to read him.

She's still a little out of it, still unsure as to what's happening, or where she is, but I notice her hand is holding her side as she looks over to where he sits, detained on the side of the road.

"What? No, Mitch didn't hurt me." Her confusion lifts as she tries to sit up again.

"Hey, hey, calm down." I try to soothe her but fail when she notices he's cuffed.

"What the hell?" Her breath is choppy as she struggles to get her words out, her face contorting in pain each time she takes in air. "Get those cuffs off him. He's only fifteen." She tries to fight me, the firecracker in her coming out.

"He's being detained right now until I can find out what is happening here."

"He was helping me, you"—she takes another deep breath— "fool. He didn't hurt me." Jesus, I can't tell if she's just winded or has a cracked rib. But something isn't right here.

"Then tell me what happened."

"Hetch, take the damn cuffs off him." She fights me, refusing to obey.

"Stop fighting. You're gonna hurt yourself more than you already are." My voice rises at her stubbornness and strong will. Remembering the kid mentioned his brother, I ask, "Did Mitch's brother do this?"

Her gaze searching out Mitch's tells me I'm right.

"What's your brother's name, kid?"

"Dominic didn't do it," Mitch answers, and I put their last name together.

Fucking Dominic Westin, street thug, gang member, a rap sheet probably longer than my dick.

74

"Jesus, you're out here on your own with the likes of Dominic Westin, Liberty?"

"What am I supposed to do? He's been hassling Mitch, trying to get him in." She takes another pained breath. "I showed up and tried to get him home."

I turn and look down at the kid. "This true? You're not part of your brother's crew?" It's not that I don't believe Liberty. I have a feeling Mitch is hiding something.

"No, sir, well, I-I mean—"

"You're either a part of his crew, or you're not. Simple answer, boy." Sterling cuts him off.

"No, sir. I'm not."

"Please, Hetch, take the cuffs off. He's only a kid," Liberty asks again, her breathing still labored. I nod to Sterling, giving him the all clear as I continue to run my eyes over her body, wondering when the hell the paramedics will show up.

"So, if Dominic didn't do this, who exactly did?" I ask Mitch this time, still not sure how to read him. He's throwing me off with his manners and concern for Liberty, but at the same time, he is Dominic's little brother. Family tends to stick together.

"One of Dominic's boys. I don't know his name." I'm about to ask Liberty if she knows them, but the paramedics finally pull into the lot.

"I don't need medical attention. I'm fine." She tries to stand, but can barely get up on her own.

"Keep still. You need to get checked over, Liberty." I'm not in the mood to argue with her, but I will if she fights me on this.

"I'm fine." She labors in her breathing, and if I wasn't worried about her, and what injuries she may have, I would laugh at her stubborn ass.

"You were passed out when we arrived. You have a nasty grazing under your eye, and you've been holding your side since you came to." She takes a second to take stock of her injuries before releasing a slow and pained huff as two paramedics start making their way over to us.

"Just let them take a look at you, and if they give you the all clear, you can come and give me your statement." She doesn't concede right away. It takes a few beats before she nods and lets the paramedic step in and help her over to the ambulance. I keep her in my line of sight, leaving them to do what they need to do, and walk back over to Sterling,

"Okay, Mitch, you're gonna give it to me straight. I find out you're not telling me the truth, you and I are gonna have issues. You understand me?" I'm not going to pussyfoot around here. Someone in his brother's crew put his hands on Liberty, and I want a name.

"Yeah." He nods, fidgeting his weight from foot to foot.

"You working for your brother?" He falters for a second, his gaze going to the back of the ambulance where Liberty is being checked over.

"Don't look at her. I want you to look at me. You've already dragged her into this mess. Let us help get you both out of it."

"He wants me to do some things."

"What sort of things?" I press.

"I don't know, just some shady things. I told him I'm not interested, but he keeps showing up everywhere I go."

"You tell your caseworker he's hassling you? Tell Liberty?"

"Nah, they're not going to do anything. Besides, he's my family, you know? Am I supposed to walk away from him?"

"Yeah, kid. You are." Sterling offers his opinion. "You don't want to be messed up with this life, do you?"

"No, I don't. I have a good thing at Boys Haven. I told Dominic that, but then he said it's not safe for me. Not safe for the people there." He nods over to Liberty.

"Liberty? He using her over you?"

"He told me if I didn't come out, it would come back on her. I can't let that happen. She's all I have right now." He kicks at the asphalt, trying to hold back his tears.

Jesus, poor fucking kid.

"Yeah, I get it, kid," I tell him the only thing I know to say. This Dominic is a piece of work. The last few years he's risen up in street cred. Working under their leader, Anton Gibson, The Disciples main revenue comes from drugs, women and using kids to hustle for them. They're yet to be picked up for anything that can stick, which means we need to be very careful. If this crew have Liberty in their sights, who fucking knows what Dominic or Anton could pull.

"Can I see Liberty now?" He manages to control his emotions and puts the tough-kid mask back on.

"Yeah, come on. We'll get your nose looked at too." I motion toward the ambulance. Liberty is still being checked over when we walk up to her, but before I come to a stop, she is already arguing with me.

"I'm not going to the hospital, Hetch." Jesus this woman is stubborn.

"Well, you are." I'm not sure how we are going to get through this one.

"I need to get Mitch home. He missed curfew, and I haven't reported it yet."

"We're gonna take Mitch back to Boys Haven," I tell her how it's going to play out.

"It's fine. I'm fine. I don't need to see a doctor, and I don't need a trip to the hospital."

"You have a nasty bump on your head. And a blow to your torso. You don't get a say in this." I turn to the paramedic. "She's going in." He looks at Liberty and me, clearly knowing protocol dictates the outcome. He only has to do what the patient wants and if she doesn't want to go, he can't make her.

"Liberty." I lower my voice, trying to reason with her. "Mitch is pretty shaken up. He's worried about you and wants reassurance that you're okay. Let us take him back to Boys Haven. You need to be checked out thoroughly. You may have a concussion, maybe broken or bruised ribs since your hand is still clenching your side." I eye her hand placement briefly before continuing on, "I promise we'll take good care of him, but you have to let us do our job." I can see her starting to slip, see how she looks between Mitch and me.

"Okay," she finally concedes.

"Good girl, we'll be up later to take your statement. Okay?" I let her know we're not done here tonight.

We're not done outside of tonight either, I think too, but push the

77

thought down and away for later.

"No, no statement. I'm not pressing charges," Mitch interjects like he has some say in the matter.

"Mitch, you know that can't happen." It's Sterling who tries to make him see some sense. Mitch needs to learn he can trust the system. Letting his brother get away with this is not doing him any favors.

"But it's only going to make him angrier. He's just trying to look out for me." Jesus, even after being hurt by his own brother, he's still trying to protect him.

"Mitch, your brother's not looking out for you like family should." I try this time, but he's not listening. He only has eyes for Liberty.

"Please, Liberty. I don't ask for much. Please don't make me press charges." His voice wavers, like he's unsure he really wants what he's asking for.

"How about we talk about this later?" I step in before Liberty can waver. "You need to get to the hospital, and Mitch needs to get home." I can see her wanting to argue, but Mitch cuts her off.

"Please, just get checked out, Liberty."

"Don't think this is over, Mitch," she concedes, her breathing becoming shallower. "I'm not letting this go." She scolds him in a disciplinary way only she manages to make hot.

Jesus, Sterling's right. She's under my skin. The only problem is, I don't have time to sit there and pick her out. There are, however, plenty of other successful ways I can get her out of my system.

My cock in her pussy is one of them.

* * *

"You're lucky it wasn't anything more, Miss Jenson," the doctor tells Liberty four hours later after giving her a diagnosis. Bruised ribs and a slight concussion.

78

"I told you I was fine." She turns to face me, pain etched over her forehead.

"Better to be safe, Liberty," I tell her, not in the slightest bit put out I made her come in. After dropping off Mitch to Boys Haven, we came back to take Liberty's statement. While she gave us what she could, we didn't get much in a way of a lead. We left to finish up our tour with a few more domestics and traffic violations before I headed back over to check in with her.

"Officer Hetcherson is right, which is why tonight I suggest you have someone around to keep an eye on you. Is there someone I can call?"

"Ahh," she pauses, "is it really necessary?" she asks, looking more put out than before.

"You're more than welcome to stay the night here," he offers, probably thinking she doesn't have anyone.

"No, it's fine. I really want my own bed. I'll call my dad," she concedes, not looking happy about it.

"Good. So I want you to take it easy for the next couple of days. No working. Headaches are normal; however, if anything becomes too severe, come straight back here. Understood?"

"Understood. Thanks, Doc."

"Let me get your release papers ready and you'll be on your way. Be sure to pick up your meds for pain relief." He hands her a prescription to get filled and steps out, leaving us alone.

"You want me to call your dad?" I ask, wondering why she hasn't called anyone already. When I rocked up earlier, I was expecting some family present.

"Honestly, Hetch, I'll be fine." The little witch had no intention of calling in anyone to stay with her.

"You heard the doctor. You're not being released without someone to look after you."

"Please, Hetch, my parents are old, they'll be asleep already. I don't want to stress them."

"Do you have anyone else you can call?"

"I don't want to bother anyone." I don't say anything right away, frustration over this woman burning stronger with every interaction I have with her.

"Then I'll take you home and stay with you," I offer blindly. She arches a brow like she's ready to argue, until the nurse comes in with some paperwork, stopping all conversation.

I step back, letting her do her thing, listening to Liberty's answers to her questions.

"Will you be taking her home tonight?" the older nurse asks me, bringing me into the conversation.

"Yes."

"No." We both answer at the same time. The nurse's brow spikes as a knowing smirk covers her face.

"Yes, I will be taking Miss Jenson home tonight," I answer again, leaving no room for argument.

"You don't have to." Of course, Liberty still argues.

"Considering I'm going the same way, to the same place, why don't you just say 'thanks, Hetch, I'd appreciate it'?" She bites her lip, holding back either a smirk or a smart retort.

Probably both.

"Thanks, Hetch. I'd appreciate it." She shocks me with her compliance.

"You're welcome." I turn back to the nurse, ready to give her any information she needs.

"Well, now that's settled, I just need a few signatures here, and you'll be good to go." She gives me a wink, letting me know she likes my play.

Liberty signs where she needs to, and within twenty minutes, we're heading down to the main lobby, Liberty in a wheelchair, me pushing her along.

"This is ridiculous. I don't need a wheelchair, Hetch." She's been bitching about the damn chair the moment it was wheeled in.

"I think I'm starting to get you, Liberty Jenson," I tell her, coming to a stop at the glass front doors.

"Oh, yeah?" She looks up as I walk around to face her.

"Yeah." I hold out my hand, helping her to her feet. "You just like to argue for the sake of arguing. Do you get off on it, Liberty?" She's a little wonky on her feet, so I keep a hold of her and walk her the rest of the way out to my truck.

"Whatever, Hetch. You won't ever get me." I don't know if she means physically or logically. My cock would more than love to get to know her physically, but what worries me more is that my head likes the thought of logically.

"We'll see," is all I say as I help her up into my truck.

"No, we won't." Again with the arguing.

"Sweetheart, I'm already halfway there." I watch her carefully. The soft sprinkling of freckles that she didn't bother to cover with makeup today makes me like her a whole lot more.

"Are you ready?" She doesn't comment on me already having her figured out, so she hides behind the uppity-snob routine she's perfected so well.

"Yeah, you hungry?" I ask, wondering if I need to stop and pick something up for her.

"Not really. Just want to get home." Her gaze sweeps around the poorly lit parking lot, revealing the vulnerable side she works so hard to hide. My chest tightens in anger.

The little punk is going to pay.

"Then let's get you home, sweetheart."

"Stop calling me sweetheart. You're freaking me out."

Fuck me. If I wasn't so opposed to love, I think I could find myself falling for her.

LIBERTY

The ride home in Hetch's truck is quiet. After a long and stressful night, all I want to do is close my eyes and find sleep, but I don't want to let my guard down around Hetch. I don't need him to see the vulnerable side of me. It's bad enough I'm back in his vehicle, not only relying on him to get me home but now he's in my business with Dominic, and he's seen firsthand what I'm dealing with when it comes to Mitch.

"You doing okay over there?" His deep rumble fills the truck and pulls me out of my thoughts.

"Yep." My reply is too chirpy, even I know it, and I wait for him to call me on it.

"Gonna get the fuckers who did this to you. Don't worry about it," he tells me, letting me know he knows where my head is at.

I hate he can see through my façade, but at the same time, I find comfort in it. In my line of work, you always have to stay neutral, and not let your emotions drive you. Add in a family who are always on my case about the dangers of what could happen with me getting too close, I never have a chance to allow the vulnerable side to show.

In a way, it's refreshing.

"You always get personally involved with these kids?" His interrogation turns, and it takes me a second to catch up.

"I'd do anything to help them, yeah." He doesn't reply right away, and it makes me wonder what he thinks about me, knowing I'm that way inclined.

"I want you to be careful, Lib. Dominic and his crew are not the type of people you want to get into trouble with."

"You don't think I know that, Hetch?" I turn a little too fast. Pain strikes through my head and slashes through my side, forcing me to flinch.

"Take it easy there. Are you okay?" He notices my discomfort and slows the truck down, pulling off to the shoulder of the road.

I take a minute to get myself together before answering. "Yeah, I'm fine." I can tell he doesn't believe me, but he doesn't press. Instead, he takes the conversation back to Dominic.

"Promise me you will stop getting in his way."

"I can't do that. I'm gonna get in his way if he keeps messing with Mitch." I hold his stare, daring him to fight me on this.

"What is it about this kid that has you so messed up?"

"He's a good kid, Hetch. He's had a tough run, and he deserves to have someone rooting for him. I'm all he has."

"Funny, that's what he said about you."

"It's the truth." He draws a sharp breath like he's resigning himself to the task at hand, before shifting the gear back into first and pulling back out on the road.

We don't talk again, my heart full of something I can't quite identify at hearing Mitch think of me as all he has. I knew I was reaching him, but this, this is more unexpected. It's not until we pull into our apartment complex I finally break the silence.

"I promise I'll be more careful." I offer what I think it is he wants to hear.

"Yeah, bullshit." He calls me on it. There's no anger evident, but his tone says we both know it's not happening.

"I will…" I start to assure him just as he parks two spots down from my car. "Wait, you brought my car home?" I turn carefully to find his face watching me, unsure how he managed to get it here.

"Sterling helped me get it back. I have your keys here." He reaches down and pulls out my keys from the console of his car.

"Thank you, Hetch." I hold my palm up and watch as he drops them into my hand.

"It was no big deal." He shrugs it off, but we both know he went above and beyond tonight. Taking Mitch home, coming back to see me and bringing me home safely. He didn't have to do all of this.

"I guess I should head up?" The question hangs between us as we continue to stare at each other. Our gazes lock as if one of us is waiting for something to happen.

"Yeah, I need to get you into bed." He opens his door to exit but quickly turns back to correct himself. "Not bed like that, bed as in rest." He falters over his words. "I mean I'd like to get you to bed, like that, but not now. Oh, fuck, never mind." He continues to ramble, and it's rather charming to see him lose the cool composure he has perfected.

"It's fine. I knew what you meant." I try to control my racing heart but fail miserably when his gaze turns hungry.

"Stay there. Let me help you down," he orders, before exiting the truck and stalking around to my door.

This is a bad idea.

This is a bad idea.

This is a bad idea, blares in my head over and over as I follow his movements. Each one is strong and with ease, while I sit here and second-guess every word, every reaction when I'm around him. The kick to the head seems to have made me lose some sense. I should call my mom. Hell, I should call Payton, but knowing my family, the last thing I need is them on my case about this.

"Come on." He opens my door and reaches across me, releasing me from my seatbelt. The warmth of his hand at my side spreads fervor all through me. I try not to react, but fail when a shiver runs right over me.

"You okay?" Anyone could have mistaken the reaction as pain or discomfort, but not Hetch. His grin tells me he knows exactly how affected I am by him. By his touch.

Smug asshole.

"A little sore, but I'll survive." I start to move out of his reach, but he holds me still, his hands at my waist, his eyes to mine.

"I'm staying with you tonight," he says, and my suspicions about the kick to the head earlier prove to be true, when instead of arguing, telling him I'm fine, my head nods in agreement.

Jesus, this is dangerous.

* * *

"I'm not sure this is a good idea, Hetch." I seem to have come back to myself twenty minutes later as I watch him turn my sofa into a makeshift bed.

"It's either your parents or me. Your call, sweetheart." I'm not sure on the *sweetheart* either, but I keep it to myself. When I told him not to call me it in the car, he laughed.

"You're too big to fit on my sofa. Won't you be more comfortable next door in your bed?" I press, hoping he sees the error of his ways. I know he wants to help, but this is too much.

"Nope, told you I'm staying, so quit hovering, take your meds, then head to bed. I'll see you in the morning," he orders and, instead of arguing anymore, I decide to let it go. If he wants to hang out on an uncomfortable sofa, who am I to stop him?

"Okay, well, thanks again. For everything." We share a brief moment, almost like the one earlier in the car, before I wave him off and head down the hall to my bathroom. Needing a shower, but craving sleep more, I quickly work through my nighttime routine. Fifteen minutes later, dressed in an old shirt and pair of short shorts, I tie my hair back in a low bun, take my pain meds and leave the bathroom. The low, dim light of the living area tells me Hetch is still up. Not wanting to face him again this evening, I slip into my room and close the door with a silent click.

I'm about to climb into bed when out of the corner of my eye, I see movement. A huge-ass spider scurries across the wall. An almighty scream leaves my mouth at the sight of it.

"FUCK!" I can't deal with spiders. Not even a little. All rational thought leaves my mind as I race out of my room and down the hall, smacking right into the hard, naked chest of Hetch.

"What's wrong?" he asks, stepping past me.

"There's a—" I can't get the words out. Between the spider, the pain of the collision and seeing Hetch half-naked, I become tongue-tied. "M-my b-bedroom."

Gun drawn, Hetch follows my pointed finger and races down the hall.

After a few short beats, he comes back, his gun relaxed at his side. "There's nothing there."

"What?" I screech, moving faster than I should back down the hall. Another scream leaves my throat when I see the creature scurry out of hiding. "There." I point at the freakishly large spider.

"That's all that's wrong?" He sounds relieved and dare I say annoyed.

"What do you mean *all*? Are you mad? The thing's fucking huge." A shiver runs over every inch of my skin at the thought of going to bed without killing it.

"Jesus, woman. I thought someone was in here."

"There is someone in here. A FUCKING SPIDER!" I want to slap him and his blasé ass.

"Fuck me." He shakes his head in a soft chuckle, stepping into my room. "You have a shoe or something?"

"Yeah, let me get one." I step around him and slowly move to my closet, grabbing the first flip-flop I see. "You have to get it, Hetch. I'm not kidding. I cannot sleep here until it's dead." I inform him on the seriousness of the situation while passing him the shoe.

"Just calm down. I have this." He sounds so sure of his spider-killing abilities, but until the fucker is dead, I'm taking all precautions.

After watching him assess the situation for a minute, he climbs up on my king bed and slowly moves in closer. It's the first chance I have to really take notice of his body. He's shirtless, wearing low-slung boxers on his narrow hips. The bunching muscles of his shoulders ripple under his tense stance.

Holy shit! He's perfection.

Perfection in my bed.

Tight.

Hard.

Corded with bronze muscle upon muscle.

In my bed.

"It's at a fucked-up angle." He pulls me out of my ogling, stressing me out further.

"Oh, God. Don't say that. You cannot miss it. Promise me you won't," I repeat, needing him to truly understand my fear.

"You keep talking, you're gonna distract me," he whispers as he slowly inches his way closer to the offending creature.

"I'm sorry. I just can't deal." I'm on edge, waiting for him to make his move.

"Relax, I'm gonna get the fucker," he promises, just as he pulls his arm back, and in one fast movement, brings my flip-flop down.

"Ahhh!" I scream at the sound of my flip-flop being slammed down on the wall. "Did you get it? Please tell me you killed it. You killed it, right?" I move when he moves.

"Fuck, did you see where it went?" he answers, letting me know he didn't get it.

I scream again. This time at him. "YOU MISSED IT. ARE YOU FUCKING KIDDING ME, HETCH?"

"Calm down, he wasn't even big." He tries to blow it off like no big deal, but the man doesn't know me. Doesn't know how badly frightened I am of them.

"Are you fucking blind? The thing could have eaten me. You

need to find it. NOW!" I demand, not caring how I sound. He looks at me like I've lost my damn mind, and he's enjoying this way too much.

"Please, Hetch," I whisper. "I'm really scared of them."

"What are you going to give me?" the smug jerk has the audacity to ask.

"Anything, please, just kill it." I don't care. At this point, I need this spider dead, or he'll be sharing my sofa with me.

"Anything?" he repeats, his gaze raking up and down my body. I know I'm only wearing mismatched clothing that does nothing for my figure, yet the way he's looking at me, I swear I feel like I'm wearing one of my Victoria's Secret negligées.

"I'm not having sex with you." I may be desperate, but I'm not that desperate. Besides, I'm staying strong on my sex sabbatical.

"I'm not asking for sex." He puts it to bed as quickly as I did and I refuse to let myself be disappointed by it.

"Well, what is it you want?" I could have sworn he was looking at me like he wanted me.

"A kiss," he simply requests, sending my heart rate through the roof.

"A kiss?" I repeat, wondering what a hardship it would be. I've been thinking about our kiss back at the bar all week. What harm could come from revisiting it?

"Yes, I want you to kiss me for getting the spider out of here." I weigh up my options. Kiss the man who has been in my dreams all week, or sleep in the same room as the creepy spider?

It's not rocket science.

"Fine. But only after you kill it." I yield, wondering how I actually get myself into these situations. It never ends with me, and now Hetch has come into my life, it's starting to become tenfold. Hetch nods, then moves back to my bed, leans over one of my many pillows and picks up the dead spider with his bare hands.

"Done, you owe me a kiss," he taunts, holding it out to me.

"Oh, my God. You're an ass. You played me." I jump back at the sight of it and duck my head from seeing it.

"A deal's a deal, Liberty." He walks past me to my bathroom, and two seconds later, the toilet flushes.

"No, Hetch. You didn't play fair. Deal's off," I call back as I begin pulling off my sheets.

No way am I sleeping in these nasty sheets.

My movements are slow as the pain in my ribs throb as soon as the threat and the adrenaline of the last ten minutes have gone.

"Deal is not off, Liberty." Hetch steps back into my room. He sweeps his gaze over the floor at the pile of sheets I've just ripped off the bed.

"What are you doing?" he asks, perplexed at my sudden need to change my linens.

"I'm not sleeping in these sheets. Dead spider juice went everywhere." I move past him to go grab a clean set. He doesn't follow me out. Doesn't tell me I'm crazy, even though he looks like he wants to. Instead, he steps back when I return and watches me as I begin to make the bed.

"You can go now, Hetch. Thanks for your help," I tell him as I awkwardly try to make my bed with a burning ache radiating through my ribs. He doesn't leave like I expect him to; instead, he takes a free corner of the fitted sheet and orders me back.

"I'll do it."

I start to argue, but the look he gives me is enough to shut me up quick smart. Instead, I stand there quietly and watch him make my bed. We don't speak, Hetch too lost in the task of fitting the second sheet.

It's domesticated and oddly arousing.

When the bed's been made, he steps back to admire his work, while I stand there and admire him.

"Thank you." I finally break the silence when his eyes move off the bed and onto me.

"You're welcome." He starts to move toward me. Unable to stand strong, I retreat, taking a step back.

"You should go now, Hetch," I warn when his gaze darkens.

"You owe me, sweetheart."

"I told you to stop calling me that. And the deal's off. You played me." I hold my ground this time. No way is he getting anything out of our deal when all along he manipulated me.

"You're so predictable." His cockiness is a turn-on more than a turn-off, yet I still retreat with a step back.

"You don't play fair." My words don't deter him. He moves in closer as I step back further.

"Babe, I play fair. The spider is dead, no? I'm just not afraid to play dirty." Another step toward me has my resolve slipping.

"Yeah, well, this proposed kiss goes against everything I believe in." I know I'm in dangerous territory here, but I'm not sure I care anymore.

"Doesn't matter. You're still going to enjoy it."

"Keep dreaming." I snort, giving myself one more step back, this time connecting to the wall. *The same wall we've listened to each other through.*

"Dreaming? Don't think so babe." He stops a whisper's breath from me. "Time to pay up." He smirks when I realize I have nowhere else to back up.

"You're an ass," is my reply.

"That's not a nice way to speak to the man who just saved your life." He has me there, considering I did make out I was going to die if the spider wasn't caught.

Ugh, asshole.

"Fine, have at it," I admit defeat. I mean, it's not much of a hardship. The man can kiss. In the quiet moments over the last few days, it still seems like I can feel his lips on me. Branding me and ruining me all over again.

"I don't think so, Liberty. You're gonna kiss me," he informs me, and I want to smack the smug look off his face. He's enjoying this way too much.

"That wasn't what we agreed to."

"It is. I asked for a kiss. Not to kiss you."

"Ugghh, seriously. Men like you are the reason I put myself on a sabbatical." I step forward. Place my hands on either side of his face and plant my lips to his. It's the most awkward kiss I've ever experienced.

Our lips stay locked. My eyes are shut until, after a few beats,

I slowly open them. Hetch is looking at me. His gaze intense, too intense for a basic peck.

He never said there had to be tongue.

I begin to pull back when the kiss becomes more uncomfortable, but I don't get far when his large hand presses into my back, holding me in place.

He doesn't speak, but it's a warning. The feel of his mouth on mine takes me back to the night at The Elephant. His lips move first, drawing me out of my stupor. The softness of his tongue shoves me back to life. Before I even reunite my tongue with his, I know this isn't going to end well. My mind doesn't care. My body takes over.

Then I know I'm done for.

9

HETCH

I know the moment she gives in. Her body molds against me, her tongue dives into my mouth and the small sigh of pleasure leaves her lips. A jolt of awareness enters me, forcing me to take over. My hands travel to her ass. Lifting her up carefully so as not to jolt her, I turn toward the bed. I don't bother asking if this is okay before laying her down on the sheets and crawling up over her.

All rhyme and reason fly out the window as my mouth finds hers again and this time, I'm not gentle. My teeth scrape her lower lip. The primal need to own them forces me to bite down.

"Ahh, Hetch," she cries out, a jumble of pain and pleasure mixed in with her own need. Her hands rake through my hair; she doesn't restrain herself, tugging in sharp and desperate need. I don't react, not with words anyway; instead, I bite down in response, before releasing her with a slow, deep suction.

"Shhh," I soothe, brushing my lips over her bruised cheekbone, over her jaw, and down her neck.

"This is more than a kiss." Liberty comes back to herself as my hand finds the swell of her breast over her shirt. They fit perfect in my grasp. Firm, full, and for tonight at least, mine.

"You want me to stop?" I ask, rolling my thumb over her nipple. Unable to wait for her reply, I rip her shirt up to her neck, exposing her rose-pink nipples. My mind conjured up an image of how pretty they would be and how much I would love them in my mouth the moment I had them pressed up against me last week. But nothing prepares me for the sight of her under me. The perfect, creamy smoothness, against my tanned, callused hands. Without a second thought, I dip down and wrap my lips around her left nipple.

"AHHH!" She arches off the bed. Pushing herself further into my mouth. My tongue and teeth fight one another in a battle of dominance. My teeth want to bite the tight pink nubs and claim them while my tongue wants to roll the perfection of the small bud around my tongue.

"Hetch, please." Liberty's hand moves to her lonely nipple. Not needing to be told twice, I release her with a pop and get to work on the second one. Latching on and rolling it between my teeth, I give this nipple the same attention, working her up with only my mouth. When my cock can't stand watching anymore, I pull back and slide her shorts and panties down her thighs.

"Ahh, shit." Her hand moves to her side, and I stop my quick movements. "No, don't stop." She douses my fire with a pained look over her brow.

"Fuck, Liberty." I growl, looking down at my hands still fisted with her delicate white lace panties. "You have no idea how much I want to sink my dick in this sweet pussy." I slow my breath, and trace the smooth skin next to her panties with the tip of my finger. "But, you're in pain." The words taste bitter coming from my mouth, especially since I'm looking at the prettiest pussy I've ever seen. I can smell her desperate need, and I can see her slick wetness.

"Are you kidding me?" Her body tenses at my rejection and the unabashed need that looks so fucking perfect on her starts to shut down.

Controlled, snobby Liberty is back.

"Liberty, you're hurt." I start to explain my reluctance, but I know she won't see past her frustration.

"Forget it, Hetch." She pushes me back, and readjusts herself, pulling her panties and shorts up her legs.

"Sweetheart, when I sink myself into your fucking gorgeous pussy, I don't want to hold back." I try again, but I know it doesn't register.

"Yeah, well, this is not happening again. It was a one-time deal, you blew it." She fixes her shirt before climbing off her bed.

"It wasn't, but I'll let you think it for now if it makes you feel better." I adjust my straining cock in my shorts and stand.

"Trust me, this"—she motions between us—"is not happening again."

"I know what you're doing, Liberty. Don't think I don't."

"You think you have me figured out? Please... you know nothing about me." I know I've hit the mark with my assessment.

Anger, frustration, and lust stirs in her eyes as she works to hide her emotions.

"I might not know everything yet, Liberty. But I know the important stuff."

"Yeah, what do you know?" She folds her arms over her chest and waits for me to elaborate.

"I know what sounds you make when you're lying in your bed at night playing with yourself." It takes her a second to realize I went there.

Before she can shut this down, I keep going.

"Know that vibrator of yours must be some heavy duty machinery 'cause some nights, baby, I swear I can feel the vibration through the wall." My grin widens as her scowl deepens. I need her to feel, to know just how much this chemistry between us has me wound up, but most of all, I need her to know this is far from over.

Even if I have to get it out of her in anger.

"How dare you!" She finds her voice, but I'm not finished.

"I also know you always go back for seconds, sometimes a third—"

"You're an ass. I want you to leave." She cuts me off this time, walking out of her room, down the hall and out of my line of sight.

"Sorry, not leaving, gorgeous." I tail her down the hall, but instead of following her to the door, I take a seat on my makeshift bed, and settle in for the night.

"I'm not joking, Hetch. I want you to leave." She opens the door expecting me to listen.

"And I want to watch you play with yourself with your jacked-up vibrator."

"Never gonna happen."

"Well then, looks like we both don't get what we want." We stare at each other longer than I expected before she reluctantly cracks.

"I hate you." She slams the door shut and stomps back to her bedroom.

"Good night, Liberty. Sweet dreams." I smile into the darkness, wondering who this woman is and how the fuck I'm going to get myself out of this one.

* * *

I wake the following morning to a note on my chest. The same neat handwriting that told me I needed to keep it down stares back at me.

Thanks for staying last night. I'm going to crash with my parents for a few days. Please lock up after you leave. Liberty.

Well fuck, now she's begging me to chase.
Game on, Liberty.
Game on.

95

LIBERTY

"We're worried about you, Bertie." That damn name comes out of my mom's mouth again, but this time, it's delivered as a scold and I know she means business. "You didn't call us, didn't come to stay with us. We had to find out from that lovely police officer."

I'm going to fucking kill him.

It's our weekly family dinner, two days after my run-in with Dominic. Two days after my second kiss with Hetch. Two days of hiding at Fee's.

Two days after my second kiss with Hetch.

To say my parents are pissed they found out I was in the hospital and didn't tell them would be an understatement. Knowing I've been hiding out at Fee's for two nights has made them lethal.

"I know, I'm sorry. I didn't want to wake you. It was late, and I know you don't like driving at night." I offer the only excuse I can give them. Yeah, it was late, and I didn't want them to worry, but the truth is I didn't want them there, giving me this exact lecture I'm getting now.

"You didn't want to wake us? How do you think we felt when the police dropped by to follow up on the statement you made two nights ago?" I find it hard not to cringe trying to envision that conversation. I can't believe Hetch showed up here. At my parents' place.

Well, I did tell him I was staying here.

"You're right, it was wrong of me. If ever I'm in that position again, I'll make sure you're the first call I make."

"I should hope you don't find yourself in this position again, Liberty." My father's customary smooth voice is thick and drowning in raw emotion. I struggle not to react to it.

"Dad, I promise you, I'm not going out trying to find trouble. I was helping one of my boys." His thick silver mustache sets in a straight line, almost parallel to the numerous wrinkles etched on his wide forehead. I know he thinks I'm on some big kick to save all the kids who come through the doors at Haven, but if he knew Mitch like I do, he would see why I'm so invested.

"Yeah, well, this kid got you hurt, almost killed." It's an exaggeration. We all know it, but I don't call him on it.

"Listen, I know you're worried. I get it. Yes, I was hurt. But so was he. He's as much a victim as I am. I couldn't walk away from him."

"You're getting too close to this kid, Liberty." My dad doesn't give in, and I don't have anything else to say so I keep quiet. The silence grows heavier the longer we stare each other down.

"We just want you to know we're concerned." Mom is the first to break the silence.

"And I understand and appreciate your concern. I do. But I need you to know, I'm not walking away from him or from my responsibility at Boys Haven." My eyes don't leave my father's, needing him to know this is my passion, and I won't step back.

"We're not telling you to walk away. I'm telling you to think smart, darling. You need to stay safe. You can't help these kids if you're not here." My gaze cuts back to my mom, at the unsteadiness of her voice, and I watch her lose her steely composure, revealing her fears.

"You're right, Mom. I'm sorry. I'm not thinking about you guys. I promise. I'll be more careful." I step toward her.

"That's all we ask." She takes me in her arms, wrapping me up in her comfort.

"You're still our baby." My dad steps behind me, circling both of us in his arms. "So don't ever keep something like this from us again." I cringe at my father's tone, letting the shame wash over me. I really should have called and filled them in before sneaking off to Fee's for two days.

"I understand." I let their love surround me, giving them the peace they need. I know they mean well, always have. They just aren't as invested as I am.

"Okay, rein it in everyone. You're gonna make me sick," my brother calls from the door, breaking our moment.

Why the hell is he here? The last time he joined us for family dinner, was months ago.

"Ohh, you're here. Excellent." Mom releases me from her vise grip, gives my brother a quick hug, and then moves past him to the front door.

"Bertie." Jett offers me his arms, and reluctantly, I step in for a quick embrace.

"Wasn't expecting you here tonight." I try to whisper into his ear, but even up on my toes, I barely reach his jaw. Just like my father, he's freakishly tall.

"Knocked off work in time." He pulls back, unable to give me his eyes. Ever since it came out about his affair with his skanky whore, he's never been able to look me in the eye.

Probably knows he can't bullshit me with his bullshit.

"Aunt B." Arabella barrels through the door, past my mother and father, and into my arms. "Daddy droves us in his car." It takes a second for me to breathe through the ache she jolted out of me.

"He did, did he?" I inhale through my nose, masking my discomfort.

"Yep." She nods up and down. "What happened to your face, Aunt B?" She steps back when she notices the small bandage concealing the graze on my cheekbone.

"I have a nasty boo boo," I tell her as her small hand reaches out and gently touches me.

"Mommy, Aunt B is hurt!" she yells out, like somehow her mother, my best friend, can fix me.

"Is she?" Payton steps into the house, her eyes scanning over my face and assessing the damage. I haven't spoken to Payton since our breakfast the other day. I'm not sure how tonight is going to go.

"What the hell happened?" Her eyes grow wide as she takes me in.

"I just—" I'm not sure what to say, so I don't say anything else. Mom, sensing the tension, ushers Arabella out of the room and into the kitchen. Leaving Dad, Jett and Payton all staring at me.

"Come on, son, come help me outside for second." My dad picks up on the stiffness between us, opting for a quick escape.

Well, this should be interesting.

"What happened?" She drops her bag down on the sofa and takes a seat.

"I ran into some trouble with The Disciples."

"Jesus, Lib, how do you get yourself into these situations." She drops her stony stare and scolds me.

"Don't you start on me, too. It's bad enough I'm getting it from Mom and Dad. I need my friend. Can I have her?" It's all she needs to hear to scoot forward and wrap me up in her arms.

"I'm sorry, girl. I shouldn't have left the way I did the other day." Her hold on me is strong, and a little painful, but I don't let her know. It feels good to have her talking to me again.

"I shouldn't have said what I did," I admit, not sure if I really mean it.

"No, you brought up valid points, Lib. I shouldn't have lashed out at you. You're right, and maybe it's why I left. I couldn't handle it. Maybe I am holding on out of guilt with Arabella. Maybe I was afraid to lose you, lose this." She motions around my parents' house. The same house we grew up in. "It's so hard to know what to do." To me, it sounds like she's made her decision.

So why did she come with Jett tonight? Like a family?

"I went home, thought hard, then spoke to Jett, and unless I make a decision, we can't move on. So I made a decision." I sit, waiting, still not sure exactly where she is going with this. "We're going to give it a second chance. But one slip up, even just a little one, he's done." It's almost too hard not to react the way she's probably expecting me to react.

"Well, I'm not sure if my brother has it in him to fix the pain he's put you through, but I hope for your sake he does. 'Cause if he hurts you again, Pay, I won't be able to control myself," I warn on a shaky breath.

"Believe me, he messes up, you can have him after I'm done with him. Trust me on this. I've laid it out. He steps out again, he loses his family." I almost make a snide remark about him not worrying about the loss of his family the first time he stepped out on her, but I only just got my best friend talking to me again. I'm not about to piss her off in less than five minutes.

"I'm happy for you, Pay. I am."

"I know you're not really, but you will be again. You'll see. I promise. He'll win you back too." It's a big call, a big chance she is willing to take. I pray more than anything, Jett can man up.

Not just for Payton's sake, but for the sweet little girl of ours.

* * *

"You sure you don't want to stay the night?" my dad asks after dinner as he and my mom walk me out to my car. Payton, Jett, and Arabella left an hour ago, but I stayed back and helped Mom clean up.

"As much as I love the thought of sleeping in the same bed I slept in when I was a teenager, my king bed is calling me after sleeping in Fee's uncomfortable guest bed for two nights.

Besides, I'm back to work tomorrow."

"Are you sure you're okay to go back to work. Has the doctor given you the all clear?" My mom worries at her bottom lip.

"Mom, it's barely a bruised rib and a slight concussion. Besides, I'm not back at the house tomorrow anyway. I'm in meetings all day at head office." I turn and wrap my arms around her, in a good-bye hug. "Love you, thanks for dinner."

"Love you, too. Call us when you get home. And make sure you tell the nice police officer neighbor thank you again for looking after you." I reluctantly agree, *stupid Hetch*, then turn and give my father the same love.

"Night, Dad, love you."

"Love you, Bertie." He kisses me on the top of the head and then releases me. They stay out the front, my mom lovingly tucked up under my dad's arm, waving me off until I turn the corner.

The drive home is quick, and soon enough, I'm pulling into my parking spot. My gaze shifts to Hetch's parking spot and I'm relieved his truck isn't there. I know we probably should discuss what happened the other night between us, and the fact he came to find me at my parents' house, and at some stage we will, but for now, I'm happy to keep laying low.

Grabbing the leftovers my mom sent home with me, I make my way up to my apartment. Climbing the stairs with a hell of a lot more ease than I had two days ago, I come up short when I notice my front door is open, slightly ajar

What the hell. Did Hetch lock up?

I slow my pace and take stock of the situation. Pulling out my phone, I contemplate dialing 911, but before I know it, I'm pushing the door open and calling out.

"Hello? Anyone here?" I step over the threshold into a chaotic mess. The place has been ransacked. Drawers and cupboards lay open, their contents littering the floor and counter tops.

Oh, God, what a state.

Ignoring my need to start tidying everything. I continue past the relatively untouched kitchen and down the hall, and into my bedroom. I'm only slightly relieved to see they didn't mess with my bed; however, my underwear drawer is another story.

"Assholes." I sigh, looking down at the hundreds of dollars' worth of panties I will never be able to wear again.

"Liberty?" My name carries down the hall, and instantly I freeze.

Shit, Hetch.

"Yeah, I'm here." I walk back down the hall to find him standing just inside the doorway.

He clocks me when I step into the room, his assessment of my living room coming to an end, his gaze burning right through me.

"What the fuck?" are his first words to me, and it takes me a second to figure out if he is asking where the fuck I've been the last two days, or what the fuck happened to my place. Taking a guess he's talking about the place, I answer accordingly.

"Welcome home gift I guess." I shrug, not sure what else to say.

"Yeah, some gift, you call it in?" He takes a step toward me but tracks my retreat. The last time I saw him I had my tongue down his throat, begging for his cock, only for him to reject me. The last two days I've been trying to get him out of my head, but the second I'm back in his presence, I know I can't trust myself.

"No." I swallow past the impulsive need to climb his stupid thick body and stick my tongue down his throat.

Hetch, oblivious to my internal dilemma, pulls out his cell and starts dialing a number.

"Who are you calling?"

"The police. This has to do with Dominic and his crew."

"Yeah, it's a warning. I knew I shouldn't have made a statement." I chance a step closer to him, wanting him to take me seriously. This is getting out of hand. I'm not going to put myself at risk.

"Liberty, I'm calling it in. This fucker is messing with the wrong person." He turns, offers me his wide shoulders, and barks his name and badge number down the line.

I stand awkwardly for a few minutes while he requests backup to our address.

Fucking great.

When he hangs up, he turns his hard gaze back to me and asks, "You touch anything?"

"No, I didn't. And I wish you didn't call it in, Hetch." I watch as he pockets his phone, and moves closer to me.

"Yeah, well, like we've already established, we don't seem to get what we want when it comes to each other, so you're just going to have to deal." He stops a whisper's breath from me, getting up in my space.

"Hetch, I'm not doing this with you right now."

"Why did you run?" He ignores my rebuff, going right for the money shot.

"Hetch." I pause, unsure what I'm going to say. Why did I run? It's the same question I've been asking myself the last two days.

"Liberty, answer the question."

"I needed a few days, that's all. It's no big deal," I lie, knowing full well it's a big deal. I ran because as much as I hate to admit it, his rejection stung more than the grazing on my face.

"Sweetheart, I'm gonna let your lie slide because I have a unit coming here any minute, but the moment they're out of here, we're talking, then you're packing a bag, and I'm taking you back to Jack and Connie's." He uses my parents' first names, shocking me into a fit of rage. *Jack and Connie?* He thinks he's on first name basis with my parents. I don't think so, buddy.

"Hetch, I'm not even going to discuss how pissed I am that you know my parents' names. Nor am I going to stay with them." I shut the idea down right away. Jesus, they barely survived the hospital visit. Finding out these guys may have been in my place will well and truly push them over.

"Liberty, someone broke into your place."

"I'm well aware of that, but I'm not going to cower away from this."

"You're not cowering away. You're being smart and sorting out a game plan."

"I don't need a game plan, Hetch. And I'm not leaving."

"Jesus, Liberty. You're the most frustrating woman I've ever met. This gang is dangerous. You think they're playing? They know where you work. They know where you live. Will you take this seriously?"

"I am, dammit," I snap, hating that he has to break me down. "I'm not trying to be difficult. My parents don't need the extra stress."

"Then I'll stay here with you again," he challenges, thinking it's going to sway me.

"Are you crazy? I don't need a babysitter and I sure as hell don't need a replay of the other night."

"Then go pack your bag."

"Hetch." My hands move to my hips, assuming the position as my father would call it.

"Liberty,"

"Hetch."

"Liberty.'

"No." I break the pattern, hoping to throw him off.

"Yes." It doesn't work.

"I'm not having sex with you." I try again, but I think the only one thrown off is me.

"You think this is what this is about? Liberty, if I wanted to fuck you, I would have fucked you the other night." The blow hurts more than I expect it to.

If I wanted to fuck you, I would have the other night.

"You know what, you're an ass."

"And you have a great ass. Quit getting those sexy panties of yours in a twist. I didn't say I didn't want to fuck you—"

"I'm fine on my own, Hetch." I cut him off, not wanting to hear the rest of what he has to say.

"I know you think you're fine, but you still have a busted lock, and at this time of night, you're not getting the super out here to fix it, so you're stuck with me. Now quit overthinking it and let this happen," he orders in his special kind of way. Where I want to punch him yet bow down to him at the same time.

"You know what, whatever." I roll my eyes and spin on my

heel.

I'm learning fast that fighting with Hetch is exhausting, so instead of going back and forth any longer, I forfeit, knowing full well this isn't going to end well.

Ugghh, stupid man.

11

HETCH

Sterling: *So you're staying at the neighbor's…*

The text comes in from Sterling. Lighting Liberty's darkened living room.

Me: *Detective Bailey's gossiping is worse than a fucking woman's.*

I type back, not in the least bit surprised the gossip has already started down at the station. As soon as Detective Bailey and his partner, Detective Sanchez, rocked up to take Liberty's statement and dust for prints, I knew they would draw their own conclusions.

Assholes.

Sterling: *Dangerous ground there. Hook, line and sinker.*

Sterling types back, but this time I ignore it. He can think what he likes. The last thing I need is to feed him with more ammunition because maybe he's right. I may be hooked. More hooked than I've been hooked before and yeah, it fucking scares me but fuck if I can't stop thinking about her. Ever since I woke up on her sofa, note on chest, I haven't stopped thinking about her or her under me, her sweet pussy glistening for me. I know I shouldn't want her as much as I do, shouldn't be entertaining the idea of anything more, but the more I try to force myself to stay away, or the more she tries to stay away from me, the more I want her.

"Fuck." I drop my phone back to the coffee table and groan into the scratchy pillow Liberty lent me and force myself not to go crawling into her bed. This shit just keeps getting out of control. Even tonight when Bailey and Sanchez were interviewing her, I wanted to hold her hand while she let them in on everything that's been happening with Dominic and the crew he hangs with.

I don't fucking hold hands.

Ever.

The need to take care of her is growing, especially now I know the crazy fucking gangbanger has her set in his sights. Ever since finding out about Dominic and his connection to Liberty, I've done everything in my power to figure out how to take the fucker down. As of today, I'm still coming up empty handed, but I'm not fucking giving up.

Deciding, for at least tonight, not to think about Liberty or how I'm going to take this fucker down, I force all thoughts of Liberty and her hold over me out of my head. It takes a while, and I'm about to nod off when movement down the hallway has my attention. I clock Liberty's pink toes, but don't let on I'm awake, unsure what has her out of her bed and back out to the living area, but intrigued all the same.

She bypasses the living room and heads straight for the kitchen. I shift a little on her God-awful sofa, searching for a better line of sight, only to regret my decision when I notice her choice of sleepwear.

Fuck me.

It's not the ratty miss-matched outfit she wore the other night. No, this little outfit is for me. She's silhouetted by the light in the fridge, her naked legs taking my attention first, followed by the pink, silk shorts which are barely covering her ass.

I repeat, fuck me.

She bends down, reaching into the fridge for a glass pitcher. My cock twitches at the sight, and to stop myself from blowing my load right then and there, I sit up and adjust myself.

"What are you doing up?" I ask when I've sorted myself out. The pitcher hits the floor in an almighty smash at my voice, and instantly I'm up off the sofa.

"Jesus, Hetch, you scared the shit out of me." She reaches for a towel to clean up the mess.

"Don't move," I warn, but in typical Liberty fashion, she doesn't listen.

"Shit!" she hisses, her foot rising up to pull out a shard of glass. I step over the mess, pick her up and place her on the counter top.

"Jesus, woman, you're fucking drama."

"I beg your pardon," she huffs out in an undignified way, her scowl morphing from discomfort to annoyance.

"You heard me." I don't try to sugarcoat it. She's drama. It's whether or not I'm digging the drama or not.

Fuck me, I'm digging it.

"I did, but care to explain what exactly you mean by drama?" Her brows rise in an expectant stare.

"I mean every time I'm near you, you're a mess. You have the worst luck."

"Please, I don't need you reminding me."

I reach for the broom and sweep the broken glass the best I can in the pool of water.

"I can do it." She starts to slide off the counter, but my gaze finds hers, relaying my order to stay put.

"I'm sure you can. You can also sit there and let me take care of you." She retreats, not saying anything. The sound of the glass tinkling against the floor is the only sound between us.

Once I've managed to clear up most of the mess, I move back to her. Kneeling down and lifting her foot to take a closer look. Her pink toenails are what have my attention first. They're almost the same color as her sexy sleepwear.

"I think you're good, no damage." I clear my throat, my thumb slightly rubbing at the smooth skin of her ankle.

"I could have told you that, Hetch." I note the tiny gasp and the familiar glazing of her eyes as she tries not to show how affected she is.

"Maybe, but where would the fun be in that?" My hand travels up her leg, carefully caressing the smoothness, painfully memorizing her softness. Instead of pulling back from my touch, she rocks forward, drawn in by it.

"You always like to take care of people?" Her voice is thick with need, almost as thick as my cock.

"Not always." I'm mildly responsive to her questions, but more fascinated with touching than talking.

"Then what's your deal with me?" It takes me a second to think my answer over. What is my deal? It's not like I'm interested in getting serious with her. Sure, I want to fuck her, but it's as far as this could ever be.

Right?

"Can I get back to you on that one?" My hand continues to travel up her leg, careful not to push too hard. A sharp intake of breath has me halting, my eyes finding hers. They burn with need, speaking to me, urging me to keep this going.

"You want me to stop?" I don't know why I ask. I'm not trying to slow this down, far from it, but I still want her to be comfortable.

"Can I get back to you?" Her head rolls to the side, exposing the creamy smooth skin of her neck. It's a smart remark; it's also not a no, so I inch a little closer, my hand wandering over her knee, and up over her thigh.

"You're gonna have to think fast, babe. I'm not sure I'm gonna be able to hold off." Her pulse quickens in her neck. A slow growl forms in the pit of my stomach, clawing its way up to my mouth.

109

I want to put my lips on that pulse. To own it. Own what I'm creating inside of her. Own her need and her want. I want to lick at it. Feel it under my tongue. Revel in the fact I created it.

"Liberty?" I press. My fingers rest on the hem of the satin shorts that had me crawling off the sofa in the first place.

"Yeah?"

"This okay?" I ask again. My tongue flicks out, licking at the erratic pulse that's driving me wild.

"Yeah," she pants, her legs spreading wider. It's all I need to slip my hand up her shorts and slide my fingers into the warm heat between her legs.

Fuck me sideways. No panties.

The soft moan coming from her lips tell me she's into it.

"Jesus, never felt something so fucking good." My dick hardens in my shorts as my finger hooks inside of her.

"Yeah." Her head lolls to the side. "I'm sure you say that to all the girls." I swallow her words, not wanting to talk about other women. Not now. Not here. Not ever.

"Liberty." My mouth moves over hers as I add a second finger and pick up my pace.

"Yes?" Her eyes roll back, her hips lifting up to meet each stroke with need.

"Shut up."

"You shut up." Her head snaps back up, giving me the same attitude I'm growing to enjoy.

"Jesus, even with my fingers inside of you, you're still bitchy." I'm not sure if I mean to say it out loud, or maybe I did.

"You did not just say that to me."

"I think I did, babe." I dip my tongue back in her mouth hoping it will shut her up this time. My play works when she fights for only a second longer before molding closer to me. Her legs wrap around me, digging her heels into my ass, and pressing me closer.

Eager to move things along, I lift her off the counter and carry her to the sofa. She doesn't protest, not even when I follow her down. Knees to the floor, hands to her silky shorts, I pull them clean off her body and throw them over my shoulder.

"Jesus, Lib." I sit back to take a better look at her. I know it's only been two days since I got a glimpse of her the other night, but seeing her again makes me want to weep knowing I could have had this already. Could have had her.

"You could have had it the other night." She takes the words out of my head as her eyes sweep down herself, assessing her body, not in the same way I see it I'm sure, but in a way that lets me know she's comfortable in her own skin. Comfortable to tease me with her body and her words.

"I didn't want to stop," I tell her what she has to know already.

"But you did."

"I did, but then you shut me out. Left me high and dry for two days." I counter her accusations with my own. "I should punish you for running." At the word punish, her pussy pulses and it takes every ounce of strength not to dive right between her legs and feel it pulse over my cock. "You like the sound of that, don't you?" My eyes lock on hers, and I don't miss the slight nod.

Yeah, she fucking loves it.

"Take your shirt off, Liberty."

"Take yours off," she fires back at me, taunting me. I reach down, pulling my old squad shirt off my back, letting it join her shorts on the floor. Her hand reaches out, running her finger down my abs and dipping into the waistband of my boxers. She glides them down my legs, freeing my straining cock from its uncomfortable position.

Expecting her to go for the main prize, I'm surprised and disappointed when she holds back, smirking up at me in some kind of challenge.

"You just gonna look at it? Or you gonna put it in your mouth and show me how fuckable those lips are." I don't mean to act like some depraved Neanderthal. It comes naturally. Especially when it's been a long time coming. Liberty doesn't seem too worried about my needs. The wicked gleam in her eyes tells me she wants to play.

"Careful, Officer." It's a gentle warning, one I want to address if she continues to play hard to get, but for now, I let it slide.

"Sweetheart, you're skating on thin ice here." I fist my cock, and give it a few tugs, relieving some of the prickly pressure.

"What's the matter, Hetch? You don't like a woman in control?" She lifts her satin top over her head, matching my nakedness to hers. My eyes track her body, giving me the perfect view of her. Completely naked, completely open to me, I draw in a breath to steady the unusual onset of nerves and memorize every smooth inch of her sexy body.

She's perfection. Hair tousled, lips swollen. Creamy plump breasts, pale pink tips. I remember the taste of them on my tongue.

Knowing I'm not going to last long with her smart mouth and naked body, I step out of my shorts, kick them to the side, then press down on my throbbing cock and point it toward the seam of her lips.

"Open."

"Say please."

"I'm not fucking with you. Open your mouth." We get lost in a stare off, both of us naked as the day we were born. Need flowing through me, want radiating from her. Neither one of us yielding to the other.

"Open your mouth before I make you… please." She laughs at my choice of words, then parts her lips in a rather dramatic fashion. Not needing another prompt, I tilt my hips and guide myself into her sweet, sassy mouth. The warmth of her tongue and the softness of her lips as they circle around my shaft have my hands moving through her hair.

"Fuck, Liberty." My grip tightens in her strands. A whimper strangles my cock, not in hunger, but pain. Instantly, I release my hold on her, but her suction stays strong, regaining back her control. It only takes two minutes—or maybe it's a few seconds—but after a few perfect strokes, she finds a flawless rhythm and the tell-tale signs of an impending orgasm start to rock through me.

"Jesus, sweetheart. I'm not sure you want to keep doing that," I warn, trying not to ram my cock down the back of her throat and blow my load before we get to where I need things to go. She doesn't heed my warning; instead, she opts to suck harder, suck wilder. I last barely another minute when a soft moan from her lips vibrates down my shaft and through my balls, setting off one of the hardest releases I've ever had. Warmth fills my bones, noise fills my head, and by the time I've finished releasing the last drop of cum, my dick is ready for round two.

"You better be ready to go again, big boy." She releases my cock from her mouth with a pop, looks up at me with the widest, most innocent eyes to ever fall upon me, and I know instantly, my normal one-time deal isn't going to cut it.

12

LIBERTY

I wake the following morning with an unexpected fright. A heavy weight covers my body. My hands are pinned above my head and Hetch is resting his thick, condom-clad cock between my naked legs.

Oh, shit.

Images of the previous night flick through my subconscious. Sucking Hetch's beautiful cock on the sofa.

Hetch returning the favor—eating me out with the same need I was feeling, before finally carrying me down to my bed and fucking me in ways I've never been fucked.

"Morning, sweetheart." His morning voice is gruff, almost husky, breaking through the sudden onset of regret rolling through me.

Oh, my God, it all happened.

"Ahh, morning." I try to lift my hands from his grasp, but his fingers tighten, letting me know we're gonna play this his way.

"How are you feeling today?" His eyes land on my torso, searching for any signs I'm in any pain.

While sex with Hetch did cause some discomfort last night, it wasn't enough to make me cry out in pain.

"Better if I had the use of my hands," I answer, trying to break his hold on me, proving my movements aren't as limited as they were three days ago.

"You won't be needing them right now." He skillfully removes one hand, while keeping both my hands secured with his other.

"Is that right?" I buck again, hoping to knock him off kilter, but the truth is he's too heavy, and I'm barely trying hard enough.

"Mmhmm." The smug bastard smirks the devilish grin I love to hate before taking his cock in his free hand and running the thick head through my lips, then slapping it down on my clit.

"Ahh." My back arches off the bed at the pleasurable sting. "What the hell do you think you're doing?" I'm not sure if I'm pissed he's restraining me or pissed he's not giving me what I want.

"Fucking you the way I want," he teases. My stomach clenches at his dirty promise.

"And you didn't fuck me last night?" A thrill rolls up my spine and heat pools between my legs when his dangerous dimples make an appearance.

"Oh, babe. I fucked you. But last night was your way. Now I know you're not in pain, I'm gonna give you a taste of my way." He slaps my clit with his dick a second time while tightening his grip on my wrists.

"Your way?" From what I remember of last night, which is everything, I know he fucked me *his* way. *Multiple times.*

"Yeah, my way." He changes strategy and goes back to running the head of his cock through my wet folds.

"What if I said I don't like your way?" I raise my hips, seeking more friction. We both know I want his way, but I'm not going to make it easy for him.

"Then I would call you a liar." He slaps my clit one final time before driving into me in one unforgiving stroke. Air leaves my lungs in a harsh cry. His thickness fills and hits the one spot I didn't realize existed until Hetch introduced it to me.

"Fuck, Liberty." He pulls out slowly, only to drive back into me. "So fucking good."

"Yeah." I think I sigh, meeting each thrust with raw need. He's not wrong; it feels good. Better than good, it feels amazing. "Is it always like this?" The question burns on my lips, but I don't have a second to worry about it before Hetch's controlled strokes become more savage.

Harder. Faster. More brutal.

My pussy clenches each time he slams back into me.

Harder. Faster. More brutal.

My breath hitches each time he pulls out of me.

Harder. Faster. More brutal.

It's never been like this before. Never so intense. Never so raw.

Hetch keeps his pace, my hands firmly locked in his grasp as he fucks me *his way*.

Harder. Faster. More Brutal.

I want to reach for him, glide my fingers through his hair, and pull back each time he strokes more pleasure from me, but his hold on me stays strong.

"Hetch," I pant as the start of my orgasm builds. "Let me touch you," I try to order, but I know it's more a pathetic plea than a demand.

"No."

"Please." I fight his hold on me, only for him to hold me tighter.

"Not happening, sweetheart." I don't have a chance to argue further when my orgasm explodes and seizes me with a rush of sensation so intense, stars burst behind my eyes.

Blinding me, igniting me, setting me alight.

"Fuck, woman. Never gonna get enough." He follows me over into the abyss of pleasure with his own release. Body tense, eyes shut, his harsh groan of masculine satisfaction drowns out my soft whimpers, almost taking me back for round two.

What is it about a man's release that makes you want to climb them all over again?

"Hetch?" I ask when he drops his forehead to mine, our breaths mixing together in the insignificant space between us. We stay connected for a long while, forehead-to-forehead, breath-to-breath, body-to-body.

"Yeah?" His lips find mine in a soft kiss. I don't want to read into the kiss, but at the same time, I can't help it when his mouth promises more than a good time.

"What's happening here?" Abrupt silence throbs between us. The *thump–thump, thump–thump* of his heart beating through his chest against mine surges between us as the quiet stretches.

"Well, I just came the hardest I've come in a long fucking time, and judging by the sexy-as-fuck blush you have going on there,"—he runs a finger down my cleavage—"you came pretty hard too." He pulls out of me so abruptly it's almost offensive. The ultimate connection now lost between us.

"Don't be smart. You know what I mean." I roll to the side, pulling the sheets up over my body.

Did I read something that wasn't there?

"Liberty, relax. We're just having fun here." He picks up on my unease, sliding the condom off his cock, and tying it off with expert ease.

"I know that. I thought—" My words fall silent when he turns and saunters his naked ass to my bathroom, ending further conversation on the matter.

I don't know what I thought, but clearly I was thinking wrong.

* * *

"So what, he just left after?" Payton asks later that evening when I'm driving home from my meetings at head office. I called to fill her in on my evening and morning with Hetch. Every hot, filthy detail. And every awkward moment after.

117

"Well, he dressed, told me he was off for the next two days so he would hang around for the locksmith to come change my locks, then he left to let me get ready for work."

"Hmmm."

"Yeah." I chew at my bottom lip, replaying the scene over in my mind. The awkwardness after. The need still pulsing through the air. The want still pulling me to him.

"Well, it's not like you're looking for anything serious. So you're having casual sex."

"That's the thing, Pay. At the risk of sounding cliché, it felt like it did mean something. I don't know how to explain it. It's this pull he has on me, even back when I first met him at The Elephant. It's been growing ever since."

"But if he's not looking for anything serious, Lib…"

"I know. Ugghh. See so stupid." I let out a frustrated breath. "I'm so stupid."

"Don't say that. You're not stupid. The man is sexy as all hell. I get it. And clearly his cock is like some fountain of youth. Instead of restoring your looks, he's restored your insatiable need for cock. Once you've had a dip in its luscious waters, you keep wanting to go back."

"Did you just compare sex with Hetch to the Fountain of Youth?"

"Well, it's the only plausible reason to justify you acting like Mother Gothel when she realized Rapunzel left her tower."

"Oh, my God, what's with you tonight?" I laugh as I pull up to my apartment complex. Even though I know there are no bounds to Payton's craziness, I still find myself shocked with the shit that comes out of her mouth at times.

"Sorry. Arabella is hooked on *Tangled* at the moment. And I've been drawing so many parallels from it." She laughs along with me.

This whole conversation has progressed to weird.

What am I talking about? Every conversation with Payton turns weird.

"Okay, you are a weirdo, and I have to go. I just pulled up."

"Ohh, okay. Are you ready to see him?" My head turns toward Hetch's car space, my eyes falling on his truck.

"Ugghh, no. I should have stayed at work. I'm not ready for this." My head hits the steering wheel in frustration.

How do I get into these situations?

"Oh, please, do you hear yourself right now? You had sex with the man. Hot, wild monkey sex. You both had a good time, don't overthink it." She makes a valid point. Things don't have to be weird. Yeah, it might have been the best sex I've had ever, but that's all there is to it. Simple.

"You're right, Pay. We're adults. I can totally move on from this." I steel myself, straightening my shoulders as I release a deep breath.

I can do this.

"Good, now before you go, are you still okay to watch Arabella this Friday?"

"Yes, all good to go. You want me to come to yours or you going to bring her to me?" Payton asked me last week if I could watch Arabella. I thought it was for a hot date with a new fling. Now I know it's for date night with Jett.

Yay me.

"I think it will be easier if she stays with you. Jett won't tell me where we're going, so I don't know what time we'll be back. Is that okay?"

"Yeah, of course. Why don't I keep her for the night? I'm off on the weekend. You can pick her up Saturday or Sunday, whenever you're ready," I offer against my better judgment.

"You would do that for me?"

"Of course, Payton. You know I would."

"You're the best. Let me double check with Jett and I'll let you know what time we'll drop her off." We chat a little more about Arabella, and some new eating habit she has acquired as I exit the car and make my up to my apartment. I'm laughing at my niece's antics when I make it up to my floor and come face-to-face with Hetch, arms wrapped around a pretty petite brunette.

"Well, that didn't take long." I can't soften my blatant disgust, nor can I control the hurt rolling through me.

"What didn't?" Payton's voice breaks through my anger

while Hetch's attention comes to mine.

Shit.

Shit.

Shit.

"Nothing, I just ran into some douchebag in my hallway," I tell Payton, my eyes still firmly on Hetch.

Jesus, two women in one day. Now I feel like a fucking whore.

"Who, Hetch? He's there?" I hear Payton ask, but I barely register it when Hetch speaks.

"Liberty." He steps back from the woman but keeps his arm resting on her shoulder.

What an asshole.

"Save it, Romeo." I push my key into the lock, only to realize I had the locks changed over today, and he has my new set. "Can I have my keys please?" I turn back, humiliation burning my insides while his stare burns me on the outside.

I shouldn't have fucking caved to him. Yeah, he made things clear we were just having fun, but he was only inside of me this morning. Now's he's seeing someone else on the same day.

"Sweetheart." His annoying name for me doesn't tighten my belly like it did this morning. Now I just want to punch his junk.

"No, Liam." I use his first name as a punishment. "Just keep yourself and your dick away from me."

"Don't even think about being bitchy and jumping to conclusions."

"Are you fucking kidding me?" I spit back, not believing what I'm hearing. The beautiful woman looks at me as if I've lost my mind, but Hetch looks like he's enjoying this. "You had your cock inside of me barely"—I look down at my watch and count down to the moment I left this morning—"nine hours ago. You're—"

"Liberty." His full-bodied baritone voice cuts me off, and I retreat at his anger. "This is Dakota, my sister." A dull ache drums through my head as the word *sister* ricochets through my subconscious.

Fuck.

"Oh, God." Heat pulses through my veins, my rage replaced

with dread. If ever there were a moment you wished the floor to open up and swallow you, it would be now.

"I'm so sorry. I didn't—"

"Yeah, I'm sure you didn't." He reaches into his pocket, pulls out a shiny new set of keys, and thrusts them into my waiting hand.

"Th-thanks." I step back to my door, unsure if I should slink away without another word or try to apologize again. Hetch clears his throat like he wants to say more, but his eyes narrow and grow darker, forcing my retreat along.

"I should probably go. Ah, nice to meet you." I wave at the woman, his sister, before I use my new key, and slip inside my apartment.

It takes a few seconds for the thumping in my head to clear, before I hear the unmistakable sounds of Payton's cackling coming through on my cell phone.

Oh, fuck me. I forgot to hang up.

Kill me now.

13

HETCH

"Oh, my God. You fucked your neighbor. That's a new low even for you, Liam." Kota shrugs off my arm and settles her best condescending look on me as soon as Liberty slams her door shut.

"Don't start on me right now, Kota." I force out a sigh, hoping it soothes the pent-up frustration building within my chest and my pants.

What the fuck was that bullshit? I don't know whether to laugh or punch the fucking wall.

No woman has ever managed to turn me on and piss me off at the same time.

"When will you learn, Liam? Seriously. She may be beautiful, but you live here. Do you know how messy things can get when you shit where you eat?"

Jesus, what is the go with women saying that phrase to me?

"Kota. You need to go." I point to the stairwell, hoping she takes the warning. I'm not going to justify to my sister who I

122

fuck and why. She has no idea what she's talking about. This, what's happening between Liberty and me, is different.

Whoa, different?

"Fine, whatever. I have to get back to work anyway. My new boss is an asshole and sent me home with hours of work. Make sure you're at Mom's this weekend." She points her skinny finger at me, waiting for some kind of reassurance.

"Already told you I'd be there, Kota." My irritated tone isn't lost on her; she just doesn't give a fuck about my mood. Or my sex life.

"And if you ignore my calls again, you're going to get more than a visit from me." She rises up onto her toes and places a kiss on my cheek. She's all bark with her attitude, but I still take the moment to wrap my arms back around her.

"Love you, stupid big brother." She squeezes me a little harder than normal.

"Love you, too, annoying little sis." I return her tight squeeze with my own, before releasing her. She turns on her way-too-high heels and saunters off without a backward glance.

I stay standing there between our two apartments for a few minutes, unsure if I should head back to my apartment and fester in anger, or go to Liberty and have it out with her.

I mean, what does she take me for? Yeah, I love the company of women, but two in a day is a bit over the top. Sure things may have looked compromising from her angle when she came up the stairs, but she didn't have to spit her bullshit disgust my way. If she took a breath before lashing out, she would have realized the situation.

I fester for a few more minutes, running the scene over in my head before my need and curiosity to see her again wins out. I make my way to her door, knocking loud enough to give her a taste of what sort of mood she will find me in.

"Open up, Liberty." She doesn't answer in enough time so I knock again, this time louder. "I'm not leaving until you open the door," I warn, then wait for another few beats before the door slowly opens and a red-faced Liberty looks up at me.

"What the fuck was that?" I cut to the chase, stepping past

her into her apartment and closing the door behind me.

"I'm so sorry, Hetch. You have no idea how embarrassed I am." She starts to pace in front of me, wearing track marks into the carpet with her sexy fuck-me heels.

"I have no idea? Are you fucking kidding, Liberty? You just told my sister my cock was inside you this morning." She shrinks back at my tone like she's afraid, but I don't have it in me to feel guilty about it. She needs to know that shit is not okay.

"I wasn't thinking. I reacted." Her wide, innocent eyes plead with me for some understanding, but I'm not sure I have it in me.

"You reacted? What are we, teenagers?" The words are a reflection on what she's making me feel, not the truth.

You're a real asshole, Hetch.

"You know what, screw you. I fucked up, okay? Yeah, I reacted. And you have every right to be pissed. But don't come in here on your high horse making me feel like shit for feeling something." My cock hardens the moment she sasses me back, and the pull I've been fighting since I walked out of her apartment this morning no longer seems like such an issue anymore.

Two large strides are all it takes for me reach her. Fisting my hand in her hair, I pull her head back in one sharp tug and crash my lips down onto hers. Her mouth opens instantly, swallowing my growl of approval. Our tongues dart out to greet each other as if the time that's passed was years rather than hours.

Her taste invades my mouth as I sweep my tongue over hers, controlling the smartness right out of it.

Ever since I left this morning, I've thought about tasting her again but wasn't sure if it was wise. Between last night and this morning, things became intense, fast. Never in my adult life have I felt such a strong connection to a woman so quickly. I knew this morning when she looked up at me, her face flushed with ecstasy, her pussy filled with my cock, I was in too deep. I freaked out. We had a moment, and when she had the balls to address it, I shut it down and shut her out.

Now what the fuck am I doing?

Not wanting to answer the question, I continue to control her mouth, drawing more of her taste into my own. After a few more seconds, Liberty's hand comes up between us. At first, I think she's gonna pull me close to her, mold her body closer to mine. But I'm left disappointed when the kiss is abruptly cut short as she pushes me back, breaking our connection.

"Hetch, this is a bad idea," she pants, as the confusion swimming in her eyes morphs into the same uncertainty I saw when she walked up those stairs five minutes ago. I didn't understand at the time, and maybe I still don't, but I know I don't like it. I don't like this unsure version of her. Where she doubts herself. Doubts my attraction to her.

"Stop that shit right now." I reach out, grabbing her hand and dragging her back into my space. She doesn't pull back, but she doesn't look up either.

"W-what?" Her voice is small and her insecurity screams back at me so I squeeze her neck, gently urging her to look back up at me.

"Where you second-guess yourself, second-guess this… whatever this is between us."

"And what is *this* between us?" Her gaze turns heated and I take a second to really look at her.

Her hair is pulled back from her face in some kind of sexy teacher twist thing, and her face free of makeup, showing the gorgeous-as-hell freckles I seem to have an affliction to.

She's fucking beautiful.

Sexy.

Addictive.

"I don't know, sweetheart, but this"—I take her hand and place it over my hard cock—"has been hard since you walked up those stairs. That little smart mouth of yours, the way your lips purse when you're angry, when you're throwing your sass my way… no one's managed to make me feel the way you do in a long fucking time." It might not be the answer she's looking for, but it's all I can give. Her fingers wrap around my shaft, and the confidence I've come to admire starts to come back.

"There she is." My hand moves back to her neck as I take

125

her lips in another rough, hungry kiss.

I'm still pissed she pulled that little stunt out there, but the feel of her fingers stroking me and the trace of her taste on my tongue is enough to make me forget how pissed I am.

"Take your panties off and bend over the sofa." I step back, waiting for her to comply.

"Hetch—" I cut her off with a sharp hand signal, urging her to follow my orders.

She only takes a second to work through her emotions before she steps over to the sofa and does as she's told. With expert grace, she shimmies out of the tiny piece of lace, hikes her dress up over her hips and presents her ass to me.

Jesus, fuck me sideways.

"I'm done talking, Liberty. Put your hands between your legs and get yourself there." I take a step back to rest my shoulders against the wall. She holds my eyes for a few beats, before finally following my orders and sliding her fingers between her legs.

"Are you wet, Liberty?" I ask, already knowing the answer. There is no fucking way she isn't as turned-on as I am.

"Yes," she sighs, her fingers working herself to the brink.

"How wet, sweetheart?"

"Dripping."

Fuck me.

"Is it for me?" I reach down and adjust myself in my jeans. I could easily take the few steps toward her and take over, but something about delayed gratification has me holding back.

"Yes." She whimpers and her hips start to move in rhythm. Even though I can't see her finger gliding between her pretty pink folds, I can picture her glistening for me.

"Show me your fingers." She groans in frustration but still complies, presenting me with a pussy-juice-coated index finger.

Fuck me, I need it in my mouth.

Done with delayed gratification, I step forward, spin her around, and wrap my lips around her finger. She tastes sweet with a hint of spice. It's all it takes for me to drop to my knees, spread her bare lips wide, and lick from her opening up to her clit.

Fuck, how could I miss her taste? It's only been hours.

She cries out in pleasure, the sound echoing around the room. Again, I repeat the action, this time ending with a light nip on her clit. Needing to make something clear, I pull back and look up at her.

"Liberty?" She looks down, her face flushed with want, her body laced in need. "Did you really think I'd have a woman in my bed the same day I was in yours? The same day I had you coming on my cock?" I know I said we were fooling around this morning, but even if she didn't feel the same connection as I did, surely she doesn't think I would fuck another woman.

She comes back to herself to answer. "Honestly?"

"Yes, honestly. Always be honest with me, babe."

"Then yeah."

Her answer guts me more than it should.

"Jesus, sweetheart."

"What do you expect, Hetch? Ever since I've moved in, you've had a bevy of women in your bed. You said you weren't looking for anything serious. I come home and see you standing there hugging a woman, all rational thinking left."

"I'm not gonna lie, Liberty. This morning scared me. I've been through my share of women. That's my baggage, but believe me this, if I'm with someone, I'm only with them.

"But you said—" Her confusion matches my own as I take a minute to think about my next words.

"I know what I said, Liberty, and maybe at the time I meant it, but now, now I'm not so sure."

"You're saying you want more?" Her hand reaches out and cups my jaw.

"I don't know what I'm saying. I don't even know what's happening here, except I want you. Clearly more than once. You've gotten to me. More than I care to admit."

"I know the feeling," she whispers, placing us both on the same page.

"So we take things slow. No labels, no decisions, and no one else."

Jesus, exclusive with a woman? What the fuck am I thinking?

My heart falls into what I assume is my stomach as I wait for her reaction. The lust swimming in her eyes is replaced with something else like she too is analyzing me for my reaction.

"Okay." She finally answers when the silence grows heavy. The word is simple, uncomplicated, yet more complex than I care to admit. Deciding now isn't the time to consider what I just proposed, I cut all conversation and continue to eat her out.

Only when I've made her come twice with my mouth and cock another three, do I truly realize how deep I am.

Fuck me, Sterling was right.

Hook, line and sinker.

* * *

"Team A will breach the front entry, and Team B is on rear," I tell Fox and Hart as we do surveillance in preparation for the high-risk arrest warrant we'll be executing later today at one of The Disciples known hangouts.

"Let me guess, you want Team A?" Fox asks from the backseat in our unmarked SUV.

"How did you know?" I almost laugh at his scowl, not feeling one bit guilty about it. The dog that guards the perimeter of the old house looks like one mean son of a bitch, one I want nothing to do with.

"'Cause your pansy ass is scared of dogs."

"There was a dog?" I ask, keeping my face straight.

"You're a pussy," he grumbles under his breath, ultimately letting it go.

The purpose of today is to do a tactical reconnaissance. On top of detailed plans provided by the detective working Liberty's case, I wanted to get some groundwork of the area and see what, if any, obstacles we might come up against, i.e. big fucking dogs. And also see if there are any lookouts we need to be aware of.

Ever since the night Dominic and his boys threatened Liberty, I've been doing some digging, speaking to a few boys down in the gang unit and turns out, while Dominic is a smaller fish in the grand scheme of things, he still has ties to some seriously dangerous men higher up the food chain. And because, like most street gang leaders, they leave the hard work up to their "soldiers", we're going to have a hard time pinning anything on him. Doesn't mean we're not going to try. Today we begin the first round of trying to flush the fucker out and get something on him.

"ETA this is going down?" Fox continues to jot down his notes.

"Tommy wants to go in after dark." Warrants at night work a little differently. While we do have the element of surprise, suspects can get away a little easier.

Richard "Tommy" Tomelson is head of the narcotics unit. His boys have been sitting on this place for a while now. If he thinks going in after dark is our best play, then we will.

"There goes my night." Fox sounds relieved more than annoyed.

"Don't know if you're happy about it or not."

"Vanessa is coming around to pick up some shit."

Vanessa is Fox's ex-wife. Wicked witch of Trebook as Fox has been known to call her. I've personally never met her, but from the stories I've been told, she definitely lives up to the name.

"You still having issues with her?" Hart asks after I tell him to head back to the base so we can brief the two teams.

"When am I not? She's just trying to get in my head. We've been divorced for two years, and she still finds a way to come over every few months."

"Seems like she has you on a short leash, Fox." I weigh in on his situation. I'm not as experienced in the relationship department as these guys; my longest relationship was in high school when I was head over ass in love with Amy Theo. I chased her for weeks before she finally relented and let me take her out. We lasted two years until her dad took a job across the country and left. We tried the long distance thing for a few months, but it never worked out. Since then, I've played the field and had a few girlfriends, but nothing serious enough to interest me in settling down.

Until Liberty.

"She thinks she has me on a leash. She comes around, throws her attitude around some, and then ends up in my bed."

"You're a sick bastard." Hart shakes his head in laughter.

"She may be a bitch, but she's a good lay." He shrugs, not in the least apologetic about it. "What about you, boss? Sterling thinks you're holding out on us with the sexy neighbor of yours."

Fucking Sterling and his big mouth.

It's been two weeks since Liberty caught the wrong idea about Kota. Two weeks of sleeping in each other's bed, fucking every chance we've had.

Two weeks of falling deeper into the rabbit hole, falling off the face of the earth, and only showing my face for work, or when Liberty complains I don't feed her enough.

Two weeks of telling myself I'm getting in too deep. Too fast.

"Sterling doesn't know what the fuck he's talking about." I shut the line of questioning down.

This week I officially received the promotion I've been waiting for: team leader of Trebook's tactical unit. To say I was shocked would be an understatement. To say I wasn't happy would be a lie. The team wanted to make a big deal out of it, celebrate the appointing with a big night out, but I wouldn't let them. While I may officially have the job, I still need to prove myself and keep my head above water in my new role.

These last few weeks have really put me on my ass. Since my chat with the lieutenant back at the training base a few weeks back, I've done a lot of thinking and realized I've worked so hard for this position, and the only person fucking up any chance of me succeeding is me.

"You're fucking whipped, admit it. You haven't been at The Elephant for two weeks." Hart weighs in on the conversation just as I see two teenage boys in a heated argument out the corner of my eye.

Is that Mitch? I twist my body back as we pass them, hoping for a better look.

Shit, I think it is.

"Who are these little punks?" Fox asks, picking up on my interest in them.

"One of them lives over at Boys Haven I think. Double back, Hart," I order, hoping it's not Mitch but some other kid who looks like him. Hart doubles the block in record time, before slowing and pulling up beside them.

It's the hoodie he's wearing that seals the deal. The black and red symbol on the back of his shoulders flashes in my mind from the night I found him leaning over Liberty.

Fuck, it is him.

"Hey, Mitch, what's happening?" I ask as I step out of the cruiser, interrupting their conversation.

"Ahh, nothing much." Mitch steps back, his eyes frantically sliding from the three of us to the punk next to him.

Okay, this doesn't look too good.

"You remember me, Mitch?" I ask, knowing full well he knows who I am. I'm the guy who convinced him to make a report against his brother.

"Yeah, you're the douchebag officer who has the hots for Liberty," Mitch retorts as Fox snickers off to my side, but I don't show any emotion.

The little shit.

"Yeah, something like that. So what are you doing on this side of town, Mitch?" His shoulders slump at my question, his hands gripping on the sides of his worn jeans.

"Just walking along, minding my own business." He shrugs like it's no big deal, but I can tell in his panicked eyes something's up.

"And what about you, what's your name?" I direct my gaze to the kid standing next to him.

The kid barely looks eighteen and thinks he has enough swagger to give me attitude.

"I don't have nothin' to say." He evades my question, his brown, sunken eyes not quite meeting mine before the little punk-ass starts to walk off, calling Mitch along with him.

"Mitch, can I have a word with you over here for a minute?" Hart steps into their path, cutting off their retreat.

"What for? Is he under arrest?" The thug steps forward, only to retreat when my hand finds my holstered Glock.

"He's not. I just want to have a chat. You stay there," I warn, giving Fox the nod to keep an eye on him.

"Nah, Mitch. Don't go with this pig. This is some bullshit."

"It's okay, Victor." Mitch steps forward, allowing me to speak to him privately.

"What's going on, Mitch? You in some kind of trouble here?" I lower my voice, so the little fucker Victor can't hear.

"I'm fine. Honestly, but you should probably go." He loses his attitude and shows his vulnerability.

Something is definitely up. This kid Victor is either packing or has something on him.

Something I can hold him on and possibly get some information traded.

"Does Liberty know you're out and on this side of town?"

"No, and you can't tell her." I look over and see Fox and Hart keeping Victor occupied and out of the way.

"You know I can't do that, bud. Now, does this kid run with Dominic?" His nonverbal reply tells me what I need to know.

"Okay, I'm taking you back to Boys Haven," I tell him, motioning him over to my cruiser.

"Please, Hetch. Don't do this. I have this sorted." I'm sure he thinks he has it sorted, but I'm 100 percent certain he most definitely does not.

"Get in the car, Mitch. I'm not gonna argue with you." I open the back door and motion for him to get in. His scowl tells me he's pissed, but I can't be worried about it right now.

Once I've closed the door, I turn back to Fox and Hart just in time to see Victor take off.

"Fox keep on him. Hart, stay with Mitch." I don't wait for his reply, but take off after Fox while calling it in. "331. We have a pursuit on foot." I catch up to Fox without breaking a sweat and overtake him as Victor cuts through a backyard.

"Go around and cut him off," I shout out to Fox, watching

the little fucker jump the fence. I follow him up, dropping to my feet while he clears the next fence.

"Remind me why we're chasing this fucker?" Fox's irritated voice comes over my lapel radio, and I smirk, knowing deep down he secretly likes this shit.

"'Cause the punk runs with The Disciples and we still need to get a lock down on Dominic," I pant back, keeping up my chase.

"So, for pussy. Got it." I ignore his jab, scaling another fence into a second backyard. Victor keeps his lead, clearing the third fence as I clear the second.

Little fucker is fast.

Upping my pace, I make it over the third fence just as I catch him crawling up underneath the house of an unsuspecting family.

"Come out, Victor, you have nowhere to go!" I shout, reaching for my flashlight and shining it under the house.

"I got nothin' to hide. I don't want no trouble," he calls out, just as Fox meets me around the back.

"Then don't make us come under there, Victor," Fox warns, his flashlight finding him first. He's in the back corner, back to us. Either searching for a weapon or dropping his stash.

My bet he's dropping his stash.

"Victor, we can play it two ways. You can come out, slowly making no sudden movement, or we can send the dogs in there."

"Don't send the dogs, man," his shaky voice pleads back.

"Aww, look at that, Sarge, he doesn't like dogs either." Fox snorts, enjoying this way more than I am.

"Then slowly come out, with your hands up," I shout, keeping my gun trained on him.

"This is fucking bullshit." He starts cursing as he crawls his ass back out. After a few choice words, he clears the house, and I step in closer, ordering him down on the ground.

"Hands behind your back." Fox wrestles him to the ground, and I follow him down.

"What am I under arrest for? I didn't do nothin'" The dumb fuck tries to fight us, suddenly more brave than ten seconds ago.

"Quit resisting." I grunt, digging my knee deeper into his back.

"I ain't resisting."

"You are. Relax your arms." It takes a few a minutes to detain him, but eventually we get him.

"What the fuck were you thinking, Victor?" I ask when he's calmed down and secured.

"I swear I didn't mean to run. You just rolled up on me out of the blue," he grunts out his reply as Fox pulls him up to his feet, giving him a full pat down. "I was scared."

"You have something to be scared about?" Fox asks when he establishes he's clean.

"Nah, man, I'm on the straight arrow."

Straight arrow my ass.

"Well, you're not on the straight arrow today. You're going to jail."

"What the hell for?"

"Well for one, making me run and two, for whatever we find up under the house."

"What? That's some bullshit. I didn't put nothin' under there." He denies any wrongdoing, but guilt is etched all over his face.

"What's up under the house, Victor?" I ask again.

"Nothin', I'm innocent."

"347. We have the perp in custody. We're gonna need a K-9 unit out here." I call in for the dog unit. If there's anything up under the house, they will find it. Almost immediately, control radios back with confirmation and an estimated time.

"I have the dog coming out, Victor, so we'll know for sure then."

"I swear I didn't drop anything." He holds his ground, not admitting to anything.

"Good, so my dog isn't gonna find any drugs up under the house then?" I push, knowing I'm gonna find something.

"No, I mean, if there is something under there, it isn't mine."

"You think there are drugs under there, but someone else put them there?" I bite his play.

134

"I mean, maybe. I-I think I saw something." He shrugs like it's no big deal.

"You saw something?" It takes everything in me not to shake the fucker out of his stupidity.

"Yeah, I mean maybe."

"How much are we talking about?" Fox steps in when he notices how hard I'm finding it to keep it together.

"Maybe, I don't know, looked like a gram. Maybe two."

"And you didn't touch it?" I gather myself enough to keep up the interrogation.

"Well, I mean, when I crawled up under there my hand might have touched it."

Seriously, you can't fucking make this shit up.

"347 to control, cancel the K-9." I decide to go up under the house on my own. We still have Mitch in the back of the cruiser to take back to Boys Haven and the less paperwork I need to file, the better off he might be in this.

"You remember where you saw it?"

"I can't be sure, but maybe up in the back corner somewhere." Fox can't hold his laughter this time, and if I wasn't worried about Mitch getting caught up in this bullshit, then I'd be laughing right along with him.

Fortunately, a few minutes later, it becomes clear we have something to hold over Victor when I find about five grams of cocaine up under the house. If we're lucky, we may be able to get Victor to shed some info on Dominic. Unfortunately, it means Mitch may be in more shit than the poor kid can handle.

Not the news I want to give Liberty.

"Look what I found, Victor," I call out when I crawl back out from under the house.

"Ahh, man it's not mine, I swear." He starts shaking his head, still denying it's his.

"This is how we're gonna play it, Victor. You're going to tell me the information I want and I'm going to drop the charges of assaulting an officer and resisting arrest."

"Nah, man, that's bullshit. I'm no snitch."

"Then you're under arrest for obstruction, assaulting a police officer, and possession of an illegal substance." I start to read him his rights, knowing he's going to cave before I finish.

"Aww, hang on, man, what do you need?"

"I need information on Dominic Westin."

"Are you fucking insane? No way I'm going against him." He shakes his head, not okay with what I'm asking.

"He doesn't need to know it's you. I just want to know where we can find him."

"Jesus, I don't know." His shoulders slump, and I know he's thinking about it.

"You think you got problems with a guy like Dominic finding out you snitched. You're gonna have huge problems with me if you don't give me what I want."

"Fuck, man. If he finds out I rolled on him…."

"He won't," I promise, knowing it's not really a promise I can keep. Hopefully, the information he gives us is enough to put the asshole away.

Then he won't be anyone's problem.

Least of all mine.

LIBERTY

"Uggg, this is hopeless." I slam the phone down on its cradle and let out a frustrated groan. *Does anything ever happen smoothly around here?*

"Bad news?" Sue asks from the doorway of my office, bringing me out of my pity party.

"Yes. The church where we were going to hold the car wash next Saturday just informed me they can't let us use the parking lot. They booked the hall and now due to health and safety, we both can't be there."

I flick through the mess of paperwork on my desk, trying to decide how I'm going to figure this out.

"Well, crap. Where else could we hold it?" She steps into the office and takes a seat across from me.

It's Saturday afternoon and once again, I'm in on my day off, dealing with this mess.

"There are a few places I can call. I know the gas station down on Parkton may let us use their lot at short notice." I flick through the folder holding all our fundraising information.

"What about your dad's car yard? That would be perfect."

"Yeah, it would be, but after what happened with Mitch the other week, I'm not sure it's wise to let him around the boys right now." I shut the idea down right away. It's bad enough I have to deal with Mom and Dad checking in on me every day. I don't need my dad getting in my business, or in the boys' business.

"Things still tense with the parents?" She smirks, knowing full well since she's fielded calls all week from both my mom and dad.

"Don't try to be funny."

The start of an argument in the recreation room at the same time the doorbell rings cuts our conversation short and has both of us out of our chairs.

"You want the fight or the door?"

"I'll take the door." I opt for the easiest option and exit first, making my way through the house to the front door. I can hear Sue sorting out the boys, just as I open the door to find a very pissed-off Mitch and an equally pissed-off Hetch standing there.

"What the—" It takes a second to register the man who's spent every night in my bed over the last two weeks is not here for me, but for something more serious.

Mitch.

"I didn't do anything wrong. Don't freak out." Mitch shrugs off Hetch's hand from his shoulder and pushes past me into the house.

"Hold on there, buddy. What's going on here?" Mitch ignores my question, stomping his way down the hall into his room.

"Ahh?" I turn back to Hetch, my mind running a million miles a minute wondering what sort of trouble Mitch has found himself in now.

Keep it together, Liberty.

"We picked him up over in Redlands. He was hanging with one of Dominic's boys."

"Jesus Christ." I run a hand over my face, completely

138

frustrated. I feel like we take two steps forward, then three back. One day he seems to be on board, and the next I have the police bringing him home.

"Can I come in and talk to you for a second, Lib?" he asks, pulling me from my freak-out and back to him.

Shit, he has more news.

"Ah, yeah, of course. We'll go to my office." I step back, letting him in, and directing him to my office.

"Let me fill Sue in real quick." He nods and I leave him there, heading into the rec room. Sue has the boys calmed down now, all arguments diffused by the time I find her. I quickly fill her in on the Mitch situation, telling her to keep an eye on him, before heading back to Hetch.

When I get back to the entrance of my office, Hetch is standing in the corner reading one of my textbooks on child behavior. He doesn't notice me right away, so I take a second to check him out in his uniform. A skin-tight navy T-shirt stretches across his back and biceps. Black military-type pants, which fit better than any pair of jeans I've ever seen on a man, and black kick-ass combat boots that for some crazy reason do something to me, complete his delectable ensemble.

Jesus.

"You okay?" Hetch turns, either sensing my presence or hearing the soft moan I let past my lips. Judging by his dimples, I'd say the moan.

"Ahh, yeah. Sorry. Umm, can I get you a drink or anything?" I ask as I step into my office.

"I'm good." He closes the book, places it back on my bookshelf, and then pulls up the seat in front of my desk.

"Right." I close the door behind me, then quickly move to my desk to tidy up a little, suddenly conscious of my mess. "Sorry about the mess. We have a lot going on around here this week with the new Big Brother program starting up in a few weeks. I wasn't expecting anyone." I know I'm rambling as I try to sort the paperwork into some sort of controlled chaos, but I can't stop

Hetch in front of me on a normal day makes me nervous.

Hetch in front of me because of issues with Mitch makes me a wreck.

"Liberty, sit down and just breathe," he orders in his special Hetch kind of way I've come to like. It's the reprieve I need to take stock of everything.

"I'm sorry, you're right." I fall into my chair, forcing myself to stay calm. "Okay, how bad is it?"

"The kid we picked him up with was carrying enough cocaine to be charged with intent to distribute."

Fuck.

"What about Mitch?"

"He was clean. But who knows what would have happened if we didn't pick them up."

"Oh, God. How could he be so stupid?" My breathing skyrockets at hearing how deep Mitch is getting involved. "After everything we've talked to him about, I don't get it. I'm trying so hard here, Hetch. I don't know what else I can do to help him." I reveal more than I probably should.

"Seems to me you're doing everything right, sweetheart." I ignore the soft flutter in my stomach at the sound of his name for me and try to stay focused on the issue at hand.

"I don't know, Hetch. One minute I'm checking in with his caseworker, letting her know he's been doing well, the next I have to pull rank and give him extra chores and take his community visits away. I don't think it's sticking."

"I think it's sticking. I just think there are other factors playing a huge part here."

"What do you mean?" I sit up a little straighter, unsure what he means.

"I mean, Dominic's hold on Mitch is a bit more complex than you might think."

"What's more complex than family? Trust me I get it."

"It's more than family to him. Mitch confided in me, but it's more to do with you, rather than him."

"Me? What do I have to do with it?" I sit back, more confused than I care to be.

"Dominic's using you over him."

140

"Me?"

"Yeah, he's found Mitch's weakness, and he's using it."

"I don't understand." I shake my head, still trying to figure out what exactly he means. "Why would he be using me over Mitch? I mean, we've had one run-in so this doesn't make sense."

"Mitch cares for you as much as you care for him. He's doing it for you. He doesn't want to follow his brother's footsteps. Dominic knows he can't make him, so he's using other forms of getting him to play."

"He's threatening harm to me to get Mitch to join his crew?" I stand, not realizing how loud my voice has risen.

"Relax, Lib. It's going to be okay." He tries to reassure me, but it doesn't help. *Mitch is doing this shit because of me? To keep me safe.*

"It's not okay, Hetch. This is getting way out of hand. I've worked so hard the last six months with him. He's come so far, and now Dominic's going to drag him down. I can't stop him from seeing his brother. Other than banning him from coming to the house. I can't stop him from getting to him at school. On rec time. I mean where does this leave me? I've no resources for these kinds of issues. The department doesn't give a shit. I'm at my wits' end." I finish my rant only to find Hetch standing in front me, holding my face in his hands.

"You need to bring it down a notch, babe. I know this is overwhelming, but it's gonna work out."

"How? Tell me how?" I want to believe things will find a way of working out, but right now, I can't see it happening.

"We're gonna bring him in, sweetheart. We have plays in motion. The little prick we picked today up is gonna flip on Dominic, so we might be able to get him on something. And I'm gonna help with Mitch." His thumb starts stroking my cheek in a soft circular pattern and for a second, it helps soothe me, until I realize him becoming involved will only complicate things.

"Hetch, you can't get involved." I try to pull out of his grasp, but his hold stays firm.

"I can and I will, Lib."

"How, Hetch? How do you propose you get involved?"

"Well for one, I can spend some one-on-one time with him."

"I can't ask you to do that."

"Why the hell not?" He pulls back, like the rejection slapped him.

"Because it's a conflict of interest. You can't walk in here and hang out, you need to be cleared. Plus, after this stunt, Mitch is gonna be on strict house lockdown." I ramble off all the reasons why it's a bad idea, completely ignoring the reasons why it could also be a great idea.

"You forget, Liberty, I'm an officer of the law. I'm pretty sure you can clear me."

"This is true." I stop trying to fight the reasons and contemplate the idea. He's right. It would be as easy as a phone call and some paperwork being filled out. "You'd do that for me?"

"For you, for Mitch."

"But why?" The question hangs in the air between us. Not in an awkward silence, but expectantly. It's only been two weeks since we fell into bed together. Granted it's been an amazing two weeks, but it's hardly anything serious. Besides getting to know each other's bodies exceptionally well, he's barely opened up to me.

"Because I like you and despite the issues you're having with Mitch and the bad decisions he's making lately, he's a good kid."

"He is," I repeat, without missing a beat.

"So figure it out and I'll do what I have to do." I nod, still not sure if this is a good thing or a bad thing. Instead of messing my head up anymore on it, I decide to let it happen. Hetch is right. Maybe having him around here, having one–on–one time with Mitch, as well as some of the boys, would be good for all of them. Especially Mitch.

"I like you, Liam," I whisper hesitantly, finally making the decision in my mind.

"I know you do." His smirk is way too cocky for the moment. "I like you too." His lips steal the words I want to say, in a soft, innocent kiss.

"I missed you." He steals my lips this time, gently soothing me with the soft caress of a promise.

"You did?" I ask before his lips whisper over my jaw and down my neck. "You only left my bed this morning," I remind him. We've been taking turns between each other's bed. One night it's my place, the next it's his.

"Mmhmm," he answers, his tongue swirling over the pulse point in my neck. "'Specially missed this. Missed seeing you come to life." His words in the intimacy of the moment stir a wave of warmth within me and push me further into his spell.

"Jesus, Hetch. You've barely touched me and I feel like I'm about to explode." I try to push him away, but he doesn't allow it.

"Go out with me tomorrow night." He pauses, more unsure than I've ever seen him before.

"Like a date?" I ask, my growing smile pauses, my heart fluttering faster.

"Yeah, like a date. You, me, food." He kisses me again, this time, harder.

"Okay," I answer when he pulls back.

"Okay." He smiles, giving me his dimples, and for the split second like every other second Hetch has invaded the last few weeks, my world seems complete.

15

HETCH

"You ready for this, boys?" I ask when we're en route in the back of an unmarked tactical van, about to execute yesterday's high-risk arrest warrant on one of Dominic's known hangouts. After getting Victor to turn on Dominic yesterday afternoon, we decided to hold off and move on the information today.

After going over the intel, and reevaluating our play, Detective Tomelson and I decided we wanted both teams on this raid. Kaighn's team will now enter through the back and deal with the dog while my team will breach the front.

"We're good, boss," Sterling answers for the team, picking up on my unease.

Normally I'm more collected before a high-risk raid, but knowing there is a lot riding on this arrest, the pressure builds.

"Yeah, we know the play. Gonna get the fucker. We're good." Fox encourages, and I force the tension out of my shoulders knowing my team has my back.

"Okay, boss, we're coming up on Garth street, twenty

seconds out," Walker tells me from the front of the van, pulling me out of my head, and back into the game. "Right, boys. Game faces and bring it in." I place my fist out in front of me and wait for everyone to connect.

"Keep it together and stay safe." I get a few nods and a couple of repeat sentiments. Seconds later, we pull up three houses down from the suspect's, exit the tactical vehicle, and stack up in formation.

Tate, Fox, Sterling, Hart and myself.

"Let's go." I squeeze Hart's shoulder, giving him the go-ahead. He in turns squeezes Sterling's shoulder. Sterling squeezes Fox's, and Fox squeezes Tate's. At Fox's go-ahead, Tate moves, and we move with him. Knees bent, rifles trained, we stay low and controlled as we breach the perimeter of the front yard.

"Team One in place," I whisper into my coms, and wait for Team Two to get into position.

It only takes a few beats for Kaighn to come through, letting us know they are in place and ready to move.

At Kaighn's order, Tate is on the door, breaching it with a battering ram, and then stepping back. Fox releases a flash bang and the noise and explosion may only give us a couple of seconds, but it's enough to get in clean and let us control the situation. Fox's fast feet lead us inside. All of us move in sync. Fox, Sterling, Tate, Hart, then myself. A second flash bang goes off in the back end of the house, letting us know Kaighn and his team have made entry.

"Police! Search warrant. Don't move." An array of shouts ring out through the house while we all move to our areas. Fox, Sterling, and Tate step to left of the entryway, Hart and myself to the right.

Instantly, my eyes train in on an unidentified male, sitting on the sofa, some bitch on her knees sucking his cock.

"Police, don't move," I shout, training my rifle on them while Hart clears the rest of the room.

"What the fuck?" We take them by surprise. The male releases the bitch's hair and stands.

"Clear," Hart calls, allowing us to push forward.

"Keep your hands above your head and get on the ground," I order both the man and the woman.

She falls to the ground, screaming at our intrusion, but the guy stays standing.

"I need back up in here," I call through my coms, keeping my weapon and eyes trained on him.

Two of Kaighn's men step in behind us, securing the woman on the ground while I step toward the difficult male.

"Get on the ground on your stomach." I inch in closer, but he doesn't waver.

"Fuck you, pig." His anger is all it takes for him not to pay attention, giving Hart an opening to reach him. Kicking his leg out in front of him, Hart drops him to the ground in one swift movement.

"You speak to your mom with that mouth?" Hart grunts, turning him onto his stomach and securing his arms behind his back.

"My mother's dead, fucker. Just like you all will be. Fucking coming to my house and fucking with me." I drop my knee to his back and help Hart secure his hands with zip ties.

"Shut up and quit resisting!" I dig my knee in deeper, my hand squeezing down hard on the back of his neck. I'm not in the mood to hear him running his mouth.

"I'm not fucking resisting."

"Then relax your arms," Hart orders, still struggling to secure him.

"Fuck you." I squeeze harder on his neck, letting him know I'm not fucking around here. After a few more seconds of fighting, he finally grows tired, and we get him secured.

"Two subjects secure and in custody," I call through the coms, waiting to hear back from the rest of the team.

"Room two, clear. Two suspects secure," Fox calls back.

"Room four clear," Sterling informs.

The rest of Kaighn's team calls through a clear on each room until the whole house has been cleared and secured.

"Where's Dominic?" I ask the punk at my feet when I realize

he's not here.

"Fuck you. I'm not telling you anything." He spits on my right boot, and it takes everything in me not to bring it back and kick him in ribs.

"House secure, suspect not here." I finally give the all clear to officers outside. "We're moving out."

"You're all fucking dead. Mark my words." The fucker starts running his mouth as soon as we pull him to his feet and start pushing him out of the house to awaiting officers.

"Yeah, yeah. Like I haven't heard that before." I hand him over to Detective Tomelson, less than impressed with his threat.

"Don't know what happened, Hetch," Tommy offers what he thinks I need to hear.

"Bad intel." I shrug, not ready to give up. "We'll get him." I know it's a long shot, the fucker seems to be a ghost, but I'm not giving up.

The longer he keeps evading us, the longer Liberty stays in danger.

I'm going to get him.

And when we do, I'll enjoy every fucking second of it.

I can guarantee it.

* * *

"You heading to The Elephant tonight?" Sterling asks an hour later when I'm filling out my reports from the earlier raid. While it was a clean bust, and the narcotics unit were able to seize a fuckload of drugs and guns after we left, I'm still pissed we didn't get a lock on Dominic.

So much for Victor's intel.

"Nah, I have plans." I don't reveal more than that. Sterling is the last person who needs to know I have a date. The fucker will read too much into it.

"Things must be getting serious with Liberty, hardly see you around."

"Don't know what you're talking about." I place my

signature on the last document. I'm not in the mood for his shit tonight, not when I'm still pissed about Dominic.

"Sure you don't. Will you be bringing her tomorrow?" he asks, still not giving up on it.

"What's tomorrow?" I file my paperwork and stand from my desk. My shift is over and I have a date to get ready for.

Fuck, a date. The thought should freak me out, but it doesn't.

"Your mom has the brunch thing going on. Don't tell me you forgot."

Fuck.

"No, I remember. I just didn't know you were coming." I cover my lie with a statement.

"Your mom invited me." I nod. Of course she did. "That a problem?" His tone has me looking up.

"Has it ever been?" I give it back. I don't know if he's pissed at my evasiveness regarding Liberty or he's got his own shit going on, but I'm not in the fucking mood.

"What the hell's your problem, bro? You're dating the neighbor, just admit it."

"What the fuck does it matter to you?" I ask, still unsure why I'm keeping it on the down low. It's not like it's a big deal. Yeah, I've dated before. Maybe not in a long time, but I have dated exclusively. I'm just not ready to share it with the world yet.

"It doesn't, Hetch. I just don't get the secrecy to it."

"You mean like the way you are with my sister?" I'm an ass. I know it. Giving him shit about Kota isn't cool, but if he's looking for a reaction, then he has it.

"What the fuck are you talking about?" His body goes rigid, his stance defensive.

"You wanted to play it this way." I shrug like it's no big deal, but I know I crossed a line.

"No, I want to know what the fuck you mean?" His hands fist at his sides and I almost laugh at his discomfort, but I don't.

"Sterling, you and I both know you're in love with Kota." I lay it out for him, no judgment, no accusations. Just pure truth.

"The fuck I am." He recoils, and I almost believe him. Almost second-guess how I've read the situation all these years.

If only he didn't get so defensive.

"Whatever you say, Sterling."

"I'm not in love with your sister," he repeats, his brow dipping in a deep scowl.

"Whatever, you keep telling yourself that." I offer a quick wave and make my way out to my truck.

I'm done. It's not my business. If they want to dance around the huge elephant in the room, they can have at it.

The drive home seems longer than normal. Running over my conversation with Sterling, I soon start to feel like an ass. I know some brothers may not be okay with their best friends going after their sister, but it's not like that with Sterling. When I say he's the best guy I know, I mean it. Kota couldn't do any better.

By the time I pull up to my apartment, my guilt has me reaching for my phone and calling Sterling. He doesn't answer, so I leave a message.

"I'm a fucking ass. Can't go out 'cause I've got a date with Liberty. Fuck me. I can't believe I just admitted that to you. Don't be an ass about it. See you tomorrow." My guilt doesn't subside right off the bat, but when I notice Liberty's car home earlier than expected, it soon fades.

I collect my mail and then take the steps two at a time.

Forgetting my apartment, I shove the mail into my back pocket and head right for her door, knocking with my standard force.

Yeah, we have a date tonight, but my need to see her now wins out.

Liberty opens her door, a huge smile on her face when she sees me.

Fuck, imagine coming home to her every day?

Whoa, calm down, fucker.

I push the thoughts out of my head and nudge her backward. Before she can argue, I kick her door closed, pick her up, and stalk to her bathroom.

"What are you doing, you big lug?" She laughs, trying to wiggle her way out of my arms.

"You and I have a date tonight."

149

"I know. I'm about to start getting ready for it."

"I need a shower."

"Don't you have your own shower next door?"

"Yeah, but I like yours better," I tell her, placing her on top of the vanity.

"What makes mine different?" she questions as I reach into her shower and turn the faucet on.

"It has you in it, sweetheart." I step back between her legs and finally kiss her. She responds immediately, wrapping her arms and legs around me.

"I want those lips around my cock." I moan against her mouth.

"Is that right?" She pulls back and rips her dress over her head, revealing one of her sexy, white lace bras and matching panties.

"Yeah, then I want to fuck you." I drop my pants and step out of them.

"Maybe if you can make me come with your talented tongue a couple times, I'll wrap my lips around this big cock of yours." She reaches down and tightens her grip around my painfully erect cock.

"Has anyone ever told you, you're a greedy little thing?"

"Only you." She laughs a carefree laugh, and I make a promise to myself that for every day I know her, I'll try to make her laugh like that again.

* * *

"Did you always want to be a police officer?" Liberty asks a couple of hours later while we're seated at the back table of Il Centro Restaurant and Bar, one of the finest Italian restaurants in Trebook.

I was lucky to get a table at such short notice. Fox managed to pull it off for me when I remembered his uncle is part owner. Even though I don't like owing anyone anything, it's still worth every bit of annoyance just to see Liberty done up. I nearly busted a fucking nut when she opened the door earlier. After fucking her in the shower, I cleaned her up and left her to get dressed. I had only been gone for thirty minutes. I wasn't expecting her to be ready when I returned. I sure as hell wasn't expecting her to look so fucking amazing. I almost didn't want to leave the apartment with her looking so fucking sexy.

A red wraparound dress molds to her body. The low cleavage makes my dick jump every time she leans forward, giving me the perfect view of her soft skin. Her short blonde curls are messy, but in a perfected kind of way. And her fuckable lips are painted the same red she wore the night I met her.

Fuck me. She's a walking hard-on.

"Not always." I clear my throat, shaking the image of those red lips wrapped around my cock away. "I actually wanted to be a youth worker for a while there," I admit, unsure why. Normally if someone asks me the same question, I always say it's been a childhood dream to join the force.

Fucking hell.

"Wow, you're serious." She sits up a little straighter at my confession.

"My dad was a youth worker." I keep my voice steady. Controlled. Even.

"Was? What does he do now?" It's the first tidbit of my personal life I've shared with her. The last two weeks we've spent learning all about each other's bodies, no private details. And while it's not by any means a new way of life for me, it is a stepping stone. Or maybe a pebble.

"He's dead." The words are like acid coming out of my throat.

"Oh, I'm so sorry." She reaches across the table and covers my hand with her small one. My heart rate shouldn't be spiked, but it is.

"Don't be." I pull out of her grasp and reach for my beer. "It was a while ago." I don't know why I thought it would be okay to talk about him.

It's never okay.

"I can picture it, you know? You with the kids, helping them out." She moves the subject along, and I don't want to be grateful for it, but I am. "Is that why you're interested in coming to the house and talking to Mitch?" I don't want to tell her the truth. That maybe I only want to do it for her. Maybe my need to keep her safe is more than I actually understand. My need to protect her is no longer about my dick, but about her welfare. I don't want to tell her any of that, so I nod instead and then change the subject.

"Everything good with getting clearance for me to come around?" Yesterday after I left Liberty's office, she started the process of adding me onto the approved visitors' list.

"Yeah, we'll need to go over everything with you, but then you'll be good to go."

"Good, just let me know when and I'll be there." I wasn't lying when I told Liberty I would help with Mitch. I know he's a good kid. Know how much Liberty cares for him. And if me coming to the house to hang with him once a week helps him realize he doesn't need to walk down the path Dominic is paving for him, then why wouldn't I do it?

"Do you want to come by tomor— Oh, my God." Her sudden change in tone and the way her body recoils has my gaze moving around the restaurant looking for the threat.

"Liberty?" I ask when she stands and slaps her napkin down on the table.

"I'm gonna fucking kill him."

I don't have a chance to ask her what she means and who the fuck the *he* is she plans to kill before she's halfway across the restaurant, getting up in some guy's face.

Well, shit. Here we go.

16

LIBERTY

"Are you fucking kidding me right now?"

"Liberty?" Jett has the audacity to look guilty as I come to a stop at his table.

"Don't Liberty me." I point my glare at the little whore who's the cause of my best friend's heartache. "Where's Payton, Jett? You know, your wife?" The smug little bitch turns her nose up at me as soon as Payton's name leaves my mouth.

"Liberty, please don't make a scene here." Jett stands and wraps his fingers around my wrist, pulling me away from his table.

"I told Payton not to trust you. I can't believe you would be so stupid." His grip tightens the louder my voice rises. I don't care we're in some fancy-ass restaurant. My no-good fucking brother is still the slime ball I thought he was.

"Shut the fuck up. It's not what it looks like."

"Let go of me. I know what it looks like." I try to pull out of his grasp, but he holds tighter.

"You can't tell Payton. I need more time," the asshole says. Ha! Fuck that.

"I'm not going to lie to your wife. My best friend. Are you fucking mad?" The table we're standing close to gasps at my choice of words, but I don't have it in me to be embarrassed.

"I swear, Lib—" he begins but doesn't get another word in because Hetch is there and in his face.

"Get your fucking hands off her now." His voice brings the rest of the restaurant which had yet to notice the tension to a standstill.

"Fuck off. She's my sister. This is family business." Jett puffs his chest out, attempting to intimidate Hetch. Only I know it won't work.

"I don't give a fuck who you are to her. Get your hands off her now."

"Hetch, it's okay." I try to reason with him when I notice the manager walking our way.

"Who is this asshole, Liberty?" my stupid brother asks, only serving to piss Hetch off more.

"Don't talk to her. You're talking to me."

"Listen—" Jett begins but doesn't finish when one minute he's standing in front of me and the next he's being dragged out of the restaurant, hands restrained behind his back. I don't have a chance to cry out and ask what Hetch is doing before he's pushing him out the front entrance and onto the sidewalk.

"Hetch." I race after them, pushing through the door just in time to see him thrust Jett up against the side of the restaurant.

"Hetch, it's okay. He won't hurt me. He's my dipshit brother." Hetch's gaze moves off my brother and turns to me.

"No one fucking touches you," he simply says before turning back to Jett.

Holy fuck, I should be annoyed he practically just pissed on me like a dog marking his territory, but I can't even begin to be. Possessive Hetch is hot as fuck.

"I don't give a fuck if you're her brother. You put your hands on her again, you and I are gonna have problems. Understand?" Jett nods, and then flinches as Hetch jerks him away from the building by his arm, and slaps him hard on the back.

"What the fuck, Liberty? You're seeing this guy?" He rubs at his arm, not giving a shit said guy is still standing there in his space.

"Not like it's any of your business, but yes," I answer, watching Hetch for any response.

"Hetch, meet my stupid brother, Jett. Jett this is Hetch."

"Can't say it's a pleasure." Jett gives him a once over, but Hetch doesn't react.

"You good here?" Hetch walks toward me, lightly touching my arm.

"Yeah. Can you give us a minute?" He looks reluctant to leave me, but I offer what I hope is a reassuring smile. It must soothe him because he leans down and gently presses his lips to my forehead before letting me know he'll wait inside. I attempt another reassuring smile, but give up when he shakes his head at me and heads back inside.

"Seriously, Liberty? You're seeing this douche?" Jett gingerly steps forward, now rubbing his wrist.

"The only douche I see here is you. What the fuck is wrong with you? What was all that shit at Mom and Dad's last week?"

"It's over. I swear." He runs a hand through his hair.

"Don't give me that bullshit, Jett." I won't play into his lies. I know what I see, know from experiences.

"She's pregnant," he whispers, knocking all fight out of me. *Fuck.*

"Is it yours?" I wouldn't put it past the little whore to pull this shit.

"I think so. The dates work out. We weren't using anything."

"You dumb jackass." I manage to work through my shock, rage, and nausea.

"She's keeping it."

I don't respond immediately. My mind is still reeling. What is there to say? I can't be angry she doesn't want to abort a child. "Does Payton know?"

"Jesus, no. We're still trying to figure things out."

"What's there to figure out, Jett? Your wife needs to know

155

this."

"I know, Liberty. But I need more time." He runs a shaky hand over his face.

"Jett, you have done some pretty fucking stupid things the last few months, but keeping this from Payton rates as top. Time isn't going to help you. You need to go home right now and tell her."

"Or what, you'll tell her?" He scoffs, knowing me well.

"Damn straight I will. She deserves to know. If you keep this from her, I'll hate you more than I do right now."

"You don't mean that, Bertie." The nickname stirs nothing in me. But instead of being upset about it, it just makes me angrier.

"I do, Jett. You have fucked up over and over with her. Hurt her and Arabella repeatedly, and now this. You need to be honest."

"I didn't mean to hurt her or Ara. You don't understand." It almost sounds like a whine, and I want to bitch slap it out of him.

"You're right. I don't understand. You had a good thing. The perfect family, work, life. And you fucked up. I don't know why she took you back, but she did, and now you're keeping this from her. I don't feel sorry for you, Jett. I feel sorry for Pay and Arabella. Tell her tonight or I will." I turn and leave him standing there, walking back inside to a waiting Hetch.

"You okay?" He takes me in his arms, holding me while I try to keep my emotions in check. Part of me wants to go to Payton right now, lay it all out for her. But another part of me can't stomach being the bearer of this news. I hope to God Jett tells her 'cause there is no way I can keep this to myself.

Jesus, what am I gonna do?

When I don't answer, Hetch grabs the attention of the waitress.

"Can we get our food to go?" If she's confused, she doesn't say anything, just tells him no problem.

"We don't have to leave. I'm fine. Promise." He knows it's a lie, but doesn't call me on it.

156

"It's fine, sweetheart. I don't wanna sit and eat while you're looking the way you're looking. You need to go to your girl?" He pulls out his wallet when the waitress comes back with some takeout containers.

"No. But maybe later."

"Okay, come on, let's get out of here." He tucks me under his arm, maneuvering me out the door and past a very sick-looking Jett. I ignore him and the slight ache that settles in my stomach seeing him so distraught, and allow Hetch to give me the comfort of his embrace as he walks me over to his truck.

"Thank you." I turn and look at him when we're both in the privacy of his truck.

"No problem, sweetheart." He takes my hands and raises it to his lips, offering me a gentle kiss. A sudden urge to tell him I'm falling for him races through me. I don't act on it, though. Even I know it's way too soon to spill those words.

Hetch doesn't pick up my small panic. Instead, he offers me a wink, starts his truck, and drives past my brother without a backward glance.

What an eventful first date.

* * *

"I'm so fucking stupid, Bertie." A snot-faced Payton sobs in greeting a few hours later when she opens her door to Hetch and me. The dreaded call came through twenty minutes ago when Hetch and I settled into bed for a movie. After taking our dinner to go, Hetch took me back to my place and served up our meals with a glass of wine. We continued our date in the comfort of my apartment. It wasn't as romantic as Il Centro's, but I wasn't complaining, especially when after we had finished eating, Hetch cleared the table and took me right then and there. It was intense, wild, and so fucking perfect I couldn't wipe the smile off my face.

Well, until Payton's phone call did.

"No, you're not." I step into her embrace, wrapping my arms around her, wishing I could take her pain away.

"He's having a baby with her." She wails into my shoulder, her body rocking with sobs. "Itookhimbackandthishappens." Her words are rushed, strung together in one fast breath, and it takes me a second or two to figure out what she said.

"Hey, now, come on. You're gonna wake up, Arabella." I try to soothe her, unsure what to say in a moment like this.

"She's awake. Jett is in there with her."

"He's still here?" The question comes from Hetch first, and it takes both Payton and me by surprise.

"Yeah, he says he's not leaving." If Payton is annoyed I brought Hetch along with me, she doesn't show it. I tried to tell him I would be fine, but he refused to let me drive out here alone. Told me it's not safe to be out late on my own, and he would drop me off and pick me up whenever I was ready. I didn't have much time to argue with him, so I gave up a good fight and let him drive me over.

Hetch and I share a look before he steps past us into Payton's house and follows the hall down to their main living area.

Closing the door behind us, Payton and I quickly follow his trail.

"Hetch, what are you—" I don't get to finish my question before he's talking, his voice taking up all presence in the room.

"You need to get your stuff and go now," he calmly tells my brother.

"What the hell, Pay? You called my sister?" Jett carefully stands from the sofa, replacing his lap with a pillow to cradle a sleeping Arabella's head.

"What did you expect me to do? You won't leave." Payton starts crying again, full-on sobs.

"I'm not gonna tell you again. Leave, or I'll make you." Hetch takes a commanding step closer to Jett.

"You're just gonna throw me out after we just got back together? What about Arabella? Don't you know how confusing this is for her?"

"You're having a baby with her, Jett. You told me things

158

were over. This isn't over."

"It is, baby. I swear. It's been over for three months." Jett steps around Hetch and takes his wife's hand, pleading with her.

"I want you to go." Payton holds her ground. Jett looks between Hetch, Payton, and me before finally conceding defeat.

"I'll go, but we aren't done, Pay. No way is this over." He picks up his jacket from the arm of the sofa, walks back over and wraps his arms around her. Payton fights him off, and before Jett can step back, Hetch has him by the scruff of the shirt, pulling him back down the hall toward the front door.

"You and I are gonna have to have a word about putting your hands on women." I hear him say before turning the corner and pushing him out toward the front door.

I don't have a second to think if I should go out and check on him before Payton is back to sobbing again.

"What am I gonna do, Liberty?" Her eyes are puffy, her nose red and runny, and I know just by looking at her, it's going to be a long freaking night.

17

HETCH

"Who are you?" a little voice asks, waking me from my sleep.

"What?" I sit up rather fast, only to find Liberty's niece standing over me, a confused look on her face.

"Umm." I clear my throat. "I'm Hetch, Auntie Liberty's friend." I look around, gathering my wits. Last night after I escorted Jett out, I came back to find a sobbing Payton and a concerned Liberty. I knew we were in for a long night when Liberty couldn't seem to keep Payton calm.

I wasn't expecting to crash on the sofa, but when the night turned into the early morning, and I found the two women crashed out in Payton's bed, I didn't want to wake her, nor did I want to leave Liberty alone. Instead, I got comfy on the sofa and gave into sleep within minutes.

"Where's my daddy?" Her little hands find her hips as she takes in my presence in her living room and the absence of her father.

"Ahhh…." I falter, unsure how to answer her question. The sun has barely risen, and the house is as quiet as when I crashed around two this morning.

"Wanna watch some cartoons?" I ask, instead of giving her an answer. I'll leave that conversation up to her mother.

"I don't watch cartoons," she smarts. Her little attitude reminds me of her auntie's, and I find myself cracking a smile at the sound of it.

"Well, what do you watch then?" I reach for the remote a little perplexed. What type of kid doesn't watch cartoons?

"Movies." She walks over to the cabinet under the TV and opens the doors, revealing a whole collection of Disney DVDs.

"They're cartoons," I tell her, watching her pick out some princess crap. It's not at all how I pictured spending my Saturday morning.

"No, they are movies," she argues right back, just like her auntie would.

Jesus, you can tell they're related.

"Right, if you say so, kid." I watch as she expertly moves through the steps of setting herself up to watch the DVD.

Once she has sorted herself out, she grabs a small teddy and climbs up next to me.

"Ahh, maybe I should go wake your mom." I stand, before she gets too comfortable. The kid is pretty chill considering a strange man is in her house.

"No, don't wake mommy yet. She's sleeping with Auntie Bertie. If she wakes up, she'll be sad again." She pats the sofa next to her, giving me her big doe eyes. The small hint of sadness is almost overwhelming and like a pansy fucker not wanting to upset her at all, I sit back down.

Auntie Bertie? I snicker at hearing the cute nickname. That's new. I'll have to remember to ask Liberty about it when she wakes up.

"So what's this about?" I ask as the opening scene starts rolling, some freaky-looking witch filling the screen with her ugliness.

"It's about *Rapunzel*." Her eyes don't leave the screen, completely missing my look of confusion.

Rapunzel? Which one is that again?

The bitch who left her shoe or the one who lives with midgets?

Fuck me, there's singing!

It's way too fucking early for this shit.

* * *

"So let me get this right. He's a bad guy, but deep down he's good. And the horse is good, but for some reason, he's being bad?" I ask Arabella thirty minutes later, trying to keep up.

"Hetch, did you listen to anyfing I told you?" she answers, growing frustrated with me.

"I'm trying to, kid. But dang, I'm confused." I'm not ashamed to admit it. Hell, any grown man who's never seen this movie would be as lost as I am.

"Ahh, am I interrupting?" Liberty's amused voice pulls me from the movie, letting me know she heard my questions.

"Shhh, Aunt Bertie." Arabella's eyes don't leave the TV, but her finger moves in dramatic fashion toward her lips.

"Yeah, Auntie Bertie." I look up, grinning wider when I notice her messed hair and crinkled face.

Fuck, she's cute.

"Oh, my God, don't you dare call me that. Ever." Her eyes grow wide, before a soft pink shade of blush coats her cheeks.

"Why? I think it's cute," I tease as I pat the sofa next to me.

"I'm serious, Hetch. If you ever call me that, I will punch you in the junk." She walks across the room and takes a seat next to me.

"What's junk?" Arabella queries, her eyes still not moving from the TV.

"Ask your mom," I offer like I've done for every question she's thrown my way the last thirty minutes.

"I'm asking you," she sasses.

Seriously, this kid is too quick for me.

"Has anyone told you she's just like you?" I turn to Liberty and catch her regarding me quietly.

"All the time." She beams like it's the best compliment anyone could pay her.

"I don't need to wonder what you were like as a kid. She's sitting right next to me." I hook my hand around her neck and drag her mouth toward mine.

"Trust me, I was worse." Her lips move against mine. A smile pulls at the corners of her mouth.

"Oddly, I believe that," I tell her, before running my tongue along around the seam of her lips.

"Thank you for staying last night. I know it's probably the last thing you wanted to do, but I appreciate it," she whispers, not quite opening her mouth to let me in.

"Don't mention it," I reply, about to deepen the kiss, only to be interrupted with Liberty's mini me.

"Auntie Bertie, you know, if you kiss with no clothes on, you make babies."

I choke on my laughter, causing a fit of coughing.

"Are you and Hetch having babies?"

"Breakfast. We should get breakfast started." Liberty stands in a rush, not answering her niece's question.

"Yeah! Can we have pancakes?" Arabella's gaze finally moves off the TV to look up at her.

"Of course, wanna help?" She holds out a hand in invitation. Arabella takes it, calling out to me on her way to the kitchen.

"Can you pause it, Hetch? I don't want to miss anyfing."

"You got it, kid." I reach for the remote and hit the pause button. I'm about to follow them into the kitchen, the call of pancakes too good to give up, when I hear the sound of the front door opening.

That fucker came back.

163

Far too exhausted to have to deal with this asshole, I reluctantly head down the hall ready to rip into him, only to find myself standing in front of two vaguely familiar faces.

"Who are you and what the hell are you doing in my son's house?"

Shit, Liberty's parents.

"Aren't you the police officer who came to our house?" Mrs. Jenson's head tilts to the side as she takes a second to place me.

"Mr. Jenson, Mrs. Jenson." I come up short, unsure how this may look to them.

A few weeks back I was knocking on their door asking how their daughter was holding up, and now I'm in their daughter-in-law's house and making myself welcome.

"Don't you Mr. Jenson me." His stance tells me he's ready to blow his top unless he gets to the bottom of this fast. "Why are you here?"

"I came with—"

"Me." Liberty steps out of the kitchen, walking past me to greet her parents.

"Hey, Daddy." She reaches for her father first, letting him wrap her up in his large arms. For an old guy, he's still in good shape. Not as tall or as built as I am, but considering he's the dad of the woman I'm seeing, it wouldn't matter in the end. I know he would kick my ass.

"What's going on here, Liberty?" he asks, pulling back and allowing his wife to greet their daughter.

"Well, it's kind of a long story," Liberty answers when her mom releases her. Liberty's mom is nothing like her. Small and dainty, she has this air of innocence around her. Almost like the way my mom was before my father died.

"Well, I suggest you start talking, darling, before your father loses it." Liberty's mother gently suggests, before the high-pitch squeal of Arabella fills the house.

"Nana!" She runs straight past Liberty and me, right into her grandmother's arms.

"Hello, darling. How are you?" she asks Arabella, picking her up in her arms. She looks almost too small to be picking up the rowdy four-year-old, but she doesn't falter, lifting her up and planting kisses all over her face.

"Hetch and Auntie Bertie slept over. And Aunt Bertie is making us her faborite pancakes," she answers, causing more confusion to fill the air.

"Will someone tell me what the hell is going on here?" Mr. Jenson bellows, his temper no longer in check.

"Hey, guys." Payton steps out of the hall, her steely composure complete bullshit.

"What's going on, darling?" Liberty's mom doesn't buy it either, picking up on the change in her daughter-in-law.

"There's something we need to talk about." Her voice starts to wobble, and I catch Liberty's worried eyes.

Fuck, what an awkward conversation this is gonna be.

"How about I take the kid back to the living room. We're halfway through *Tangled*, and oddly enough, I need to know how it's going to end." I manage to get an out.

"Yay!" Arabella shouts, wiggling her way down out of her nana's arms and making a run for it toward the living area.

"You guys talk." I offer Liberty a smile. She mouths "Thank you," and before I know it, half an hour has passed and I'm shouting at the TV, devastated she cut the bitch's hair off.

Fuck me, who makes these movies?

* * *

"Okay, well, thank you for calling me. No, no, I understand. Next time for sure. Okay. Thanks. Bye." Liberty hangs up the call and lets out a frustrated sigh.

"What's up?" I ask from her sofa later that night. After being subjected to a Disney movie this morning, I told Liberty I needed some hardcore action movie to wipe my mind clear of all those catchy tunes.

165

"Ugghh, I'm having a hard time finding a new place for our car wash next week." She plops her ass down next to me, tucking her feet up under her.

"What sort of place you need?" I pause the movie, pulling her into my lap and against my chest before wrapping my arms around her waist.

"Anywhere at this stage. All I need is access to water and space for the cars. It's not like we normally get a huge turnout, but it's still enough for us to be able to fund some things at Haven."

"I might have a place," I offer, wondering if it will work.

"Yeah?" She sits up, her eyes growing wide with possible excitement.

"Why not down at the station? It's not far off the main road. We get heavy traffic, and I'll make sure the boys bring their trucks in for a clean."

"Oh, my God, are you serious?"

"Yeah, if you think it's a good spot."

"It's a perfect spot." She captures her lip between her teeth, working through the idea. "Can you clear it with whoever you need to clear it within the next few days?"

"It's a done deal. I'll sort it out," I tell her, knowing the Captain will be onboard.

"Seriously, Hetch,"—she throws her arms around my neck, squishing her tits close to my face—"you're a lifesaver. The kids will love it. But are you sure?" She pulls back, taking her tits with her.

"Yeah, sweetheart. I'm positive." I tug her back, hoping to get reacquainted with those sexy tits of hers.

"Have I told you you're amazing?" she whispers, before pressing her soft lips to mine. I let her lead, enjoying seeing her become more confident.

"You did this morning after I slept on the sofa, survived a Disney movie, and then had breakfast with your pissed-off father, but you *can* still show me." I rest back, allowing her room to straddle my lap completely.

166

"You gonna let me be in charge?" She pushes my shirt up over my head then gets to work on my belt.

"Depends," I answer, lifting my hips so she can strip me free of my pants.

"Depends on what?" she asks, taking a step back.

"If you can handle it." I fist my cock, stroking myself to relieve some pressure.

"Oh, I'm more than capable." She reaches behind her. The brief, sharp hiss of the zipper opening is the sweetest sound I've heard all day, but it's what she reveals underneath the dress that's the sweetest sight I've seen *ever*.

"Jesus, sweetheart." I stroke my cock a little harder, taking in her lace boy shorts and bare breasts.

It's simple. But fuck me, it's perfection.

She smirks down at me, before walking over to the end table and reaching into the drawer.

"What are you doing?" My leisurely assault of my cock slows when she pulls out a pair of department-issued handcuffs.

"Showing you how capable I can be." She turns, stalking her way back to me.

"I don't fucking think so, sweetheart." I reach forward, wrap my fingers around her tiny wrist, and pull hard. She comes willingly, falling sideways back into my lap.

"What's the matter, honey? You don't like to be restrained?" It's the first time she's called me honey, and I don't know why I like it so much, but I fucking do.

I like it.

A lot.

"No. I don't like to be restrained. That's your job." I tug on the handcuffs as she straddles me once again, releasing them from her grasp before she knows what's happening.

"No fair." She pouts, rolling her hips against my stomach.

"Life isn't fair, but it sure as hell is fun sometimes," I taunt, capturing a wrist in my grasp while snapping one cuff closed. She fights me for a second, not sure what I'm up to, but when I grind my hips up to meet her pussy, she loses all train of thought, and her arms relax.

That's my girl.

"Here's how we'll play it," I tell her, taking her other wrist in my grasp and snapping on the second cuff. "You can be in charge, first," I explain, liking this play much better than hers.

"And how am I supposed to be in charge if I can't use my hands, Hetch?" She raises her hands in front of her and pushes out a huff of air when she realizes how restraining cuffs can be.

"Words, baby. I'm at your beck and call right now. You just gotta know how to ask." I slip my finger through the cuff, making sure it's not too tight.

"You're gonna do what I say?" She doesn't sound so sure, but fuck me, looking at her right now, hands restrained in front of her, lace-covered pussy pressed against my stomach, I'd fucking do anything she asked.

"Sweetheart, there's nothing sexier than a woman who's not afraid to ask for what she wants." She rolls her hips, and I have to bite back a groan when I feel her wetness through her panties, coating my stomach. "Tell me what you want, Liberty, or you get nothing." She wiggles back, taking her wetness with her and stands. Fingers locked, wrists bound, her tentative gaze flicks over my face and down my naked body. It doesn't take long before the hesitancy is lost and she is standing before me a different woman.

Strong. Confident. Hungry.

"Rip my panties off," are her first words.

Not unsure. Not meek.

Strong. Confident. Hungry.

I'm not prepared for such a strong visceral reaction to her demand.

"Fuck, sweetheart." My dick jumps and my stomach tightens in need. Not needing any more cues, I sit forward on the sofa, my hands immediately reaching for the sides of her panties. I dig in, yanking them apart with robust need. The lace doesn't stand a chance of surviving when the harsh tear purrs between us.

"Now, sit back."

I continue to follow my orders, my cock too invested in the end game to be put out by her demands. Only when I've sunk back into the sofa does she step forward, place a knee beside my outer thighs, and straddles me for the third time tonight.

"Jesus, Lib. I don't have a condom." I groan when her hips start moving back and forth. Her wet pussy slides along the length of my dick. It's the first time my cock's been acquainted with this kind of intimacy. The heat of our skin, the wetness of her arousal. I nearly blow my load like a fifteen-year-old kid.

"Where are they?" Her breath is wispy and quick. Her movements slow and deliberate. One wrong move here could have my cock sliding home, and I'm not sure once he's had a taste he'll ever come back.

"Fuck, in my wallet." I think quick but make no move to retrieve the safety net.

"It feels so good, Hetch." The cool metal of the cuffs digs into my chest, but I don't let it take away from the heaven I'm feeling along my cock.

"So fucking good, sweetheart." My hips start to rise in unison, in need. In hunger. Her hips continue to roll over me, spreading her arousal over my cock and balls.

"I'm clean and I'm on the pill," she adds, hitting the proverbial nail.

I shouldn't want this as much as I do. Yeah, it's like the holy grail to all cocks. Bareback and a tight, wet pussy, but it also means more to me.

A trust. An understanding between two people.

Am I ready for this?

"I'm clean. Always used one," I tell her, my head hazing in and out of pleasure.

"Are we sure?" Her movements are slow and her head drops to my forehead, allowing us a moment to think this through.

This is not how I saw this going.

One minute I was a man in control.

The next I'm a slave to the feel of her around my bare cock.

"Your call, sweetheart." I hand the decision over to her.

Liberty doesn't answer with words. Instead, she rolls her hips one more time at just the right angle and before I know it, my cock is nestled at the opening of her pussy. On instinct, my hands move to her waist. Lifting her up, I position her at the head of my cock, and slowly, oh so fucking slowly, I slide her down my shaft.

"Fuck me." I force my eyes to stay open and watch as her pussy swallows my cock whole.

"Holy shit," she pants when I no longer can see my shaft.

"Yeah," I say because I don't know what else to say. It's as if the whole world has shrunk down to just the two of us and nothing else matters except her tightness hugging me, and the wet warmth encasing my cock.

And then she moves.

At first, it's a small roll of her hips. Shy and exploratory. I don't move while she adjusts to me in a different position before slowly moving up and down. My hands haven't left her waist, and once I manage to descend from what I can only call heaven, I get my shit together and help her along, lifting her up and pulling her back down just as fast.

"Feels so good." She groans as our bodies collide. Her slamming down, me pushing up.

"Fuck, babe. Don't want to fucking leave here." I push out each word, the start of my release beginning to boil in my balls.

"Don't leave." Her eyes grow wide the harder we collide, and I know I'm hitting the right spot.

"Not gonna last, Lib." I hate this is gonna end way too fucking soon, but the indefinable itch rises and surges within me.

"Me either. So close." She picks up her speed, forcing me to control myself. I'm on the edge of experiencing perfect ecstasy, but I need to hold on. Just a little longer.

"Fucking hell, I'm gonna blow." I slam her down with extra force then repeat it, harder the second time.

It's all it takes to take her over. Her body jerks, her pussy clenches, and then she's coming.

"FUUUCCKK!" she screams and for a second, I think I've

hurt her until her eyes open, and bliss finds mine. It's the anchor I need to take me over. Releasing the tension I created to hold myself in check, I let go. Heat coils in my balls, shooting from the base and exploding up my cock.

"Fuck, yes." I grunt, then thrust my hips up and slam her down, riding out the explosion. Every little ridge and muscle inside her pussy almost painfully caress my orgasm out of me. Tightening in perfect unison. Milking me till I'm dry.

"Wow." Liberty sighs when we both fall into the abyss of post-orgasm. Breathing in sync, sweat covering our bodies, I reach forward and pull her to my chest. The shift in angle forces my cum to seep out of her and down my balls, but I can't be fucking worried about it.

My head and my body need a minute to gather myself. I've just come the hardest I've ever come, with a woman who's slowly meaning more to me than just fun.

Fuck me. I think I'm falling for her.

Or maybe I've already fallen.

Either way, I'm not ready to address it.

"Wearing a condom is like licking a lollipop with the wrapper still on." The words fall out of my mouth in a fluster. Silence throbs between us before her body starts to shake with laughter.

"So, you're saying you want to taste the lollipop from now on?" she asks into my chest.

"Yeah, that's what I'm saying, but only your lollipop, babe." I kiss the top of her head, holding her tighter in my grasp.

Yep.

I've definitely fallen.

18

LIBERTY

"Hey, Sue, can you grab me another bucket?" I call out across three cars and probably ten people, hoping she can hear me.

It's carwash day, and after a stressful week of not knowing where we were going to hold this damn fundraiser, Hetch was able to come through for me and get us approved to set up outside Trebook's police station.

It's a brilliant location. Considering we're only halfway through the day, we've already raised more money than we probably have the last three years combined.

"You need something, sweetheart?" Hetch's smooth voice dances over my shoulder, and up the side of my neck.

"I need another bucket." I look up from the wheel I'm cleaning and find him standing directly over me. Today he's wearing a Trebook police department T-shirt, and dark basketball shorts. Not his normal attire when at work, but nonetheless, still sexy.

172

"I'll get it for you." He gives me a wink and then saunters off to where we stocked our supplies. I force my eyes away from his retreating back and back to the wheel. I don't want to give the kids the wrong idea, plus the parking lot is packed, and at this rate, we won't be stopping for lunch.

Everyone is here today, as well as a few extra volunteers. Payton, Sterling, Fee, and Hetch have all pitched in along with Sue, myself, and the rest of the Haven staff and boys.

"Hey, Liberty, do you know where I can find another cloth?" Brooklyn asks across the roof of the car behind the one I'm working on.

"If you follow Hetch, he can grab one for you," I reply as I stand and take a step back to look over the wheel, making sure I got everything.

"Wow, looks good, Liberty. I don't think it's been this clean since I drove it off the yard."

"Ha, please. You're too kind." The owner of the truck is one of Hetch's teammates, and while I remember him from back at The Elephant, I can't remember his name.

"I'm serious. Thanks so much. Where do I pay?" He pulls out his wallet.

"You can pay me." I smile, sifting through all the names I have cataloged. I know he's the youngest one, blond hair, blue eyes. I'm sure Sophie was the one who thought he was cute....

"Tate," he offers when I come up blank.

"Right. So sorry. It's been crazy here today." I push down my awkwardness and move on.

"I'm not surprised. The boss made sure we all dropped in; otherwise, we would have our asses handed to us in PT on Monday," he reveals, explaining why we are so damn busy.

Bloody Hetch.

"He didn't." I gasp, feeling all kinds of awkward about it. "I didn't ask him to."

"Hey, it's for a good cause." He shrugs, like it's no big deal and then hands me a fifty-dollar note.

"Keep the change."

"Oh, my gosh, Tate. That's way too much." I try to hand it

back, but he doesn't accept it.

"Like hell it is." Hetch steps in beside me and takes the fifty from me. "I'll make sure it goes in the kitty," he tells Tate with a nod, before handing me the bucket I asked for.

"No, Hetch. Seriously, it's way too much." It's the second time I've seen one of his guys pay too much. Earlier, Fox paid a hundred for Mitch and Sue's detail on his truck.

"It's fine, Lib. The boys and I want to help. Let us." He doesn't give me another chance to argue it further when he calls out and motions for the next car to pull in.

"Come on, we've still got about six more cars to do before you clock off." He throws a wet rag at my face then side steps me when I throw it back.

"You so did not just do that," I call out, picking up the hose from the ground and turning it on him.

"You're going to pay for that, Liberty," he shouts when I manage to drench him. I quickly take off between two cars. The kids are all laughing, and the volunteers are egging us on.

"Don't you dare." I slow my pace and slip in behind the last car in the line where Sterling, Payton, and Garrett are working together. "We don't have time to play games," I call out just as I see Hetch filling a bucket of water.

"You should have thought about that before you turned the hose on me."

Oh, God, this is going to get messy.

"Please, don't let him get me, guys," I plead like a little girl to Sterling and Payton and, for a minute, I think they're going to keep me safe. That is until Sterling drops the cloth he was using, grabs me around the waist, and carries me back toward Hetch.

"YOU TRAITOR!" I scream over the catcalls from Payton and the whoops from the boys.

"What do you think, kids, does Liberty need to cool down?" Hetch shouts so everyone can hear him.

"YES!"

"Do it!"

"Get her...!" are called out among them all, and I have to say even though I know I'm about to get it, I can't help but smile at how much they're all having fun.

"I thought you all loved me, boys!" I cry out when Sterling plants me on my feet in front of Hetch.

"Sorry, sweetheart. The tribe has spoken." Hetch smirks, and it's sexy, but I don't stick around to see it, darting between him and the bucket. I don't get very far, the smaller hand of Mitch, reaching for my shirt, has me halting.

"I've got her, Hetch. Do it," he calls, and I chuckle at how eager he is to see me pay. Ever since Hetch brought Mitch home last week, he's been in a perpetual mood. He's been taken off the program. House bound for two weeks, and his chore roster has grown until he earns his privileges back. It may seem harsh, but sometimes, tough love is what they need.

"How could you, Mitch?" I fake my shock, knowing I would probably do the same if I were him.

"Sorry, us boys have to stick together," he tells me, as a bucket of water is dumped over my head.

"Ahh!" I yelp as the cold water drenches me through and through.

The kids holler and yell, finally getting what they wanted.

"Okay, you got me, show's over," I try to move this along, knowing if we don't get a handle on it now, we may lose them to a twenty-person water fight. "Lunch is in an hour, and if we get it done, pizza is on Hetch," I lie, knowing I've already placed the order and paid.

"Thanks, Hetch, you're the best!"

"Yeah, pizza!" A couple of the boys high five Hetch as we turn and start walking back to the car we are meant to be working on.

"Sorry about getting you all wet, sweetheart." The soft whisper of Hetch's voice tracks over my skin and a shiver follows its same path.

"Oh, you will be sorry, later."

"Oh, yeah? Is that a threat or a promise?" He walks alongside me, voice low and unsuspecting.

"A promise." I wink, picking up the cloth that started the whole water fight.

"Shit, babe. I need to go work on another car. I can't deal."
He groans under his breath while he looks down at my chest.

"Get out of here." I roll my eyes when I notice there's nothing revealing or sexual about what I'm wearing, even if it's wet. I made sure I wore all black today, and nothing would become see-through.

"I'm not kidding. Here. Put this on." He rips his damp shirt over his head and hands it to me."

"Umm, no. Put your shirt back on, you crazy man." I push the shirt back into his chest.

Seriously, is he trying to kill me here?

"I have another in my truck," he argues, offering it to me again.

"Okay, fine. But seriously go and put it on then, or I won't be able to work on this car with you."

His grin deepens at my confession, his pecs dancing in a taunt.

"What's the matter, Lib. Can't concentrate?" He mocks me, before sauntering off to his truck. I force my eyes not to follow; instead, I turn and use the side mirror to track his movements.

"Hey, Lib. You got something here," Payton calls out, pointing to the corner of her mouth.

"Huh?" I reach up, and wipe it, only to realize she's implying I'm drooling.

Fuck me, everyone's a comedian today.

"No, still there." She laughs when I shake my head at her.

"Go back to work," I call back, not in the mood for her teasing.

Today isn't the time or the place to be getting caught up in Hetch and his tempting tactics. I need to keep it professional.

Who am I kidding? The man is a walking sex dream. I'll be lucky if I survive the day.

* * *

"I can't hold it. I'm going to come, Hetch." I squirm, fighting the need, trying to hold off until he gives the order.

We're in bed later that night. Hetch is on his back in the middle of my bed, while I sit on his face and wait for the all clear to come.

"Don't you fucking dare." His words take hold of my orgasm, managing to hold me suspended between free falling and exploding.

"Hetch, I'm serious, I can't handle it." His grip on my thighs tightens and bites into my skin. I know I'm going to bruise, but I don't give a shit about it right now.

"Hold it, sweetheart." My hips buck when he doesn't let me give in, a growl falling from my lips in frustration.

"No, I can't." I fight it, my orgasm already starting to implode. Hetch's frustrated growl drowns out my moan while his hands move to my waist, and before I know it, he lifts me off his face. Flips me so I'm on my back. Straddles my chest and rests his cock between my breasts.

"What the?" Confusion filters through, my orgasm abruptly cut short.

"Told you to wait." He shakes his head as he presses his hard cock along my cleavage.

"Come on, Hetch," I complain, not really sure what the issue is.

What did he expect me to do? I was sitting on his face for Christ's sake. After a day of secret innuendos, sneaking glances and promises of payback, I'm a walking firecracker ready to ignite.

"No, sweetheart. I told you to wait, but you got greedy. So you don't get to come until I have. Now squeeze your tits together for me." He continues to roll his hips. Pre-cum beads at the head of his cock, coating my tits with his very own lube.

Not one to disobey twice in a row, I cup the side of both breasts, pressing them together, and encasing his cock between them.

"Fuck, baby," he groans, slowly picking up his pace. Squeezing tighter to keep him trapped, I lock eyes with him and watch as he loses himself to the pleasure.

"Fuck, baby. You look so fucking sexy right now." He moans, the sounds traveling right through my body and down to my core.

"You're the sexy one, honey," I repeat his sentiment, becoming more turned on than I expected to. The pleasure is coming from watching him as he watches his cock slide between my tits.

"You got great tits, sweetheart." His breath hitches, and if I didn't pick up the drop of his voice, I wouldn't know he's close.

"Yeah? You like fucking them?" I move things along. Working myself deeper into arousal. Who would have guessed this shit makes me wild?

"Fuck, yeah, been thinking about fucking them from the moment I saw that shirt of yours today, wet and plastered to you."

"Is that what your issue was? You were thinking about fucking them?" I ask, unsure if he's messing with me, or this is a fantasy of his. Titty fucking isn't high up on my list of must-dos, but with Hetch doing it, I could easily make it a weekly occurrence.

"Fuck yeah," he grunts, the sound urging me to squeeze him tighter.

"Would have taken you around the back and sucked on those tight nipples, but we kind of had an audience." I laugh, picturing how things would have gone down if we were caught in a compromising position like that.

"You're always thinking about sex." For some reason, my breath starts to rise, as if I'm doing all the work here.

"If I'm with you, yeah." His balls slap against my skin, tightening my core even more. "Fuck, squeeze harder," he orders and my hands push in at his command. "You ready, baby?" he asks, and if I wasn't ready before, I am now. Ready for whatever he wants to give me.

"Yeah," I pant, blowing warm air over the head of his cock.

"Don't look at it, look at me." My eyes rise up to his, just as the first spray of warm cum hits my neck. "Fuck yes!" He grinds, the muscles in his neck pulsing as he tenses and flexes with his orgasm.

A second spurt of cum hits my chin, a third on my neck.

Fuck me.

My core convulses with each groan, each hit of warm cum pushing me further into a frenzy.

"Jesus, Hetch." I whimper under him. Watching him come apart has to be one of the sexiest things I've ever seen.

He continues to push his hips forward, sliding in and out of the tight place I've created for him until he starts to slow his pace.

"Sweetheart, I think you just topped my spank bank material." He reaches down, runs a finger through his cum and circles my nipple.

"Get it off me." I release my hands, letting my tits fall naturally apart. The sexy part now over, I'm left with the aftermath of his release all over me.

I'm all for swallowing it, spitting it, even taking it, but wearing it, not so much.

"I don't think so, babe. I'm gonna fuck you like this now." He moves his body down mine, taking his cock and leaving his cum.

"I'm serious. Get it off." I start to wiggle out of his embrace wanting to be cleaned up before we go any further. Hetch, having other ideas locks his grip on my thighs, spreads me open then lines himself up at my entrance.

"It's staying there while I fuck you. Maybe next time you'll learn not to be a greedy little thing," he taunts while gliding himself into my wet and waiting pussy.

My body wants to argue some more, my mouth open and ready, but before I get a chance, he picks up his pace and all thoughts of cum and where it doesn't belong have left my mind.

"Ahh, harder," I groan, lifting my hips to meet each one of his thrusts.

"You have no idea how fucking sexy you look right now. My cum all over your tits and my cock filling your pussy. Maybe I should fuck you like this every day, sweetheart," he teases some more, pushing into me with harder, longer strokes.

"You wish." I gasp, body coiling up ready to find my own release.

"Are you going to obey me next time I tell you not to come?" he asks, but my orgasm is barreling toward me in record speed, and I don't want to lose it.

"Answer me, sweetheart, or this ends," he warns, and it's all the incentive I need to let go, screaming out my release with my answer.

"Yesss! Yes. Yes, I'm going to obey." I tell him what he wants to hear, but I'm not sure I mean it.

Maybe disobeying every now then wouldn't hurt.

Even if it means a repeat of what just went down. Sticky mess and all, there was no denying I would do it again.

Hell, I'd do anything Hetch asked me.

Now that is a dangerous thought.

19

HETCH

"You know what I think?" Mitch pulls me from my staring and back to the moment at hand where I should be paying attention.

"What do you think?" I focus back on the game in front of me, wondering how the fuck he could enjoy this.

"I think you love her."

"W-who?" I'm at a loss for words. Unsure where his assessment comes from, and how to respond to it.

"Liberty. You haven't stopped looking at her since we came out here." He raises a brow looking way older than his fifteen-year-old self.

I'm at Boys Haven a few days after the fundraising car wash, having some one-on-one time with Mitch.

"Yeah, not something I'm talking about with you." I make my move on the chessboard we have set up on the patio table. I'm not very good at this game, my confession ringing true when Mitch makes his move and calls out "Checkmate."

181

Fuck.

"Seriously, where the hell did you learn to play?" I ask, more than impressed.

"My dad." He shrugs like it's no big deal, but I know that shrug. I think I might have invented that shrug.

"Oh, yeah? He good?" Liberty briefed me on how to act and what to expect when talking to the boys. Generally, they tend to keep to themselves, only sharing information when they are comfortable. I'm not expecting any miracles, but something tells me Mitch is comfortable enough to share.

"He was. Before he stopped playing." He pauses for a minute, twirling the king piece between his fingers. "Before the drugs." I don't know what to say to his confession. I'm not trained in the whole how-to-talk-to-a-teenage-kid thing, but something tells me he wants to open up to me.

"When did things start getting bad?" I might not know what he's been through, but if his dad slipping away due to drugs is anything like my father slipping away due to a mental illness, I may have something to work with.

"It kind of happened so fast, you know? One minute he was the best dad, taking me to baseball practice, and the next he was strung out."

"It must have been tough." I recall the first time my father tried to kill himself. I was fifteen. Mitch's age. I walked in on my mother giving him mouth-to-mouth in his office. She screamed at me to call 911. I think I froze for a second. Seeing him lifeless. Seeing my mom try to save him. Seeing my sister rocking in the corner. Confused. Scared. Broken. I had only left to hang out with some friends down at the basketball courts a few hours before. Dad seemed his normal happy self when I said good-bye.

How did he go from laughing at breakfast to swallowing a whole bottle of pills by lunch?

"Yeah. I mean, he was a good dad. We had a good life. Seeing him become a different person, it messes with ya."

"I hear you. I get it. My dad, he had some issues too." I pick up the knight piece and like Mitch, roll it between my fingers. I

182

hadn't planned on revealing anything about my past, but sitting here with him letting me in, it flows out.

"He an addict too?" Mitch pauses, waiting for my confirmation.

"No, but he had some pretty hard knocks," I tell him, not sure how much I should reveal.

"He kill your mom?" The question is laced with a challenging tone, so I give it to him straight.

"No, he killed himself. In front of me," I add, maybe to get his attention, maybe because it feels good to tell someone who won't judge or pity me.

"Fuck. That's brutal." He sits a little straighter.

"It is." I ignore his language, knowing if I try to educate him on manners right now, I'll lose him.

"How old were you?" His voice drops along with his eyes.

"Thirty."

"I was nine."

Fuck, this kid is killing me.

"It stays with you, Mitch. Always will, you know?" His head rises at my honesty.

"How do you deal?"

"Honestly? Some days I don't. Some days it's all I see. The blood. The fucking mess. It can play over and over in my head. But I still have to make a choice, you know?" I watch as he nods, taking in everything I am giving him. "I choose to get up, and go to work and do good. Like you have a choice. You can choose to do better. Not walk down the same path as your brother, you know." My dig about his brother may be a low blow, but I'm still pissed we haven't been able to get him on anything.

"What if I don't have a choice?" he asks, amplifying my concerns.

"There is always a choice, Mitch." His Adam's apple bounces twice before he asks his next question.

"What if there is no right choice? What if no matter what I choose, someone gets hurt?"

"Then you choose the best one for you. The one that keeps you safe. The one you can live with. You get me?" I want him

183

to know he doesn't have to worry about Liberty. That I have her back, but something tells me if I say it aloud right now, I'll lose him.

"I don't know what's best for me." He places the chess piece back on the board, setting it back up for another game.

"I think you do, Mitch. I think you know what's good for you, but you're scared."

"He's my family, Hetch. I walk away from him and I have nothing." The words gut me, but not because I feel for him, but because hearing him say them hurts for Liberty. She loves him. Jesus, anyone can see it. "Seems to me you have a good family here too, you know?" I look around the backyard, seeing the tight knit group they have here. It's evident as they stick close together no matter what they're doing. "They might not be blood, but when they've dug their way so deep in here,"—I pat my chest, covering my heart—"you can't get them out. They're the family you hold onto, son." He nods, before holding out his hand for the knight. I don't give it right away, taking a moment to word my next sentence carefully.

"Just promise me, Mitch, whenever you decide to make the decision, you make it for you. And if you can't make the decision yourself, then you call me. Any time. Any place. I'll be there. No matter what. And we'll make it together. You think you can handle that?" I ask, hoping like hell I'm getting through to him.

"Yeah, I can."

"Good." I hand over my knight.

"So, you want another game?" he asks, and even though I've been here for over an hour and am so fucking over chess, I still say yes.

"Yeah, but go easy on me this time. My rep is at stake here."

"Dude, I have been," he says, and for a brief second, I see the carefree teen he should be, right before he laughs loud enough to gain Liberty's attention. She smiles, then waves, and like every other time she looks at me, I'm sucked back into her hemisphere.

LIBERTY

"Can I get a double cheeseburger with fries and a strawberry milkshake?" Mitch looks over the top of his menu to gauge my reaction.

Boys.

"I'll get the same, but no milkshake. I'll have a diet soda, please." The waitress smiles as she takes our menus, and tells us she'll be right back with our drinks.

"Snack, huh?" I ask Mitch, sitting back in my chair.

It's a Saturday afternoon, and after spending a few hours at the library with Mitch so he could get some studying in, we decided we would stop in for a drink. Which turned into a snack. Which clearly to a fifteen-year-old, means a meal.

"Well, I did work up an appetite with all the work I've put into my English assignment." He shrugs and then moves back to his cell phone. I have to agree. He has been working hard these last few weeks.

Ever since the car wash and spending some one-on-one time

with Hetch, it's like he's a different person.

"How are you doing in the rest of your classes?" I ask, taking the opportunity to have my own one–on–one time with him. While Mitch has been back on the program for two weeks, he still has to have a chaperone everywhere he goes. Despite Hetch's persistency, Dominic still hasn't been picked up, and my commitment to keeping him away from Mitch is still strong.

"It's getting a lot easier," he answers, while his fingers dance over the keyboard, typing at expert speed.

I want to ask who he's texting, ask if Dominic has contacted him, but before I have a chance to address it, he finishes up his text and slides it into the pocket of his hoodie.

"That's good. You keep studying and working hard, you'll be on track for college," I tell him, as he reaches for the ketchup bottle and starts spinning it in front of him.

A lot of kids who grow up through the system don't think they are capable of that sort of opportunity. But if Mitch keeps going the way he is, away from his brother, applying himself, and staying out of trouble, I truly believe he has a real shot.

"I don't know, Lib." His eyes don't quite meet mine, and I wonder if he's as worried about his brother getting in the way as I am.

"Has your brother been in contact with you, Mitch?" I come right out and ask him. If I wanted to check his phone, I could, but I want to give him a chance to talk to me about it first.

"No, I haven't heard from him since Hetch picked me up a few weeks back." His spinning of the ketchup bottle ceases when the waitress returns with our drinks.

Mitch digs into his milkshake right away, while I decide to wait for my meal.

"Do you know where he is?" I press a little more.

"I already told Hetch I don't know anything," he snaps, and I realize I might have pushed too far.

"Okay, I just wanted to check with you. So, how do you like your one-on-one time with Sergeant Hetcherson?" I ask, hoping I haven't ruined our easygoing conversation.

"You know, he's pretty, cool." I nod because I do know.

Hetch is way cool. All the boys at Haven are in love with him. They hang on every word he says when he comes to visit with Mitch.

I've tried asking Hetch how his time with Mitch is coming along, but he hasn't revealed anything since they've been spending time together. Just keeps telling me Mitch is opening up more and more with each visit and he has everything under control.

"I think he loves you." He pushes his milkshake back and folds his arms over his chest, with a smirk on his face.

"What are you talking about?" My voice starts to rise on the last word, but I manage to catch it in time.

"Hetch, he totally loves you." His brows bounce with humor, his grin spreading wider.

"No, Mitch." I shake my head and reach for my soda.

"Aww, come on, Lib. I know y'all think you're hiding it, but I've seen the way you look at him when he's at the house." He laughs when my face burns in embarrassment.

"I don't know what you're talking about, Mitch." I sip on my soda and pretend not to be affected.

Shit, have I been obvious?

"If you say so, Liberty."

"I do say so."

Mitch opens his mouth to continue but shuts it when the subject of our conversation coincidently strolls into the diner with three other officers.

The air stills and a calmness, which wasn't there before, settles over the place.

Hetch clocks us instantly. A slow smile steals over his face when his eyes connect with mine.

Jesus, he's handsome.

Tallest of the four, his strong, powerful presence commands not only attention but respect. I know I say it every time I see him in his uniform, but holy shit.

Somehow, his navy shirt seems tighter today, and the black military pants that had me wanting to climb him this morning when I watched him dress, has me wanting to climb him all over again.

"What were you saying, Liberty?" I ignore Mitch's jab and focus my attention on Hetch until he's standing directly in front of us.

"Hey, Mitch. Liberty." He offers me a wink before sliding in next to Mitch.

"What are you guys doing here?" I ask when Sterling slides in next to me and the remaining Fox and Hart occupy the booth next to us.

"We dropped in for lunch." A quick flick of his gaze to Sterling, and a few snorts from the booth over tells me he's lying.

"How did you know we were here?" I ask Hetch, but my eyes track Mitch's sudden tensing.

He was texting Hetch.

Well, there's my answer to who he's been chatting to.

"Don't be mad, Lib. I was chatting with him, and told him we were hanging out here," Mitch confesses right away. Hetch doesn't say anything, just calmly takes a menu from the waitress and starts looking it over.

"So you thought you would invite yourself." I point my gaze to Hetch. I'm not angry at Mitch for texting him. I think it's great he's been spending time with him and connecting with him. I just wish he didn't come around while I was working.

I find it too hard to concentrate, and I need to stay focused.

"We were in the neighborhood."

Another lie.

Another few snorts.

"So what did you guys order?" He changes the subject, moving his attention back to the menu, and forcing me to let it go.

Seriously, I don't know if I want to kiss him or smack him.

Maybe both.

"Cheeseburger and fries. They have great burgers here, right, Lib?" Mitch looks over at me, gauging my opinion.

"They're pretty good." I nod, backing him up.

"Okay, you sold me." Hetch drops the menu back to the table as the radio attached to his belt comes to life.

"All units in the vicinity of Westchester and Vine, Code Three. Shots fired."

Hetch and the boys stand in record speed before the dispatcher finishes his words.

"Rain check, Mitch?" Hetch asks, dropping a fifty-dollar bill down on the table.

"Yeah, for sure." Mitch beams up at him, more excited than I've ever seen him before.

"Okay, lunch is on me. See you later." He offers me a wink and a grin, and as fast as he entered the place, he's gone. Mitch smiles and waves, watching them with me through the glass window as they climb into their SUV.

"Liberty?" Mitch asks, still turned at the waist, watching them pull out and speed off down the street.

"Yeah?"

"I think I know what I wanna do when I finish school." He turns back and faces me.

"Yeah? What's that?"

"I wanna be a cop," he tells me proudly, and I can tell he's serious from his posture.

"I think you would make an amazing police officer," I tell him as our cheeseburgers arrive.

"You think so?" He pauses. "Even with Dad and Dom?" He doesn't have to finish the question, but I know what he's asking.

Even if my father is a murderer and serving twenty-five years. And even if my brother is a street thug who's heading down the same road.

"I do, Mitch. You should never let anyone's actions define what you want out of life. Okay? You can be anything you set your mind to. Regardless of where you come from or who you are related to." He responds with a nod and I know he's listening. Know he's thinking.

And it's all I can ask for.

These boys need to think about their future. Think about doing better for themselves so when they leave they have the tools and the resources to keep off the streets.

We spend the rest of lunch talking about what sort of things Hetch and the men of SWAT deal with on a daily basis and by the time lunch is over, and our table has been cleared, Mitch is adamant he has decided his career path.

Okay, so maybe I don't need to smack Hetch for dropping by unexpectedly.

I'll just kiss him later.

Way later.

HETCH

Liberty: *I was going to smack you for showing up like that today, but judging by the change in Mitch's attitude since you left, I think I'm going to have to kiss you.*

I read the text over again and quickly respond.

Me: *Sweetheart, I'd like to see you smack me.*

Liberty: *I so could smack you. I just don't want to. :P*

"You gonna put your phone down so we can finish this workout, or you gonna keep being a pussy?" Sterling flicks his towel at me, causing me to drop my cell on the ground.

"Fuck you, asshole." I bend down and reach for it, then place it into the pocket of my gym shorts.

He's right, though. It's been a long day and as much as I

would prefer to sit around sexting Liberty, the quicker we get through this workout, the quicker I can head home and sex her.

While the tactical unit is required to participate in group PT three times a week, a typical week for the boys in our unit includes those three PT sessions, but also an extra two group sessions in the gym. This afternoon happens to be group training.

"Ahh, leave him alone, Sterling. He's in love," Fox taunts from across the gym, starting up a round of catcalls and collective *awws*.

Assholes.

They've been on my back all afternoon, ever since I walked into Betty's Diner like a fucking puppy.

When I received the text from Mitch letting me know they were out for lunch, I couldn't drive fast enough to catch up with them. The boys and I had finished weapons training out at the firing range, and we were heading back to the station when I told the boys we were stopping for lunch in town.

They didn't catch on to why I needed to backtrack three blocks to Betty's Diner until we walked in and they found Liberty sitting all fucking innocent and sexy in the back booth.

"Fuck you all." I ignore their taunts and move back to the bench press.

"Come on, admit it, boss. You love her," Tate chimes in with his jab, bringing it three to one.

"I don't have to admit anything." I lie back on the bench, ignoring their snickers, and continue with my set.

"It's always the hard ones who fall so fast." Hart enters the gym, bringing their tally up to four.

"Who would have thought the blonde would bring him to his knees?" Fox asks as he comes to spot me.

"I knew he was a goner the moment she sent the drink back," Tate announces.

"Boy, you didn't know what his extracurricular activities were." Fox snorts, dismissing Tate. "I didn't know how far gone he was when he made me chase the punk-ass thug down two streets. It wasn't until he wanted the reservation at Il Centro I knew he was hooked."

"Damn… he took her to Il Centro?" Hart asks. "Shit. If I didn't already suspect he was hooked when he started having us bust down doors to get Dominic Westin, then that info would have sealed the deal." I finish my set and sit up, raising a brow at him. I'm not surprised Hart's playing along, but I did expect more from him.

"I knew when you ordered our asses to the damn car wash," Walker shouts across the gym, giving his opinion. "Then made us pay fifty dollars for a lousy detail." I grin, realizing, yeah, I did threaten them with unfavorable consequences if they didn't show up. Boys Haven made a pretty penny on the guys from the department who came down and made a donation.

"Fucking highway robbery is what it was," Fox grumbles.

"Fuck you, it was for a good cause."

"Yeah, if that's what you're calling it these days." He nudges me off the bench so he can knock out his set.

"What about you, Sterling?" Hart asks.

I turn my head in his direction. "Yeah, Sterling. Seeing as though you all seem to think you have it figured out, you wanna throw in when you think I fell?" I don't know why I'm encouraging this. Maybe it's my way of wondering when I really did fall. If I have fallen at all.

I think I have, but how can I be sure? It's been so long since I've been in this situation, my feelings are almost foreign.

"You take her out to the house yet?" He holds my stare in challenge.

The fucker has a way of messing with my head.

"No."

"Then I'm not sold." He shrugs like that settles it.

"What?" A collective cry rings out amongst the guys.

"I'm not saying he's not whipped. I'm saying I don't think it's love." He stands and rubs his towel over his face.

Fuck him. He's trying to get in my head.

"Whatever you say." I focus my attention back to my reps and ignore the niggling feeling that maybe he's right. Maybe I need to open myself up to Liberty more.

She sure as hell has with me.

The boys continue to chat amongst themselves, ribbing Fox over his ex-wife, and Tate over a new woman he's been seeing. We're only halfway through, and I find Sterling's dig has put me in a foul mood.

"Come on, boys, you all keep running your mouths, you're not gonna like me when I run PT on Monday," I warn them. Running PT is my favorite pastime. Making the boys run the obstacle course in full SWAT gear might be on the cards.

The gym soon quietens down. The threat of me kicking their asses in PT is enough to allow us to finish the rest of our workout in silence. It also gives me a chance to get my shit sorted.

By the time I've finished, showered and heading home, I've made a decision.

Maybe this weekend I'll take her out, show her my house.

Maybe this weekend I'll tell her about my dad, tell her everything.

Maybe Sterling can fuck off.

* * *

"It doesn't have to be like this. I know you can't see it at the moment, but we can work this out. There are other ways." I ignore all my training and step closer. "Let me help you." He doesn't retreat as I take another step closer, and my chest expands in determination.

I'm almost there.

His vacant stare holds my gaze as a flicker of something passes between us.

Him understanding my fears.

Me understanding his weakness.

"Dad, NO!" I don't recognize my voice, yet I recognize it's too late.

"I love you, Liam, always know that."

It happens so fast.

The change of his aim.

194

The discharge of his gun.
The fall of his body.
The agony of my screams.

* * *

I wake in alarm. My muscles tense in anticipation of its ending, to the outcome that I witnessed and to the nightmare I can't stop myself from reliving.

Fuck.

It's always the same.

A recap.

A reminder.

My reality.

"Hetch?" Liberty stirs next to me as the dream replays over and over in rapid succession.

The gun.

My screams.

The blood.

The end.

All of it smashes into me with violent force, like a battering ram used to tear through a door on a SWAT raid. Tremors rack my body while my heart slams against my chest as I force the memories back down to where they don't hurt me.

"What's wrong?" Her sleep is lifting, and I need to sort my shit before she completely wakes.

"Shhh, go back to sleep, sweetheart." I lift an unsteady hand and graze my thumb along her cheek. She doesn't fight the pull. Resting back down to the softness of her pillow, I count ten breaths before she slips back to sleep gracefully.

Fuck me, an afternoon of talking about my future and I'm back to dreaming of him again.

Lifting her hand from my chest, I carefully roll out of the bed, and trudge my way to the bathroom.

I fucking hate it when it comes back to me like this.

So unexpected. So fucking raw.

I wash my face in the basin, splashing cold water over me to calm myself down. I know it's eating away inside of me, but I don't know how to control it.

I don't know how to fucking calm it.

I was doing okay until Sterling brought up the house.

Fucker.

"Hey, you okay?" I look up at her voice, annoyed she's interrupting my moment, but relieved at the same time.

When I'm with her, I don't feel so goddamn lost.

"Tomorrow, what do you have planned?" I ask as my answer.

Fuck Sterling.

"Nothing, I'm off. Why?"

"I want to take you somewhere."

"Ohh, sounds fancy." She steps into the bathroom and wraps her hands around my neck.

"Barely, but you might enjoy it." I don't reveal anything. Giving myself an out if I decide I'm not ready for it.

"Aren't you on tomorrow?"

"I'm on call, but it's only fifteen minutes out of town. We'll be good. Now come on, let's get back to bed."

"Okay, but you sure you're okay?" She pauses, not letting me escape.

"Never been better." I lean forward and kiss her, stopping any more questions and arguments.

I don't need to think right now, not anymore.

I need to feel.

And the perfect way to manage it right now is with her.

"Actually, there is this one thing…." I trail off watching her hips sway as she pulls away.

She laughs on the way back to my bed.

Not a *ha ha ha* funny laugh.

A knowing laugh, a laugh that promises a good time.

Fuck me.

I love her.

LIBERTY

"So you own this place, but you still rent in town?" I ask Hetch as we stand in the middle of his house twenty minutes outside of the city.

Last night when he said he wanted to take me somewhere, I had no idea we would end up here.

"Yeah, I haven't had a chance to finish it." He moves to a hallway closet and pulls out some sheets.

"How long have you been working on it?"

"A few years. My dad was helping me fix it up before he—" He stops talking and silence falls between us. It's the second time in the last few weeks we've had a conversation stop with the mention of his father.

Unsure if I should ask for more information or let it drop, I let the silence stretch between us.

"I need to spend more time out here," he continues, as if there was no pause.

"How often do you get to come out here?" I ignore the huge elephant in the room and let it pass. I know things between us are getting serious, but if there is an issue here, I don't want to push him. I would rather he told me.

"I usually try to come out every weekend, but I've been a little preoccupied." He reaches for me, wrapping his arms around me.

"Oh, yeah? With what?" I play along, raising my arms up around his neck. The last few weeks have been a whirlwind of craziness. Between keeping a close eye on Mitch, the other boys in the program, dealing with the Payton and Jett drama, and Hetch's intense schedule, we've barely had any free days.

"Your pussy." He's so blunt in his answer but it doesn't surprise me he uses those words. What surprises me is how I feel about his choice of words.

Is this all I am to him?

All we are?

"Oh, is that all?" I try to mask my disappointment, and maybe I do, but either way, he doesn't read into it.

"What do you mean is *that* all? It's not just any pussy, sweetheart. It's Platinum Pussy." I don't know if anyone has ever called my pussy platinum before, but platinum is good, right?

"Platinum?" I ask.

"Fucking perfection." He kisses me deeper while his hands pull my dress up over my hips, revealing my naked ass.

"Jesus, you're not wearing panties?" He doesn't give me a chance to reply before he slides a finger between my wet and wanting folds. "You're killing me here." He moves his finger through my wetness a few times before driving two fingers into me. My leg comes up, wrapping around his body, seeking more friction. My head falls back at the sudden burst of pleasure.

"Hetch," I moan, my body tight with need and my head loose with passion.

"Gonna fuck you now, B. Right here on the floor." It's the first time he's called me B and my heart skips a beat when I realize how much I like it.

"Right here on the ground?" I know the sheets are clean, but is he for real?

"Right here, sweetheart. You can present your tight sexy ass to me on all fours, or lay back and spread them wide." He holds me up against his body while dropping to a knee and lowering me to the ground.

Already knowing how I want it, I turn, find my knees, and present my ass to him. Arching my back, I spread my legs a little wider, hoping he gets a good view. Judging by the low moan he breathes out, I know he does.

"Don't know if I want to eat this platinum pussy out or fill it with my cock." His hands come to my ass cheeks, roughly pushing them apart.

"Cock." I pant when he blows a warm breath over me. I know he's right there. Can feel his soft breath over my wetness as he stares at his prize.

"I think I need a taste first." He ignores my request, spreading me wider, his tongue hitting my clit first. A spark ignites on impact, burning through me slowly. Skillfully, he glides through my folds, over my opening, and up to my asshole.

Holy Fucking Shit!

I tense at the sensation of Hetch's tongue where it's never been before.

"Relax," he soothes, his finger replaces his tongue and travels in the same path.

"How am I supposed to relax? Your tongue just licked my asshole." I try to sound offended, but it only comes out breathy when he pushes his finger into me.

"You loved it." He taunts, removing his finger. He dips back to my clit, dragging my wetness back through my folds and up to my asshole.

"I didn't," I lie, unable to stop myself from tensing when he presses against my tight hole.

"Has anyone ever taken you here, sweetheart?" He pauses, waiting for me to answer.

"No." I don't have a second to worry if I should be embarrassed by the fact when a deep, painful moan vibrates over me.

"Fuck, yeah." He groans, burying his face back between my legs, repeating his earlier path.

"Doesn't mean you're getting in there." The taunt falls from my lips with ease. His fingers dig harder into my flesh as he spreads me even wider, but there's not time to call out because his tongue starts spearing into my pussy.

"Fuck, Hetch." I moan, unsure if I can come this way. He continues to fuck me with his tongue, more convinced than I am. I think I'm almost there, almost to the precipice when a startled gasp comes from the front door. My head rears back, my eyes falling on someone I quickly recognize as Hetch's sister and an older version of her.

A scream rips through my lips at the sight of them. Hetch's tongue vacates my pussy in expert speed, then pulls my dress back down to cover me up.

"Get out!" Hetch booms. The women turn, bumping into each other on their way out the door.

"Oh, my God." I drop my head to the ground. The embarrassment is almost threatening to bring up my breakfast. "Please tell me that was not your mother."

He doesn't answer and somehow through my panic, I know without a doubt it was.

"Hetch?" I turn back. He has my arousal all over his face, and his gaze is on me.

"It was my mom and you've met my sister." The bastard chuckles while helping me to my feet.

"I want to die." My stomach rolls at the thought.

"Relax, it's fine." He smirks. His dimples don't make me feel better.

"Relax?" I think I'm in shock. His mom just saw his head between my ass cheeks and all he has to say is relax?

Is he mad?

"What the hell is wrong with you?" I drop his hand and adjust my dress back into place.

"What do you want me to say, Liberty? I can't change her walking in. It happened. No point getting yourself worked up over it." He has a point, but it still doesn't make me feel any more relaxed. In fact, his blasé attitude is making me less relaxed.

"Where are you going?" I ask when he starts walking toward the door.

"I'm gonna go find out what the fuck they are doing here. You coming?" He motions me forward.

"What! Are you mad? You want me to meet your mom, now?" I know things have been moving pretty fast the last few weeks with Hetch, but meeting the parents wasn't on my radar.

"If my mom is here, then she ain't leaving. Seeing as she walked in on me out here with a woman, she ain't gonna want to leave until she meets you." He takes my hand and pulls me into his chest, offering me a chaste kiss. I can smell my arousal on his face and I die a little more.

"Go wash your face off." I push him back and point to the kitchen. He looks confused for a minute before understanding filters through. Returning to the kitchen, he turns the faucet on and dips his face under the running water. After he dries his mouth with the front of his shirt, he walks back over to me and wraps an arm around me.

"Come on then, the sooner we get this over with, the sooner we can finish what we started."

"Seriously, how can you be thinking about sex at a time like this?" I scold him as he opens the front door.

"How can I not? It was fucking hot, sweetheart," he whispers low in my ear as my eyes connect with a woman who looks older than I originally thought and much more polished than I wished. I step out from Hetch's arm, the moment too real for me to handle, and distance myself from him. Hetch doesn't seem to mind. Instead of tucking me back into his arms, he folds them over his chest and directs his stare down at his much shorter mother.

"Mom. Kota," he simply says, before his sister blurts, "I told her to knock."

I think I'm going to be sick.

201

HETCH

"I told her to knock," Kota blurts, throwing Mom under the bus. I don't bother to comment. Keeping my stare on my mom, I force her to address me first.

"I'm sorry, Liam. I wasn't expecting you to have company." Her words are hesitant, unlike her vibrant self, but she doesn't cower away from my stare.

"We were on our way to lunch, and I saw your truck out front. We thought you were working on the house." She steps up into my space and I drop my brashness long enough to lean down and give her quick hug.

"Knock next time," I tell her as she steps back and gives me a flustered nod. She then turns her attention to Liberty.

"Hi, I'm Brianna. Liam's mom. I'm sure you feel every bit embarrassed right now, but don't, he is my son after all." She tries to put Liberty at ease, but I'm not sure it works.

"Mom. Just stop." Kota puts a hand on Mom's arm, ready to

pull her away at a moment's notice.

"No, it's okay." Liberty finally speaks up. "I'm so embarrassed to meet you like this."

"You're telling me. But hey, at least we didn't walk through the back door." She attempts a joke. Kota snorts, while I hold in my laugh. Liberty must not get it at first until the ball drops.

"Oh, God!" It finally clicks. Her embarrassment travels over her skin in a perfect shade of red. "Well yes, I guess there's that. I'm Liberty, by the way, and it's nice to meet you, Mrs. Hetcherson?" She doesn't sound so sure, but Mom doesn't seem affected by it.

"Please call me Brianna. And this is my daughter, Dakota."

"Yes, we've met." Kota offers Liberty a small wave.

"You've met?" Mom looks taken back, before turning her questioning eyes on my sister.

"Only briefly a couple weeks back." Kota smirks at Liberty, obviously replaying the scene over in her head.

"Yeah, it was almost as awkward as this meeting." Liberty chuckles, relaxing a little.

"What? Are you kidding me? It was awesome. That sassy mouth of yours laying into Liam. Girl, you and I are going to be great friends." Kota winks, only confusing Mom more.

"What am I missing?"

"Nothing," both Liberty and I answer right away, making Kota laugh harder.

I know this is quite sudden. Meeting my family isn't something we have discussed, but now it's happening, I'm enjoying seeing her squirm a little.

"Okay." Mom looks between us like we've lost it before dropping it. "Have you guys had lunch? You should join us." It's not worded as a question because she knows I would say no. Instead, it's a careful encouragement. One I won't agree to if Liberty isn't okay with it.

"Ahh, no. We haven't," I answer, searching out Liberty for her reaction.

Meeting my family is one thing, subjecting her to lunch with them unprepared is another.

"Well, you should come. We're heading to Naples," Kota persuades this time.

"You hungry?" I ask Liberty, trying to get a read on her.

"Yeah, I could eat." She doesn't seem stressed or put out by the change of plans. So I agree, telling Mom and Kota we will meet them there.

"You should ride with us, Liberty." Kota smirks at my scowl. She's enjoying this way too much.

"We will meet you there." My tone doesn't leave room to argue.

"Oh, Liam. This is way too much fun." Kota laughs, following Mom back to the car. Only once they've left, and I've locked the house up do I ask Liberty if she's really okay with this.

"We don't have to go if you don't want." I pull her against my chest and cup her face with my hands.

"Are you kidding me? Why wouldn't I want to have lunch with your mom right after she saw you eating me out?" she sasses.

"I'll call her, tell her we aren't coming." I step back and reach for my cell.

"No, seriously, don't. It's okay. I want to go. They seem nice."

"Nice? Woman, tell me what you really think in another couple of hours." I grin, knowing full well how my mom and sister can get.

My mom will have her telling her life story in less than half an hour, and Kota will have made plans by the end of lunch, excited she made a new friend.

My family is crazy.

But so is Liberty.

So I know even before they do, they will be smitten by the end of lunch.

Oddly enough, this doesn't frighten me.

* * *

204

"So tell us. What do you do, Liberty?" Mom asks Liberty twenty minutes later when we're settled at our table in the small Italian pizzeria we've been coming to since we were kids.

Liberty's eyes come to mine first before answering. I know she remembers my reaction a couple of weeks back, and now she's searching for my approval. I give a quick nod, letting her know it's all good.

I'm the only sorry bastard who's still messed up by my father's death.

"I'm a youth worker," she answers, and I find myself anticipating it. Mom's eyes take on a memory, and she gets lost in it.

"Oh, wow, so you're pretty, funny, and amazing. Where do you work?" Kota takes over the questions when she notices Mom's small lapse into the past.

"Over at Boys Haven." Liberty notes my mom's reaction but doesn't ask about it.

"That's great. Do you work full time?" Kota continues the conversation, not drawing attention to Mom. Not sure what else to do, I reach out and grab Mom's hand, giving it a light squeeze. She comes back at my touch, turning her head to look at me. It's a silent question. One I'm not sure I understand. Before I can read into it any further, my cell rings.

"Sorry, need to get this. I'm on call," I tell the ladies as I stand and hit accept.

"Yeah?" I bark into the phone once I am far enough away to hear clearly.

"We have a hostage situation on the William Jones off-ramp." The voice on the other end is Sterling. He gives me the rundown, letting me know kids are involved, and the full team is needed on this one.

"I'm fifteen minutes out. I'll meet you on scene." I hang up the call and stalk my way back over to the table.

"I'm sorry, Mom. We gotta run." I lean down, drop a kiss to her forehead and move on to my sister.

"Oh, do you have to? We just ordered," my mom asks, not

understanding the situation.

"SWAT call out. You know how it is."

"Well, Liberty can stay. I'll take her back after lunch," Kota offers. My head turns to Liberty, trying to get a read on her.

"You wanna stay?" It's not something I would normally impose, but I'm time sensitive, and I need to get on the road.

"Yeah, you go. I'll stay." Liberty offers an uncomfortable smile.

"Okay, I'll see you later." I lean down and press my lips to hers, offering a quick, chaste kiss before turning and heading out to my truck.

It's only when I'm speeding along the freeway back into the city, I catalog the smile. It's a smile that says 'whatever is coming out of my mouth right now is all a lie. Do not do what I am suggesting you do.'

I half chuckle, half swallow my unease. Jesus, I can just picture how annoyed she is going to be later. Knowing I don't have time to worry about Liberty, and whether my mom and sister are taking it easy on her, I push it to the back of my mind and spend the rest of the drive focusing on the task at hand.

SWAT has been called in. A hostage situation involving kids.

Me and my boys needed to be prepared.

These call-ins were the ones that could really mess you the fuck up.

* * *

"What are we looking at?" I ask the lieutenant and the on-scene commander as I step into the tactical operations vehicle ten minutes later. The familiar sounds of Velcro grates in the air as some of Team One and Team Two begin to suit up in their tactical gear.

"Norman James, father of three, picked his kids up from Trebook Elementary," the on-scene commander, Parker, commences filling me in. "Custody arrangement only gives him access every other weekend. Mom called it in after getting a text from him saying he was taking them and not coming back." He points to one of the monitors, showing a picture of Norman James. White male in his early forties. Though he's fighting a slightly receding hairline, I would have placed him in his early thirties.

"Amber alert went out as well as a bolo on his car." Parker continues to give me all the information we have to work with. "Patrol officer picked up his tail over on Kensington. When he failed to stop, he led them on a chase through town, ending when he pulled up to a stop on the off-ramp, and one of his kids jumped out, making a run for it." My eyes move back to the monitors' live feeds from the overhead chopper. The closest police cruiser fills two of the six screens we have available.

"The kid give us anything?"

"No, too shaken up to talk."

"Weapons?"

"Patrol officer thinks he saw a handgun. Kid's not saying so can't be sure."

"Have we established any communication?"

"We tried his mobile, but he's not picking up."

I take everything in. The initial rush of the moment settles within me as I pull up a chair in front of the monitors.

"You want lead negotiator on this, Sargent?" my lieutenant asks, and I nod, letting him know I'm the right man for the job. He takes my nod, then steps back, allowing me to take control of the situation.

"Walker, I want better eyes in the car and keep trying him on his cell 'til he picks up."

"On it, boss." Walker starts clicking away on his keyboard, getting settled in.

"Okay, boys, our main concern is those two kids. We need to figure out if he's acting out in anger, or suffering a mental break. Fox, what are our tact options here?"

"He's out there, open and exposed." He steps forward and points at the monitor. "I think our only play here is to have a sniper's perch set up over here on the adjacent side ramp." I nod, agreeing with the play. I turn to face my lead marksman.

"Tate, you're lead sniper." Tate nods, adjusts his rifle firmly in his grip, and then exits the command vehicle ready to do his job.

"Perry, you're second," I order one of Kaighn's men out to follow Tate. From what I know about the kid, he's just as good as Tate, and if I can get two sets of eyes up there, the better off we will be.

"What's your play on this?" I ask Kaighn, Team Two's leader, opening up the lines of communication. This isn't just any rescue. It's a sensitive situation. A father clearly on the edge, three innocent children caught in the crossfire.

"Only way I see this happening, we box him in. Use the BearCat to get up close." A BearCat is a Ballistic Engineered Armored Response Counter Attack Truck. Simply put, an armored personnel carrier.

I think over Kaighn's play, working it out in my head.

It may work. It's probably our only shot.

"Okay, boys, that's our play. Team One, you'll take the north end of the ramp. Team Two, you're south. Let's get to it. You know what needs to be done." The two teams exit the command unit, setting up the play with no other questions.

"Is the ex-wife close?" I ask Kaighn, hoping she may be able to help talk her ex-husband down.

"She's en route."

I nod, making a note. "Let's have some of the patrols move back, so the boys can—"

"Got a connection." Walker cuts me off, switching my coms over to the call.

"Mr. James, this is Sergeant Hetcherson of the Trebook PD tactical unit—"

"You all need to stay back. You're getting too close." He cuts right to the chase, giving me the first glimpse into his frame of mind.

"We're working on it right now, Mr. James. In the meantime, you want to tell me what's going on here today?"

"I'm not talking to anyone till you back the fuck up. You're scaring Lucy," he repeats his order, and I take note of his daughter's name.

"How is Lucy?" My eyes find Walker, and I circle Lucy's name then write 'brother's name' with a question mark next to it.

"She's fine."

Walker has the kid's name up in less than ten seconds.

"And Conrad? He doing okay too?"

"They're fine. But we would be better if you all pissed off."

"You know we can't do that, Norman." I test his name on my tongue. "It's okay to call you Norman?" I ask, hoping to establish some kind of rapport with him.

"Yeah."

"Okay, good. Now you want to tell me what's happened today that's brought us to this point?" I open the conversation up to him, hoping he will inadvertently expose himself.

"The bitch. It's all her fault. She doesn't care about them. She only cares about hurting me."

"Who are we talking about Norman?" I already know he's talking about his ex-wife, but I need to keep him talking while the two teams get into position.

"My bitch of an ex-wife."

"Okay, wanna tell me about it?"

"No, I have nothing to say. You'll only use it against me."

"I'm not going to use anything against you, Norman. I want to help. Help you get out of this situation. Help you get what you need."

"Bullshit. You don't want to help me. You're like the others. You'll only listen to her side."

"It's not true, Norman. I'm here talking to you. How about you tell me your side?"

"In position, boss." Tate's voice comes through my earpiece, letting me know he's set up and has eyes on Norman.

"I want my kids. She's trying to take them from me."

"How is she doing that, Norman?"

"She lied. Told the court some bullshit stories. Now I only get to see them twice a month! Do you know what that does to a man? They're my life, and that bitch takes them from me." I can hear his anger through the phone, but that's not what worries me; it's his desperation.

"It's got to be hard, Norman. I get it. But is this the right way to go about it? The kids don't need to see this, Norman."

"They have to see what their bitch mother has done to me. What she has done to us."

"Team One in position," Sterling checks in.

"Look, I know you're hurting now. I understand it, but why don't you let the kids out of the car and we can talk about this some more."

"And let them go back to her? No fucking way. If I can't have them, neither will she." It's the threat I didn't want to hear, but I knew it was coming.

"You don't mean that, Norman. Nothing has been done today you can't come back from," I tell him, still waiting on Team Two to get in position. Until we have both teams in position, we can't move. "We can figure this out—" My words get cut off when the back door of his car opens, and Conrad slips out, making a run for it. Lucy tries to escape next but is yanked back, and the door is slammed firmly shut.

"Hold your fire!" I shout, ordering the surrounding officers not to discharge their weapons.

Sterling steps out from behind the BearCat, shield out in front of him, he runs forward and scoops the kid up in one fast movement, turns and runs back, firmly tucking him under his arm. He makes it out of range safely, handing him over to a waiting officer.

"Norman, you still there, buddy?" I bring Norman's attention back to the moment. "Is everything okay in the car?"

"I need you to get my wife down here, NOW!" he answers, Lucy's crying growing more frantic.

"We're still waiting for her to get down here. In the meantime, how about you let Lucy go too?"

"Not until she gets here."

"In place." Team Two finally comes online, letting me know everyone is ready. I mute my call with Norman to speak to my team.

"Okay, boys, we go in slow. Team Two, you need to inch in close. Team One, not until Team Two comes up over the crest of the overpass do I want you to move."

"Copy that."

"Roger," I get back in response, and then I flick the line back over to Norman.

"How's Lucy doing there, Norman?" I ask, hoping to bring his attention away from the team closing in on him.

"What's going on? Why are they moving?" The play doesn't work. Norman catches the movement as Team Two comes into view. "You need to stay back." The line falls silent, cutting off our communication.

Fuck!

"Do we have an ETA on the wife?" I ask Walker, watching as Team Two inches closer.

"She's a few minutes out."

Knowing I don't have much time, I pick up the phone and call Norman back.

"Is Sharon there?" he answers on the second ring.

"She's two minutes out. But I need you to know we're not going to be able to let her on the bridge, Norman."

"I don't need her on the bridge. I just want her to see." He ends the call short, throwing the cell out the window.

Fuck. This is going to escalate fast.

"Okay, guys, we lost communication. We need to move this along," I order as the front driver door opens and Norman exits the car. With Lucy held close to his chest, he makes a run for the side of the bridge.

Both teams step out from their positions, forming a basic formation they slowly inch forward.

"STAY BACK!" Norman screams, reaching into his jeans and pulling out a gun.

Fuck. He's going to jump.

Acting on instinct, I step out of command, crossing over the perimeter and run toward him.

"You all need to stay back." Norman spins when he makes

it to the ledge, his left arm holding Lucy close to his chest.

"Drop the weapon, now."

"Do it now."

"Drop it." A barrage of demands and shouts fill the air as both teams close in, guns drawn, as Norman draws his pistol up to Lucy's temple.

"Norman, you don't want to do this." I push past Hart and Fox, hands raised in front of me. Lucy is screaming as she tries to claw her way out of his hold.

"Boss, you need a shield," I hear Hart call out, but I keep my focus on Norman.

"Is she here? Can she see?" He frantically looks around, stepping back further toward the edge of the bridge.

"Let Lucy go and we can let you talk to her, Norman." I inch closer. I don't believe he wants to harm his daughter. He's hurting, and sometimes desperate people go to extremes for something they love.

"I have the shot." Tate's controlled voice comes through on my earpiece.

I weigh up our options here. He's close to the ledge with Lucy held tight to his chest. If Tate takes the shot, we risk him falling back with Lucy.

"Norman, take a step away from the edge for me." I risk another step closer to him.

"Stay back. I'll throw her!" he yells, forcing another petrified scream from Lucy. I risk a quick look, regretting it instantly. Wild eyes, pupils dilated, her fear speaks to me in its cackling voice, telling me I'm not going to save them while taunting me with the idea I might.

I wish I could reach out and yank her from him, but it doesn't work like that. I need to keep calm and in control.

"You won't. I know you love her, Norman." I force another step. "You would do anything for her." Norman nods, his crazed stare slipping into realization.

"I just want to be with my kids."

"Look at me, Norman." I take a final step. "Give me the gun."

"Why did she have to lie? I just want to be the best dad." His voice drops to a whisper.

"Norman, give me Lucy." He takes another step away from my voice, just as I see Sterling give me a hand signal in my peripheral vision.

I signal back, letting him know I'm reading him.

On his count of one, he takes a step to his left. On two, I take a step to the right. By three, we both lunge.

I grab for Lucy—Sterling for the gun. It becomes a tangle of arms and legs, and in a quick flurry of movements, I manage to rip Lucy from his arms as Norman dives over the edge.

"Daddyyyyy!" She tries to fight my hold, reaching for her father. I tuck her head into my chest, obscuring her view, and start moving her away.

She clings to me like a lifeline. Her small body is shaking harder than my composure.

"I've got you. It's okay." I try to soothe her, but as hard as I want to believe it to be true, I know it's not.

The fear in her scream tears at me, taking me back to the moment I lost my father.

The moment he gave up.

And in that second, I know no amount of time will ever make this okay.

She will never be okay. Never forget this moment, and never forget the pain.

No amount of okays will take it away. It will be forever ingrained in her soul, like a piece of her.

Just like it is with me.

LIBERTY

"Oh, my God, your face when you walked up those stairs. I thought you were going to punch me." Kota laughs as she drives me home later that day.

We finished lunch hours ago, but between her and her mom wanting to know everything about me, the hours flew by and before we knew it, it was edging closer to dinnertime.

"No way. Now Hetch on the other hand…." I trail off and Kota laughs, probably thinking I'm joking. I'm not. Before I found out he was hugging his sister, I could have easily punched his junk.

"Why do you call him, Hetch? Did he tell you to call him that?" She continues with her questioning.

"I don't know. I guess when we first met, he introduced himself as Hetch, and it stuck. I notice you and your mom only call him Liam."

"Yeah, Mom hates it, especially since Dad died. It's what his friends called him too." The air in the car stiffens, not in the same way it may have if Hetch had told the same story, but in a way which tells me their loss is still very fresh.

"Do you mind me asking how your dad died, Kota?" I whisper, hoping to get some kind of insight into what Hetch is dealing with.

"Liam hasn't told you?" Her head whips around briefly to get a read on me.

"No, he told me he passed away. But since then every time it comes up, he kind of shuts down." I tell her the truth. Whatever happened to Hetch's father has defined the type of man he is. I just want an understanding of the matter.

"Umm, well, I don't know. I mean, I don't have a problem talking about it. It's just Liam might not be okay with it."

"Oh, okay. Of course it's fine." I push down my disappointment.

"I wish I could tell you, Liberty. But I think it's probably better coming from him," she offers, only confusing me more. *What does Hetch have to do with it?*

"I shouldn't have asked, I ju—" My words get cut off by the ringtone of Kota's phone through the car speakers.

"Sterling." Her smile grows as she accepts the call, as if him calling is the highlight of her day.

Okay, something is definitely going on there.

"Hello?"

"Hey. Where you at right now?" he replies, less excited to speak to her than Kota seems to be by receiving his call.

"Driving back to town. Why, what's up?" Her tone loses its spark. It's only subtle, but I pick it up instantly.

"You see the news?"

"No why?"

"Good," is all he says.

"What's going on, Sterling. Is Liam okay?" My heart clenches at his name. It takes a second before Sterling answers before I can take a breath.

"We're at The Elephant. We had a bad call. Surprised you didn't see the news."

"Shit," she curses. Obviously clicking on to something I'm not getting. "How bad?"

"Lost the dad."

"Shit. How is he?"

"What do you think, Dakota?" The way her name is delivered in a smooth, smoky tone makes my senses come alive.

Holy shit, there is something seriously going on with these two!

"Don't be an ass, Sterling. I'm coming now. I have Liberty with me. Maybe she can talk him down."

"I don't think it's a good idea."

"Well it can't hurt, can it?"

"Fine. Just hurry." He cuts the call without a good-bye.

"What's going on, Kota?" I ask, hoping like hell Hetch is okay, and Kota reveals something. Anything.

"Okay, so maybe I should tell you how our father died. If things are as serious with my brother as I think they may be, you need to know what you're dealing with." Her confession sets my nerves on fire.

What the fuck is going on?

And why do I get the feeling what she's about to tell me will change everything?

* * *

"Oh, Shit." Kota pulls into The Elephant parking lot ten minutes later to find a very drunk Hetch taking a swing at Sterling. On the drive over, Kota filled me in on everything regarding Hetch and what their family has been living with the last few years.

To say I was shocked wouldn't be a stretch. From the last few weeks of spending time with him, I knew there was something he was dealing with. What, I wasn't sure. Never in a million years would I have guessed it was witnessing, and not being able to stop, his father's suicide.

"Stop!" I call out as Sterling's fist connects with his face,

216

knocking him down on his ass.

"Sterling, what the fuck is wrong with you?" Kota rushes forward with me, but instead of kneeling down to check on her brother, she gets up in Sterling's face.

"Stay out of this, Dakota."

"Like hell, Sterling."

"Hetch?" I ignore their bickering and reach for him. "Are you okay?" He looks up at my voice, the haze clearing in his blank stare.

"What the hell are *you* doing here?" He finally notices me.

"What the hell is going on?" I answer with my own question.

"You shouldn't be here." He starts to stand, a little wonky on his feet.

"Well, clearly I should be. Look at you. You're a mess." I reach for his hand to help him stay steady.

"I didn't ask you to come, Liberty." He pulls back like my touch burns him. "You need to go."

"Not without you I won't be."

"Kota, get her the fuck out of here."

"Liam, you're drunk. Don't be an ass." Kota gives up her argument with Sterling and joins ours.

"Why would you call her, Sterling?" He turns and narrows his eyes on his best friend.

"I don't know, 'cause you were talking shit for the last hour."

"What sort of shit?" Kota presses.

"Will you all just fuck off and leave me alone." He turns and starts walking in the direction of home.

"What sort of shit, Sterling?" Kota presses while I jog to catch up with Hetch.

"Hetch! Will you talk to me? Tell me what's happening here?" I don't recognize this man. He's normally so self-assured, has it together, and yet tonight he's someone else.

"I don't think I can see you anymore, Liberty." His words slap the air, and even though he is drunk, and probably doesn't know what he's talking about, it still stings.

"What?" My pace slows as I try to get my head around the change of events.

This morning we were heading out for a drive, I met his mom, spent the day with her and Kota, and by the evening, we are over?

"You heard me."

"I did, but I was hoping the second time you said it you would realize you're full of shit." I catch up, my earlier shock morphing into anger.

"I'm full of shit?" he mocks, and I know I shouldn't engage him, shouldn't be discussing it in his state, but he's baiting me.

"You know you are."

"How so, Liberty?" The way he speaks my name makes me feel unsettled, like he's distancing himself from me and the easiest way to do it, is to act cold and heartless.

"I'm getting too close, aren't I? Getting under your skin?" I know I hit the nail dead on when he physically recoils.

"That has nothing to do with it." *Does he think I'm stupid?*

"No? Then tell me what it is?" My voice rises and I catch Sterling and Kota's presence in my peripheral vision.

"I don't do relationships. I don't take women out to my house, and I sure as hell don't do lunch with my mom and sister. You brought all this on."

"Liam—" Kota starts to talk, but I don't want her involved.

"And it scares you?"

"No, I just don't want this. I don't want any of this shit. I was happy before you came along."

"No, you don't want it because you're scared. Admit it. You're running scared right now."

"No, it's because I don't love you," he corrects, and my body flinches at the rejection. "I don't need to be dragged down with your bullshit drama. I don't need the stress of having to worry about you. About the boys. I'm done. I'm so fucking done."

"That's enough, Liam." Kota steps in front of me, blocking me from his line of sight, but it's too late. He's already hit his mark.

He's trying to hurt you, Liberty.

Maybe he doesn't love me the way I thought he did, but he still cares. He's just too lost in his head right now.

"No, it's fine, Kota." I step around her and take three steps toward him. "You know what you are, Liam Hetcherson?" His nostrils flare when I spit his name at him. "You're so lost you can't see what's in front of you. You think a night out on the booze fixes everything? Makes it all go away? You're only hurting yourself here." I turn and start to walk back to Kota's car. There's no getting through to him tonight. The best thing for all of us, especially me, is to walk away.

"You don't know what you're talking about, Liberty!" he shouts, only because I hit a soft spot.

"Right, I wouldn't have a clue, 'cause I'm just some platinum pussy who has no idea what you could be dealing with right now? I couldn't possibly know what I'm talking about." I spin back, using the words he used this morning.

"How could you? You weren't there. None of you fucking were. So why the fuck do you get to judge me?" His voice starts to rise, and I wonder if this is going to be it for him.

Rock bottom.

"No one is judging you, Hetch." I keep my voice low and calm as I risk a step back to him. "I wasn't there, but it doesn't take a trained professional to know you need help, Liam. You need to talk about it with someone."

"YOU DON'T GET TO TELL ME WHAT I NEED!" I recoil from his scream, feeling ridiculous for it. Hetch may want to hurt me with his words, but I know he would never physically hurt me.

"Enough, Hetch." Sterling steps in front of him, his voice carrying a warning with enough menace to scare me. "Liberty's right. You need to talk to someone. If you don't, I'm gonna report your ass." His finger pokes his chest, pushing his opinion literally into him.

"Fuck you, Sterling."

"No, fuck you. I love you, man. I do. But this shit has to end. You have a family who cares about you. A woman who's holding on, even though you stand here pushing her away, and friends who would do anything for you. What more do you fucking want?"

"You know what, I don't want anything from any of you. I'm done. Kota,"—he points to his sister—"I'll see you later. Sterling,"—he flips his middle finger toward him—"fuck you very much, and Liberty,"—he steps up into my space, reaching for me. He holds my face so gently I can feel my heart skip a beat—"I'm only gonna hurt you." He kisses me once. "It's for the best." He kisses me twice. "Don't make it harder on me." Then a third before he steps back and drops his hands.

"You don't have to hurt me." My voice is small, weighed down with pain.

"Damn it, I already am!" His shoulders slump forward, his hand rubbing through the mess of his hair like he's trying to rein in his emotions.

"Hetch." I reach for him, only for him to brush me off.

"Kota, make sure she gets home." He turns without another word and starts walking away from us. I want to call out to him. Want to tell him he's not hurting me, but it would be a lie.

He is hurting me. He's hurting us.

And I'm not sure if we can come back from it.

"I'll make sure he finds his way back home. Kota, make sure you get her back too," Sterling orders before taking off to find him.

"Come on, babe, let's get you home." Kota reaches for my hand, but I pull away.

"Maybe I should follow too." I look over at her, despising the pity I see in her eyes.

"I think you should let him be, give him some time. He'll come back to you. I know he will."

I want to believe her, believe that he will find his way back to me, but I'm not so sure.

I'm not sure about anything anymore.

* * *

"Sweetheart, open the door." Hetch finds his way back to

220

me four hours and seventeen minutes later. My eyes open from my broken sleep, adjusting to my dark living room before slowly sitting up.

"Liberty." He knocks harder while I try to force my racing heart down. I've been sitting here since Kota dropped me home, wondering where he was and when he was getting back. Praying he would come to me. But now he's here, I'm not sure I'm ready to see him. I'm not ready to see this other person who's a stranger to me. A broken man. A heartless man. A man who doesn't care who he hurts.

"Please open the door, Liberty. I need you." The desperation in his voice calls to me and all concern and worries I may have been feeling are left behind as I move to the door.

"Hey." I open up, keeping my body inside the doorframe and my hand on the door.

"Baby, you opened." He looks shocked; his bloodshot eyes tell me he either continued drinking wherever he walked off to, or he's been crying.

My guess, both.

"Don't make me regret it." I open the door wider to let him pass.

"Sweetheart, I—" He reaches for me, but I step out of his way.

I'm not sure I'm ready for him to touch me.

"Please don't." I close the door and move back over to the sofa. I didn't let him in so we could fuck. We need to talk. We need to be real.

Following my lead, Hetch walks around and takes a seat next to me.

Not too close.

Not close enough.

"I don't know where to start." He looks so defeated, so rejected. A little less self-assured. A little less cocky.

Not the man I've fallen in love with these last few weeks.

"Maybe from the start," I offer, wanting him to lay it all out for me. Is this something that happens all the time? Is it a one-off? So many questions fill my head, but I keep them to myself and wait for him to share.

"My father died three years ago." He takes a breath. Moving his hands from his lap, he rubs his palm over his mouth. "He shot himself in front of me." His voice cracks for a second, but he holds himself together long enough to clear it.

"I'm so sorry, Hetch." I tell him the same thing I told Kota when she filled me in. And just like with Kota, I sound awkward and unsure. I mean, what do you say to someone who's lived through that? I can't imagine what they've been going through, or the emotions they may have harbored.

"I always thought I was coping, you know?" he continues, gaining more conviction along the away. "Dealing with things in my own way. I mean, most days it doesn't hit me. Sure, I think about it. But I do my job. I live my life." He pauses and I count the beats between. "Then the look on that kid's face today." He drops his gaze to his lap. "It all came back. I was that kid. I was screaming for my dad again." He falls silent, his body trembling in silent sobs.

"Hey." I slide closer, unsure if I should touch him. I've never seen a man cry before. Never seen anyone so utterly defeated, so cut down and broken that my stomach aches for them.

"I fucked up, sweetheart." He looks up. "I fucked up so bad." He reaches for me, and this time, I don't pull away. Instead, I welcome his embrace.

"No, you didn't." I pull him in closer, needing him to know I'm okay. We're okay.

"I don't know what I'm doing. I don't know what anyone wants from me anymore. I just don't know."

"Hey, it's okay. It's gonna be okay." My eyes burn, and my face heats, as a tear escapes my eye. First one and then two, and before I know it, they are falling rapidly. I cry along with him. For him. For his loss. For the screaming kid inside of him.

"It's not okay, Liberty. I'm not okay." He pulls back, wiping his face with the sleeve of his shirt.

"I know, but it's okay to hurt, Hetch. It's okay not to be okay."

"But don't you see? I don't want to be *not* okay, Liberty. I don't want to have to be fixed or changed. I just want you. I need you." The sentiment should warm me and give me some kind of sign he cares for me like I care for him, but it doesn't. I can't become his crutch. He needs to address the issues with his father. To finally release the hurt and the anger he's been holding on to for so long.

"You have me, honey," I tell him what he needs to hear. The man doesn't need to be told he's hit rock bottom. He needs someone to help him climb back up.

"I think I'm falling in love with you, Liberty." He holds my face between his hands. So gentle. So tender. "I'm not saying this because I was an asshole earlier."

"I know, Hetch." My hands cover his as his lips caress mine. I don't tell him I feel the same way, or the fact I'm already in love with him. It's not the time or the place. Tonight is about him opening up to me, accepting whatever it is he needs to accept. And letting him know I'm here for him.

"I'm so tired, B. I'm so tired of all of this." He rests his forehead on mine, exhaustion seeping from the both of us.

"I know you are, honey." I take his hand and stand. "You have to be so tired. Come with me," I urge and he stands without hesitation, following me into the bathroom.

"Are we having shower sex?" He cocks a brow while I reach in and turn the shower faucet on.

"No." I smirk at his ability to lighten the mood. "You're going to have a shower while I go and get you a change of clean clothes. Then we're going to bed." I help him out of his shirt and make quick work of his jeans. He helps me along, kicking off his boots, and stepping out of his jeans and boxers.

When he's finally naked, and the water is ready, I motion him into the shower, hoping he's lucid enough to stay standing while I grab him clean clothes.

"You gonna be okay for a minute?" I ask, closing the glass door. He doesn't answer right away. His eyes are closing as he steps under the spray of the water. "Hetch?" I step forward, unsure if I should leave him.

This is more than I can handle, him standing in front of me.

I know I haven't even caught a glimpse of the broken man fighting his way out.

"I'm good," he finally speaks.

"Okay, I'll be back." I hang around for a few beats, before leaving and heading over to his apartment.

It only takes two minutes to grab a pair of boxer briefs, an old SWAT shirt, and a pair of loose-fitting black pants.

But those short two minutes in the shower are all it takes for his defenses to wash away.

"Hetch, honey?" I whisper when I step back into the bathroom and find him on the floor of the shower. Head in hands, his body shaking in grief.

"Hey, you okay?" He looks up at my voice, but it's as if he doesn't register I'm here.

"Why did he do it, B?" There's a rawness to his question, like an open wound that refuses to heal. I open my mouth to answer, but he doesn't let me, cutting me off and firing off another desperate question.

"What kind of father does that to his son?" His head rears back against the tiles, and a sob rips past my lips at the force of it.

"I don't know, honey." I rush toward the shower and open the glass door. Not bothering to undress, I crouch down to his level and hold him against me.

"A man who was sick? He probably didn't think very far ahead. When you try to pull someone out of their horror show, they have a way of dragging you into their nightmares. Maybe your father thought he was trying to save you from his darkness." I don't register the words I'm telling him. I just need to get through to him.

"You really believe that?" He looks up, his eyes searching for more than I can give him.

"I do, Hetch. And maybe one day you will see it like I do, too. You're just hurting right now."

"Jesus, Liberty." He reaches for me, leaning forward until he is an inch from my face. "How can you bear to look at me?" His question hurts my heart and burns my throat.

"How could I not? You're an amazing man, Liam." I use his first name, needing him to know I see him. The real him.

He doesn't respond, lost under the stream of the warm water. Lost to the storm inside his head.

"I think we need to get you to bed." I place my hands over his and start to stand.

"Don't leave me, B," he whispers. It's so gentle I almost don't hear it until I look down at him, and he speaks again. "You're the only person I trust."

"I'm not going anywhere," I promise, meaning it more than anything I've ever promised.

In my thirty years of life, death has never touched me. I've never truly grasped the complexity of it, nor have I comprehended how grief could tear a man down. But the depths of pain someone can live through is unfolding in front of me.

I'm not walking away from him.

I'm in love with him.

Flaws and all.

I am in this for the long haul.

The only problem being, when I wake the following morning, Hetch is gone. No note, no explanation, no word.

Deep down a part of me knew he wouldn't be here. A proud man like Hetch would be hurting more today.

But if I knew how long it would be before he talked to me again, maybe I wouldn't have made him leave the shower.

Maybe I would have held on a little tighter.

A little longer.

Maybe I shouldn't have let go.

HETCH

"How are you today, Liam?" Dr. Anderson, the force-appointed shrink my lieutenant sanctioned, asks as he sits across from me in his leather armchair. Left leg crossed over his right, right arm bent at the elbow, his long fingers wrap around the stainless steel barrel of his ballpoint pen. He's the epitome of arrogance, with his stuffy suit and pointy shoes, but give him a few minutes, he'll be a list of contradictions.

"Okay, I guess." I shrug, not really sure how I'm feeling today.

A little less messed up than yesterday.

A little more desperate today.

"Just okay?" he presses with the right amount of query, then waits.

"Well, I'm not pissing rainbows yet, Doc, but I don't feel like I'm having a heart attack every five minutes this week. So yeah, just okay." I don't know why I'm fighting it today. While it's protocol for me to talk about the incident that happened three weeks ago on the overpass, it's my choice to take it seriously this time. My choice to sort my shit out and for once, be honest.

So why am I being an asshole today?

Because you miss her.

"Well, it's an improvement on your first visit." He nods, not giving a shit about my foul mood.

It's my third visit. What started out as a debrief session, soon turned into a standing appointment every Monday for mandatory sessions until Dr. Anderson clears me. If I want to stay on in the tactical unit, this is where I need to be. One slip up, one missed appointment could have me off the team. I knew it was coming. While the mandatory part pisses me off, I still welcome it. After everything I've been through the last few years, I'm surprised I lasted this long.

"So, what's been happening since you stormed out of here last week?" I should hate the way he's so frank, but I don't. It's refreshing for once. It also keeps me in check.

"Nothing," I answer honestly.

I've done fucking nothing other than working out with the boys in our group training sessions. Eating, sleeping and missing Liberty sums up my life. On top of that, I've been here, telling this fucker all about how I've been doing fuck all.

"Well, that sounds boring as shit." He continues to roll his pen between his fingers.

"Tell me about it." His timely, uncensored comment settles me enough to relax back into my chair. "How about you approve me for work and I won't be so bored?"

"Let's see how we go today." He doesn't reject the notion completely, so there's still hope.

"Deal." I nod, a little extra spring in my voice.

"Okay, how are we going to play it today, Sergeant? You want me to try and pry everything out or do you want to cut to the chase and get started?"

He starts the session the same way each time.

Same question. Same bluntness. Same result.

Trepidation trickles through me as I try to figure out which way is less painful.

I've done both ways, and to be honest, neither way is pretty.

"I don't know. How about you start? I'll try not to be a dick, and we'll see how we go?" It's all I can offer.

"Have you spoken to her?" He opens with the sucker punch.

Liberty.

He knows a little about her. It's the one thing I've been reluctant to talk about; however, judging by his play, he's about to tackle it today.

"Not yet."

"Communication is key here, Liam. Not only with me but also when you leave here. For me to clear you for work, I need to know you're talking not just in here, but out there too."

"You don't think I know this? Why do you think I'm here? I know I need to talk to her, but I don't know how."

"You answered your own problem. All you have to do is talk."

"She's going to be pissed." I reveal a little more.

Do you blame her? You left in the middle of the night and haven't been back since.

"Why is she going to be pissed?" He presses for more.

"Because I've shut her out."

"And why have you shut her out?"

This is how he works, and maybe before now, his style of peppering me over and over with question upon question would have had me shutting down, but I can't keep doing that. I need to be able to work through this. I need tools to deal.

"I don't know why I left."

"Oh, come on. Yes, you do. You need to be honest with yourself."

"I don't know," I lie as my brow starts to sweat.

"Why have you shut her out, Liam?"

"Because I'm embarrassed." I pause, waiting for three longer-than-normal beats, then another two before I realize he's expecting more from me.

"By how I acted. By how unpredictable my grief is," I blurt before I can censor myself. "One minute I'm fine, and life seems

228

to be moving on, and the next, I'm in a fucking shower, breaking down in front of my woman."

"You broke down in front of Liberty?" *Fuck, there I go, getting carried away. I was hoping to keep that little tidbit of information to myself.*

"I shared some things." I don't delve too much into it. For one, I'm unsure if what I shared was real or if somehow I made it all up. The night is an array of broken images. Sterling and Kota played a part, but most of it flashes to Liberty climbing into the shower, holding me while I burdened her with my shit.

"What did you share?"

"I don't know. Things…."

"Okay, let's leave it there for a minute and talk about your father." He changes tactics. Hitting me with another question, equally as frustrating. "Tell me something you've never told anyone before."

"Sometimes I dream about saving him." The words spill out of my mouth before I can process them.

"How do you feel in those dreams? When you save him."

"Happy. Relieved."

"And do you talk to him after?"

"No, usually, it's the end of the dream, and then I wake up."

"And what do you feel after you wake up?"

"Anger." I pause. "Then heaviness here." I thump my hand over my heart and tap it twice. The dream is rare. Normally, it's a replay of what did happen, rather than what I wish would happen.

"What did you tell Liberty that night?" I don't see the ploy to get me to open up. My head is still in disarray with the dream talk.

"That I didn't understand why he would do that to me. That I don't know what people want from me anymore. That I don't know how to act. How to be."

Fuck.

"How do you think you should be?" He doesn't give me a chance to be annoyed, hitting me with another tough question.

"Over it? Fuck, I don't know." I adjust my position in my chair, irritation surging through me.

"Do you think you'll ever be over it?" His twirling of his pen stops, and the uncrossing of his leg alerts me to his change in observing me.

"Isn't that why I'm here? To get over it?" I shrug while I pick at a hangnail on my thumb.

"I'm not asking you why you're here. You know why you're here. We both know there is a lot of pain underneath this façade you have constructed. I'm asking you, do you think you will ever get over your father's death—"

"Suicide," I correct him before he can finish.

Death to me was cancer or dying in your sleep. Something you had no control over. My father did. He decided to die. He decided to kill himself.

"Why do you do that? Correct me every time I say he died. Did he not die?"

"He killed himself."

"Is there a difference?" I don't know how to answer his question. Is there a difference? Part of me says no. Like cancer, my father was sick, and his illness killed him. But the other part of me—the angry and guilty part—says yes. He didn't have to stop taking his meds. He could have tried harder.

"I don't know," I end up answering. He doesn't push the issue of death, instead notes something down before continuing with his questions.

"Tell me. What's one thing about your father *dying* that has stayed with you? I'm not talking about the scene, or how he died. I'm talking about you as his son. What's one thing you've missed, or something you realized?"

It takes me a minute to think it through before I come up with something. Normally, if I do think about my father, it's about the moment he left. I never think about anything else.

"I wasn't expecting to find myself still losing parts of him months, even years later," I finally answer.

"What do you mean?"

"Him dying didn't sever the connection we had." He holds my stare for a moment, not responding how I expected him to.

"Can you explain that to me?"

"You know, like the house. He was helping me work on it. I didn't go out there for so long and the first time I did, I couldn't remember where he had put something. I guess I didn't, and I still don't realize how connected to me he was."

"And you to him." He picks up my twist of words.

"And me to him."

"Has anyone ever told you it's okay to be angry at your father, Liam?"

"No. Usually, it's used against me."

"Why did you leave before Liberty woke up?"

"I was scared. I woke up, realized the fucked-up mess I was in and didn't want her to see it. Didn't want her to see me."

Fucker did it again.

"But you let her see a part of it, in the shower?"

"Right. It was rock bottom. She already saw too much. She doesn't need to see any more of this shit. I'm meant to be looking after her, not the other way around. What type of man breaks down like that?"

"What type of person, you mean? Because I see a man, even when we've been deep in session. You're still a man. You're still someone's child. A son. You're allowed to feel pain, Liam. You're allowed to break. You're allowed to cry. It doesn't make you any less of a man. The only way you can move on and find peace with this is to allow yourself to let it happen."

"By freaking out my woman? By breaking down to the point I have trouble breathing?" I ditch the hangnail and start flexing my fingers. Opening and closing, to calm myself.

"Those are normal reactions to have. I'd be worried if, after the incident with the father and his children, you didn't have some kind of reaction. What you have been through will always stay with you, Liam. And yes, I know the job has to be black and white, but unfortunately, our lives are not. There are going to be days where you question things. The how's and whys won't ever stop coming. You have to realize that. But you also have to realize you can control it. You can work through it and not let it control you."

"So how do I control it then?" I sit forward, almost eager for

231

the magic cure.

"You do it by going back to work, by continuing to live. And by accepting you couldn't save your father. You couldn't then, and you sure can't now. You do it with the help of people you love. By talking about it all with them. And by letting them in.

"I want to let her in. I want to open up to her—"

"Then let's take it back to the first question." He cuts me off before I can continue. "Why are you avoiding her, Liam?"

"Because..." I think about it for a second. "...because she deserves a happy ending, and I'm not sure I can give it to her."

LIBERTY

Sunday.

Me: *Talk to me Hetch.*

Tuesday.

Me: *Don't push me away.*

Wednesday.

Me: *Please, Hetch...*

Friday.

Me: *Just tell me you're okay.*

Sunday.

Me: *I miss you.*

I scroll through my phone's history willing a reply to appear.

Give it up, Liberty. He's not going to answer.

"So, what's new with you? It seems like you've dropped off the face of the earth these last few weeks." Payton's foot kicks me under the table, pulling me out of my moping.

"Sorry, what?" I drop my phone into my handbag and zip it up, locking it away from me.

We're at Lotus café. It's my favorite coffee shop, on the account they have the best coffee around, and we're catching up before I head to work.

"What's going on with you? You're not yourself. How's Hetch doing?" The question seizes my heart, his name like a death grip, squeezing it tightly to remind me how much he owns it.

"He's good," I lie, not wanting her to know I haven't seen or spoken to him in three weeks.

Twenty-one days since I woke up alone in my bed.

Five hundred and four hours of not knowing how he is.

Thirty thousand something minutes spent wondering if he's ever coming back.

And almost two million seconds thinking he won't.

Three weeks is a long time when someone you love ignores you.

"Why don't I believe you?" Payton's question douses my stalkerish countdown.

"I don't know. Why don't you believe me?" I challenge, forcing a light tone.

You can do it, Liberty. Don't crack now.

"Because you're sitting there with the same look as you had when you were nineteen and Bobby Tannersville dumped your ass back in college."

234

"I am not." I scoff with a grin because she's right. But Bobby Tannersville was a grade A asshole who didn't deserve my tears. Hetch does.

"Lib." She reaches across the table and covers my hand with hers. "You know you can talk to me about anything."

"I know, I promise I'm fine. I'm just so busy with work is all." I return her hand squeeze with my own and pull out of her grasp.

I don't know why I haven't told anyone Hetch and I are in limbo. Maybe I'm holding onto some kind of false hope that he's going to sort his shit out, and everything will go back to the way things were.

Or maybe I'm not ready to say good-bye yet.

"Enough about me, how about you? How's everything with Jett?" I've been so lost in my own drama the last few weeks. I don't even know what's going on with my own brother.

"He's moving in with *her*."

"Are you fucking kidding me?" The news is like a shock paddle to my depressing life, jolting me into feeling something other than self-pity.

The stupid motherfucker.

"Yeah, he came around the other day to collect the rest of his stuff. Told me all about it." Her voice is a mixture of pain and disgust, and for a second, I think she's going to break right here in the coffee shop. Until her chin juts out and her shoulders square, keeping herself in check.

"I don't know what to tell you, Pay. I'm embarrassed he's blood-related to me."

"Don't say that. God, your mom would have a freak-out."

"My mom would be equally embarrassed," I counter. Knowing it might be a stretch, but I would put money on it that she's probably had the thought once at the very least. "In all seriousness, Pay, you know we don't support anything he is doing."

"I do. And I promise I'm okay. I'm just so over it now. You were right. I need to move on."

"I hate I was right." This time, it's me who reaches across

the table and gently covers her hand with mine.

"I know, but at least I know now, right? I mean, yeah I really thought we were going to make it this time. I mean hell, we were talking about having another baby." She shakes her head and stops herself from saying any more. "Anyway, what's done is done. Time to focus on Arabella and me. We need to get right with our lives now."

"How is Arabella taking everything?" I miss the little cutie. Having her smiling face around would have been too much for me, so I've been keeping myself busy with the boys at Haven.

"Oh, well, that's the one good thing about it. She's not upset. I think maybe a little confused, but honestly, she's more concerned when Hetch is coming around again so he can watch another movie with her. She hasn't stopped asking about him." My throat restricts at his name and my previous calm exterior cracks under the pressure of keeping this façade going.

"Liberty?" Payton picks up on my change in demeanor, scooting closer toward me. "Hey, what is it?" I think she asks, but I can't be sure over the start of my breakdown.

"Iliedthingswithusarenotokayeverythingisamessandidon'tkn owwhattodo." I manage to sob all of it out in one long breath, before dropping my head into my hands.

"Okay, you're going to have to try that again, I can't understand crying Lib." I snort through my tears at that one. And take the moment to gather myself before trying again.

"I lied," I tell her once I've calmed down enough to talk. My eyes do a quick sweep of our area and realize we don't have an audience.

"I gathered. Now, what exactly did you lie about?"

"Hetch and I haven't spoken in three weeks." Saying the words aloud brings on another round of tears. Payton reaches into her bag then hands me a tissue when she catches me using my sleeve to dry up my tears.

"Okay…?" She prompts for more.

"Things have been messy. He's dealing with some serious issues Pay, and I don't know what to do."

"What sort of issues? What are we talking about here?" She

pulls out anther tissue when the tears won't stop.

"His dad shot himself three years ago."

"Fuck," she softly curses. The word pretty much sums it all up for us.

Fuck.

"Yeah. Hetch was there. He tried to talk him down. He couldn't."

"Oh, God, I had no idea he was dealing with that."

"Neither did I. It all came out after the jumper on the overpass in the city three weeks back. It brought up those issues with his dad. Next thing I know, he's drunk and breaking things off with me." I leave out the part about him coming back to me and the moment in the shower. It was a private one. I know Payton would never reveal anything I told her but I still don't feel comfortable telling her.

It was our moment.

"So, that's it? It's over?" She sounds as confused as I am.

Is Hetch not talking to me his way of saying it's over? Did he regret coming back to me that night? The questions play out over and over, and like every day of the last three weeks, I have no answer.

"I don't know, Pay. I haven't spoken to him since he left. He's been avoiding me." I cringe as I recount how many times I've knocked on his door over the last twenty-one days, only to be left standing there rejected.

"How is that even possible? You live next door to each other."

"He hasn't been there. All I know is, he's not working. Kota, his sister, messaged me saying he took a leave of absence."

"Did she say anything else?"

"Just told me not to give up on him." My mind recalls the text messages with her. I wish I had the balls to ask her where he is. If he is staying with her, or out at his house. If I knew where he was, maybe this would be easier.

"So maybe he's working through it all and needs time."

"Maybe, and I'm trying to be patient, and I'm trying not to take offense to him ignoring me. He has a lot of shit to work through, and I'm not sure where I fit in with all of it."

"What do you mean you don't know where you fit in with it all? You love him, don't you?" She sounds annoyed now, so I brace myself for it.

"Yeah." I wipe my eyes again when the tears start back up.

"Then you find a place. You get in there and you fight for it, babe. He's hurting. I can't imagine what he's going through. Don't give up on him."

"You're right." I draw a calming breath into my lungs. "I'm just emotional and overthinking things. I can give him more time."

"There she is. You're damn right you can. But if he takes longer than six weeks, I'm gonna kick his ass."

I force a smile or maybe it's a disguised grimace at the thought of waiting another three weeks.

Jesus.

"We're a couple of messes, aren't we?" She accepts it with a wink, trying to make light of our situations.

"Hot freaking messes. *Sex and the City* and ice cream have our names on it." I blow my nose, vowing it to be the last time. I need to get my shit together. We're in a damn coffee shop for Christ's sake.

"No, I'm thinking more cocktails and dancing." Her brows dance up to her hairline, taunting me with a good time.

"I don't know, Pay. I'm not going to be the best dance partner right now." I wish I didn't have to knock her back like this, but I know I'm not going to be much fun.

"What? Come on, Lib, you have to. It's your duty as my best friend to take your newly single friend out after she finds out her husband knocked his secretary up."

"It is?" I sigh, knowing this isn't going to end the way I hoped.

"It is. Come on, it will be good. This Saturday Jett has Arabella for the weekend. It will be her first weekend away from me. Can you imagine how hard it's going to be for me?" I know she's putting it on, but I don't miss the panic flash in her eyes.

Jesus, she's killing me here.

238

"Okay," I concede. "But only if we go somewhere else. I don't want to go back to The Elephant." I can't imagine what I would do if I ran into Hetch there.

"Sold." Her hands drum down on the table in jest before she softly claps them together.

"It's going to be fun. You'll see, B. One night out like old times and all our worries will be on the back burner."

I'm not as certain as she is.

One night out isn't going to fix my broken heart, nor my worried soul.

At least not until Hetch and I have closure will I be able to function. Until then, I guess I have to put it aside for the sake of my friend. It's the least I can do, considering the douche who broke her heart is my brother.

Dick.

* * *

"Excuse me, Lib, can I have a word with you?" A knock at my door later in the day has my head moving from the files I'm working on, to find Mitch standing in my doorway.

"Sure can. Come on in." He pauses on the threshold, letting his eyes roam around my office before stepping inside and taking a seat across from my desk. Today I'm in the office catching up on paperwork while Renee is on shift with the boys.

"So what's up, Mitch?" I press, after watching him for a few beats. There's something different in the way he's holding himself today. As if he's unsure how to act in order to appear relaxed.

"Umm, I have a favor to ask." The quiver in his voice doesn't hide his nerves, which in turn makes me uneasy.

Please, don't let it be anything serious.

"Okay then, ask away." I try not to let my concern show. For all I know, his question is something personal and maybe he's embarrassed to ask.

"Umm, well I'm hoping maybe you could tell me why Hetch stopped coming around." A flush of adrenalin tingles through my body at the mention of his name.

Crap, I should have realized this was coming.

Hetch not only has dropped out of my life, but he's dropped out of Mitch's too.

"Oh, Mitch." I shift my weight briefly and take a second to think about how to word my next sentence. "I know he's really busy at the moment. If he could be here, I'm sure he would." I try to soften the rejection for him.

If only someone could soften it for me.

I haven't told Mitch what's been happening with Hetch. The first week he missed one-on-one, Mitch took it fine.

The second week, I could tell he was confused, maybe even a little hurt, and by the third, he was angry.

"Yeah, he said he's been busy, but I thought maybe I had done something wrong."

"You've spoken to him?" My question slaps the air with contempt, and I have to remind myself not to react the way I want.

I had no idea they were still in contact.

"Yeah, he's texted me a couple times." Mitch somehow misses my annoyance, revealing how often he and Hetch have been keeping in contact.

Of course, he's messaging Mitch. He's only ignoring you, Liberty.

"Well, I'm certain you have done nothing wrong, bud. I know Hetch has a lot going on and when things calm down for him, he'll be back." I surprise myself with my easy tone, despite the tightening of my chest.

While I am relieved he hasn't abandoned Mitch completely, I still have to squash down the disappointment he hasn't contacted me.

"Well, maybe you could still talk to him. 'Cause you know, the big brother program starts next week, and I thought you know, he's already like my mentor, and I don't want anyone else. Maybe he could do it." He continues to break my heart.

"You want me to ask him to join our big brother program?"

I have to repeat the question slowly to allow myself some time to control the rolling heat spiraling in my belly.

The big brother program is one of our main volunteer programs at Haven. It kind of works the same way as what Hetch does for Mitch. Only it's a little more hands on, and more frequent. Committing to the program means committing to two hours, every week. Joining in on group outings, plus being readily available if needed.

I'm not sure Hetch is up for it.

Mitch is going to get hurt here.

"You think he would?" His hands clasp in front of his stomach, twisting his fingers to crack each knuckle. It's a habit he does when nervous and even though there is nothing wrong with it, I can't stand the sound.

"Gross, Mitch. Don't do that, you know I can't handle it," I scold while I figure out how to deal with his request. I don't want Mitch to think he has no chance, but I also don't want to give him false hope.

"Sorry." He releases his hands and shakes them out in front of him. "So do you think you can talk to him?" he presses, impatient for my answer.

"I'll talk to him, Mitch," I concede, because what else can I say?

I'll talk to him all right, maybe with my fist.

"Thanks, Liberty." He stands, his earlier tense stance relaxing from his shoulders. "He's not going to say no to you." He starts to walk out, his swagger a little too cocky.

"Hang on a minute, Mitch," I call him back. "I don't want you to get your hopes up, okay? I'll ask, but if he has too much going on, I don't want you to be upset." I try to lay it out for him the best way I can. He needs to know there is a possibility Hetch may not even be able to commit to the program, or *want* to commit to the program.

"It's all good, Liberty. I know he'll want to do it." He doesn't heed my warning, only making my belly coil tighter.

Fucking Hetch.

I don't bother pushing the issue; there's no point. Mitch has made up his mind. In his head, Hetch hangs the moon, and even if he hasn't been by in three weeks, he's still the best thing since sliced bread.

"Okay, kid. We'll sort it out. Now get out of here. Don't you have rec time with Renee?" I check the activities board over to my right to see if I'm correct.

"Yeah, I'm going. Thanks again, Lib. You're the best." He gives me one of his rare smiles, then leaves, unaware of the inner turmoil boiling through me.

"Damn you, Hetch." I sigh when I'm alone and Mitch is out of sight.

"Damn you. Damn you. Damn you."

I find myself pacing a few minutes later, repeating the words.

"Damn you. Damn you. Damn you."

When my pacing and ranting only serves to frustrate me more, I do the only thing I know to do. I reach for my phone and with trembling fingers, I dial his number.

There is no way I'm letting Mitch get hurt in all of this.

The phone rings once, twice, three times and like every other time I've called him the last three weeks I'm expecting his voicemail. It doesn't come; instead, the line clicks over and Hetch answers with my name.

"Liberty?" My heart slams against my chest, and my legs fill with lead.

I open my mouth but nothing comes out, the shock of his voice disorientating me.

"Liberty, are you okay?" This time his voice rumbles. Calm and tender, but still powerful enough to send chills through my body.

Speak, Liberty.

"It's one thing to ignore me and walk out of my life, but don't you dare think I'm going to let you do it to Mitch." My voice is wobbly and unsure. My head is foggy and confused.

"Sweeth–" My irrational fear doesn't allow him to finish the word, cutting him off before it's too late.

"Don't, Hetch." It's not the word that scares me. It's how I know I will react to hearing it. It's a reminder of everything he's ever touched in my life.

"If you're going to walk out on him, at least be a fucking man about it and tell him why you've stopped coming around. I'm not covering for you, Hetch. He's hurting. Sort your shit out and either show up and be the man I know you are or tell him you're not coming back." Still trembling, I hang up the call and stumble to my chair before I fall down.

My cell phone rings back, Hetch's name flashing on my screen, but before I can answer, the room falls away. Tears sting my eyes, and sobs wrack my body. For the second time in one day, I break down.

Damn you, Hetch.

27

HETCH

"I was beginning to think you weren't coming back," Mitch casually remarks while he waits for me to make my next move.

"Either show up and be the man I know you are or tell him you're not coming back."

"What? And miss out on a good ass kicking in chess?" I move one of my pawns, trying to figure out if he's pissed, upset, or genuinely curious why I've been blowing off our sessions.

"If you're going to walk out on him, at least be a fucking man about it and tell him why you've stopped coming around."

Mitch stares at me for what feels like forever before he drops his gaze to the board to ask his next question.
"Did I do something wrong?"

Jesus, Liberty was right. He's hurting.

"Nah, bud. You didn't do anything wrong." I try to fix the fucked-up mess I've put us in. "I've had some issues I've had to deal with the last few weeks." Not wanting to lie to him, I give it to him straight.

"So it has nothing to do with me?" He toys with one of my chess pieces he captured earlier, rolling it between his fingers and thumb. I've noticed this trait of his before. Nerves. Frustration. Anger. Whenever overwhelmed by certain emotions, he starts to fidget.

You're a real fucking asshole, Hetch.

"No, kid. In fact, you're the only one I've been talking to through it all," I reveal, telling him the truth. I haven't talked to anyone other than Dr. Anderson in therapy and Mitch via text.

I knew our situation was tricky. I didn't want to cut off all communication, but I wasn't ready to come here.

"I am?" He makes his move on the chessboard and for the first time ever, I can see his play forming.

"Yeah, you're kind of easy to talk to, kid," I admit, moving my bishop to capture one of his knights.

"I find it easy to talk to you, too," he admits then somehow captures my bishop.

Fuck me. I'm never going to win a game against this kid.

"I'm sorry I haven't been around, Mitch. I have it all sorted now, and if you still want to keep kicking my ass at chess, I'll be here." I wait a couple of beats, thinking I've blown it.

Finally, he finally replies, "All good. Just don't leave me hanging again." It's a gentle warning, one I take seriously.

"Got it." I make a promise to myself not to let him down again. "So, what's been going on around here the last couple of weeks?" I ask once we've gotten the awkwardness over with.

"Nothing much. Same as always."

"Have you had any problems with your brother?" I know Sterling and the boys haven't been able to get any more tip-offs on Dominic, but it doesn't mean we're giving up. We'll get him on something. Eventually, he's going to fuck up.

"Nah, I haven't heard from him in weeks." He captures

another one of my pieces without a second glance.

"Well, sounds like I haven't missed too much then." My eyes do a quick sweep of the backyard for probably the tenth time, taking in my surroundings and hoping to catch a glimpse of her.

"She's not here." Mitch catches my spying, even though his eyes remain on the board in front of us. "She went to the store," he answers my next unasked question.

"I wasn't looking for her." I maintain an even tone while I push down the disappointment.

It's not like I'm expecting to sort things out today with her. My main goal is to make sure Mitch and I are still good.

But I still want to catch a glimpse of her.

Ever since I took her phone call, and had her lay it out for me, I knew I'd fucked up. I mean I knew I fucked up the minute I walked out of her place three weeks ago, but hearing the tremble in her voice, and the finality to her words was enough to wake me up and figure out I couldn't lose her.

I couldn't lose them.

"It's one thing to ignore me and walk out of my life."

"Sure you weren't, Hetch." Mitch grins because he thinks Liberty and I are still hiding our involvement with one another.

Jesus, I wish it were so simple.

It's so complicated now that I'm not sure we'll ever get back.

Knowing I can't keep thinking about Liberty while focusing on Mitch, I keep my head in the clear, and concentrate on him and the game I vow to give my all.

Later I will figure out how to win her back.

Now I have to win this one.

Two minutes later, Mitch calls, "Checkmate," and issues a rematch. I take it, and the following two, not because I want to but because I need to.

I have a lot of groveling to do. Both with Mitch and with Liberty.

I just hope Liberty is as forgiving.

* * *

"To being reinstated." Sterling holds up his beer in celebration, once we've settled into the back booth of a hole-in-a-wall pub just outside of town.

"Thanks, man." I reach for my water and tap it against his glass.

"Gonna be good to have you back."

"You have no idea." I place my glass back on the table and take stock of the pub Fox picked out.

I've never been here before. With a décor older than The Elephant, it's bigger in size and subsequently louder.

"Why are we here, again?" My eyes find Fox, Hart, and Tate over by the bar. They're talking to a group of girls, not in the least bit interested in celebrating my new reinstatement.

"You told me you wouldn't go back to The Elephant. We had to find a new place." Sterling shrugs as if it's a perfectly good reason to change our hang out.

While I'm not sure The Elephant is the issue, I just didn't want to risk falling into bad habits.

"You didn't have to do that," I tell him, wondering if we're going to address the issues between us.

"You're the team leader. Can't have team bonding without your ugly mug." He knocks my shoulder, before taking a pull of his beer.

"Sterling, before the boys come back over, I want to tell you how sorry I am." The mood becomes somber with the need to get it all out.

The week has been a whirlwind of commotion, between visiting Mitch yesterday, the force shrink clearing me for duty, and having my team welcome me back with open arms, I may as well get it all out and lay it on the line.

"Hetch, you don't–" He shakes his head, not wanting to hear it.

"Yes, I do." I cut him off before he can let me off the hook. "I've had my head up my ass for so long, and I took our friendship for granted. I know you have my back, and I appreciate everything you've done for me. But I want you to know I don't want you to do it anymore. Okay?" I wait for him to respond, hoping he reads between the lines.

"You want me to kick your ass every time you're an asshole," he jokes, but I know he's listening.

"I want you to do whatever it is you need to do, regardless of our friendship." I don't plan to find myself so fucked-up again, not now when I'm learning how to deal with my issues. But if it ever came down to it, I don't want Sterling risking his ass for me.

"Well, considering you're not gonna find yourself there, we won't have a problem." He doesn't give me the answer I want, but his slight nod tells me he understands.

"Thanks, man." I knock my water to his beer again as Fox, Tate, and Hart join us back in the booth.

"You won't fucking believe who's here." Hart shakes his head, sliding in across from me.

"Who?" Sterling asks, but I don't need to wait for them to tell me. I know who by the way all three of them are watching me.

Liberty.

Did the fuckers set this up? What are the chances of meeting her out of town? Who is she here with?

The desperate knot in my stomach tightens. The questions swarming my mind only serve to second-guess my resolve.

"She here alone?" My jaw locks, waiting for the answer.

"She's with a group of girls."

Thank God.

"Have you spoken to her yet?" Fox inquires while I search her out.

Fuck, it's the question of the week.

"I'm working on it," I tell them, unsure exactly how I'm working on it. After hanging with Mitch yesterday for three hours, I was disappointed to find Liberty didn't come back from the store. Knowing she wasn't going to show up while I was there, I gave up waiting and told Mitch I'd be back in a couple of days.

"Well, you have the perfect chance now." Tate nods toward the booth they're sitting in, giving up their location.

Not giving one fuck what the boys think of my lack of self-respect, I turn to get a better view and take her in. Chest expanding, pulse quickening.

Fuck me, I almost forgot how beautiful she is.

Her blonde hair is down tonight, just the way I like it. The mess of curls perfected in a tidy way. Red lips that have haunted my dreams are spread into a wide smile as she laughs at something Payton says.

Fuck, I'm the biggest fucking dickhead to walk this earth.

She is mine.

All fucking mine.

And I left her.

I was wrong thinking I was doing the right thing by walking away from her. All I did was delay the inevitable.

She's *it* for me, and even if it still scares me a little, as God as my witness, I am prepared to do anything to make it right.

Beg.

Grovel.

Fight dirty.

She is mine, and fuck, I need to claim her back.

LIBERTY

"Here's to my sabbatical, take two." I raise my fifth shot for the night, bring it to my lips, and throw my head back. The amber liquid stopped burning after the third shot, my tongue and throat numb to the elixir.

"Didn't you learn your lesson last time you subjected yourself to that horrid idea?" Fee slams her glass down on the table and motions the waitress for another round.

"What? Icansoooooodoitthistime." My words roll together in a jumble of barely distinguishable syllables.

"Girl, you're so drunk, you think you can take on the world." Sophie nudges beside me, cradling the same drink for over an hour.

She lucked out and was dubbed designated driver.

"I'm not drunk!" I yell. I think I'm offended or maybe winded.

Okay, maybe on my way to being drunk.

Each shot Fee feeds me offers me a new lease on life. A new kind of promise.

No men.

No sex.

No Hetch.

"Lib, you just downed your seventh shot." Payton giggles and I giggle along with her.

"Shit. Okay, I think I am drunk." I quickly take stock of my bearings. We're at some pub Payton dragged me to. What was meant to be one celebratory drink, has turned into not five, like I originally thought, but seven.

"Isn't it great? You were all tense and uptight, and now you haven't a care in the world." Payton, oblivious to my sobering state at the mention of my troubles, wistfully smiles and reaches for her cocktail.

I'm about to tell her I'm still a little tense about my exchange with Hetch yesterday when a tall glass of water is delivered to our table and placed down in front of me.

"Ahh, what's this?" My curiosity piqued, I look up at the pretty waitress.

"I thought you could do with some water." She offers a smile, one I don't know how to read before she turns and walks back toward the bar.

What the heck?

"I think you have an admirer." Fee's eyes dance along with her brows, the insinuation the woman has a thing for me dangles in front of me.

"What? No way," I refute, but still turn my head to see if there is some truth to Fee's words. The waitress doesn't pay me any more attention, going about her shift like I'm not even on her radar.

"Well, this is weird." Payton laughs, confused like me. I eye the glass of water wondering what the hell she's up to. Why did she only bring me water, and not the rest of them? I mean, sure, I'm a *little* drunk, but I'm not dancing on the table.

I'm still eyeing the glass when my phone vibrates in front of me. Turning it over, my chest constricts when I see Hetch's name flash across the screen in a text.

Hetch: *Drink the water.*

It takes a few calming breaths, and an internal pep talk to realize he sent the water over, and in turn, is here in the same pub.
Crap.

Me: *Thanks, but I'm good.*

I manage to type back, before casually looking around to find him. See, I'm not that drunk if I can still text efficiently.
A burst of adrenaline rushes through me when three dots dance in the bottom left-hand corner telling me he's typing.

Hetch: *Don't be difficult. You're drunk, and there are at least five fuckers around you waiting to pounce.*

This time, I don't hide my blatant searching.
Where the hell is he?
My eyes scan the bar hoping to spot him. When I only find three seedy men eyeing me off, I quickly type out another reply.

Me: *Why does it matter to you?*

My inner sass comes out full force.
"Who are you talking to?" Fee notices my strange behavior, before Hetch can reply.
"Ahh, Mom. She's checking in," I lie, forcing my eyes not to stray. Taking my lie for the truth, the girls go back to talking about a new store they found over in the mall, while I hold my phone in a death grip, bullying it to come to life.
It only takes a few seconds for it to happen.

Hetch: *Don't be a fool.*

My fingers tap hard on the touch screen, my head shaking at his audacity.

Me: *You did not just call me a fool.*

I don't know how I ever fell in love with this frustrating man. Three weeks of no contact and he calls *me* a fool.
The ass.

Hetch: *I think I did, sweetheart.*

Seeing the word has the same loosening effect on my resolve.
A lingering want. A fluttering need.
I have to stay strong.
A few simple text messages are not going to sway me.

Me: *Don't call me that either.*

Hetch: *Drink your water.*

Me: *I think I'm good!*

Hetch: *Liberty*

Me: *I'm not doing this with you. Leave me alone.*

I lock down my phone and my resolve and place them both on the table out of reach.
For a few intense minutes of trying to absorb the conversation happening around me, I manage to hold back from reaching out and checking if he replied. But when compulsion wins out, and curiosity taunts me, I give in and reach for the phone.
Disappointment clenches my stomach and defeat burns my throat when I find the screen empty.
Seriously, I feel like I have whiplash.
I'm about to shut the damn thing down completely and put

it in my purse when it vibrates in my hand.

Hetch: *You're killing me here, sweetheart.*

Me: *What am I doing?*

I type out too eagerly, but clearly, I'm not too concerned about my quick reaction when I hit send. HIs own reply comes back instantly.

Hetch: *Drink the water.*

Knowing we're only going to keep going back and forth, I give in. Reaching for the glass and in dramatic fashion, I raise it in the air—high enough for him to see where ever he is—then bring it to my lips and down it in one large gulp.

"Okay, I think we should probably get her home." Sophie hands me a napkin when I realize I let a little water spill out the side of my mouth.

"What? No, we haven't danced yet," Payton sulks. It's almost identical to one of her daughter's pouts.

"Yeah, I'm not ready to go," I tell them, though not because I want to dance like Payton. I'm not ready to stop talking to Hetch.

Even if it's only via text, he's finally engaging with me now and honestly, I don't want it to end.

Sophie is about to argue some more when my phone vibrates again.

Hetch: *Thank you, sweetheart.*

My mouth moves into a grin before I can control it.

"Seriously, who are you talking to?" Fee reaches across the table and snatches the phone out of my hands.

"Fee, give it back!" I react, but she's too quick. Her body leans back and curves out of my reach.

"Fee," I try again, stretching my arm out further. Knowing

254

I'm close, she raises the phone at arm's length above her head and continues to read through my messages.

"Oh, my God! Hetch is here." Her eyes whip around the pub, searching him out like I did only a few moments ago.

"Hetch is here?" Payton turns in her seat, following Fee's gaze.

"Give me my phone back, Fee." I don't bother answering Payton. My main goal is to stay calm against my rising panic and retrieve my phone.

"What's he doing here? Is he following you?" Payton stands, trying to get a better look.

Seriously, I'm going to fucking kill her.

"Ohh, you have another text." My mouth dries and my hand tingles while she reads it over. "He says, Fee, give Liberty the phone back."

I don't have a chance to laugh like Pay and Sophie, my panic still barreling forward when Fee starts typing out a reply.

"Don't, Fee." The words are a plea, one she doesn't heed, so I stand, ready to crawl across the table to grab my phone if I have to.

"Fee," Sophie warns, "give it back to her." It's barely a reprimand, laced with no anger and definitely not a threat, but Fee must see something in it, something big enough for her to stop typing and reluctantly hand it over.

"Fine, you're no fun." It's her turn to sulk. She slides my phone across the table, and I reach out, snatching it back.

"This isn't a joke, Fee. It's my life."

My phone vibrates again, cutting off her reply. And like an addict scoring a fix, I briefly close my eyes and allow the thrill of this soothe me.

Jesus, I think I need help.

Hetch: *Meet me near the restroom.*

Every muscle down to my toes flexes ready to stand and meet him, but something stops me.

My heart.

Am I ready to see him?

It's one thing to engage with him via text, but it's another to see him face to face.

"What's he saying now?" Sophie asks, but unlike Fee, her query is gentle, not mocking.

"He wants me to meet him." I glance around again, still unable to find him.

"Ohh, a booty call," Fee teases, not understanding the seriousness of our issues.

Of Hetch's issues.

"Seriously, Fee. Shut up." I stand, not in the mood for her judgmental juvenile bullshit. Fee shifts uncomfortably in her chair, while a heavy silence, thicker than my own frustration, settles over the table.

There's no logic to my irritation with her. I know she doesn't get it; it's who she is. Fee can always find a way to inject her unique humor into anything with her smart mouth, and normally I can take it. Normally, it doesn't rattle me. But tonight, she hit her mark.

Is Hetch only looking for a hookup?

Realizing the night is getting away from me, I direct my eyes down at Sophie.

"Can you take me home, Soph–?"

"Lib." Fee cuts me off. "I'm sorry. I didn't mean anything by it." Her apology seems genuine, but I'm done.

"Come on, Lib. Sit down." Payton tries this time, but it's one of those moments where there isn't a way to come back from it.

Not right away.

"It's fine, Fee. I just don't think making a joke out of my situation is funny." I don't make eye contact, knowing it's going to upset me to see her hurt by my coldness. "You guys can stay. I can take a cab if you're not ready to go, Sophie."

"No, I'll take you. You're sure, though?" She thinks I'm leaving because of Fee, but the truth is it's not Fee who has me running.

It's Hetch.

I'm not ready to see him.

Just like yesterday when I discovered he was coming to visit Mitch. I ran.

"Yeah, I'm sure." I reach for my bag, tucking it under my arm, then lean down and kiss Payton's cheek.

"Thanks for getting me out. It helped." It's a lie, one I offer anyway because I know she's disappointed I'm leaving early.

"Message me when you get home." She stands and gives me a hug. Glancing briefly at Fee, I watch her slide out the booth, coming to stand in front of me when Payton steps away.

"I'm an asshole, you know? I feel terrible you're leaving." She wraps me up in her arms and squeezes hard.

"You are an asshole, but I still love you." I return her hug and then let her go.

"You guys have a good night," I tell them before following Sophie out to the car.

Not risking a peek around me, and with my phone carefully locked away in my purse, I have no idea if Hetch knows I'm leaving.

Is he waiting for me? Will he be upset with me? Should I have gone to him? The questions roll over and over, each one casting more doubt over my need to run.

It's not until Sophie pulls up at the front of my place I see him pull in behind her. He followed me home.

"You want me to stay?" Sophie's eyes track Hetch when he exits his truck and hangs back, waiting for me.

He looks good, too good.

Dark jeans, tight Henley, five o'clock shadow. He stands tall, legs apart, arms crossed over his chest. I almost smile at how strong and handsome he looks until I remember he broke my heart.

"I have to talk to him at some point, right?" I lean over and kiss her cheek good-bye. "I'll be fine." I offer what I hope to be a reassuring nod and then exit her car.

She idles in the drive for another minute or two, before taking me for my word and backing out. Not ready to turn, I stay unmoving, my back to Hetch, my eyes on the retreating red taillights of Sophie's car.

Finally, when the lights fade to nothing, the car no longer in sight, I force a reassuring breath, turn, and make my way up to my apartment.

I don't make eye contact with him, unsure of what I can say. I almost expect him to ignore me until he calls out, ruining my easy getaway.

"Liberty." His voice travels across the darkened parking lot and wraps around me like I imagine his arms want to. "Can we talk?"

"Oh, you're ready to talk?" I spin around with the same amount of grace a three-hundred-pound linebacker would have on a balancing beam.

"Sweetheart, I know you're angry, but I just want to explain." He risks a step closer to me, and like a caged animal, I react.

"For three weeks I've been sitting around waiting for you to explain." I sweep my arm out in front of me, my finger slicing through the air. It's almost like I have no control of my limbs. No control over my words.

"Every day wondering where you were, if you were okay. I called, messaged, and knocked, and you ignored me." He takes another step closer, but I don't stop. I won't stop. I can't stop. I've been allowing my anger to fester for so long I need a release.

"I wasn't asking for much, Hetch. Just to know you were okay. I was worried. Fuck, I thought you were going to do something stupid." I hate the shake in my voice, hate I even had the thought. Hate the heated flush of rage that covers my body from the inside out. But I was there. I held the man while he cried for his father. "Jesus, I had your mom and your sister out looking for you. Do you even care how sick to the stomach I've been? Do you care I couldn't eat for days?"

"Baby, I fucked up." He brings a shaky hand out in front of him like he's worried I'm going to make a run for it and he needs to approach with care.

"Yeah, you fucked up. You fucked up so badly, I'm not sure you can fix it." He's in front of me now. My pulse is speeding and my muscles quiver, and in a brief moment of clarity, I see my own fear reflected back at me.

"Please don't say that, baby." His hands cup my jaw, holding me steady in his grasp. I want to slap him away, scream at him not to touch me, but the warmth from his touch anchors me there. The gentleness of his voice, robbing me of any more fight.

"Say anything you want, but don't say we can't fix us." His eyes glass over, like the lake down behind my parents' house in the middle of February, and it's a stark contrast to the warmth I've grown to love.

"You left, Hetch." I fight the wobble in my chin, the crack in my resolve. "You left me after you begged me never to leave you." This time, I can't control it. Over three weeks of anguish holding me hostage, finally pours out of me. I lash out, hitting him against his hard chest, releasing my anger and my heartache.

Hetch doesn't move, just stands there, taking everything I give: every hit, every word, every tear. It's not until my head becomes too heavy, and my sobs too quiet do I realize he has me in his arms, holding me steady from my own volatile storm.

"I'm sorry, I—" I start to pull away, his embrace too much for my broken heart, but like my soul, his arms don't allow it.

"I hate I did this to us, Liberty. But I'm here now, and I'm not leaving again. I'm fighting for you. Fighting for us. Can't you see?" A calmness settles between us, yet uncertainty still churns viciously around us. We're stuck in the eye of the storm. One wrong move here could tear both of us apart, destroying everything we had and could have been in its wake.

"Hetch, I nee—" I start to say, attempting to fight against my own wants.

"Whatever you need, sweetheart."

"I need some time." My words are the resistance my body doesn't want to hear. Seconds seem to drag into minutes, and like a criminal serving time, I feel each and every one of them.

"Then time is what you'll have, sweetheart."

A simple promise with a simple concept.

Time.

It all comes down to time.

A temporal length of an event or an entity's existence, period. I'm not sure how it's going to end, nor do I know for certain the duration of us, or the continuance of him and me, but judging by his curt nod and set jaw, he has a plan.

And I don't expect any less of him. After all, having a course of action and being able to see the big picture in order to focus on the outcome is Hetch's specialty.

Different scenario, but the same strategy.

Something tells me I'm not going to stand a chance.

I am his end goal.

Hetch will find a way to cement his way back into my life.

I just don't know how or when.

HETCH

"What the hell do we need to go there for?" Fox grumbles beside me after I tell him to head to Cherry Lane Flowers across town.

"Why else do you visit a fucking flower shop, Fox?" I try to keep my patience in check, but after four hours with Fox and his perpetual mood, I'm not doing too well.

The minute I turned up for my first shift back and discovered I was patrolling with Fox instead of Sterling, my partially good mood was in jeopardy.

"So, you're still groveling like a fucking puppy?" He thinks we're heading to Cherry Lane to order flowers for Liberty, but he would be wrong. The flowers are for my mom. Not only have I been a stupid fool with Liberty for the better half of a month, but I've also been a dick to my mom.

For three years.

From ignoring her calls months on end and missing

memorials for my dad, to letting her knock on my door for hours only to leave her on the other side begging me to let her in. Thinking back on those moments, I wish I had answered the phone, showed up on the dreaded anniversary, but most of all opened the door and let her in. Maybe if I had let her in, the one person who hurt like me, I wouldn't have pushed everyone else I love away.

Maybe I would have let Liberty in from the get go.

"They're not for her." I don't know why I clarify. Fox doesn't need to know I've not only fucked up with Liberty, but I've also fucked up in every aspect.

My mom. My sister. My job.

"So, you've sorted things out with Liberty then?" he presses, like every other time he's tried to engage with me today.

"I didn't say that."

It's only been two days since I promised Liberty space. Two days since I stood there, holding her in my arms while she laid into me. Two days of trying to figure out how I'm going to fix this mess I've put us in. I wish I knew what I was doing. If I could go back to the night I walked out on her, I would. But I can't. And now I don't know what to do. I'm torn. Part of me wants to march over there and demand she let's me back into her life, but the other part—the part that's scared I'm going to lose her completely—has me holding back. I have to figure out what she needs from me to trust me again.

"Well, in that case, maybe you should open your wallet up a little wider and order two bouquets of flowers." Fox, oblivious to my inner turmoil, continues to play with me.

"Liberty's not the kind of woman you win over with flowers." I reject his jab. If my fuck-ups were fixed by a simple bouquet of flowers, I'd have dropped into Walmart for a ten-dollar bunch last week when she ripped me a new one about not showing up for Mitch.

No, I need more.

Something deeper.

I need to be smart here and think this through before making my move.

"Well, you got me there," he agrees, clicking his tongue. "So, what *are* you doing to win her back?" The question is loaded. Careful, but also challenging.

"I haven't figured it out yet."

"Figures." He laughs outright, and I weigh up the dangers of what a blow to his arm while traveling at eighty miles down the freeway might cause.

Too much danger. I'll get the prick later.

"Shut the fuck up, Fox. Like you have any better advice." It may be an insult, but it also may be my way of prodding. Either way, I'm not about to admit I'm hoping he will share some sage advice.

"I'll have you know I was very romantic when I was married." He takes my bait, and the downtown loop exit, driving us closer to our destination.

"She turned out to be a bitch, so I stopped." It's my turn to laugh now. He shoots me a look that tells me while he may prefer to be rudimentary, there is well-hidden charm in there somewhere.

"Okay, so what the fuck should I be doing?" I swallow my pride and finally ask for help. I've always been the type of person who's never been comfortable asking for things. Before I started seeing Dr. Anderson, I would have shut down this line of conversation, but if I have learned anything in the last three weeks, it's that asking for help isn't a sign of weakness. Isolating myself for self-preservation doesn't work. I needed help, in any form.

"You need to remind her why she fell in love with you. Show her you're willing to do anything she wants." The concept sounds simple, but there is one fundamental flaw.

"Yeah, well it's hard to remind her of anything if she won't talk to me." I cringe, recalling how the last two nights I've resorted to talking to her through our bedroom wall. She hasn't acknowledged me yet. But I'm not giving up.

"Patience is overrated, Hetch. Stop being a pussy. Just claim her back."

Just claim her back?

That's all he has?

"We're not talking about a lost piece of property here, Fox. We're talking about my woman. The woman I hurt."

"The woman fell in love with your demanding ass, didn't she? She *thinks* she wants time. She doesn't know what she wants."

He has a fair point. I did manage to get her in my bed by claiming what's mine, but this is different. This is about respecting what Liberty needs. Sure, I've wanted and needed things so desperately before that I've taken them without any worry or repercussions, but there's a saying my father used to quote, "You get the chicken by hatching the egg, not by smashing it."

Pushing Liberty too fast would smash everything we have. I'm not willing to do it, no matter how desperate I may seem.

"She won't go for it. I need something else. I need to prove to her I'm serious."

I wait for his wise words, but they don't come.

"Are you serious?" His words are dragged out, each one enunciated clearly. Not because he's unsure of the question, but because he wants the question to be heard. "Or is this some pussy you've got your head messed up with?"

"Fuck you, asshole." This time, I do punch his shoulder, the cruiser only shifting a little unsteadily from the impact. Fox curses before righting his arms back on the steering wheel.

"Don't talk about my woman's pussy ever again, fucker." He doesn't have a chance to reply before the radio crackles with a code ten SWAT pre-call up and our conversation comes to a grinding halt. Fox turns the SUV away from the direction of Cherry Lane Flowers, heading straight to where we're needed.

It looks like Mom isn't getting flowers today.

And I'm not getting any advice.

And now, I'm back to square one.

* * *

264

"You still awake, sweetheart?" I ask the wall, hoping tonight is the night she replies. It's a few days after my first shift with Fox. I just finished my weekly session with Dr. Anderson, and even though I'm drained from working a ten-hour shift, and surviving the one-hour session with the doctor, I still find myself wanting to talk to Liberty more than anyone else.

"I know you're there, sweetheart. I can hear your breathing from here."

"Hetch, I'm really tired tonight." Her voice is low and trails slowly, revealing her presence behind a wall that's been acting as her emotional barricade. I sit up and move closer. It's the sign I've been waiting for, a small step in the right direction.

"How long are we going to keep this up?" I ask, wondering how much more I have in me. I need to find a happy medium here. Liberty needs time but at the risk of jeopardizing everything, not too much time.

"Hetch, I told you, I need some time. You can't push this." It's a deflection if I ever heard one.

Knowing I'm not going to get her this way, I'll try to hit her from a different angle.

"Do you remember the night I saved your life? You know, after I risked my own killing that huge spider for you?"

"I remember it differently, but yeah." There's a lightness to her tone, one I've missed so fucking much.

"I told you I had you figured out."

My mind tracks back to the night in question, replaying the encounter over in my head.

"Yeah, what do you know?" She folds her arms over her chest and waits for me to elaborate.

"I know what sounds you make when you're lying in your bed at night playing with yourself."

"You said something to me. Do you remember?" I pull myself out of my recap.

"Yeah."

"What did you say to me, B?" I'm on the edge of my bed now. Hand to wall, I try to make any connection with her I can while I wait for her answer.

"I don't know." She's hesitant in her reply. I know she's lying; the shake in her voice a dead giveaway.

"Yes, you do. Like me, I know you remember every word. So humor me, sweetheart."

"I said you know nothing." She caves and the statement is becoming appropriate now. I have no idea about anything anymore, but I refuse to let it stop me from getting back what is mine.

"Right. And then I said, I might not know everything yet, but I know the important stuff." The wall stays silent as I figure out where I'm going with this. "Ask me what I know now, Liberty." A plan starts forming, one I hope works.

"What do you know, Hetch?" Irritation laces her question rather than arousal like it did all those weeks ago. Disappointment treks its sorry ass back to me.

You fucking dumb shit.

"I know I've never loved anyone as much as I love you." I let my confession hang in the air. Let the truth give us something to work with. "But I fucked up. I hurt you. You're the last person I ever want to hurt. I know I'm haunted by my past, but when I'm with you, you take it all away. And most of all, Liberty, I know time is what you *think* you want, but it's not what you need." It's Fox's cocky statement, but it doesn't mean it's not the truth.

She doesn't respond, her silence speaking louder than denial.

"I'm giving you a week," I state plainly, deciding what's best for us. I'm not smashing the egg; I'm adding extra warmth to move things along.

"That's not how this is meant to work." She fights it, of course, but I can hear the quake in her voice and my excitement spikes.

"A week, Liberty."

Then I am coming for her.

"One week and then you're mine."

266

LIBERTY

Hetch: *I know you're hurting, and I know I caused you this hurt. If I could take it all away, I'd do it in a second.*

I read the text over, memorizing every single word he says, and stressing over every single word he doesn't.

If I could take it all away, I'd do it in a second.

It's not the first text I've received in the last few days. They started the night after he told me I had one week.

At first, I thought they were a little cheesy; I mean we've been there, done that, the night at the pub. But I played along regardless. Gave him his play, and ever since, I haven't been able to stop reading them. Every day this week, I've received an "*I know*" message. And every day, he picks at my resistance and cracks my determination.

Hetch: *I know you want to talk to me, but you're too stubborn to cave. I love that about you.*

Another text comes through. Another crack in my resolve.

Jesus, he's right. I am too stubborn. I was stubborn when I asked for time. I didn't want to put this distance between us.

So why did I ask for it?

Because you didn't think he would give it to you.

Hetch: *I also know I love the way you're scared of tiny spiders, but you're the strongest woman I've met.*

He hits me again. My reluctance wavers, and in its place, a new kind of want forms.

I'm ready for more.

I'm ready to take him back.

Closing my eyes, I hold my breath and prepare myself to respond, but before I can be sucked back into his vortex, I'm abruptly interrupted.

"I'm worried about Mitch."

The four words are as effective as being doused in ice-cold water.

"Why, what's wrong?" I look up from my phone to find Sue in the kitchen, standing at the opposite end of the breakfast bar.

I had come in here to get something to eat, but Hetch's texts disrupted me. Now I'm so flustered, I've lost my appetite.

"We found this in his room today. Had it hidden in a tear in his mattress." She steps around the breakfast bar, stopping an arm's length away from me and hands me a small pocketknife.

Jesus.

"You confronted him?" I turn the knife over in my hand, taking a closer look.

"Yeah, and that's what I'm worried about. When we asked him why he had it, he wouldn't tell me. Just said he needed it for protection."

"From his brother?"

"He didn't say, but who else would have him scared?" The implication that Dominic is a part of this seems fitting. I'm just not sure we see it right.

"Hetch said Dominic and his crew moved underground when they raided one of his places. It could be someone else, someone his brother is mixed up with." Jesus, I don't know what's worse: Dominic still threatening Mitch or someone else who's out to get revenge.

"Well, either way, we need to keep a close eye on him. When I took it off him, he lost it. Said he can't leave the house without it. I've never seen him like this."

"Okay, I'll have a word with him today." I place the knife in my pocket, making a mental note to lock it away in my office so no one else can find it, and make a call to his caseworker before my shift ends. "Maybe I can get him to open up to me about what's going on."

"Or maybe you could have a word with Hetch. I know he's been coming around a lot more. Maybe he might have something else to offer. He may be able to reach Mitch in a way neither one of us can."

My body locks at the sound of his name.

"Ahh, yeah," I ease out, hoping she didn't notice the change in me at his name. "It can't hurt to involve him, give him a more active role as a mentor around here. I'll have a word with him, see what he thinks." I step away from her, effectively ending the conversation of Hetch. My earlier need resurfacing right now is not what I need.

"Okay, I'm leading rec time today. I better get out there."

She walks out without a backward glance, leaving me alone with too many thoughts and too many concerns.

Later in my shift, another text comes through. I contemplate ignoring it, but curiosity gets the better of me.

Hetch: *I know you don't want to hear this, but my cock is hard for you right now, thinking about the last time I had you.*

Seriously, I'm screwed.

31

HETCH

"Hetch?" The knock comes through the wall unexpectedly, causing a spike in my heart rate. I just got home after a long twelve-hour shift where my SWAT team were smashed with high-risk arrest warrants most of the day. After receiving an elbow to the jaw from some cracked-up meth head, my head still pounds, and my body aches from tackling said meth head down a flight of stairs. But as much as I want to sleep for the next two days straight, the sound of my name coming through the wall takes every one of my issues away.

"Yeah, sweetheart?" I sit up in my bed and move closer to the wall. Normally. I'm the one who instigates these talks, but something tells me after my risqué text today, she's finally coming around. Perhaps knowing I still get a hard-on for her was all she needed to hear?

"Do you ever have days where you think you don't know what the hell you're doing?" Her voice is quiet, unsure, and a

270

little unsteady.

"Ha, you do know who you're talking to, right?"

She lets out a shaky laugh before clearing her throat. "I'm serious, Hetch."

"What's going on, Liberty?" There's a pause on her end before she replies.

"I'm worried about Mitch. He's pulling away, and I don't know what to do."

"What's been happening?"

"Sue found a pocketknife in his room today. When she took it off him, he freaked out, said it was for protection."

"You think his brother is pressing him?" I don't doubt he might try, but with an arrest warrant out for him, the dickhead would be stupid to try anything.

"He said he isn't, but I don't know if I believe him. I think he's hiding something."

"Sometimes you just have to trust they will come to you when they need you, Lib. He's not a kid, you know? He's a young man, and if he's going to make something of himself, you need to realize he has to make mistakes, and he has to learn from them."

"He had a pocketknife, Hetch." I understand her concern, but I only spoke to Mitch two days ago. We had our normal one-on-one time; and like all our other sessions, he was polite and talked about school with ease. He assured me his brother hadn't been hassling him.

"So did I at that age. And I lived at home with my parents. He lives in a group home setting. You have to realize these boys are never going to be normal teenagers. They're bound to slip up, most kids do."

"I know. It's just, I–I don't know. I'm probably over thinking it. I worry about him."

"I know you do. It's one of your strengths, but also one of your weaknesses."

"What's that supposed to mean?" I can't see her face, but I can just imagine it pinched, eyebrows raised in a "how dare you say that" way.

271

"You know what it means, B. It's great you care. I love that about you. But sometimes I worry you're too close. My dad was the same with his kids when he was a youth counselor. He'd become so invested, they were almost as important to him as Kota and I were." I pause, amazed I didn't freeze up. "It didn't upset us, but sometimes I wondered why he cared so much when he had his own family."

"You know, that's the first time I've ever heard you talk freely about your dad," she states cautiously, and I can hear she's unsure if she should even bring it up.

"Yeah, well, the quack I've been seeing seems to be helping." My laugh is forced, uneasiness weighing my body down.

"You're seeing someone?" Her tone is hopeful, and I can't help feel it along with her.

"Yeah, it's helping. A lot."

"I'm glad, Hetch. That's really good."

"I'm trying hard here, sweetheart," I offer all I can.

"Will you tell me about him? Your dad, I mean." I don't answer right away, too busy focusing on my raised heartbeat and trying to ease it.

"Ahh, what do you want to know?" I answer when I've managed to clear my throat, and push down my anxiety.

"What was his name?"

It's a simple question. Easy enough to answer, but still, it takes a few beats before I can.

"Samuel. Sam for short." The same ache that's rooted deep within me whenever I think about him starts to throb. Only this time, I'm not going to bury it. Instead, I'm going to let myself feel it, allow myself to mourn. If I've learned anything in my sessions with Dr. Anderson, it's that death is something you never heal from. Unlike how a scab heals, or a scar fades, the absence of someone you love never disappears. His death will be a part of my life forever, a part of me. And if I want to prove to Liberty I'm the man she deserves, then I need to let it be a part of us too.

"Dad wanted to name me Sam Junior, but Mom wanted Liam. Clearly, Mom won. Samuel is my middle name, though. I guess they both kind of won."

"Yet, both of you went by Hetch?"

"Yeah. He just wanted his kid to have the same name. Mom never understood it. I thought it was cool."

"I wish I could have met him," she whispers, and all of a sudden, I do too. Wish he could have met the woman who changed my life, who pulled me out of my own darkness and forced me to see the light.

"Me too, sweetheart. He would have liked you. Not because of your job, just you as a person."

"Thank you for calming me down." She doesn't ask anything else about my dad, and I'm neither relieved nor disappointed. I'm content.

"No problem, I charge by the hour."

She laughs at my response, and my gut tightens at the sound. My joke, though lame, makes her laugh that carefree laugh of hers I haven't heard in what seems like forever, so I can't be too embarrassed with myself.

"I should get to sleep. I have an early day tomorrow." Disappointment floats over me, but I don't let it show.

"Miss you, B." She doesn't reply right away, so I press on. "You don't have to tell me you miss me too. I know you do."

"You're incorrigible."

"I'm right. Admit it."

"Goodnight, Hetch." She ignores my bait, but I don't let her get away too easily.

"Only one more day, Liberty," I warn, wishing it would hurry the fuck up.

One more day and she is mine.

* * *

"The boys and I are heading to The Elephant after this. You in or has your woman taken you back finally?" Sterling asks the following afternoon. We're sitting in the staff room at SWAT

273

headquarters. After a full shift of training today, we were getting ready to call it a day when we were called in by the lieutenant for an impromptu meeting.

No reasons were given.

"I'll come for one drink. Then I'm out." It's the last thing I want to do tonight, but after my first full week back with the team, I should try and make an effort to hang with them outside of work.

"So, she hasn't taken ya back then?" Tate sticks his jab in. "You're losing your touch, boss."

"Shut the fuck up," I growl. Yes, growl, because sitting around waiting for some bullshit meeting is pissing me off.

"Jesus, I think she's broken you," Sterling comments just as the lieutenant steps into the room.

"Hetcherson, we're ready for you." His eyes only come to me and even as he keeps his stare on me, it's unreadable.

"Coming." I stand and nod for the boys to follow me.

"You know what this is about?" Hart asks as we make our way down to the briefing room.

"Nope. I'm as clueless as you," I tell him before stepping into the room we use for briefings before call outs.

"Sergeant, you remember Detective Katie Marsh from organized crime division." The lieutenant motions to the redhead at the head of the briefing table.

"Good to see you again, Katie." I keep my annoyance out of my voice. Her presence here tonight means she has a job for us, and as much as I love the thrill of taking down whichever crime boss she has her sights set on, irritation bubbles just below the surface. It looks like my grand plans of knocking on Liberty's wall one last time are going to have to wait.

"Yeah, I'm not sure you'll be happy to see me after this." She clicks a button on the small remote in her hand and brings up the case file on the large monitor.

"Nah, we're always happy to see you." Hart enters the conversation, taking the seat closest to her, and I catch Katie's slight blush.

Hmm, interesting.

"Right. Okay, well, we don't have much time, so let's get started." She shakes her head as if she's clearing something from her mind and moves her eyes back to mine. "We've been gathering intel on Miguel Morales for a couple of months now." She hands me his file and continues. "Morales started out a low-level drug dealer, cooking in the basement of his mom's house. Over the last six months, he's risen up and got ahead in the game by producing an identical, recognizable, and reliable product to match his competitors at a fraction of the cost."

"Making him a major player in the drug underworld," I murmur, checking over his rap sheet. Other than a few misdemeanors, they have nothing on him.

"A major player with no ties to any organization. He's a one-man show and making a killing."

"Okay, so why the sudden move now?" I press on, wondering what they have on him to warrant a risky bust with no planning.

"He's stepping up to the next level. Joining forces with Anton Gibson." She pushes another file across the table to me. "You might know him. The leader of The Disciples." The man Dominic answers to. *Fuck.*

"Yeah, we know him."

"Anton has caught on to Miguel's way of business and wants in. With ties to international crime syndicates, Anton is a major player in heroin and gun trafficking in this area, making him one hell of an asset to someone like Miguel."

"That happens?" I can't imagine two heads of crime joining together.

"We've seen it happen a lot. Groups with diverging interests, goals, and philosophies are working together to capitalize on each other's specific skills or assets."

"So who's our target here? Miguel or Anton?"

"Both. A meet like this is a one-time deal."

"When does it go down?" I ask, placing Anton's file back down.

"Tonight in a nightclub over in Morningston." She clicks on her remote, pulling up the blueprints of the nightclub on the

275

screen.

"How much are we talking?"

"Street value is in the millions."

Jesus, this is huge.

"The meet will go down in this room." She points to a back room on the bottom level. "Two entrances, here and here." She moves her finger to the entry door from inside the club and to the exit that leads out to the street. "You guys will come in through here."

"It's Saturday night. The club will be packed. How do we keep it contained?" Sterling enters the conversation when he sees how close the entry door is to what looks like a dance floor.

"Inside will be covered with my undercover agents keeping watch. My informant will be manning the internal door. We give him the signal to lock it from the outside, automatically eliminating the entry as a possible exit."

"And how reliable is this CI?" Fox asks the question running through my mind. It's all well and good to base a raid on this information, but we need to know we aren't walking into a trap.

"Dominic Westin." She pulls up a picture of Mitch's brother, and my heart constricts in my chest. *What the fuck?*

"Yeah, told you, you wouldn't be happy." She tracks my expression.

"You're telling me Dominic Westin is your informant? He's a street level thug." I can't believe this shit. No wonder we haven't been able to get a hold of him over the last few weeks.

"He *was* street level. But he's been moving up the ranks. He came to me six weeks ago with talks of a big deal happening."

"And you trust him?" I scoff, not believing it.

"He's given me no reason not to. The information he's fed us the last few weeks is more than we could hope for, and he is the one who brought this meet to our attention."

"And what is Dominic getting for this information exactly?"

"We get what we need, he gets probation and is asking for visitation rights with his brother."

"No, not happening." I stand, pushing back my chair. This is the last thing Mitch needs.

276

"Sergeant," my lieutenant warns from across the room.

"His brother is off limits." I shake my head as I sit back down, forcing myself to stay calm.

"I'm sorry, Liam. It's a done deal. We get these guys, then we're ultimately disabling two drug rings at the same time. And I honestly believe him when he says he wants to get out of the game and turn over a new leaf."

"Yeah, turning over a new leaf my ass. He was only pressing his kid brother to join his crew two months ago. He attacked my woman and had her place broken into." I shift in my chair, growing more irritated by the second.

"He was trying to keep him protected. He still has to play the part."

"Bullshit. His brother is scared out of his fucking mind of him."

"And that's the way we wanted to play it. Until he realized he had you around, he wanted eyes on him. When you situated yourself in his brother's life, he backed off. Listen, I know you don't know him like I do, but trust me, he wants out, Liam. I'm giving him a chance."

The room sits in silence for a beat while I work through this change of events.

Jesus, how is this going to affect Mitch? I'm not the type of person to keep anyone apart from their family, but can we trust Dominic?

"Is this going to be a problem for you, Sergeant Hetcherson?" Detective Marsh asks when the seconds click over to minutes.

"Not at all," I respond as nonchalantly as I can when it's the complete opposite of what I'm thinking.

Fucking A it is, my mind screams, but I push the thoughts away. Later, I'll sort this out.

"Good. Then we have four hours. Let's get started."

* * *

277

"Okay, listen up, boys. It's been a long night, but we've got this. Stick to the plan, quiet feet in. Tate and Hart, you're on the two men arming the doors. Fox, we want an explosive entry, and then we move." I reposition my rifle across my chest and then lower my goggles down over my eyes, adrenalin pumping through my veins.

"Copy that, boss."

"10.4," is relayed back as the last of the boys fall into line.

Tate, first. Followed by Hart, Fox, and Sterling while I take up the rear.

"Team One is in position. Waiting for a go," I whisper into my com.

"Stand by." Detective Marsh comes through my earpiece. "We're waiting on confirmation for the locked door."

I wait for a beat, then another before the order comes through.

"Confirming door is locked. Door is locked." It's all we need to take action and in two seconds, we're moving.

"Go, go, go, go, go!" We move together as one unit, descending on the two bodyguards. Before they have a chance to reach for their weapons, Hart and Tate pull them out of the line of sight to waiting officers.

"On my count of three, we go," I whisper, my fingers counting down the beats.

Three. Two. One.

Fox, knowing what he needs to do, rams the door once and throws in the flash bang.

It's the same drill every time: Fox moves to the left. Sterling to the right, and I take center.

"Police! Search warrant!"

"Police, stay down!"

"Drop your weapons! Put your hands in the air!" Every command is screamed out by the three of us. The smoke from the flash-bang barely clears before a hail of gunfire descends upon the room.

It happens so fast. Bullets tear through the air around us, as shouts and warnings are screamed out. Instinct kicks in as our unit falls back, taking cover to reassess our options.

"What the hell, Marsh?" I shout down my com. Adrenalin pulses through my veins at the realization we walked into an ambush. This was never meant to be a lethal entry, but a simple raid, with no loss of lives.

"Get out of there, now!" The possibility this is turning into a standoff grows stronger with the continuation of gunfire.

"Fuck!" The word comes out as a grumble, the world tilting on its axis.

My feet turn to lead in my boots and my steps become sluggish. I urge my legs to work, to pump faster and get out of the line of fire, but they refuse; instead, they give out beneath me and I hit the concrete hard on my knees.

"Shit, boss. You okay?" The question knocks me back, and it takes me a minute to realize I've dropped. Pain slingshots through my body and a ringing sounds in my ears before fading out. For a moment, I think I've gone deaf, but it comes back in a roar as I hear shouting.

"Officer down, officer down!" someone screams out, but scanning each of my men, I can't find anyone shot.

"Who the hell's been shot?" I ask Sterling when he comes to lean over me.

"We're getting you out. Hold on for me." He pulls me out and away from the warehouse by the back of my Kevlar vest.

"I've been hit?" A burning itch in my neck springs to life. Awareness has my hands searching to find the issue.

"Just stay calm." Hands push mine away, revealing warm blood staining between my fingers. But still it doesn't register. Instead, my world has become the slow beat of my heart pounding in my ears. Darkness takes hold and starts to pull me away. Everything numbs. The pain. The light. The noise.

"Come on, Hetch. Stay with me." A voice, barely a whisper now, swirls around me in a turbulence of nothingness. Time no longer anchors me to my body. Darkness is now my keeper.

"Tell Lib, I lov…." The last word becomes stuck in my mouth as my throat closes up. With each intake of air, breathing becomes harder.

Liberty in my arms. Liberty kissing me. Liberty loving me.

Every moment I've spent with her replays in my mind as the beat of my heart slows even more.

I'm losing her and her me.

"He's crashing!"

LIBERTY

"Tell me what you want, Liberty, or you get nothing." His words are all I need to step back and demand him to take my panties off.

"Rip my panties off." His throat constricts, his Adam's apple bobbing as he swallows.

"Fuck, sweetheart, is that the phone?"

What the fuck? That's not part of the dream.

The annoying ringtone of my house phone next to my head pulls me out of my dream and back to reality.

The hell?

"Seriously?" I grumble as if the rude caller can hear me and cover my head with my pillow. I'm not on call this weekend, and work rarely calls my house phone, so my guess is it's Payton. No one else I know calls this early on a Sunday morning. Deciding I'm not in the mood for her chirpy ass this morning, I try to block out the offending ringing, but it doesn't help. She's persistent. The phone rings again; this time, it seems louder.

With more energy than I thought possible, I reach across the bed and yank the phone from its receiver.

"Do you know how early it is, Pay?" I groan into the phone, pulling my duvet up over my head.

Normally, I would never answer her call with this much attitude, but after the dream she just interrupted, she deserves it.

Clearly, I'm mean when I'm horny.

"Liberty," Kota's voice replies, pulling me out of the mood. The unexpected shock of hearing her voice strips me of any lingering sleep and jolts me to life.

"Kota?" I find myself tangled in my sheets as I twist around, confusion slamming into me. I imagine I look like a fish when it's first thrown down onto the bottom of a boat. Twisting and squirming to find freedom.

"Lib…." Her voice takes on a tone I can't decipher, but the hair on the back of my neck stands to attention, a dizziness that makes no sense sweeping over me.

"What's wrong?" I find my feet as dread weaves its way through my mind, like a spider weaving its web.

Slowly and meticulously.

"It's Hetch." Beneath my feet, the ground becomes unsteady. Or maybe it's just me. Her words are knocking the balance from me.

"What happened?" I force my body to steady and move into action without any guidance. Ripping my nightgown up over my head, I quickly dress in the first outfit I can find.

Dark skinny jeans and one of Hetch's old SWAT T-shirts.

"I don't know much, just that he's in surgery."

"Surgery?" The ground tilts again. This time, I have to sit down. "Where are you? What happened? Is he okay? He has to be okay. He's a fucking cop, for Christ's sake!" Every scenario of how he ended up in surgery runs through my head.

"Liberty, you have to stay calm. Freaking out is not going to help him. We're at the hospital. He just went in. Fox is coming to pick you up. He should be there any minute. He's closer than me, so wait for him." The only word I take in from her sentence is wait.

Wait?

Wait while the man I love needs me?

Is she mad?

"No, I can drive. It's okay." I don't know what I'm saying. I can barely stand, let alone drive.

"Liberty, the guys don't want you driving. Please wait for Fox." I don't bother answering her when a knock at my front door cancels any argument I may have.

"Doesn't matter, he's here. I'll be there soon." I hang up the phone, push my feet into a pair of flip flops, and open the door to find Fox standing there.

"Fox?" His name acts as the main question when a thousand different thoughts are running through my head.

What happened? Is he going to be okay? Tell me he's going to be okay. Tell me *we're* going to be okay.

"He was shot." The words hit me hard, like a fucking sledgehammer to the stomach.

"Is he? What? How?" My stomach tightens and a deep ache takes root, forcing me to bunch over and hold my stomach.

"We need to go now, Lib," is all he replies, but it's not enough. I can't get my feet to move.

"I-I can't. I can't." I don't know what I'm saying, what I'm asking. It's like time has ceased and everything around us has frozen.

"You can, darlin'. Just take my hand." He holds it out, but the simple task of moving my hand to his has me completely lost.

"Please, Liberty. He needs you." The words are exactly what I need to jolt me back to some semblance of myself. Fox, noticing my return, steps forward, takes my hand and gently maneuvers me out of the doorway so he can close the door behind me.

"You need anything else?" I think I shake my head, or maybe the ground moves again, and I move with it, but whatever it is, Fox takes it on board, and starts directing me down the stairs.

"Does Hetch need anything?" I ask, stopping our descent,

the thought hitting me fast.

"Other than you? Not right now. Let's just get you to the hospital." There's no annoyance in his tone, but I can tell he's tense.

"Okay, yeah," I continue and he follows, keeping close like Hetch would. When we reach the parking lot, he takes the lead. Walking past me, he opens the passenger door of his truck. The step up is not as high as Hetch's truck, but for some reason, this one seems harder for me climb into. Fox, noticing my reluctance, places his hands on either side of my hips and helps me up.

"Thank you. I'm sorry, I'm just…." I trail off, not looking at him. I'm barely holding on by a thread; I've already lost it in front of him once. I don't need to do it again.

"Hey." He reaches out a comforting hand but stops himself midair. "He's going to be okay, Liberty." His reassurance does nothing to calm me. If anything, it makes me want to ask him how he could possibly be so sure. Two minutes ago, he said he didn't know. Now he's reassuring me he's going to be okay.

Instead of lashing out at someone who doesn't deserve it, I sit back and silently work through the same breathing exercises I teach my boys when they're worked up and can't contain their emotion.

One hand rests on my chest, the other on my abdomen and I inhale steadily through my nose.

Please, don't die, Hetch.

Exhaling through my mouth.

Don't you dare die.

Inhaling through my nose.

Please don't die.

Exhaling through my mouth.

Don't you dare die.

By the time Fox pulls up at the front of the emergency room fifteen minutes later, I'm no calmer than when I took Kota's call. If anything, the coil of tension snaps tighter inside my stomach.

Please don't die, my mind screams loudly.

Not prepared to wait for Fox to shut off the truck, I release my seatbelt, throw open my door and I forgo any help down. Fox doesn't call out for me, or maybe he does and I'm too lost in my own head to hear him. Instead, he picks up his pace to stay close behind me.

Reaching the double entry doors before he does, I make it into the waiting room out of breath and immediately search for Kota, or anyone familiar. It doesn't take long for me to find Kota first. She's standing on the far side of the waiting room, shoulders resting against the wall, hands crossed over her chest. She's talking to Sterling and her mother, and at the sight of them, I instantly feel like I shouldn't be here.

You pushed him away, Liberty.

"Kota?" My voice is unsure, across a waiting room of police officers. Her head, followed by Sterling's and Brianna's, come up at my voice and I move toward them, anxious for information.

"Oh, thank God you're here." Kota steps away from the wall first, followed by Sterling and Brianna.

"Is he okay? Where is he? What happened?" The questions fire out as I move toward them, and I can't stop them.

Please be okay. Please be okay.

"Whoa there. Slow down, darlin'." Sterling reaches for me just as I reach them on wobbly legs, and takes me in his arms, holding me steady.

"Tell me what happened? Fox said he was shot. How? Is he going to survive?" My heart rate can't keep up with the questions. Pounding against my chest, I fight the tightness with large deep breaths.

Please don't take him away from me.

"Come here." He pulls back, and motions me over to a vacant chair. The last thing I want to do is sit down, but I don't voice my concern. My need to know everything that's going on anchors me down into the chair.

"He was hit twice in the neck. They're operating now." He gives it to me straight, and instantly, I wish he were more gentle.

"The neck?" Last night's dinner threatens to come up, but I manage to keep it down by sliding back in my chair and looking up at the ceiling, squeezing my eyes shut. *The neck?* How serious is the neck? My mind takes stock of my own body, connecting everything together.

"That's not bad, right? He can survive, right?" Tears hit the back of my eyelids, and before I can control it, they're rolling down my face.

The neck is bad. I know it. It's connecting to his throat. To his head. His face. His handsome face.

Sterling doesn't answer me right away, the silence screaming louder than my mind is.

"It's touch and go, babe. He lost a lot of blood." His voice shakes, setting off a tremor through me.

"But he can still survive. *He* can, right?" A small, cold hand finds mine, and I open my eyes at the contact to find Brianna sitting down next to me, wearing the same stare Hetch had on his face the night I found him in my shower.

Lost. Broken. Scared.

"We need to be strong, but we also need to prepare for the worst, Lib." I want to reject the words, ask her how could she say such horrible things to me, but I can't. I can't because the way she's looking at me tells me she's just as scared as I am.

"I think I'm going to be sick." I release her hand and find my feet. "Yes, I'm going to be sick." I stumble in the direction of what I hope is the bathroom, but get stopped by an older man I don't recognize. Grey hair, wide shoulders, he could almost pass as my father if he wasn't wearing police blues.

"Here, darling." He hands me a sick bag and steps back. When I turn my back to him, my stomach convulses, bringing up the small amount of food I had for dinner last night.

A bottle of water is handed to me next, this time by Hart. I want to cry when I see him standing close to me in his SWAT gear, but I don't. My focus is solely on keeping myself from vomiting again.

"Thank you," I croak out, swallowing down mouthfuls of water to get the putrid taste out of my mouth.

"You gonna be sick again?" he asks, and I shake my head. With gentle fingers, he takes the bag from me, twisting the end,

286

and handing it off to someone else.

Jesus, is everyone here? I look around the waiting room and realize there are more than a few officers here. More like twenty. All are wearing the same look as Fox. As Sterling. As Brianna and Kota. *As me.*

"I shouldn't have pushed him away. I should have taken him back when he came to me," I blurt to no one in particular. Maybe Hart. Maybe Brianna or Kota. Maybe all of them.

"What if he doesn't survive this? What if I never see him again?" I'm pacing now, my world turning from color to darkness in simple seconds.

How could I be so stupid? Tears hit the back of my eyelids, and before I can control them, they're rolling down my face. "I didn't even tell him I love him. I made him play this stupid 'need time' game. Why? Why would I do that?" The tears don't stop now, sobs wracking my body, twisting and contorting me with their strength.

"Hey, hey. Come on, you need to keep it together, Lib." Arms come around me, Fox's voice coaxing me away from hysteria.

"What if he dies, Fox?" I turn in his arms and push my face into his chest. It's not the chest I want, but it's the only one I have.

"He's not going to, okay? He's going to pull through, and you're going to tell him you love him." I almost believe him. Almost take comfort in it. Until his voice shakes with the same unease pressing within me. "He's going to be okay." He moves me back to the chair, pulling me down onto his lap and holds me while I hide from the world.

"I can't lose him, Fox. I can't."

He doesn't reply, or maybe he does, but nothing gets through the muffled sounds of my sobs.

For the next four hours, I stay like that.

Held in Fox's arms, I cry, and pray, and wait.

Inhale. Exhale. Wait.

Please don't die, Hetch.

HETCH

"Liam?" a voice I didn't think I'd hear again whispers and settles over me.

"Dad?" A black haze fixes itself against an endless sky, but even concealed behind an inky darkness, I still know it's him.

My father.

"You shouldn't be here." His words are more than a whisper across the unusually frigid air and this time, my body tries to react. To search for him, find where he is. But no matter how hard I force my limbs to move, I can't.

I'm stuck. Frozen. I'm nothing.

"Where *is* here?" I give up fighting when the haze slowly lifts, and he's there, standing in front of me.

"Hello, son." He steps toward me, his face coming into the light. He looks different from how I remember him.

Younger. Brighter. Alive.

His salt-and-pepper hair looks as thick as the day I graduated high school and the groomed mustache he'd worn since the day I was born is still tidy and neat.

"How?" I close my eyes, opening them again to make sure I'm seeing things right.

How is he here?

Why is he here?

Where *is* here?

"You shouldn't be here, Liam. You need to go." Seeing him again splinters something deep and raw inside of me.

The change of his aim

The discharge of his gun.

The fall of his body.

The agony of my screams.

"Son, you really need to get out of here before it's too late." His pained stare captures me as the black haze builds again, the brightness I noticed about him before dims.

How come he can move and I can't?

"Too late for what? Where are you going? Please don't leave," I ask him frantically.

I'm not ready for him to leave. I only just got here.

Wherever *here* is.

"We don't have time for this, Liam. Just promise me you'll open your eyes."

Open my eyes? What the hell is he talking about? My eyes are open.

"Why did you do it?"

"There is no time for this, Liam. Just rem—" He shakes his head, still caught up in what he wants to say.

Then as soon as he was there, he's gone.

Darkness wins out again.

34

LIBERTY

"Family of Liam Hetcherson?" A short, older woman wearing blue scrubs steps into the private waiting room we've been moved into and closes the door.

At first, I thought it was a good thing when they herded us into the small room an hour ago. Then I remembered I once saw a movie where they moved the family of a car crash victim to another room to let them know he had died. I don't share my concern with anyone, though. Even if I want to, I can't. Hell, I can barely manage a whisper at this point. My voice is no longer mine, lost to the violent sobs that wracked me four hours ago.

Instead, I've sat quietly, tucked into Fox's chest. Brianna to the left of us, Kota to the right.

"Yes, how is he?" someone asks, but I can't be sure. Maybe it's the older man from earlier, or maybe it's Hart. Everything bleeds into each other. Faces. Voices. Time.

"He's out of surgery and in recovery." A collective sigh

settles through the room, releasing an invisible band of tension that's been restricting us all.

"Is my son going to be okay?" Brianna stands and steps closer. I want to follow her up, but I'm mentally incapable. Body spent, mind lost, I hold on to Fox like a lifeline.

"Your son is very lucky, Mrs. Hetcherson. The first bullet penetrated what we call zone 1." She motions to the lower part of her neck. "And the second bullet entered what we call zone 2." This time, she motions higher up her neck. "The first bullet penetrated his left common carotid artery. And while serious, we were able to reconstruct and repair the artery, using a vascular graft. Now the second bullet being higher was a little more complex. There was complete disruption of the internal carotid artery, as well as a small laceration in the internal jugular vein. The degree of the injury was such that to control the bleeding, the internal carotid artery had to be ligated."

"What does that mean?" My voice croaks, burning raw, and even though I know no one can hear me, I still ask.

"What does that mean?" Fox asks the question for me, his voice vibrating against my cheek.

"It means we couldn't repair the artery. Laymen's terms, we tied it. Now, arterial repair is reported to achieve better neurological outcome and survival rate compared to ligation. However, patients like Liam who present with a normal neurologic examination can still have an excellent prognosis."

"So, he's going to be fine?" It's Kota's turn to ask.

"We won't know for sure until he wakes up."

"When will that be?" Kota presses. I can't see her from my position, but I know she's standing there, holding her mother's hand, staying stronger than I ever could be.

"Right now he's sedated and intubated. Over the next twenty-four hours, we will know more. In the meantime, I suggest you all go home, get some rest and come back in a few hours. He won't be taking any visitors just yet." There's a flurry of movement, a few calls of resistance, but I stay sitting there, hiding.

"I'm not leaving," I croak against Fox again, thinking he's

going to force me to leave. "Not until I see him."

"I wouldn't dream of moving ya, Lib. Hetch would kick my ass if I sent you home." He rumbles against my back, and it's the first smile that slips free. "Just don't get too comfortable. I do have to give you back."

I don't answer, nor do I move. Stuck in a trance of time as it stands still. Seconds could be minutes, minutes could be hours. Exhaustion tugs at the edges of my mind and before I can put up a good fight, it wins.

35

HETCH

"Shoot me. Or I'll have to do it." His voice teeters between a moan and a tremble. While my hand rests ready on top of my gun belt, prepared to arm myself at a moment's notice, my gaze stays trained on a man I don't recognize, yet love.

"That's not going to happen, Dad," I tell him with all the conviction I can muster. It's almost surreal, like we're reenacting the play-by-plays we used to run when I was going through the academy.

"I'm telling you it's happening, Liam. Don't think I'm not going to end today the way I intended." He takes a step back from me as I step in closer. The gun he's pointing at me wavers as his free hand moves to his hair, tugging in irritation.

"What way is that, Dad? What exactly is the end goal here?"

"It has to. It does. It has to. You know it. You know it," he mutters. I'm not sure to himself or to me.

"Dad," I call him back; I need him to stay focused and in the moment. "Don't do this to me, Dad." This isn't my father, the man who raised me.

This is someone else. Another version of him. The version he's been struggling with for the last few years.

"Talk to me. Tell me what's happening here." I take another small step closer, my mind trying to figure out how to stop this.

Maybe I can bring him down with my Taser.

"Stop right there, Liam." He jerks back. "Stay out of range." He might not be of sound mind, but he knows my training.

"Dad, please...." My voice cracks, not sure how I'm going to get us out of this, but I can't stop till I have tried.

"Hetch?"

The scene fades, and a black haze swirls around us returning me to the place he keeps meeting me.

"What are we doing back here?" I turn to face my father. Only this time there's no gun, no threat of suicide. Just us.

"You know every time you relive it, I'm there with you. Every dream, every encounter. I'm there with you." Silence beats between us as he stands there across from me.

"So you're aware of what it did to me? What it did to all of us?" In my mind, the question comes out as an accusation, but the truth is, I'm just a kid, standing in front of the man I thought hung the moon for thirty years, asking why we weren't enough.

"I do, son. And if I could take it back I would. But at the time, I wasn't thinking about you. I wasn't thinking about anything but stopping the pain in here." His hand rubs his chest, and it's almost like I can feel his pain inside of me. "I was sick, and I was hurting. But you have to believe me, the last thing I wanted to do was hurt any of you. You were all my life, but no matter what I did, or how hard I tried to be the person you all needed me to be, I couldn't. I couldn't do it."

Time stretches between us as I wait. Wait for understanding. Wait for clarity. When it doesn't come, panic rises to the surface. I've waited three years for this, and his words aren't the magic fix I thought I needed.

"It never goes away, you know? No matter how hard I try to forget, no matter how hard I fight it, it's always there." Every minute of pain he's handed to me comes back, and for a second, it's almost too much.

"I know, son. And if I could go back and change things I would. I'd do it in a second and vow to live through the pain all over. If I thought sorry would ever be enough, I would say it a million times over to you. But, Hetch, I can't do that, and sorry isn't enough. Nothing will ever be enough." I don't know what I was expecting from his words. Maybe a moment of understanding. Maybe relief. But the truth is I get neither. His words don't take the pain away, his presence doesn't soothe the ache.

I'm still me, and he's still him, and together we're here.

Wherever *here is*.

LIBERTY

"In my head, there's this woman. She's brave and she's smart. She has it together." The monitors next to Hetch's hospital bed beep loudly between us. "She's nothing like me, you know? She's so positive, so optimistic…" I trail off when the door opens and the doctor walks in.

"He hasn't woken up yet. Why isn't he waking up, Doctor?" I don't bother with the sequential greetings as I stand and give her room. It's been two days, and I haven't left Hetch's side. I know every doctor on the roster, every nurse who's come in. I know all the gossip. Who's screwing who. Who hates who, and who's not talking to who. In the beginning, it helped. A distraction to keep the minutes from dragging, but now the days are ticking by and I'm done with the small talk. I'm done with the gossip. I'm done with the waiting. I want him to wake up. I'm ready for him to wake up. I *need* him to wake up.

"There's still time." She starts to do her doctor thing. Picking up his chart, she moves around the right side of the bed before pressing some buttons on the screen attached to his monitors. It should all be really scary—the tubes, the sounds, the wires— but sitting here watching, I don't see anything but him.

"But you said twenty-four hours. It's been over forty-eight." My voice shakes as I count the hours off in my head. Every single one of them.

From the family who've come by to pray and cry, to the officers who've told me to be strong, the unknown faces, the known faces... every one of them represents a long minute, a dragged-out second.

"The waiting is always the hard part, but like I told you, this morning everything looks good. His brain function is clear. He's breathing on his own, and there are no signs of complications from the surgery. We have to be patient now." She writes some notes down on his chart before replacing it in the rack at the end of his bed. "I'll be back later tonight. Keep talking to him. It helps." She offers me what I like to call the pity smile and leaves me alone to think again.

Talking helps? I'm not sure I believe her. I've been talking for two days. Two days of not shutting up, and I'm not sure it's working.

"I hate her, you know? Not the doctor, the girl in my head." I continue with my ranting and take my seat back beside him. "I hate her because I used to be her. I was her. But the problem is I can't be her anymore, not without you. You already left me once, Hetch. And I know everyone makes mistakes. I know this. Jesus, I know this. It's the after that matters. How you come back. And you came back. You came back and I pushed you away. So now I'm asking you to give me *my* after. Give me my chance. Don't stop fighting. Please wake up. You have to come back to me. I'm not finished loving you, Liam Hetcherson."

I need more time.

The girl in my head needs more time.

We *both* need more time.

* * *

"Please, Hetch, please wake up. I need you to wake up now. Okay?" I squeeze his hand, waiting for something. For anything.

Three days.

Three days of back and forth with these doctors and I'm going crazy.

"Come on, Lib. Will you just try?" Sterling taps my shoulder, pulling me out of the bubble I've created for Hetch and me.

"I'm not hungry." I look up to find Sterling, Hart, Brianna and Kota staring down at me.

"Liberty, you need to eat. Just try a bite." Hart tries to reason with me, but the last thing I want to do right now is eat.

"He's like glasses," I blurt, clearly still not myself. Three days of hell and I've barely slept more than an hour at a time. I'm also in desperate need of a shower, but I refuse to give up on him. Refuse to leave his room. "Hetch. He's like glasses," I tell them all, probably not making any sense.

"Glasses?" Hart's eyes move to Brianna's before coming back to mine. I know they're worried about me. I heard them talking about me outside the door before they came in. I know they mean well, but I can't seem to care about anything other than worrying when Hetch is going to wake up.

If he is going to wake up.

"Yeah. Like when someone doesn't know their vision isn't perfect. They think they can see fine. But the moment they put those glasses on for the first time, they see everything so clearly, so vivid. They realize how much detail and beauty they've been missing. That's Hetch. He's my glasses." No one says anything for a beat, and I wonder if they're thinking about having me committed. I smell, I haven't eaten, and I've started talking in metaphors and similes.

"I get it. Ava was my glasses," Hart finally answers, filling the silence.

"Ava?" I sit a little straighter, relieved I'm not going completely crazy.

298

"My wife." His eyes glaze over briefly before he shakes his head and clears it. "She died a few years ago. But even on the darkest days, the days I didn't think I had anything left in me to fight with her, she was the clarity my life needed." His voice shakes a little, and for a second, I feel like a complete ass.

How did I not know his wife died?

"I don't want to walk through life thinking I can see when I know I can't," I whisper, unsure if it's the right thing to say. He lost his glasses; he knows what I'm going through, but I shouldn't rub it in.

"You won't, Lib. He is going to wake up. And when he does, you'll see so much; you'll wonder why you ever doubted."

I don't answer, not sure if I can believe it; instead, I hold my hand out for the sandwich they've been trying to make me take a bite of for the last twenty minutes.

"Thank you." He hands me the sandwich and steps back.

"I'm not gonna lie. I probably won't even eat half," I warn before they think they won the battle.

"Well, I'm not gonna lie, I wish I had some of these magical glasses," Sterling murmurs beside us, and like the other day when Fox made a joke, I smile. Then maybe I laugh.

It's not the laugh Hetch would have given me, but it's something. And for that, I'm hopeful.

37

HETCH

"Hetch, please. You need to come back to me. I can't do this on my own." The soft sound of Liberty's voice fills the still, dark air. Breaking through my peace and calm, it wraps its panic around me.

"Liberty?" I turn, trying to find her. "Liberty, where are you?" Panic sets its claws into me.

Why is she here? What happened?

I don't know how much time has passed. Seconds could be minutes, minutes could be hours. Time bleeds into nothingness, scenes run into each other.

"She's not here, Liam." My father steps in front of me, halting me from my search. Each time he comes to me now, I'm less shocked and more relieved.

"Well, why can I hear her?" I push past him, needing to find her. Something is wrong. I need to get to her. She needs me.

"Because she's waiting for you. They're all waiting for you."

My fast feet slow, and I turn to face him.

"What are you talking about?" The words don't make sense.

"Hetch, I tried to tell you. You're running out of time. You need to open your eyes. You have to go back. Your mom, Kota, Liberty, they need you. They need you to fight, son. If you don't open your eyes soon, you're not gonna see her again."

"What do you mean?" The possibility of never seeing Liberty again burns so hot, I want to scream. "I don't understand what's happening here." Part of me knows something isn't right. I'm in some kind of alternate universe, talking to my dead father, but at the same time, it feels right.

"Son, where were you before you came here?" He takes my hand and starts walking us through the fog.

"I don't know. I don't remember." I fight the darkness, trying to think.

"Think harder. Where were you?" My mind flashes to Sterling, and distorted images of the raid come crashing in.

Bodies moving. Guns firing. Pain searing.

"I-I died?" The realization hits me just as painfully as the first bullet I took to the neck.

I'm dead? Is this death?

"You died twice, Hetch. But they brought you back." Relief floods my body. I'm not sure I'm ready to die yet. I'm not ready to leave Liberty.

"So, if I'm not dead, what is this place?" I look around, the scene changing before me. No longer are we surrounded by darkness, but a room, a hospital room. It's quiet, but I can hear her.

"What's happening?" My mind can't keep up. I'm standing next to my father, looking down at Liberty holding my hand in a hospital bed.

"You're stuck, son, in the in-between. And unless you wake up, it's going to be too late."

"Liberty?" I step toward her and reach out.

"She can't hear you."

I don't pay myself any attention. My gaze is firmly locked on her. She looks tired like she hasn't eaten in a week. She's wearing one of my SWAT shirts with a pair of jeans, and even in this fucked-up state, I want to reach out and kiss her.

"Is she the one?" My father's question breaks my staring.

"I don't know. I think she is, but how do I know for sure?"

"The fact you're standing here asking me is a pretty clear indicator she's the one, Liam." He cracks a smile and disturbingly, it warms me. I can't remember the last time he smiled.

Years. *So many years ago.*

"She's the one, Dad."

"Then you need to go back to her."

"Tell me how. Tell me what I need to do." I turn to face him, eager to be taught.

"You need to let me go." A flash of pain crosses his face, but he quickly hides it.

"What? No. What if I'm not ready? What if I want to stay with you a little longer?" Logically, I know it's not possible. I don't want to be here, but the thought of leaving him is too hard. I just got him back.

"You can't, son. It's not your time." He wraps his arms around me.

"I can't leave you. I can't do it."

"You can and you have to. You need to wake up, Hetch. You need to fight." I start to pull back, but stop when he holds me tighter.

I'm not sure who's slipping faster this time, him or me, all I know is I need more time.

"Please, Dad. I love you. Don't make me choose."

"I love you too, son. But this isn't a choice. I'll always be with you. In here." His hand moves to my heart. "But you need to fight now. You need to let me go and fight for your girl. Fight like you've never fought before. Open your eyes, son! Do it."

Darkness fades and the numbness I've grown accustomed to these days takes me.

38

LIBERTY

"So there's this moment I keep coming back to." I climb up onto the bed later that night when everyone has gone home, and the doctors have done their final rounds. "It was right after the day of our car wash. Do you remember it? We were having a quiet night in, just lying around and talking, and you stopped and looked at me. You looked at me like no man has ever looked at me before." I run my fingers through his hair, careful not to jostle the monitoring cords. "It was like you were seeing me for the first time." I take a breath, hoping to keep the tears away at least for a few hours. "It's the moment I keep going back to. I want you to look at me like that one more time. Just one more time. That's all I'm asking." I lean in closer and breath him in. "Please, Hetch. You have to wake up."

"You shouldn't be up there." Avery, my favorite nurse, walks into the room, intruding on our personal bubble.

"You gonna make me get off?" I whisper back. If she thinks

I'm getting down off this bed, she has another thing coming. She's a little thing, and if I had to take her on, I would.

"I wouldn't dare. But don't let the doctors see you up there." She reaches for his chart and walks around to his other side. We don't talk while she does her thing. The routine's become so predictable. I know what buttons she'll press, what tests she'll run, and what she'll put down in his file.

"How is he tonight?"

"Same. Just like yesterday." She picks up on my tone and pauses in her notes.

"Have you eaten today?" I almost roll my eyes. If it's not the boys or Brianna trying to feed me, it's the nurses.

"I ate today." If you call two bites of the sandwich Hart brought me today eating, then yeah, I've been eating.

"Okay." She doesn't look convinced, but she drops it and moves on. "Well, everything looks good here. I should be a good nurse and tell you that you should head home for some sleep, but you're not going to listen to me, are you?" She replaces his file and offers me a sad smile, or maybe it's a hopeful one. It's hard to read them today.

"No, I'm not."

"Didn't think so." She walks toward the door. "Okay, I'll come back later. Buzz me if you need anything." She waves, then leaves us alone again.

Taking Hetch's hand, I settle back into his side. I don't know how long I have alongside him. I might get away with it with Avery, but if a doctor catches me, it won't be good.

Closing my eyes, I take in a deep breath. My heart beats in sync with his, his warmth heating me to the very core. I take in his scent, basking in the memories that filter in and out of my head.

Liberty.

I imagine my name falling from his lips, and it's the sweetest sound I've ever heard.

Lib.

The deep baritone of his voice wraps itself around me and vibrates through me.

"L-Lib?" The word is croaky, more like a question and barely above a whisper, but I still hear it. I still hear him, clearer than the previous times.

Louder.

"Hetch?" I sit up, not trusting my ears. His eyes open, and his face grimaces in pain, but still, he manages one of his dangerous grins.

"Hey, sweetheart." Time passes without thought as I look down at him. He's awake. He's here. He's talking.

"Y-you. Y-you talked. Oh, my God. Talk some more." I reach across his body for the nurse call button.

"How long have I been out for?" he rasps, trying to sit up.

"Don't move. Wait for the nurse to come back." I gently hold his shoulder so he doesn't try to sit up again.

He takes my lead and rests back, pulling me down next to him. "How long?" His voice is still barely a croak, but I'm not worried. The man took two bullets to his neck. He's not going to have too much of a voice for a while.

"You've been out three days. How are you feeling?"

"Sore." He winces a little when his hand finds the bandage on his neck.

"Well, getting shot tends to do that to you." The tears I thought I managed to keep at bay fall when his beautiful eyes find mine.

He woke up.

Hetch is awake and everything is going to be okay.

We are going to be okay.

"Hey, I'm okay, sweetheart." I can tell it hurts him to talk, but three days without his voice has taken its toll on me, and right now, it's like a balm soothing the ache inside of me. Three days of waiting. Three days of not knowing, three days of thinking the worst, pours out of me.

"I was so scared, Hetch. I didn't think I'd ever see you again."

"Shhh, sweetheart. I'm here now. I'm not going anywhere." His words calm me, talking me down from the brink and wrapping around me like a comforting embrace.

"I sh-should call your mom and Kota. The boys. They've all

been here around the clock, waiting for you to wake up."
Everything rolls over in my head, and I know I need to get up
to make those calls, but having him awake in my arms, holding
me, makes it hard to move.

"J-just give me a few more minutes." He doesn't let go, and
I don't make him. Not even when the nurse comes running to
my call and finds him awake. Or when the doctor arrives and
checks him over. Holding me harder against his side than he
probably should, we stay like that until we're left alone and
exhaustion wins out.

Connected, grounded, and *together*.

HETCH

"I'll always be with you. But you need to fight now. You need to let me go and fight for your girl. Fight like you've never fought before."

I wake with a startle, my father's words ringing in my head as I struggle with a wave of nausea rolling through me.

Fuck, it's just a dream. I'm not back there, inside my head with my father standing in front of me.

"Hey, it's okay." The nurse, who came in when I woke up last night, calms me as I try to control my breathing.

"Sorry," I croak, my throat still raw and scratchy. I've been told it's normal after a gunshot wound to the neck and being intubated. The doctor warned me it might take a few weeks for my voice to come back.

"What time is it?" I try to sit up, but stop when she uses the control to bring the bed up instead. I'm still getting used to the idea I was shot, survived surgery, and was out of it for a few days.

"It's after twelve." She hands me a cup of water with a straw.

"Where's Liberty?" I take a sip, the cold water soothing the roughness in my throat.

"She went down to get some coffee with your mom and sister. You fell asleep on them." She takes the water when I'm done and moves back to my chart. I vaguely remember talking to them this morning. After a tearful hello on Mom's part, the drugs they have me on took effect, and as hard as I tried to stay awake, I didn't last very long.

"These drugs you have me on keep spacing me out." With the dream still fresh in my mind, I decide to blame the drugs on the whole talking to my father business.

"Yeah, enjoy it while you can." Her voice is soft, almost singsong, and when she laughs, she reminds me of a cartoon character. "How are you feeling this morning?"

"Besides feeling spaced out by the drugs, okay. Think I can go home?" It's a long shot, I know it, and her cartoon laugh confirms it.

"You're a funny one." She shakes her head as the door pushes open.

"Well, well, well, look who decided to grace us with his presence, boys." Nurse forgotten, I look up at Sterling's voice to find my teammates walking through the door and taking up too much space in the small hospital room.

"Hey." My eyes move over each of them—Sterling, Fox, Hart, Tate, and Walker—making sure they're all here and okay. The last time I remember seeing them was when we walked into a hail of gunfire.

"How are you feeling, boss?" Tate steps forward first, lifts his fist, and waits for a connection.

"Hanging in there, Tate." I bump my fist to his and watch as Walker steps forward next.

"Scared the shit out of us, boss." He reaches out and squeezes my shoulder. I push down another wave of nausea and keep my face neutral.

"Glad you pulled through." Hart comes forward next

followed by Fox.

"When I told you to claim the girl, I didn't mean go get shot so she doesn't leave your side." His smartass remarks are funny, but I don't let him know it.

"Fuck off, Fox." He laughs at himself. Dropping his fist, he steps back over to a free chair.

"Where's your girl?" Sterling is the last one to step forward. His hand grips onto my wrist.

"She's gone to get a coffee with Mom and Kota."

He doesn't release his hold as quickly as the others did, his eyes drilling into mine in a silent question.

Are you doing okay?

I nod back, my own silent answer passing between us.

Yeah, I'm good.

"Okay, everything looks fine here. Give me a buzz me if you need anything," the cartoon nurse interrupts our silent conversation and steps out of the room, leaving us alone.

"Dang, I should get shot if it means having cute nurses looking after me." Walker whistles loud enough to ensure the nurse heard him.

"Knowing your luck, you'd get the old bag who's been manning the nurses' station for the last three days." Hart shuts his fantasy down.

"You all been here every day?" I try to clear my throat again, only to aggravate it more.

"On shifts," Sterling answers, the dip in his brows telling me how concerned he's been. Liberty filled me in on a little, but I still haven't received the full run down.

"So, what happened?" I ask the question of the hour when Sterling moves back over to a spare wall space. My visitors so far today have consisted of Mom, Kota, and the lieutenant. While Mom and Kota filled me in on what happened after the surgery, and the lieutenant filled me in on what's been going on since the raid, I still want a play-by-play with my team.

"What do you remember?" Fox answers first.

"We cleared the entry." I push my groggy mind through the haze and try to bring up my last memory. "We took fire. I pulled back, but before I knew it, I was down." The scene plays out in my head.

Hands push mine away, a warm blood staining between my fingers, but still it doesn't register. Instead, my world has become the slow beat of my heart pounding in my ears. Darkness takes hold and starts to pull me away. Everything numbs. The pain. The light. The noise.

"I don't remember much after that." I clear my head when the image of me going down rushes to the surface.

"You didn't have Morales. He wasn't there. You went down by one of Anton's guys." Sterling fills in the blanks. "We walked into an ambush set up by Anton."

"Dominic set us up?" I'm not surprised. I knew we couldn't trust the fucker.

"No, it looks like Anton played Morales. He didn't want to do business. He wanted to take out the competition." Tate picks up on the sudden rage pulsing through me. My head wants to fight the notion that Dominic didn't have a hand in this, but when I think about it, it makes sense. If Anton wanted Morales out of the picture, he could have set up a meet on false pretenses and taken him out.

"So the raid was a bust. Trebook may possibly have a gang war brewing. Detective Marsh doesn't have a case, and I took two bullets for the fuck of it?" I summarize what we know.

"We did get Anton." The only silver lining of the night is delivered by Sterling. Anton off the street is good news.

"Oh, and Detective Marsh is pissed at you for getting shot," Tate adds, looking over at Hart.

"She's not pissed. She's just not looking forward to the clean-up," Hart defends her. His quick support of the feisty detective confirms my suspicions of the two.

"You have a thing for Marsh, Hart?" I ask outright. No point in fucking around with suspicions.

"No." His scoff and fast-delivered scowl tells me different.

"Come on, Hart. You're fucking her, admit it." Fox stirs the pot.

"Fox, I'm not kidding. You keep running your mouth and you're gonna regret it." Hart pushes off the wall and steps to the middle of the room. I'm getting way too much enjoyment seeing Hart get worked up over the dig.

"What's the matter, Hart? Am I hitting a nerve?" Fox keeps his stance, not intimidated by Hart's threats. My eyes move to Sterling and watch him roll his eyes at their petty bickering.

"So Dominic hasn't been exposed?" My concern isn't for the safety of Dominic; it's for his brother. I don't want anything to touch Mitch. If Dominic is exposed, there is definitely no way I'm letting him anywhere near Mitch.

"No. As far as Anton knows, Morales turned on him too and instead of turning up for the meet, he sent the cops. Dominic's cover wasn't questioned."

"Jesus, what a fucking mess. I should have realized this wasn't going to end well." I shake my head, forgetting about my neck until the tightness hits me right before the pain.

"Yeah, well it's out of our hands now. Marsh isn't going to give up until she has Morales. So you just worry about getting yourself back together," Walker assures me, but I feel anything but reassured. There's still the issue of Dominic coming back into Mitch's life.

"Well, the sooner I get out of here, the sooner I'm back," I tell them, wondering how long I have to take off.

The doctor explained my injuries last night but didn't confirm how long I'd be out of work for. My guess is a few weeks.

"I'm sorry, but no talk of going back to work while you're still in the hospital, Liam," my mom scolds from the doorway.

"Yeah, listen to your mommy, boss," Fox taunts from the corner of the room, clearly intent on pissing everyone off today.

I don't bother arguing with him or my mother. The fact she has Liberty and Kota at her back makes the decision a whole lot easier.

"How are you, boys?" Mom steps into the room and walks around to all of them, offering a hug and kiss on the cheek. They all take it with a quick, "Hi Mrs. Hetcherson." Kota hangs back, her eyes moving between Sterling and me, while Liberty comes straight to me.

"Hey, sorry I wasn't here when you woke up. I had to organize some things for the boys at Haven. Sue called just as we made it to the coffee shop. Your mom and Kota sat down with me." She offers me a quick kiss.

"It's okay. I'm good here. Do you need to go in?"

"No, just trying to delegate some things. Then Mitch wanted to talk. He's been on my case about coming up to see you. I told him I'd talk to you about it." I can tell she's unsure about the prospect of bringing Mitch in, but I don't want to ask her about her reservations while we have a room full of people.

"I'd like that," I tell her, and it's the truth. Mitch and Liberty are cut from the same cloth. They wear their heart on their sleeves. Until he sees for himself that I'm okay, he's going to be taking it hard. Besides, I need to talk to him about Dominic. Detective Marsh might think she's done a good thing by making this deal, but if Mitch doesn't want this, then I'm not going to let it happen. I need to figure out if he's in the right head space for it. Mitch is a good kid. If Dominic is going to be coming back into his life again, he's going to need someone who has his back. I'm his person. I've grown attached to him, and I hope I'm making a difference in his life. He is without a doubt, making one in mine.

LIBERTY

"So you're saying I have no say in this?" Mitch stands and paces the length of Hetch's hospital room. It's been three days since Hetch woke up and after coordinating with Sue the last two days, she was finally able to drop him off at the hospital for a visit.

"We're not saying that, Mitch. We're just telling you what we know. So you're prepared." Hetch tries to calm him, but I can see Mitch starting to work himself up.

The pacing.

The way his hands clench, opening and closing tightly.

The panic in his eyes, the quick rise and fall of his chest.

He's not taking this the way I thought he would at all.

"Well, I don't want to see him." He stops his pacing and turns to face us, his cheeks holding a red flush. "I refuse to."

"You don't want to at least try, Mitch? You won't be alone. The visitation will be monitored." I try to reason with him.

When Hetch told me about Dominic and his involvement in The Disciples, I suspected Mitch would be confused, but the last thing I expected was for him to be this angry about it.

"The last time I saw him, he almost broke my nose, and one of his crew put you in the hospital, Liberty. I don't care if he was playing a part. He put you in the hospital." My heart warms at his loyalty, but I try not to let it show. Instead, I look to Hetch, hoping for some kind of help.

"What? He has a point, sweetheart." My eyes grow wide in a silent are-you-kidding-me stare. I told Hetch this morning we should wait to tell Mitch, but he said something about him being his person, and it would be better coming from him. He went on about how we shouldn't keep this from him a moment longer.

"Well, you don't have to make any decisions right away. We still have some time before we have to set something up. Maybe you should think it over." I try a different tactic.

"I'm not changing my mind. I'm not seeing him. I don't trust him. You can go back and tell them no." I understand where he's coming from, and don't blame him. But the last thing I want for him is to make such a rash decision without thinking about it. "No one asked me what I wanted." It's the change in his tone, the vulnerability in his voice that has Hetch speaking up.

"Well, tell us. What do you want, Mitch?" His eyes lock onto Hetch's as he finally chimes in on my side. The room fills with even more tension as they stare one another down. Like this moment is too important to be spoken, so instead of using words, they're talking with their eyes. "Because the only thing B and I want is for you to be happy. Remember the day I said sometimes family is in here?" I watch as he pats his chest with his hand right over his heart. Mitch's stare drops down to Hetch's hand with a slight nod. It's so slight I almost don't catch it. "We're always gonna be your family. Rebuilding a relationship with him won't change that. You don't have to choose between us because we aren't going anywhere." I see the realization of Hetch's words as they hit Mitch. How the tension all but evaporates.

Did he think we wouldn't be there for him if he wanted to see Dominic?

Before I can dwell on the question, Mitch steps toward Hetch and wraps his arms around him. But it's not what pulls me out of my own head. It's the fact there is no uneasiness in Hetch, no hesitation at all as he wraps his arms around Mitch.

A few seconds pass us by before they finally release one another and Mitch's eyes land on me. His silent words wrap themselves around me.

Please don't make me.

I don't want this.

And it's the raw honesty that has me relenting.

"Okay, Mitch," I tell him. It's for the best anyway. There won't be any getting through to him today. The whole ordeal has too many wild emotions spiraling around all of us to be settled in one day. "I'll talk to your caseworker. We'll set a meeting up for you two so you can explain everything you're feeling and what you want, even if it's nothing at all." I don't know how that conversation is going to go down. But it is what it is. At least it gives Mitch a chance to get some things off his chest to the people who can actually change this outcome.

Happy with my stance on the matter, Mitch takes a seat back beside Hetch's bed and reaches for his backpack. "I brought the board. You want a game?" He pulls out his chess set and starts setting it up on the small table in front of Hetch.

"Only if you let me win. I *am* at a disadvantage here, you know?" He points to the bandage on his neck.

"Sorry, not going to work on me. I don't do special treatment." He doesn't seem as affected as everyone else who has walked through the door these last few days, but I see it. I see the slight flash of panic in his eyes every time they land on Hetch's bandage. The way he's been quietly regarding him. He's been just as scared. But unlike the rest of us, he's kept himself together.

"Harsh." Hetch lets out a gurgle for a cough. I'm starting to get used to the sound and am no longer panicked at hearing it. I reach for the water and hand it to him.

"Okay, well I'm gonna head down and get a coffee, leave you boys to it." I stand, wanting to give them some space.

"You don't want to stay and watch me kick his butt?" Mitch looks up, his teasing tone much easier to hear than the panicked one.

"Nah, you boys have fun. I'll be back in a few. You need me to get you two anything?"

"We're good." Hetch reaches for my hand and squeezes briefly. I squeeze back before pulling away with one thing on my mind.

We are good.

And nothing will change that.

41

HETCH

"You two like to break the rules, huh?" The nurse I've come to know as Liberty's favorite, whispers across a sleeping Liberty as she checks my blood pressure and vitals.

"Don't blame her. I made her climb on up," I whisper back, careful not to wake her. It's been seven days since I woke up and not only did Liberty not leave my side the three days I was out of it, she hasn't left me since.

"I think she loves you." She continues to write in my chart, not looking up. I see why she's Liberty favorite. Even though she may be a little too chatty and maybe a bit too nosy, she does have a way of putting you at ease.

"I don't know. She still hasn't said it." I feel Liberty tense beside me, but she doesn't stir or wake. We haven't had much alone time these last seven days. Between my mom, my sister, and my teammates, my room has been a revolving door for visitors. Doesn't mean I don't think she does. I'm just waiting to hear where we stand.

"The fact she hasn't left your side since you've been in here says a lot."

"You picked up on that? Here I was thinking she was sneaking past you nurses every night." I give her a wink then watch her hide her blush.

"You're a very lucky man, you know?" She takes off the blood pressure cuff and writes down the results.

Lucky. The one word I've been hearing over and over for the last seven days. Lucky I survived the gunshot. Lucky I woke up. Lucky I have such a supportive family.

While I am still trying to work through everything that happened to me, I still feel like luck had nothing to do with it.

More like fate.

"Well, I'll feel a lot luckier when they let me get out of this place." As much as I appreciate the whole "saving my life" thing. I'm ready to go home. The visitors, the food, the poking and prodding every other hour, I'm done. Although my neck is still stiff, the pain has diminished to a dull ache, my dizziness and nausea gone, and after no longer dreaming about my father, it's safe to say my brain is in good working order.

"Well, there you go, getting lucky again. A little birdy tells me you might get your discharge papers today." She replaces my chart at the end of the bed and starts walking out.

"You're saying he gets to go home?" Liberty sits up, her sudden alertness way too bright to have only just woken up. The earlier tension I picked up on when the nurse mentioned love, runs through my mind. The little witch has been listening in on our conversation the entire time.

"Morning, Liberty." Avery laughs at her eagerness but doesn't comment on it.

"Don't morning me, Avery. Does he get to go home today?" Liberty turns her puppy dog eyes up at her, her excitement spilling onto me.

Seriously, I love this woman. Not only does she know everyone who comes into my room by first name, she's become fast friends with most of them.

"Put it this way, if all goes well on Dr. Fenteir's rounds this morning, you should be able to sleep in your own bed tonight. Now, if you'll excuse me, I have other patients to attend to." She offers us a brief wave before leaving us alone.

"Oh, my God, honey. You're going home!" She wraps her arms around my waist, careful to keep away from my neck, and presses her lips to my cheek.

"So you heard, you little faker." I pinch her side, watching her face light up with a shy smile.

"Sorry, I didn't mean to eavesdrop. I was waiting for her to leave." Without hesitation, I lean forward and press my mouth to hers.

"Liar." My lips move against hers in a chaste kiss. The room slips away when her mouth parts and her tongue meets mine first, surprising me and exciting me. I take over the kiss. I devour and savor the first burst of her taste; nothing has ever tasted as good.

This is what I've missed the most. These quiet moments where we can just connect again.

"Oh, God, not this again." My sister's voice interrupts our morning make-out session, but I don't pull back, not even when Sterling adds in his two cents.

"Leave them alone, Dakota. They're like teenagers who've been grounded for a month. They have a lot to catch up on." I might not be able to see them, but I'm betting his grin is as big as my sister's. It's all my family and friends seem to do around us lately. *Grin.*

"Yeah, leave us alone," I moan against Liberty's mouth, still caught up in her sweet taste. Who needs pain meds when I have her kisses to give me a high?

"Sorry, can't do. Mom is outside the door talking with your doctor, and apparently, you might get to go home today. So I'd take your tongue out soon, or you might find yourself grounded again."

It's all Liberty needs to pull back and end the kiss.

Seriously, if I'm not released today, I'm going to lose it.

* * *

"Can I get you anything else before I leave?" My mom fusses with a throw pillow after tidying up the living room and fidgeting with the remote controls.

"Mom. I told you, I'm in good hands," I reassure her, but we both know it's not happening tonight.

"Come on, Mom. We need to go, leave him be. Liberty will look after him." Kota steps in, trying to move things along.

It's my first night home in ten days, and after a long, dragged-out day of waiting around for my discharge papers, I'm ready to fall into my bed with Liberty by my side, and finally have some peace and quiet.

"I know she will, darling. I'm just making sure you're settled." She fusses some more, tidying up things that don't need to be tidied.

"Mom." I step in front of her. "I know you're worried, but I'm fine. Even if Liberty wasn't here looking after me, I can handle it." Me being home is what everyone has been waiting for. Now I've been discharged, they're all starting to hover.

"I thought I lost you, Liam." Her lip wobbles and her voice shakes. "You're my son, and I thought you were gone."

"Mom...."

"No, don't 'Mom' me. You know I worry." I cut her off with a hug before she starts breaking down in front of me and I never get her to leave. She's been okay the last week. I think having me in the hospital helped. Now I'm home, I think the reality of the entire situation is hitting her hard.

"I know you do, Mom. I'm sorry I scared you. But I'm good. And tomorrow when you drop by unannounced, you'll see I survived." I give her my best comforting smile and a wink for good measure. "Now go, before Kota loses her cool and drags you out." I carefully lean forward and give her cheek a kiss. She doesn't release her grip on me right away, holding on a little tighter than normal.

"Are you sure I can't get you anything else before I go?" I know she doesn't want to leave me, but if I let her stay one moment longer, she'll never leave.

"I think B has it under control." My eyes find Kota's and silently ask her to wrap this up.

"Okay, let's go. Let's go." Kota's impatient tone eventually breaks Mom's reluctance. Herding Mom toward the door, she blows me a kiss and tells me they'll be back tomorrow.

"You will call me if you need anything?" Mom starts pestering Liberty next.

"I promise." She accepts my mom's hug then my sister's.

"Love you, son," she calls out as Kota pushes her out the door.

"Love you, too, Mom." I lock up behind them and turn to find Liberty standing there, carefully regarding me.

"You're not going to fuss over me like my mother and sister just did, are you?" I step in front of her and pull her close. While I was given the all clear to head home, I'm still a little tender and for the next few weeks, I'm meant to be taking it easy.

"Depends." She rises to her toes and offers me her soft, warm lips. It doesn't get old. The touch of them. The taste of them.

"On what?" I smile against her, but she doesn't open like I want her to.

"If you behave."

"Well, you know that's not happening." I try harder to deepen the kiss, to ignore the throb in my neck as I lean in closer to get a better taste. She doesn't let it progress. Pulling back before I can get too far, she takes my hand and walks down the hall to my room.

"I'm serious. You heard the doctor. Nothing too strenuous for the next few weeks."

"So you're saying no sex?" I follow her down to my room, only a tad disappointed. As much as I want to take her, I know we have a lot to talk about first.

"No sex, Hetch."

"Okay, fine. But are you opposed to sleeping naked?" We

clear the doorway to my room as I play with her some more, and like every time I do, that cute blush of hers kisses her cheeks.

"Seriously, who would have thought you were shot eleven days ago?" Her words tell me she finds me charming, but the drop in her smile shows me she's still a little shaken up by it.

"Come here, baby." I climb into bed and move over to make room for her.

"Hetch, I still have a few things I need to do before bed." Her reluctance doesn't concern me. She's fought me every step of the way in this relationship. Why would she stop now?

"Sweetheart, it's my first night out of the hospital, and I just want to hold my woman, in my bed, with no interruptions." I pat the bed, encouraging her up. It only takes a couple of pats before she eventually gives in and climbs in with me, resting her cheek on my chest.

"Thank you," I whisper when she settles in and makes herself comfortable.

"For what?" She doesn't look up, but I can still picture the confused look on her face.

"For not leaving me. For not leaving Kota and Mom, and the team alone in all of this." I know we have some issues we need to work through, but she was there when I needed her, when my family needed her, and that alone tells me more than what hasn't been said between us.

"Ahh, I don't know if you've noticed or not, but I was kind of a mess. If it weren't for your mom and sister, and the guys, I might have been committed." Her forced laugh does nothing to take away from the fact she isn't exaggerating. Both Kota and Fox have filled me in on how hard she took it. Imagining her broken and lost, hurts my heart, so I shake the image away.

"I know I can't take it away, but I'm sorry I put you through it, Lib." It's barely enough, but it's all I can offer.

"Don't you dare apologize to me. You were doing your job. You have nothing to be sorry for." Her voice is steady, but I don't miss the shake in her hand as she brings it to rest on my stomach. Yeah, it's my job. I'm a police officer, but we weren't in a good place when I was shot. The last thing she needed was

322

the extra stress of not knowing where we were at.

"Does my job frighten you?"

She doesn't answer right away, but I don't panic. The concern isn't if my job frightens her; it's if she can handle it or not.

"I'm not going to lie. I've never been more scared in my life sitting in that hospital waiting to hear if you survived. But I knew going into this what you did for a living, and the risk that comes with it. What scared me the most was the possibility of never being able to tell you how much I love you." The room pulses in unmasked tension as I process the words I've been waiting to hear. I know she hasn't left my side through all of this, but she's been yet to say it and, after the mess I put her through, I wasn't sure if she was hanging around out of obligation or if she really did love me.

"You love me?" I sound like a pussy, even to my own ears, but the truth is, I need to hear her say it so badly right now I'd be willing to beg for it.

"I'm so deeply, deeply in love with you, Liam, that the thought of you never knowing how much I loved you, broke me. It shattered me. The only reason I recovered was because you opened your eyes." Her lips find mine in a kiss which stops me from replying. It's not soft, or warm; it's not even comforting.

It's urgent and forgiving, and by the time she pulls back, I'm so far gone I can't process if it's her tears on my lips or my own.

"I love you, Liam Hetcherson. But don't ever leave me like that again or I will hunt you down." She wipes my face while I wipe hers.

I don't answer her with a promise. Because the promise of something so big is too dangerous to lie about, especially with my job. Instead, I hold her against me and promise never to stop loving her. To never stop making her laugh, and to always come home when I can.

42

LIBERTY

"Do you believe in heaven?" The question comes out of left field as we lie together in bed.

"Umm, yeah. I guess I believe there's something bigger out there." It's dark in my room, but the low light of the moon filtering through the window shows me enough to see he's on his back, not looking at me. Coming up on my elbow, I rest my head in my palm and wait for him to respond.

"I think I saw my dad when I got shot." His gaze stays locked on the ceiling, but his hand moves to find my free one.

It's been four weeks since Hetch came home, and while we still haven't fallen back into old routines, we're slowly getting there.

"You mean like in a dream?" I press on.

"Maybe." He shrugs. "I mean it felt like a dream, but sometimes I think I remember hearing you talking to me. Asking me to come back." He risks a look at me, concern etched into

324

his brow.

"I've heard of things like this before. I mean you were out of it for a few days. Your subconscious can give you dreams like that." I offer what I hope is some reassurance. I'm not saying he didn't experience what he's saying, I'm just trying to understand it.

"We talked about you. We talked about Mom and Kota. He told me I had to wake up." He releases my hand to rub his face a couple of times.

"Are you freaking out about it?" I ask, wondering if I should be concerned. This is the first time he's brought this up in four weeks. Maybe it's bothering him.

"Not really. In the beginning, I was a little freaked out. But, since coming home, I've stopped dreaming about him. Before, I would replay the same dream over and over a couple of times a week. Now, it's gone."

"Well, maybe it was your way of finally letting go?" I whisper, hoping it's true.

With Hetch being off work the last four weeks, it's given him more free time to see Dr. Anderson. I've noticed a huge difference in him. From opening up more about his dad and his past, to barely flinching when I ask questions about him.

"Yeah, maybe." He doesn't sound convinced, but he doesn't sound worried either. Not sure what to say, I don't say anything and let the quiet fall between us again.

"I miss him." He shakes his head and rolls to face me. "I hated that dream, but now it's gone, I'm missing him."

I scoot closer, placing my open palm against his heart. "It's okay to miss him. I don't ever expect you not to miss him. He's your father, and you're his son, regardless if he is here in the flesh or not. But what you need to remember"—I pat his chest, drawing his attention to his heart—"is that he is always in here." Reaching up, I then cup his jaw.

"Have I told you I love you today?" I ask, changing the subject before he has time to dwell on it too much.

"Maybe." His hand covers mine. "But I'm not opposed to hearing it again."

"I love you, Liam Hetcherson." I smile when he smiles. "You are the most amazing man I've ever known." I kiss him before he can say anything. My sudden need to show him all the love he deserves is too strong to stop.

He deepens the kiss. The hand resting on my hip digs in and pulls me against him while his tongue thrusts past my lips and entwines with mine.

Seized by a rush of need, I press closer to him. My legs part and I lift one up over his side, rolling my hips against him. It's probably the worst thing I could do. Since leaving the hospital, we've yet to have sex, the doctor giving Hetch strict instructions on no strenuous activity. *Sex included.*

"Wait." I stop, realizing my mistake, but Hetch doesn't obey.

"No, not stopping tonight." His lips leave mine and travel down my jaw, and to my neck.

"The doctor hasn't cleared you." My words may be rejecting him, but my hips are still rolling against him, searching for friction.

"We'll be careful." His teeth sink into my neck, sending a ripple of goose bumps over my skin.

"Oh, God. We shouldn't." I fight a little harder.

"Please, baby. I need you." His plea is followed by another quick bite to my neck.

Fuck, how can I resist him?

"Hetch, this isn't a good idea." He rolls both of us so I'm on my back, and he's covering me.

"See, that's where you're wrong. My cock and I think it's the best idea of the day." His hands push my nightie up and over my head while mine find the waistband of his boxers. Our heads collide while we try to undress each other.

"Fuck."

"Shit."

We both curse, rubbing our heads.

"We seem to be a little out of practice," I whisper, watching him carefully.

"We just need to slow it down." He pulls back and stands by the side of the bed. I watch as he drops his boxers, freeing his rock-hard erection.

The thick veins running through his cock throb in front of my eyes.

Jesus.

"Are you sure you want to?" My fingers dip into the sides of my panties, but I don't pull them down until he gives the okay.

"What sort of question is that, sweetheart?" He widens his stance, fists his cock, and strokes himself. My core throbs and my nipples harden. Even if I wanted to resist this man, the sight before me pushes every bit of willpower left in me away.

Making quick work of my panties, I kick them off and move down the bed so I'm lying in front of him. Exposed and waiting.

"Jesus, I've missed you." His voice is husky with need. His stare is scorching with want.

"Touch yourself, sweetheart." My hands obey. Reaching between my legs, I part my lips and glide my finger through my wetness.

"Tell me how wet you are." His eyes don't leave my pussy while mine don't leave his cock. Both of us transfixed with the other, getting ourselves off.

"Take a look yourself." I spread my legs wider, giving him a better view.

"Fuck, baby." The half groan, half grunt washes over me, and anchors me to the point I almost don't feel him climb up over me and settle between my legs. "Need you so bad."

I spread my legs wider, making room for him. Coming up on my elbows, I look down my body and watch him line up his cock at my entrance. Risking a glance up at him, I find his gaze locked on me.

"Watch, sweetheart. Watch me come home." My gaze slides back to his cock as he pushes himself inside me.

"Oh, God," I pant as he throbs inside of me, my core pulsing around him.

The sting of him stretching me coils in my stomach, but is soon forgotten when he moves his hips in a slow, deliberate pace.

"Harder," I encourage as an orgasm builds faster than

expected.

"No, baby." He takes my hands and secures them over my head, keeping me restrained. "We're not fucking tonight. I'm making love to my woman." His words whisper over my skin like the heat of a fire on a winter's night. Tremors of excitement pulse from my toes and work their way up to my heart.

"Hetch." I moan. The start of an orgasm dances in front of me, the promise of ecstasy teasing and taunting me.

"Look at me, Liberty." My eyes open on command and connect with his. Each one of his thrusts remain controlled, but still, it manages to spiral me out of control.

"I'm so deeply in love with you, B." My mouth swallows his words. Our tongues make love with the same amount of passion as our bodies.

I don't get a chance to confess my love before my orgasm takes hold of me and drags me through an abyss of pleasure.

"God, yes!" This time, his mouth captures my cries. Keeping up his perfect pace, it takes only a few more beats before his release seizes him. His cry of pleasure rings out, prickling my skin in a second wave of want.

"Jesus, I've missed you." He drops his forehead to mine while he tries to catch his breath.

"I'm so deeply in love with you, too." His eyes open at the quietness of my words and lock onto mine.

"Move in with me, B," he replies, knocking the wind out of me harder than the orgasm he just gave me.

"What?"

His lips curve up at my panic. "Move in with me." Even repeated a second time, they don't soothe my unease. Maybe being trapped under him with his cock still pulsing inside of me makes it harder to focus, but it's like the words have wiped my brain from functioning.

"B-but I live next door." My answer is stupid, even I know it. If I could slap myself, I would.

"I'm not asking you to move in with me here. I want you to move in with me, in my house." He whispers soft kisses over my face, like he's easing me into the idea.

"But it's not livable. You said it's too cluttered." I don't know why I'm fighting it. Of course I want to move in with him. It's just so sudden and unexpected. And he still has his cock inside of me.

"I did, but then you came along, sweetheart. You crashed into my life with your jacked-up vibrator, and your inappropriate notes, and you saved me. You saved me when I didn't know I needed saving."

A wave of tears burst free, but I try my hardest to control them. "Hetch–"

"I realize I can do anything when I'm with you, sweetheart. The darkness seems a little less dark, the pain is a little more manageable, and the clutter... the clutter fades and what's left behind is the beauty of the moment. So yes, I know it's soon. But you're mine, and I'm not letting you go ever again."

I let the room fall away from us as I imagine us together in his home. I can see it. I can see us living there in the beautiful home, even through the chaos of all the renovations. But most of all, I can feel it.

"You've gone quiet." He pulls me out of my vision.

"Did you practice that speech?" I blurt, my heart beating wildly in my chest. In my head, I see myself reacting differently, but I can't seem to switch off the stupid.

"Yeah, with hand gestures and all, but I dropped them last minute," he replies, letting the heavy tension fall away from our easy candor. "Did it win you over?" he asks when the silence grows too wide.

"You didn't have to win me, Hetch. You had me already."

His hands cradle my face as he slows the moment down. "So that's a yes?" His eyes track mine, holding me frozen to him as if he's willing the right answer from within me.

"Yes, it's–" His lips crash to mine before I can finish my reply.

It's not a simple everyday kiss, but one that changes our lives. Changes our future.

"I love you, sweetheart," he says as he pulls away, but even breaking the kiss, our eyes stay locked on one another.

"And I love you."

I never thought the night he interrupted me and my "jacked-up vibrator" as he puts it, we would be where we are right now. Hell, I never thought I'd fall in love again, but here I am. Here *we* are.

The paths we traveled separately brought us to one another.

He thinks I saved him from himself, but he saved me. And when I close my eyes, I see the faces of all the people who love him; and I see, even if briefly, how he saved each one of them: his mom, Kota, the guys on his team, Mitch. And it makes me love him more.

Harder. Deeper. Stronger.

Forever.

EPILOGUE

HETCH

FOUR MONTHS LATER

"So we have a bit of a dilemma."

I turn at Payton's voice. "Please tell me she isn't here." My eyes scan the back deck, hoping the surprise isn't ruined."No, no. She's not here. But neither is her mom or dad."

"Have you heard from them?" I look down at my watch, checking how late they are. Everyone was meant to be here an hour early so this wouldn't happen.

"Yeah, they're running late. They're not going to be here for another ten minutes.

Crap. Liberty should be here in less than fifteen.

"Okay, so I'll call B, see how far away she is." Stepping away from the noise of the house, I pull my phone out of my pocket and bring up her name. She answers on the third ring, less chirpy than when I sent her out the door to work this morning.

"Hello, birthday girl." Her grunt of a reply only proves she's trying not to be pissed that no one has called her today to wish her happy birthday. "Have you left yet?" I ignore her attitude. Soon she'll realize why everyone has stayed clear from her today.

"Just getting in my car now." I grin because even though I can't see her, I can picture the soft pout on her lips, and the crease in her brow that deepens when she's sulking.

"How did it go?" I brave her attitude, because as much as I want to get her to this party, the meeting she's been at for most of the afternoon was with Mitch's caseworker regarding visitation for Dominic. While Mitch originally stated he wanted nothing to do with Dominic, these last few months have given him time to think it over some more. Surprisingly, like us, Dominic has been supportive of his brother's decision and hasn't pushed the issue of seeing him. In the beginning, I didn't buy it, but now, it's not hard to see he's trying. I'm not saying I trust the situation completely, but Dominic has kept himself out of trouble. Got himself a job at a local mechanics. He's passing his random drug tests that are a part of his probation and from the intel Detective Marsh has been giving me, he hasn't been affiliated with The Disciples since he testified against Anton.

"Yeah, it was fine. Everything is set for next week." She sighs. A rush of breath pulses through the phone, tickling my ear with its vibrations.

"You okay?" I press, knowing she's not. She's trying so hard to be supportive of Mitch in whatever he decides, but welcoming Dominic back in his life is a big step, one neither of us have taken lightly. It's nerve wracking. We're all wondering if this is going to be a huge mistake. If Dominic is going to undo all the good Mitch has achieved these last few months.

"Just tell me this is a good thing." The plea is desperate, so I give her what she needs.

"This is a good thing, Lib. Mitch is ready. He's taken his time to come to this decision. Thought it through. He's not a kid, and we need to respect his need for family in his life." The soft sigh of relief washes over me, as my words do their job.

"You're right. I'm just worrying."

"I know you are, sweetheart, and that's why Mitch is lucky. But please don't worry about this too much. I've got Mitch's back, and if Dom fucks up, even once, I'm there."

"Thank you." I'm not sure if she's thanking me for having Mitch's back or for reassuring her. Either way, I accept it.

"You're welcome. Now, how far out are you?"

"Ten minutes." Her tone is less tense now, and I'm cringing for what I'm about to ask next.

"Ahh, okay. Are you able to stop by the store on your way home and pick me up some beer?" I pause, waiting for her reaction. The last four months of living with this woman has taught me a lot. But nothing more than when she is sulking, you don't poke her.

"W-what?" Liberty questions me while I smirk, watching Payton's jaw drop as I try to buy us some more time.

"Well, it just so happens that I started the grill up then realized I needed beer, and you're already out." I bite my lip to stop myself from laughing.

"We're eating in? I thought we were going to Il Centro's?" Guilt sneaks its way into my reasoning, but I fight the urge to let the surprise out of the bag.

"Ahhh, yeah about that, they were booked when I called. We couldn't get a reservation." I'm going to boyfriend hell, front row seat.

"Oh, my God, this is the worst birthday ever!" she huffs in a fit of rage.

"I'm sorry, baby. I know you were looking forward to it. But I promise I'll make it up to you." I try to soothe her annoyance, but there's no use. She's been looking forward to her birthday all month, and now we're ruining it.

She doesn't say anything for a while, her heavy breathing a clear indicator she is trying to calm herself. "Okay, so you just want the beer?" she somehow finds her Zen and asks.

"Yes, please, sweetheart."

"Right, well, I'll be home in twenty then." She hangs up without a good-bye, and if it were any other day, I would call back and give her shit for it.

Pocketing my phone, I let Payton know the good news.

"We have twenty minutes." I head back inside, ready to let everyone know we're twenty minutes out.

"You're so bad. You know that, right?" She follows close behind me, not letting me off the hook.

"What did you expect me to do, Pay? This whole night was your idea." At first, I was opposed to Payton's idea of throwing a surprise party for Liberty, but soon I learned saying no to Payton was almost as maddening as saying no to Liberty.

"Hey, this is a brilliant idea. Trust me, she is gonna–" She's cut off when Arabella comes running into the kitchen, crying out for her.

"What's wrong, baby?" She bends and scoops her up like a momma bear ready to pounce.

"The mean man told me to go away." Her little lip wobbles and my own papa bear instinct comes out at the sight of it. Over the last four months, Arabella has completely cemented her way into my heart as the baddest little chick I know. With quick wit and a big heart, it's hard not to fall in love with her.

"What mean man, baby?" Payton turns, looking for the culprit. My eyes follow the direction of Arabella's pointed finger, centered right on Fox.

Jesus, here we go.

"What's your problem, Mason?" she yells across the room, gaining the attention from our guests. The house is packed with my teammates, my mom and sister, some of Liberty's extended family, and with permission, Sue and the boys from Haven.

"My problem is your kid. You should keep a better eye on her. She shouldn't be talking to strangers."

I've never seen Payton and Fox exchange more than a few words. So the fact that she uses Fox's first name isn't lost on me. But what's more interesting is the slow smirk I see grace Fox's face when he has her complete attention and the fact that he cares that Ara is apparently talking to strangers.

"You did not just say that to me." Payton hands Arabella off to me and stomps her way over to him. In all the years I've known Fox, he's never warmed to kids. Hell, the idea of having kids broke up his marriage. So while his attitude toward Arabella frustrates me, it doesn't surprise me.

"Pretty sure I did, Payton."

Jesus, just what I don't need tonight. These two at each other's throat or worse, in each other's bed.

"Come on, Ara. Let's go find Della." I move us out of earshot, from her mother ripping Fox to shreds, and into the living room where Hart is watching a movie with his six-year-old daughter, Della, and Mitch.

"Should I be worried about those two?" I nod back over to Fox and Payton, who are still in the middle of arguing.

"I don't know about them, but those two are freaking me out." He points over to Sterling and Kota, who seem to be in a heated argument as well.

"Jesus, I don't have time for this crap. I have twenty minutes to get everyone ready before my pissed-off woman gets here. Everyone seems to be forgetting why we're even here."

"Hetch said a bad word." Shit! I forget about small ears listening.

"Sorry." I cringe, not needing to be tattled on.

"I told you this was all a bad idea." Hart looks far too smug for a father stuck watching a Disney movie.

"A little help would be appreciated."

"Do you need help, Hetch?" Mitch looks up, forgetting the movie for a second.

"Nah, I'm okay kid." I turn my eyes back to Hart, a silent warning that I need *his* help.

"Sorry, boss. I have my hands full." Before I can call him out, Liberty's parents come racing through the door, followed by Liberty's asshole brother, Jett.

Seriously. One drama averted only to have another land in my lap.

Leaving Ara with Della, I move toward Liberty's mom and dad.

"What the hell is he doing here?" I don't hide my distaste of seeing him. This is the last thing I need right now.

"Now, come on, Liam. He's family." Jack steps in closer so

only I can hear.

"Hey, I understand. But Payton is gonna be pissed. Which will only make Liberty more pissed." I'm not telling them anything they don't know. The girls are tight. Tighter than blood. An upset Payton equals an upset Liberty. It's pretty simple.

"It's going to be fine, Liam. We will sort it out," Connie reassures me in a way that only a mother can.

"We have ten minutes to get everything ready."

"Okay then, let's get started." Her smile is warm, comforting and offers me the reprieve I've been waiting for.

If anyone can fix this mess in less than ten minutes, it's Connie Jenson.

She will make it all right.

She has to, otherwise, this will be all for nothing.

Seriously, why the hell did I agree to this?

* * *

LIBERTY

TWENTY MINUTES LATER

The house is dark when I step through the door. Beer in hand, I call out for Hetch, only to hear nothing in return.

"Hetch, what's going on?" I drop my handbag on the hall table and kick my heels off. "Seriously, you better freaking be here, because I swear to God if you were called in, I'm gonna lose it," I continue to rant as I walk toward the darkened kitchen and flick the light switch on.

"SURPRISE!" The screaming and hollering from over thirty people startles me enough to drop the six pack of bottled beer on my feet, and my own scream to escape my mouth.

"Oh, God!" I jump back in pain and shock as a sea of faces stand before me with bright grins and outstretched hands.

"Shit, sweetheart. Are you okay?" Hetch is there in front of me, pushing everyone back and crowding my space. The tears come right away as pain shoots up my foot in a dull ache.

"I don't know?" I look down at the mess of beer and broken glass, to find my foot swelling and bruising. Hetch assesses the situation and then picks me up in one fluid movement, planting me on the counter.

"Someone get some ice," he calls out while checking out the damage.

"What? What's going on?" Confusion, pain, and embarrassment fill me as I look down at him squatting in front of me.

"I'm sorry, baby. This was a bad idea." I wince as he clears glass from my foot. I'm mildly aware of the blood, but I'm more focused on the faces I see crowding me. Mom, Dad. Payton. Family I haven't seen in ages. Even Sue and the boys are here to celebrate with me.

"This is why none of you called me today?" I cry harder, my tears falling freely as I put it all together.

How did I not pick up on this?

"Hey, don't cry." Hetch stands and wipes at my face, just as my mom comes forward with an ice pack.

"Don't cry? Do you know what I've been thinking all day?" The sobs prevent me from being able to talk clearly, but I don't stop.

"I thought you all forgot about me." A low lull in conversation tells me everyone is witnessing my freak-out. "How crazy is that?" A bubble of laughter fills the air as I realize how stupid it was of me to think that.

"Aww, Bertie." Mom looks almost as stricken as I feel. "I'm sorry, sweetie. We just wanted it to be perfect." Her eyes flick to Hetch before coming back to mine.

"This is…. You did all this?"

"With the help of Payton." He shrugs like it's not a big deal. But this is a big deal.

"I don't know what to say," I whisper so only Hetch can hear me.

"You can say thank you and not be pissed at me."

"Oh, I'm still pissed at you." I level my best you-are-in-big-trouble stare at him. "You made me stop for beer." *The beer I just dropped on my foot.*

"For the record, he thought of that dumb move on his own," Payton shouts from the back of the crowd. Her confession pulls out a surge of laughter from everyone around us.

"Yeah, that was mean. But I'm gonna make it up to you." He kisses me deeply before I can tell him it's not needed.

Yeah, I had a shitty day, followed by the start of a shitty night, but none of that matters. Not when I have everything I want here.

Family, friends, my boys from Haven, and him.

Hetch.

The man who risks his life to save others. The man I almost lost.

He's a survivor and a fighter, but most of all, he's my glasses.

* * *

HETCH

FOUR HOURS LATER

"How's the foot feeling?" I ask when the last of our guests have left for the night, and she's sneaking a second slice of cake.

"It's okay. The alcohol helped." She looks down at her now bandaged foot and shrugs. After icing it for an hour, one of her aunts, who happens to be a nurse, patched her up and gave her the all clear to move about. Me, concerned more than I probably should have been, never left her side, carrying her around whenever she let me.

"You have no idea how terrible I feel about that." I step in close. My eyes lock onto her mouth as she wraps her red lips around the fork.

"You can make it up to me now." Her tongue comes out, licking at a dab of icing on her bottom lip. I don't know if she's doing it on purpose or if she has no fucking clue how sexy she is.

"Whatever you need, baby." My cock hardens, and my balls tighten.

"You, I just need you, Hetch." Her words shift something inside of me. Her acceptance warming me. Her simple need calling me.

This woman, she's given me grace when I didn't deserve it, peace when I didn't know I wanted it, and love when no one else could.

Because of her, I've been given a life I never knew I was missing.

"Ask me what I know," I whisper, knowing not what I want to do, but what I need to do. Her eyes close briefly before she opens them at my words. They fall on the faint scars on my neck. She does that sometimes, just stares at them as though she needs it to anchor herself.

"What do you know?" She's smiling now, our little "I know" game becoming a part of who we are.

"I know I love you." I gently press my lips to hers, kissing and breathing her in. "I know you're the most important person in my life." My lips move to her nose, gently pecking the tip. "I also know because of me, you've had a really shitty day." I pepper each kiss over her jawline, working my way up to her mouth.

"No, it was amazing." She tries to deny it, but we both know it's true.

"But most of all, Liberty, I know more than anything this is it for me, sweetheart. This chaotic, crazy life is it." I release my hold of her and drop to one knee right in front of her. I hadn't planned on doing it tonight, especially not in the kitchen of our

339

house, but there's no stopping it now. I am so in love with this woman I can't wait.

"Hetch? What are you doing?" She steps back, her hands move to her mouth as her eyes track me.

"Sweetheart, I know you deserve so much more than what I'm giving you right now, but waiting another minute to ask you is going to kill me." I pull out the small box I've been carrying around for the last month, waiting for the right time. "Liberty Jenson, I am so deeply in love with you, most days it hurts. The only way you could cure me is by marrying me."

She waits for a beat, then another two, then her mouth moves but nothing comes out.

"Sweetheart?" I press, wondering if I'm reading it all wrong.

"D-did you practice that speech?" She grins down at me, and my heart kicks up a beat. It's the same response she gave me when I asked her to move in with me.

I can't help but grin back up at her. *Fuck, I love this woman.*

"Yeah, this time with props." I lift the ring her mother and father cried over, when I showed them last month, out of the box and present it to her. "Did it win you over?"

"You didn't have to win me, Hetch. You had me already." Her hands move to either side of my face. Cupping my jaw, she leans down and presses her lips to mine.

"Is that a yes, sweetheart?" My lips move over hers, not willing to accept anything else.

"Yes. Yes, Liam Hetcherson, I will marry you." My lips crash to hers, owning them like she owns me.

Tension flows from her body into mine as I take it all from her.

Her taste.

Her acceptance.

Her love.

My father used to say to get to the end, we have to go back to the start.

This is one of my moments. She is one of my people. Her love has redefined the type of person I have become.

And because of her, I am never going to be the same again.

THE END.

ACKNOWLEDGMENTS

Alissa Evanson-Smith: Girl, these just get harder and harder! Thank you for all you do. I wouldn't be where I am without you. Love you lady.

Brie Burgess: Gahh, my little savior. Thank-you for everything you do. You know just what I need, when I need it.

Stewart Jones: Ahh Stu. Thank you for putting up with my consistent questions. For letting me go back and forth with you and not giving me too much trouble when I wanted to argue with you. this is hollywood damn it!

Gillian Grybas: Gikky, oh, Gikky. You know how much I love you right? Woman you rock. Thank you for loving Hetch, even when I didn't. Love you babe.

Cassia Brightmore: Thank you for all your hard work woman. Love you so hard.

JJ: My sister wife. You rock. That is all.

Tania: Thank for your help and extra attention to detail. Wouldn't have been able to do it without you.

Abbey: Oh Abbey, my toughest critic. Lady, that's for kicking my ass.

Priya: Priya, Priya, Priya, you rock lady. Thank for being awesome. Miss seeing your face babe.

Louisa from LM Creations: Lady, this cover! You rocked it.

Thank you for your hard work. You are amazing.

Becky Johnson: Thank you for all your hard work. You make editing a breeze. Even when I feel like losing it, you're there to calm me down.

Rebels: I know heaps of authors say this, but all the others are lying. I truly have the best readers. You all rock!

To ALL the Bloggers: Thank you for your support. I wouldn't have been able to get my name out without you guys pimping my work, reviewing, and loving the Knights Rebels boys just as much as I do.

My Mr. Savage: You're the only one who knows how hard this one was. Thank you for being there for me. We got there in the end. I LOVE YOU!

ALSO BY
RIVER SAVAGE

KNIGHTS REBELS MC SERIES.

INCANDESCENT
AFFLICTION
RECLAIMED
DESERTION
INFATUATION
PARADOX

MEN OF S.W.A.T. SERIES

HETCH
FOX (coming soon)

HELP SOMEONE. HELP YOURSLEF

The **World** Health Organization (WHO) estimates that each year approximately one million people die from **suicide**, which represents a **global** mortality rate of 16 people per 100,000 or one death every 40 seconds. It is predicted that by 2020 the rate of death will increase to one every 20 seconds.

Life can be painful and problems can seem overwhelming at times. Some people may think about suicide but do not act upon it. For others, suicide seems like the only way out of their situation or the feelings they are experiencing. They generally feel very alone and hopeless. They believe nobody can help them or understand what they are going through.

If you are concerned that someone you know is considering suicide, act promptly. Don't assume that they will get better without help or that they will seek help on their own. Take immediate steps to obtain help and keep the person safe. It is also important that you care for yourself through the process.

If you are feeling suicidal it is important that you take immediate steps to keep yourself safe.

- Tell someone how you feel and, if possible, have them stay with you until you get help.
- Contact a health professional and tell them you are feeling suicidal and need urgent assistance.
- Take practical steps to keep yourself safe by connecting with people, and managing your thoughts.

If you, or someone you are with, is in immediate danger call 911

ABOUT THE AUTHOR

An avid reader of romance and erotic novels, River's love for books and reading fueled her passion for writing. Reading no longer sated her addiction, so she started writing in secret. She never imagined her dream of publishing a novel would ever be achievable. With a soft spot for an alpha male and a snarky, sassy woman, Kadence and Nix were born.

Made in the USA
San Bernardino, CA
07 September 2017